THE TIME OF INDIFFERENCE

BY ALBERTO MORAVIA

THE TIME OF

INDIFFERENCE

ALBERTO MORAVIA

Translated by

ANGUS DAVIDSON

FARRAR, STRAUS AND YOUNG

NEW YORK

Manufactured in the United States of America by
American Book–Stratford Press, Inc., New York

THE TIME OF INDIFFERENCE

1

CARLA CAME into the room. She was wearing a brown woolen frock with a skirt so short that the movement she made in shutting the door was enough to pull it up several inches over the slack wrinkles her stockings formed about her legs; but she was unaware of this, and advanced cautiously, peering in front of her as she moved clumsily and uncertainly forward. Only one lamp was lit, showing up Leo's knees as he sat on the sofa; the rest of the drawing-room was wrapped in a gray gloom.

"Mom's dressing," she said, coming up to him; "she'll be down soon."

"Then we'll wait for her together," said the man, bending forward. "Come here, Carla, sit down here." But Carla did not accept his offer. Standing beside the little table with the lamp on it, her eyes turned down towards the circle of light cast by the lampshade. Inside it the knickknacks and other objects, in contrast to their dead, unsubstantial fellows scattered about the darker parts of the room, displayed all their color, all their solidity. She was feeling with her fingertip the movable head of a Chinese porcelain figure—a heavily laden donkey upon whose back, between two baskets, sat a kind of rustic Buddha, a fat peasant with his belly wrapped in a

[3]

flowered kimono; the head went up and down, and Carla, her eyes lowered, her cheeks lit up, her lips tightly pressed together, appeared wholly absorbed in this occupation.

"Are you staying to dinner?" she asked, without raising her head.

"Certainly I am," replied Leo, lighting a cigarette. "Perhaps you'd rather I didn't?" Bending forward as he sat on the sofa, he was examining the girl with interest—her legs with their slightly crooked calves, her flat stomach, the little shaded valley between her big breasts, her fragile looking arms and shoulders, and the round head that looked so heavy on its thin neck.

What a pretty girl she is! And he repeated to himself: What a pretty girl she is! The lust he thought had been assuaged for that afternoon reawoke, the blood mounted to his cheeks, and he wanted to cry aloud from desire.

She gave one more little push to the donkey's head. "Did you notice what a dither Mom was in at tea today? Everyone was looking at us."

"She's worried over business matters," said Leo. He stretched forward and, in a casual way, lifted the hem of her short skirt.

"D'you know what nice legs you've got, Carla?" he said, turning towards her a stupid, excited face where a falsely jovial smile struggled unsuccessfully to appear. But Carla neither blushed nor made any reply; with a sharp movement she thrust down her dress.

"You make Mom jealous," she said, looking at him, "and that's why she makes life impossible for all of us." Leo waved his hand as much as to say: "And what can *I* do about it?" Then he threw himself back again on the sofa and crossed his legs.

"Do as I do," he said coldly. "As soon as I see that the storm is on the point of bursting, I don't say another word. Then it passes over and everything's finished."

"Finished, for *you*," she said in a low voice, and it was as though the words he had spoken had reawakened in her a blind and ancient rage. "For *you* . . . but for *us* . . . for *me*," she burst forth, her lips trembling, her eyes dilating with

[4]

anger, one finger pointing at her breast, "for me, who live with her, nothing's finished." There was a moment's silence. "If you only knew," she went on in that same low voice in which the words were emphasized by resentment, assuming a strange, foreign sounding, accent, "how oppressive, how miserable, how shabby all this is, and what kind of a life one leads, having to listen to it all every day, every single day." A deadly wave of bitterness seemed to come sweeping forward out of the gloom that filled the other half of the room, to lap against Carla's breast, and then to vanish, black and foamless; and she was left with staring eyes, breathless, struck dumb by this flood of hatred.

They looked at each other. The devil! thought Leo, somewhat shocked at such violence, evidently it's a serious matter. He leaned forward and held out his cigarette case: "A cigarette?" he suggested kindly; and Carla took one, lit it, and, in a cloud of smoke, came a step nearer him.

"And so," he asked, looking up at her, "you really can't stand it any longer?" She nodded, appearing slightly embarrassed at the confidential tone the conversation was taking. "Well, then," he went on, "you know what one does when one can't stand a thing any longer? One breaks away from it."

"That's what I shall end by doing," she said, with a rather theatrical decisiveness, but she felt she was acting a part that was both false and ridiculous. Was this the man towards whom the sloping path of her exasperation was imperceptibly carrying her? She looked at him. He was neither better nor worse than others—in fact, there was no doubt he was better than many; but there was, in addition, a certain fatal quality about him, since he had waited ten years for her to develop and mature so that now, on this particular evening, in this dark room, he might lay siege to her.

"Break away," he repeated; "come and live with me."

She shook her head. "You're crazy."

"Ah, do!" Leo stretched out and took hold of her skirt again. "We'll part company with your mother and send her to the devil, and then you can have everything you want, Carla." He kept pulling at her skirt, and his eye travelled excitedly from her frightened, hesitant face to the little strip of bare leg that could just be seen above her stocking. Take her home with me, he was thinking, possess her. His breath almost failed him. "Everything you want . . . clothes, lots of clothes, travelling. We'll travel together. It's a wicked shame that a lovely little girl like you should be sacrificed in this way. Come and live with me, Carla."

"But this is all quite impossible," she said, trying unsuccessfully to free her skirt from his hands; "there's Mom. It's impossible."

"We'll leave her to her own devices," repeated Leo, taking hold of her, now, around the waist. "She can go to hell, it's high time all this was finished with. And you'll come and live with me, won't you? You'll come and live with me, because I'm your only real friend, the only person who understands you and knows what you want." He clasped her closer to him in spite of her movements of alarm. Oh, to be at home, he was thinking, and these swift ideas were like bright flashes of lightning in the storm of his lust, then I'd show her what it is she wants. He raised his eyes towards her dazed face and felt a desire to say something tender—anything would do—to reassure her: "Carla, my love."

Again she made the futile gesture of trying to push him away from her, but more feebly than before, for now a kind of resignation had taken possession of her: why should she refuse Leo? Virtue would merely throw her back into the arms of boredom and the distasteful trivialities of everyday habit; and it seemed to her, furthermore, owing to some fatalistic taste for the moral rounding-off of a situation, that this present adventure, with its air of familiarity, was the only epilogue her old life deserved; afterwards, everything would be new—both life and herself. She looked at the man's face, close to her, held out towards hers. End it all, she thought, ruin everything. And her brain whirled as though she were about to hurl herself head foremost into space.

But instead, she besought him, "Let me go," and again tried to free herself. She thought, vaguely, that she would first rebuff Leo and then yield to him—she did not know why, unless perhaps to have time to consider the whole of

[6]

the risk she faced, or perhaps from some remains of coquettishness. She struggled in vain; her subdued voice anxious, mistrustful, hurriedly repeated the meaningless request: "We'll go on being good friends, won't we, Leo?—good friends as we've always been"; but the pulling at her skirt uncovered her legs, and her whole attitude of unwillingness, the gestures she made to cover herself up, to defend herself, the sounds torn from her by the man's licentious grasp, all were imbued with a sense of shame, of embarrassment, of confusion that no mere setting at liberty could have dispelled.

"Very good friends indeed," echoed Leo, almost joyfully, twisting the thin woolen stuff of her skirt in his fist, "extremely good friends, Carla." He clenched his teeth, with an exaltation of all his senses at the nearness of that deeply desired body. Now at last I've got you, he thought, twisting on the sofa so as to make room for the girl; and he was on the point of pulling down the head that hung over him, above the lamp, when a tinkling sound from the glass door in the darkness at the far end of the room warned him that someone was coming in.

It was her mother; and the transformation her presence caused in Leo's attitude was suprising. He immediately threw himself back against the back of the sofa, crossed his legs and looked at the girl with complete indifference; in fact, he carried the pretence to the point of saying to her, in the important tone of voice of someone concluding a conversation already begun: "Believe me, Carla, there's nothing else to be done."

Her mother entered. She had not changed her dress but had tidied her hair and generously powdered and painted her face; she walked forward from the door with her usual faltering step; and in the gloom her blank face, with its undecided features and its vivid colors, looked like a silly, pathetic mask.

"Have I kept you waiting very long?" she asked. "What were you two talking about?"

Leo, with a wide gesture, pointed to Carla standing in the middle of the room. "I was just telling your daughter

[7]

that there's nothing to be done this evening except stay at home."

"Indeed there isn't," she agreed, with haughty, commanding approval, sitting down in an armchair facing her lover; "we've been to the movies already today, and there's nothing at the theatres except what we've seen. I shouldn't have minded going to see *Six Characters* with Pirandello's own company. But really, how could one? It's a popular price evening."

"I can assure you you're not missing anything," Leo observed.

"Oh, I don't know about that," she protested languidly: "Pirandello can be very good, sometimes. What was that play of his called, that we saw not long ago? Wait . . . Ah, yes, *The Mask and the Face*. I enjoyed it immensely."

"Well, perhaps," said Leo, throwing himself back on the sofa, "personally, I've always been bored to death with him." He put his thumbs in his vest pockets and looked first at the mother and then at the daughter.

Standing behind her mother's chair, Carla received this heavy, inexpressive stare like a blow that smashed her own numbness to pieces as if it had been made of glass. She noticed then, for the first time, how stale, how ordinary, how distressing was the scene in front of her—her mother and her mother's lover sitting opposite each other in a conversational attitude; the half-darkness, the lamp, the blank, stupid faces, and she herself leaning affably on the back of the armchair to listen and talk. Life doesn't change, she thought, it refuses to change. She wanted to scream; she lowered her hands and wrung them together, against her belly, so violently that her wrists ached.

"We can certainly stay at home," went on her mother; "all the more so since we've got engagements every day of this week. Tomorrow there's that *thé dansant* for the orphanage; the day after there's the fancy dress ball at the Grand Hotel . . . and on the other days we have invitations all over the place. Oh, Carla, I saw Signora Ricci today. She's terribly aged. I looked at her carefully; she has two deep lines that start from her eyes and go right down to her mouth,

and as for her hair—you can no longer tell *what* color it is
. . . *too* horrifying!" She twisted her mouth and waved her
hands in the air.

"She's not quite as bad as that," said Carla, coming forward and sitting down beside the man. She was bothered with
a slight but distressing impatience; she foresaw that her
mother, by indirect and devious ways, would in the end—as
she always did—arrive at the moment when she made a little
scene of jealousy with her lover; she could not tell when and
how it would happen, but she was as certain of it as that
the sun would rise next day and night follow in its turn. And
this foreknowledge brought with it a feeling of fear; there
was nothing to be done, for everything was immutable,
everything was ruled by a kind of shabby fatality.

"She told me a great deal of news," went on her mother.
"She told me they've sold their old car and bought a new
one . . . a Fiat. 'You know,' she said to me, 'my husband has
become Paglioni's right-hand man, at the Banca Nazionale
. . . Paglioni can't get on without him, Paglioni points him
out as his most probable partner.' Paglioni this, Paglioni that.
Really it's disgraceful!"

"Why disgraceful?" observed Leo, gazing at her between
half-closed eyelids. "What is there disgraceful in all that?"

"Don't you know," she retorted, looking sharply at him
as if to urge him to weigh the words carefully, "don't you
know that Paglioni is Signora Ricci's lover?"

"Everyone knows it," said Leo, and his dull eyes rested
heavily upon Carla as she sat there in a state of dreamy resignation.

"And you know also," insisted Mariagrazia, carefully
enunciating her syllables, "that, until they knew Paglioni, the
Riccis hadn't a penny. And now they have a car."

Leo turned his head. "Ah, so that's it, is it?" he exclaimed.
"Well, what harm is there in it? Poor people, they work
very hard."

It was just as if he had put a match to a carefully prepared
train of explosive.

"Ah, I see," she said, opening her eyes very wide in irony.
"So you justify a shameless woman—and not even a beautiful

[9]

one, just a mere bag of bones—who exploits her lover without any scruples at all, gets him to give her cars and clothes, and even finds means of advancing her husband, who is either an imbecile or extremely cunning—one doesn't know which. So those are your principles, are they? That's fine, that's really splendid. There's nothing more to be said, then. Everything is perfectly clear. Evidently that's the sort of woman you like."

Here we are, thought Carla. A slight shudder of impatience ran all through her, she half-closed her eyes and threw back her head out of the light, away from the conversation; into the shadow.

Leo laughed. "No, frankly, that is *not* the sort of woman I like." He cast a swift, covetous glance at the girl beside him—at her full bosom and pink cheeks and youthful figure. *That's* the sort of woman I like, he wanted to shout at his mistress.

"So you say now," persisted Carla's mother, "so you say now. But the disparager is often the buyer. And when you're with her—as you were the other day at the Sidoli's, for instance—you're full of compliments, aren't you? You talk all sorts of nonsense to her. Get along with you, *I* know you. You know what you are? A liar."

Here we are, thought Carla again. This conversation might go on for a long time; and she had recognized that life was rooted stubbornly in fixed habits and did not change, and she had had enough. She got to her feet. "I'm going to put on a woolly; I'll be back in a minute," she said, and without looking around—for she could feel Leo's eyes fixed on her back like a couple of leeches—she went out.

In the corridor she met Michele. "Is Leo in there?" he asked her. Carla looked at her brother. "Yes."

"I've just this moment come from Leo's agent," said the boy calmly. "I got to know a whole pile of pleasant things. And, in the first place, that we're ruined."

"What d'you mean?" asked the girl in amazement.

"It means," explained Michele, "that we've got to hand over the house to Leo, in payment of the mortgage, and go somewhere else, without a penny in our pockets."

They looked at each other; a dismal, forced smile crossed the boy's face. "Why d'you smile?" she demanded. "D'you think it's a thing to smile at?"

"Why do I smile?" he echoed. "Because all this is quite indifferent to me. In fact, it almost pleases me."

"That isn't true."

"Certainly it's true," he retorted; and, without saying another word, he left her there, stupefied and frightened, and went into the drawing-room.

His mother and Leo were still quarrelling. Michele had just time to notice, as he came in, a rapid change from a familiar to a more formal mode of address, and smiled with pity and disgust. "I think it's dinner time," he said to his mother, without greeting or even looking at Leo, but the man was not disconcerted by this cold demeanor. "Oh, look who's here," he cried with his usual joviality, "it's our own Michele. Come here, Michele. It's such a long time since we met."

"Only two days," said the boy, looking straight at him. He made an effort to appear cold and tense although he felt nothing but indifference. He would have liked to add, "The less we see of one another, the better," or something of that kind, but had neither the quickness nor the sincerity to do so.

"And does two days seem nothing to you?" cried Leo. "One can do so many things in two days." He thrust his broad, jubilant face forward in the lamplight. "I say, what a nice suit you've got on! Who made it for you?"

It was a dark blue suit, well cut but considerably worn, which Leo must have seen him wearing at least a hundred times, but, smitten by this direct assault upon his vanity, Michele forgot in an instant all his previous determination to display hatred and coldness.

"D'you think so?" he asked, making no attempt to conceal a half-smile of complacency; "it's an old suit. I've been wearing it for a very long time. Nino made it." And instinctively he turned round to show Leo the back, pulling down the edges of the coat so that it would cling tightly to his body. He could see his reflection in the Venetian mirror on the wall opposite him: it was a perfect fit, there could be no doubt about that; but it seemed to him that his attitude was just as full of ridiculous, fixed stupidity as that of the well-dressed models in shop windows, with price labels on their chests. A feeling of disquiet crept into his mind.

"It's good . . . yes, really good." Bending forward, Leo was now feeling the material. Then he straightened himself up again: "He's a fine fellow, our Michele," he said, slapping him on the arm; "you can't find any fault with him. He does nothing but amuse himself, and never has a thought of any kind." From the tone in which these words were spoken and the smile that accompanied them, Michele saw, too late, that he had been astutely flattered and thoroughly made fun of; and where were the indignation, the resentment that he had imagined he felt in the presence of his enemy? Vanished, into the limbo of his good intentions. Hatefully embarrassed by the meaningless attitude in which he found himself, he looked at his mother.

"What a pity you weren't with us today," she said, "we saw a magnificent film."

"Oh yes," said the boy; then, turning towards Leo, he said, in the driest, tensest voice he could produce, "I've been to see your agent, Leo. . . ."

But Leo interrupted him with a sharp movement of his hand. "Not now. . . . I understand. We'll talk about it later. After dinner. Everything at its proper time."

"As you like," said the boy with instinctive mildness; and immediately he realized that he had been outwitted for the second time. I ought to have said *at once*, he thought. Anyone else would have done that. *At once*—and then argued with him—yes, and even insulted him. He wanted to scream with rage. Vanity and indifference—in the course of only a few minutes Leo had contrived to make him fall into both these shabby pitfalls. In the meantime his mother and her lover had risen to their feet.

"I'm hungry," Leo was saying as he buttoned his coat; "very hungry." She was laughing; and Michele, automatically, followed them. After dinner, however, he thought, seeking in vain to instil some measure of bitterness into his somewhat distracted ideas . . . after dinner I shan't let him get away with it so easily.

At the door they stopped. "Please," said Leo, and Michele's mother went out. They were left face to face with each other, the man and the boy, looking at each other. "Come on, after you," insisted Leo with extreme politeness, laying his hand on Michele's shoulder, "the master of the house must go first." And with a fatherly gesture, and a smile so friendly as to appear mocking, he pushed the boy gently forward. The master of the house, thought the latter, without a trace of anger . . . that's a good one. It's you who are the master of the house. But he said nothing, and went out into the passage behind his mother.

2

BENEATH THE THREE-BRANCHED chandelier the white mass of
the table glittered with minute splinters of light from dishes,
carafes and glasses, like a block of marble newly scratched by
the chisel. There were stains on it—the red of wine, the brown
of bread, a green soup steaming in bowls; but the dazzling
whiteness blotted them out, shining immaculate between
four walls where, by contrast, everything—both furniture and
pictures—was blurred in one single blackness. And at the
table, in her usual place, her astonished eyes fixed upon the
piping hot food, Carla sat waiting, without any sign of impatience.

The first of the three to come in was her mother, with
head turned towards Leo close behind her. She was declaring,
in an ironical, excited voice, "One doesn't live to eat, one
eats to live. But you do just the opposite. Lucky you!"

"No, no, no," said Leo as he came in, touching with a mistrustful hand, out of pure curiosity, the barely warm radiator.
"No, you didn't understand me. I said that, when one is
doing a thing, one shouldn't think of something else. For instance, when I'm working I only think of working. When
I'm eating, I only think of eating. And so on. Then everything goes right."

And when you're stealing? Michele, just behind him, would have liked to ask; but he found himself unable to hate a man whom, unwillingly, he envied. Really and truly, he's right, he thought as he went to his place. *I* think too much.

"Lucky you!" the woman repeated sarcastically. "With me, on the other hand, everything goes wrong." She sat down, assumed an attitude of mournful dignity and, with downcast eyes, stirred her soup in order to cool it.

"Why is everything wrong?" inquired Leo as he took his seat. "In your place, I should be happy. A pretty daughter, and intelligent son with a fine future in front of him, a charming house. What more can one want?"

"You know exactly what I mean," she said with a half-sigh.

"No, I don't; at the risk of being mistaken for an ignoramus, I must confess I don't understand at all." His soup was now finished, and Leo put down his spoon. "And in any case you're all of you unhappy. Don't imagine you're the only one, Signora. D'you want proof of it? Now you, Carla, tell the truth, are you happy?"

The girl looked up. This spirit of joviality and false good nature aggravated her feeling of impatience. There she was, sitting at the family table, as on so many other evenings; the usual remarks were being made, there was the usual objects in the room, stronger than time itself, and above all the usual electric light, devoid of illusion, devoid of hope, utterly commonplace, worn by use like the stuff of a garment and so completely inseparable from their faces that sometimes, when she had suddenly turned it on over the empty table, she had had the vivid impression that she could see their four heads, her mother's, her brother's, Leo's and her own, hanging there in that mean halo. There were present, therefore, all the objects of her irritation, yet in spite of this Leo must come and prick her exactly at her sorest point. She restrained herself, however. "Yes indeed, things might be better," she admitted, and then she lowered her head again.

"There you are!" cried Leo triumphantly, "I told you so. . . . Carla too. But that's not all; I'm sure Michele says the same. . . . Isn't it true, Michele, that things are going badly for you too?"

The boy, also, looked at him before answering. Now, he was thinking, now I ought to tell him what I think of him, insult him, start a quarrel and end by breaking off all relations with him. But he hadn't the sincerity to do it; all he felt was a deadly calm; irony; indifference.

"You'd better answer that one yourself," he said quietly; "you know how things are going better than I do."

"Ah, you're a clever one," cried Leo; "you're a clever one, Michele. You want to avoid answering, you want to pass it off. But it's quite clear that you're not happy either; otherwise you wouldn't be pulling a long face like that." He helped himself to the dish that the maid was handing to him, then said: "I, on the other hand, ladies and gentlemen, I, personally, wish to make it clear that all is going well for me, —extremely well, in fact—and that I am extremely happy and contented and that if I had to be born again I would want to be born just as I am and with my own name, Leo Merumeci."

"Lucky man!" exclaimed Michele ironically. "Tell us how you do it."

"How do I do it?" repeated the other, his mouth full. "Well, well. But what you really want to know," he added, filling his glass, "is—why aren't you three like me?"

"Why is it, then?"

"Because," he said, "you get into a rage over things that aren't worth it." He broke off and drank some wine. There was a moment of silence. All three of them, Michele, Carla, and their mother, had a feeling of wounded pride. The boy saw himself as he was, pitiable, indifferent, discouraged, and said to himself: "Ah, I'd like to see you in *my* present situation." Carla thought of the unchanging quality of life, of the trap the man had set for her, and wanted to cry out: "*I* have *real* reasons." But it was their mother, impulsive and talkative, who spoke for all three.

To be associated with her children in this general tendency towards discontentedness had seemed to her—owing to the very good opinion she had of herself—to be as cruelly wounding as a downright betrayal; her lover was not merely abandoning her but was making a fool of her into the bargain. "All right," she said at last, after this significant silence, in the metallic, malevolent voice of one who wants to pick a quarrel, "but I, my dear good man, have very good reasons for not being happy."

"I don't doubt it," said Leo.

"We don't doubt it," echoed Michele.

"I'm no longer a girl, like Carla," she went on, in a resentful, emotional tone, "I am a woman who has been through a great deal, who has had sorrows. Oh yes, many sorrows," she repeated, excited by her own words, "who has been through many troubles and many difficulties, and who nevertheless has always been able to preserve intact her own dignity and maintain her superiority over everybody. Yes, my dear Merumeci," she burst forth in a bitter, sarcastic tone, "over *everybody*, including yourself."

"I never thought . . ." began Leo; they all realized, now, that her jealousy had found a direction and would pursue its course to the very end; they all foresaw, with irritation and disgust, the pitiful storm that was gathering in the calm light of the dinner table.

"You, my dear Merumeci," went on Mariagrazia, staring at her lover with frenzied eyes, "you spoke very lightly just now. I am not one of those smart lady friends of yours without many scruples in their heads, who think about nothing except amusing themselves and getting on in the world, with one man today and another tomorrow, just as suits them best. Oh no, you're quite wrong. I feel myself to be completely and utterly different from ladies of that kind."

"I didn't mean that."

"I am a woman," she continued with growing exaltation, "who might teach you and lots of other men like you how to live, but who has the rare delicacy, or the stupidity, not to plant herself in the front row, not to talk much about herself, and who is therefore almost always ignored or misunderstood. But even so," she cried, raising her voice to its highest pitch, "even if I *am* too kind, too discreet, too generous, even so, I repeat, I have just as much right as other women to expect not to be insulted, every moment, by anyone who pleases." She flashed a final glance at her lover, then lowered her eyes and started mechanically moving the objects on the table in front of her.

Consternation was visible in all their faces. "But I never thought of insulting you," said Leo calmly. "I merely said that the only one among us all who is not discontented is myself."

"Oh yes, of course," she answered, obviously hinting at something or other, "it's quite easy to see that *you*'ve no reason to be discontented."

"Really, Mom," Carla broke in, "he hasn't said anything insulting." Since this last scene, the girl was overwhelmed by a sort of terrified desperation. I've had enough of it, she thought, looking at her childish, middle-aged mother who, with head bent, seemed to be ruminating over her own jealousy. I must get away from all this, I must make a change at any cost. Absurd resolutions passed through her mind—to run away, to disappear, to vanish into the world, into the air. She recalled something interesting Leo had said: "What you need is a man like me." It was the end—he or another one, she thought—the end of her patience; and her unhappy eyes passed from her mother's face to that of Leo. These were the faces in her life, she thought, hard yet pliable, uncomprehending; and then she looked down again at her plate where the food was growing cold in the congealing wax of the sauce.

"As for you," commanded her mother, "you needn't say anything. You can't possibly understand."

"Really, my dear Signora," protested her lover, "I didn't understand anything, either."

"*You*," she replied, stressing her words and arching her eyebrows, "*you* understood me only too well."

"So be it, then," began Leo, shrugging his shoulders.

"All right, be quiet!" she interrupted him scornfully. "It's better for you not to say a word. In your place I should try and hide my head, or disappear altogether."

There was silence, while the maid came in and removed the plates. Now, thought Michele, seeing the angry expression on his mother's face gradually relaxing, the storm is over and the sun's coming out again. He lifted his head and, without the slightest suggestion of gaiety, "I say," he asked, "is the incident closed?"

"Completely closed," answered Leo with assurance. "Your mother and I are reconciled." He turned towards Mariagrazia: "Isn't that true, Signora? We're reconciled, aren't we?"

A pathetic smile trembled hesitatingly on the woman's painted face; she knew that voice and that insinuating tone from happier times, when she was still young and her lover still faithful. "Do you think, Merumeci," she asked, looking daintily at her hands, "that it's so easy to forgive?"

The scene was becoming sentimental. Carla quivered and lowered her eyes, Michele smiled scornfully. There, he thought, there we are; give each other a kiss and don't talk about it any more.

"To forgive," said Leo with mock gravity, "is the duty of every good Christian." (To hell with her! he was thinking. It's lucky that there's the daughter to compensate for the mother.) Covertly, wtihout turning his head, he examined the girl. A sensual type, more so than her mother, lips red, fleshy, obviously disposed to yield; he must try, after dinner, strike while the iron's hot, not wait till next day.

"Well then," said the mother, entirely reassured, "let us be Christians and forgive." The smile, so far withheld, now expanded, pathetic and brilliant, showing two rows of teeth of a doubtful whiteness; the whole of her tired body palpitated. "And, by the way," she added, in a sudden access of maternal love, "we mustn't forget. Tomorrow is our dear Carla's birthday."

"We don't keep it any more, Mom," said the girl, looking up.

"Oh yes indeed, we're going to celebrate it," her mother answered solemnly. "And you, Merumeci, consider yourself already invited for tomorrow morning."

Leo made a sort of bow over the top of the table. "Delighted," he said, then, turning to Carla, asked, "How old will you be?"

Their eyes met. Her mother, who was sitting opposite her, raised two fingers and moved her lips as though to say "twenty." Carla saw, understood, hesitated; and then a sudden hardness played havoc with her mind. She wants me, she said to herself, to understate my age so as to make her appear less old. She disobeyed. "Twenty-four," she answered unblushingly.

An expression of disappointment crossed her mother's face.

"As old as *that?*" exclaimed Leo, in playful surprise. Carla assented. "Yes, as old as that," she repeated.

"You shouldn't have told him," scolded her mother; and the sharpness of the orange she was eating increased the acidity of her expression. "One is always as old as one looks . . . and you don't look a day more than nineteen." She swallowed the last segment of the orange. Leo brought out his cigarette case and offered it all around; blue smoke began to ascend in thin spirals from the disordered table. For a moment they sat motionless, looking into each other's eyes; then the older woman rose. "Let's go into the drawing-room," she said. And the four of them went out.

3

DURING A BRIEF but painful passage along the corridor Carla
kept her eyes fixed on the floor, thinking how this daily tread
of feet must have worn threadbare the old carpet that covered it, and how the oval mirrors on the walls must surely
have preserved some trace of their faces and figures which
had been reflected in them several times a day for years—
but only just for an instant, of course, just time for her
mother and herself to examine their makeup, Michele the
set of his tie. In this corridor habit and boredom lay in wait
and pierced the soul of anyone who passed along it, as
though the very walls exhaled poisonous fumes. Everything
here was immutable—the carpet, the light, the mirrors, the
glass door of the vestibule on the left, the dim space of the
staircase on the right; everything, here, repeated itself—
Michele stopping a moment to light a cigarette and blowing
out the match, her mother complacently inquiring of her
lover, "Don't you really think I look tired this evening?";
Leo, answering indifferently, without taking his cigarette out
of his mouth: "Why no, not at all, I've never seen you look
so bright"; and herself, suffering from it all. No, life did not
change.

They went into the cold, gloomy, rectangular drawing-room, which was divided into two unequal parts by a kind of arch, and sat down in the corner opposite the door. Curtains of dark velvet concealed the closed windows; there was no chandelier but only lamps, in the form of sconces, fixed to the walls at equal distances, three of which were lit and diffused a mediocre light in the smaller half of the room, while the other half, beyond the arch, remained plunged in a shadowy blackness in which reflections from mirrors and the long shape of the piano could barely be distinguished.

For a moment they did not speak; Leo was smoking apologetically, the Signora was gazing with mournful dignity at her hands with their enamelled nails, Carla, almost on all fours, was trying to light the lamp in the corner and Michele was looking at Leo. Then the lamp went on, Carla sat down and Michele spoke. "I've been to see Leo's agent and he's told me a whole lot of things," he said. "The gist of the matter is this: apparently the mortgage falls due in a week's time, and we shall accordingly have to clear out and sell the house in order to pay Merumeci."

His mother opened her eyes very wide. "That man doesn't know what he's talking about. He's acted merely according to his own ideas. I've always said he had something against us."

There was silence. "That man spoke the truth," said Leo at last, without raising his eyes.

They all looked at him. "But really, Merumeci," implored the Signora, with joined hands, "surely you're not going to turn us out like that, at a moment's notice? You must give us a little respite."

"I've already done that twice," said Leo, "and that's enough —especially as it wouldn't help to avoid a sale."

"How d'you mean—not avoid?" she asked.

Leo raised his eyes and looked at her. "I'll explain," he said. "Unless you can manage to get together eight hundred thousand lire, I don't see how you could pay except by selling the house."

She understood, and an immense fear opened like an abyss before her eyes. She turned pale, and looked at her lover; but Leo, absorbed in contemplation of his cigar, gave her no

[22]

reassurance. "This means, then," said Carla, "that we shall have to leave the villa and go and live in a small flat?"

"Yes," answered Michele, "exactly."

There was silence again. The older woman's fear became vast and over-powering; she had never wanted to know anything about poor people, not even to know any of them by name, she had never wanted to admit the existence of people whose work was laborious and whose lives were dreary. "Their lives are happier than ours," she always said; "we are more sensitive and more intelligent and therefore we suffer more than they do." And now, lo and behold, she was forced to mingle with them, to swell the throng of the poor and wretched. She was oppressed by the same sense of repugnance, of humiliation, of fear that she had once experienced when driving a car that was very close to the ground through a dirty, menacing crowd of strikers; she was terrified not so much by the discomforts and privations she would have to face, as by a burning sense of shame, by the thought of how the people of her acquaintance, all of them well-off, respected and elegant, would treat her, of what they would say; she saw herself poor, lonely, with these two children of hers, with no friends, since everyone would desert her, with no amusements, no dances, no lights, no entertainments, no parties, living in obscurity, in complete, naked obscurity.

Her pallor increased. I must talk to him alone, she thought, clinging to the idea that she might be able to seduce him, without Michele, without Carla. Then he will understand.

She looked at her lover. "If you, Merumeci," she proposed vaguely, "will grant us another respite, we'll find the money somehow."

"How will you do that?" he asked, with a faint knowing smile.

"The bank . . ." she hazarded.

Leo laughed. "Oh, the bank." He bent forward and stared straight into his mistress's face. "Banks," he said slowly and clearly, "do not lend money without safe guarantees; anyhow, with the present scarcity of ready money, they now don't lend at all. But supposing they did lend, what kind of guarantee could *you* give them, dear Signora?"

"This discussion is meaningless," observed Michele. He felt he ought to be working himself into a passion over this vitally important question, to be making violent protests. After all, he thought, it's a question of our very existence. At any moment we may find ourselves with literally nothing to live on. But, however hard he tried, this threatened ruin remained alien to him; it was like seeing someone drowning, and looking on without moving a finger.

His mother, however, behaved quite differently. "You must give us this respite," she said with haughty intrepidity, pronouncing each word separately and drawing herself up, with her bosom thrust out, "and you can be sure that at the date it falls due, you'll have your money—yes, down to the last penny. You needn't worry."

Leo laughed softly and lowered his head. "Yes, I'm sure of it," he said. "But what's the point of a respite, then? These methods you'll adopt to raise money—why don't you make use of them now and pay me at once?"

That lowered face was so calm and wise looking she was afraid of it, and her eyes moved irresolutely away from Leo to Michele, and then to Carla. There they were, those two defenseless children who would now know the hardships of poverty; and an exalted feeling of mother love came over her. "Listen, Merumeci," she began in a persuasive voice; "you're an old friend of the family, and I can say anything to you. It's not only for myself, it's not for my own sake that I ask for this respite; personally, I should even be prepared to go and live in a garret." She raised her eyes to heaven. "God knows I'm not thinking of myself, but I've got to find a husband for Carla. Now you know what the world is like; the very same day I leave the villa and go live in some little flat, everybody will turn their backs on us. People are like that. And then, what will be the use of thinking of my daughter's marriage?"

"Your daughter," said Leo, with false seriousness, "has a beauty which will always find her suitors." He looked at Carla, and winked at her. A deep, restrained rage had taken possession of the girl, and she wanted to cry out to her mother, "Who do you think is going to marry *me*, with this man about the house and you in the situation you are?" She was hurt and humiliated by the coolness with which her mother, who customarily took no trouble at all about her, now dragged her into the discussion as an argument favorable to her own ends; she must stop it, she felt, she'd give herself to Leo, and then nobody would ever want her for a wife. She looked her mother in the eyes. "Don't think about me, Mom," she said with firmness; "I don't come into all this, and I don't want to."

It was at this moment that a peal of laughter, so acid, so false that it set the teeth on edge, came from the corner where Michele was sitting. His mother turned towards him. "You know," he said, making a great effort to cover the indifference of his voice with a tone of sarcasm, "you know who will be the first to desert us if we leave the villa? Guess!"

"Why, I don't know."

"Leo!" he burst forth, pointing at the man, "our dear Leo."

Leo made a gesture of protest.

"Ah, Merumeci?" repeated the Signora, hesitant but clearly impressed, looking at her lover as though she wanted to read in his face whether or not he were capable of such treachery. Then, her eyes and smile glittering with pained sarcasm. "Of course," she said, "of course. How stupid of me not to think of it! Of course, Carla," she added, turning to her daughter, "Michele's quite right. The first person who'll pretend never to have known us—after having first pocketed his money, naturally—will be Merumeci. Don't protest," she went on, with an insulting smile, "it's not your fault, all men are like that. Yes, I could swear it, he'll walk past with one of those perfectly charming, smart lady friends of his and will barely see me. He'll turn his head the other way. Of course, dear man, I would put my hand in the fire." She paused for a moment. "Well, well," she concluded, in a bitter, resigned tone; "well, well. Christ, too, was betrayed by his best friends."

Overcome by this flood of accusations, Leo put down his cigar. "You," he said, turning towards Michele, "are only a boy, and for that reason I don't take you into consideration.

But that you, Signora," he added, turning back to her, "could possibly think that I should desert my best friends on account of any sale whatsoever—that I did *not* expect . . . no, really I did *not* expect it." He shook his head and took up his cigar again.

How false he is, thought Michele, amused; then suddenly he remembered that he himself was the man who was being robbed and mocked and outraged, in his patrimony, in his dignity, in the person of his mother. Insult him! he thought; start a scene! He realized that, during that evening, he had missed numberless opportunities for picking a quarrel more favorable than this one, for instance when Leo had refused to grant a respite; and now it was too late. "You didn't expect it, eh?" he said, throwing himself back in his armchair and crossing his legs. He hesitated, then, without moving, added: "You swine!"

They all turned towards him, his mother in astonishment, Leo slowly, at the same time taking his cigar out of his mouth. "What did you say?"

"What I mean is—" Michele started to explain, gripping the arms of the chair and failing, in his indifference, to rediscover the reasons that had urged him to throw out this vehement insult; "what I mean is that Leo . . . that Leo has ruined us, and now he pretends to be our friend. But he isn't really."

There followed a silence of deep disapproval. "Listen, Michele," said Leo at last, fixing a pair of completely inexpressive eyes upon the boy. "I noticed, some time ago, that you wanted to start a quarrel tonight, goodness knows why. I'm sorry, but let me tell you at once it won't work. If you were a man I'd know how to answer you, but you're nothing but an irresponsible boy, and therefore the best thing you can do is to go to bed and sleep on it." He paused and took up his cigar again. "And you say this to me," he added brusquely, "just at the moment when I was going to propose the most favorable terms possible."

There was silence again. "Merumeci is right," the Signora chimed in. "Really, Michele, he hasn't ruined us and he's always been friendly to us. Why insult him in this way?"

Ah, now you're defending him, thought the boy; and he

was filled with a violent irritation both against himself and against the others. If you only knew how completely indifferent all this leaves me, he wanted to cry out. His mother, excited and concerned, Leo deceitful, even Carla who was looking at him in astonishment—they all seemed to him, at that moment, to be ridiculous, and yet enviable just because they clung to their own kind of reality and really considered the word "swine" to be an insult, whereas to him everything, both gestures, words and feelings, was nothing more than an empty game of pretence.

And yet he was determined to go to the end of the road on which he had started. "What I said is perfectly true," he remarked without conviction.

Leo shrugged his shoulders in disgust and dissatisfaction. "Will you be so kind," he broke in, violently shaking the ash from his cigar, "will you be so exceedingly kind?"—and already Michele's mother was preparing to give him her support, with "You're completely wrong, Michele,"—when, at the far end of the room, in the feeble light that reached it from the corner where they were sitting, the door was half opened and a woman's blond head appeared round it.

"May I come in?" asked the head, and everyone turned round.

"Oh, Lisa!" exclaimed the Signora. "Come in, come on in." The door now opened completely and Lisa entered. Her plump body was enveloped in a blue coat that reached down almost to her minute feet; her head, on which was a small cylindrical hat of blue and silver, looked even smaller that it really was above those full shoulders further widened and rounded by the thick, winter material of the coat; and even though the coat itself was ample, the curving, swelling lines of her exuberant bosom and hips were abundantly visible. The extremities of her figure, on the other hand, were astonishingly small, and it was very surprising to observe the thinness of her ankles beneath the wide, bell-like shape of her coat.

"I'm not interrupting?" she asked, coming forward into the room. "It's late, I know. But I was dining in your neighborhood, and since I was passing along your street I couldn't resist the temptation of paying you a visit, so I came."

"Why, of course," said the Signora. She rose and went over to meet her friend. "Won't you take off your coat?" she asked.

"No," answered the other woman; "I'll stay just a moment and then run away. I'll just undo it—there! Then I won't be too hot."

She undid the belt of her coat, revealing a showy, glossy black silk dress adorned with large bluish flowers. Then she greeted Carla: "Good evening, Carla. Ah, Leo too: impossible *not* to find Merumeci here! And Michele: how's Michele?" She sat down on the sofa beside the Signora.

"What a pretty frock you're wearing!" said the latter, pulling Lisa's coat aside. "Well, what news have you to tell me?"

"None at all," replied Lisa, looking around. "But why are your eyes all starting out of your heads? You look as if you'd been having an argument and I'd interrupted it."

"No, no," protested Leo, looking at Lisa through his cigar smoke with a glance of deliberate mystification, "not at all. The greatest gaiety has reigned here, so far."

"We were just chatting about nothing in particular," said the Signora. She took up a box and handed it to her friend: "Will you smoke?"

At this point Michele, in his usual inopportune manner, broke in. "You're absolutely right," he said, bending forward and gazing intently at Lisa. "We were having a violent quarrel and you interrupted our argument."

"Oh," said Lisa, with a forced and malicious laugh, "then I'll go away. I wouldn't, for anything in the world, disturb a family council." She made no move to rise.

"Please don't *dream* of going away," the Signora protested, and added with an angry grimace at Michele, "Idiot!"

"An idiot, am I?" repeated the boy. That suits me exactly, he thought. An idiot . . . yes . . . an idiot to try and work myself up into a state of excitement over these problems of yours. He was oppressed by an odious sense of futility and boredom. He moved his eyes around, over the hostile half-darkness of the room, until finally they came to rest on the faces near him. Leo was looking at him—ironically, it seemed to him—with a barely perceptible smile on his fleshy lips, a smile that was insulting. A strong man, a normal man, would have taken offense and made a protest, but he—he did nothing. He, with a depressing feeling of superiority, of pitying contempt, remained indifferent. But he was determined once more to assert himself against his own true nature. I must make some protest, he thought. I must insult him all over again.

He looked at Leo. "I say," he began, in a colorless voice, "what need is there for you to smile?"

"I . . . well, really . . ." replied Leo, feigning astonishment.

"I say . . . went on Michele, raising his voice with a painful effort. This was the way to begin a quarrel. He remembered having been in a streetcar, while a violent argument went on between two equally fat, equally important gentlemen; each of them, after calling all those present to witness, and stating in the most feeling terms, his own respectability, his own profession, his own war wounds, and, in general, all those details that might possibly move his audience, had finished—still in the hope of overwhelming his adversary—by shouting at the top of his voice and attaining a degree of genuine anger. That was what he, too, ought to do. "Don't imagine," he went on, "that just because Lisa's arrived I'm unable to repeat what I said before. I *do* repeat it, in fact—Swine!"

They all looked at him. "But really!" his mother exploded in indignation.

Lisa was examining Michele with curiosity. "Why . . . what's happened?" she asked. Leo neither moved nor showed any sign of being offended: he merely uttered a high-pitched artificial, contemptuous laugh. "Ah, that's magnificent . . . magnificent," he repeated. "One isn't even allowed to smile any more." Then, brusquely, "Joking's all very well," he went on, getting up from his armchair and hitting his fist on the table; "but that's enough, now. . . . Either Michele apologizes to me or I leave the house."

They all understood, now, that the matter had become

serious, and that Leo's laugh had been only the livid flash of lightning that precedes the breaking of the storm.

"Merumeci is absolutely right," said the Signora, her expression hard, her tone imperious; she felt cruelly exasperated at her son's behavior because she feared her lover might seize this opportunity of breaking off relations with her. "Your conduct is disgusting. . . . I order you to apologize."

"But . . . I don't understand. Why is Merumeci a swine?" asked Lisa, with an obvious desire to complicate matters.

Only Carla neither moved nor spoke. A miserable, irritating disgust oppressed her; she had a feeling that the distressing tide of the day's little events was about to overflow and finally submerge her patience; she half-closed her eyes and peered unhappily between her eyelids at the stupid, annoyed faces of the other four.

"Oh," said Michele ironically, without moving, "so you *order* me? And supposing I don't obey?"

"In that case," replied Mariagrazia, not without a certain touching, if theatrical, dignity, "you would be causing your mother great displeasure."

For one moment, without speaking, he looked at her. "You would be causing your mother great displeasure," he repeated to himself; and the phrase seemed to him at once ridiculous and profound. That's right, he thought, with a distaste that was only superficial. It's a question of Leo . . . of her lover . . . and yet she doesn't hesitate to drag in her position as mother. But that was what she had said: "You would be causing your mother great displeasure"—a phrase both repugnant and irrefutable. He removed his eyes from that sentimental countenance and he momentarily forgot his intentions of truthfulness and indignation. In the long run, he thought, nothing matters in the least to me. Why not apologize and spare her this famous displeasure? He raised his head; but he was still determined to tell the truth, to display the whole of his own insulting indifference.

"Do you really think," he began, "that I'm incapable of apologizing to Leo? If you only knew how little all this matters to me."

"That's a nice thing to say!" his mother broke in.

[30]

"You can't possibly imagine," continued Michele, almost excited, "how utterly indifferent I am to it all. So don't be afraid, Mom. If you like, I'll not only apologize to Leo but kiss his feet too."

"No, don't apologize," said Lisa at this point; she had been following the scene with close attention. They all looked at her.

"Thank you so much, Lisa," said the Signora, in an offended, dramatic manner, "thank you so very much for setting my own son against me."

"Who's setting your son against you?" answered Lisa calmly. "But it doesn't seem to me to be worth it."

Leo looked at her sideways. "I don't care to be called names like that by a boy," he said in a hard voice. "I've asked for an apology and I shall have it."

"Wouldn't it be better to forget the whole thing and make it up?" suggested Carla, leaning forward with a half surprised, half ingenuous look on her face.

"No," answered her mother; "Merumeci is right: Michele must apologize."

Michele rose to his feet. "I'll do it, don't worry. . . . Well then, Leo," he said, turning towards him, please accept my humblest apologies for having insulted you. . . ." He paused a moment; how easily the humiliating words had fallen from his lips! "And I promise I won't do it again," he concluded, with the quiet voice and the indifference of a child of six.

"All right, all right," said Leo, without looking at him. Imbecile! Michele wanted to shout at him, seeing him so assured, so completely engrossed in his own role. But it was Michele's mother who, deceiving herself, was more pleased than anybody. "Michele is a good son," she said, looking at the boy with sudden tenderness, "Michele has obeyed his mother."

The flame of humiliation and shame, which had not lit in Michele's cheeks while he was offering his apologies to Leo, now suddenly scorched him in face of this lack of understanding. "I did what you wished," he said brusquely; "and now, if you don't mind, I'll go to bed, because I'm tired." He twisted on his heel like a marionette and without saying good night to anybody, went out into the corridor.

As he came into the hall, he noticed someone was following him. He turned, and there was Lisa. "I came on purpose to tell you," she said, panting and looking at him with a curious, impassioned expression, "that whenever you like I can introduce you to that relative of mine . . . and he'll be able to find you a job of some kind . . . in his own firm, or elsewhere."

"Thank you so much," said Michele, staring at her in turn.

"But you must come to my flat . . . then you can meet him there."

"All right." As Lisa became more embarrassed, the boy seemed to grow calmer and more attentive. "When?"

"Tomorrow," said Lisa. "Tomorrow morning, early . . . *He*'s coming about midday . . . but that doesn't matter . . . We'll have a bit of a talk, shall we?" They were both silent, looking at each other. "And why did you apologize like that to Leo?" she demanded boldly. "You oughtn't to have done it."

"Why?" he asked. Ah, he thought, that's what you're coming to, is it?

"There's no time to tell you the reason now. Besides, they might start wondering," explained Lisa, becoming all at once very mysterious. "But if you come tomorrow I'll tell you."

"All right then. Till tomorrow." And he shook her hand and went off upstairs.

Lisa went back into the drawing-room, where the other three were still sitting in the corner, around the lamp. The Signora, whose face, with all its colors, was exposed to the full light, was talking about Michele. "It was obvious," she was explaining to her lover, who was lying back in his arm-chair, listening to her with a completely stupefied expression, without moving an eyelid, "it was obvious that it cost him a great deal to make that apology. He's not a person who yields easily. He's very proud," she added, with an air of defiance; "he has a proud, upright soul like mine."

"I don't doubt it," said Leo, raising his eyelids and taking a long look at Carla. "But this time he did right to yield." All three remained silent; the incident was over and done with; and now Lisa, on noiseless feet and with the least meddlesome expression in the world on her face, came forward into the room.

"Have you got your car here, Merumeci?" she asked.

All three turned towards her. "My car?" repeated the man, rousing himself. "Yes, of course, I've got my car here."

"Then you'll take me home, won't you?" said Lisa, "—providing, of course, that I'm not being a nuisance . . ."

"But of course not, the pleasure is entirely mine." Leo got to his feet and buttoned up his coat. "We'd better go, then . . ." he began. But secretly he was chafing with rage; not merely had he failed to do anything about Carla, but now he had to take Lisa home into the bargain.

But he was saved by the obtuse jealously of Mariagrazia. Between the two of them, Leo and Lisa, there had been, many years before, a relationship, a love affair—they had, in fact, been engaged to be married—when Mariagrazia, already a widow, had appeared on the scene and had stolen her best friend's fiancé. It was a very old story now, but . . . suppose those two had the idea of starting the affair all over again? She turned towards Lisa. "No, don't go away just yet," she said. "I want to talk to you."

"All right," Lisa looked at her in false embarrassment. "But then I shan't have Merumeci to drive me home."

"Oh, don't worry about that." This time the pleasure was truly all on Leo's side. "I can wait for you in the corridor, or here. You can go on talking to the Signora. I'll wait for you. Carla," he added, looking towards the girl, "Carla will keep me company."

Indolently Carla rose to her feet and, shaking her big head, walked towards him. Now, she was thinking, if I'm left alone with him now it's the end of everything. Leo was looking at her in what seemed to her a knowing way, and this taking for granted of her complicity was hateful to her; but what would be the use of resisting? A distressing impatience took possession of her. Make an end of it, she repeated to herself, looking at the dimly lit drawing-room where so many days of fire had burned themselves out in ashes, and at the solemn, ridiculous group around the lamp, make an end of all this. And she felt herself falling slowly and hesitatingly into a state of resigned acceptance, like a feather fluttering down the shaft of a staircase.

She made no protest, therefore, and said nothing.

"But you don't know," objected the Signora, "how long I'm going to keep Lisa. You'd much better be going. We'll get a taxi for Lisa." It was an insinuating voice, the voice of jealousy: Leo was polite but inflexible. "I'll wait," he said. "What does it matter? A minute more or less. I'll wait with pleasure. . . ."

She saw she had lost, and that it was going to be impossible for her to separate these two, Leo and Lisa. It's quite obvious that he wants to wait for her, she thought, examining their two faces, so that they can then go together to her flat. This idea seemed frightful to her, and jealousy shone openly in her eyes. "All right, then," she said at last, "go on . . . go and wait outside. I'll give you back your dear Lisa in a moment— in just one moment, don't worry." She waved her hand threateningly, and a bitter, spiteful smile trembled on her painted lips. Leo looked at her fixedly, then shrugged his shoulders and, without saying a word, went out, followed by Carla.

In the passage, without making any fuss about it he put his arm around the girl's waist; and she, although well aware of it, resisted the temptation to free herself. It's the end, she thought, the end of my old life. The mirrors gleaming in the shadows reflected their two interlaced figures as they passed.

"You saw," she said aloud, "Mother's jealous because of Lisa." There was no reply beyond a pressure of the arm that brought her side close against the hard side of the man: and so united they came into the vestibule—a small, cube-shaped room with high, white walls and diamond-shaped tiles on the floor.

"And who knows?" she added, with a humiliating sense of futility; "I daresay it may be quite true." This time he stopped and, without releasing her, came face to face with her.

"On the contrary," he said, with an awkward, silly, ex-

cited smile, "you know whom she *ought* to be jealous of?
Why, you . . . yes, you . . ."

Now we're in for it, she thought. "Of me?" she demanded
in a clear voice. "Of me? Why?"

Their eyes met. "Will you come and see me?" Leo asked,
in an almost paternal manner; and saw that she lowered her
head without saying yes or no. This is the right moment, he
thought; and he was already pulling her towards him and on
the point of bending to kiss her when a sound of voices in
the corridor warned him that her mother was approaching.
He almost choked with rage; it was the second time that day
that his mistress had come and spoiled everything just at the
most delicate moment. The devil take her, he thought; he
could hear her talking and arguing with Lisa in the passage,
and although there was still no sign of her appearance Carla,
in agitation, made motions to break away from him. "Let me
go," she murmured, "Mom's coming." Leo, furious, looked
at the door, looked all around the room and yet could not
make up his mind to let go of that supple waist; then suddenly his eyes fell upon a curtain that concealed a door on
the right hand side of the vestibule. He put out his arm,
switched off the light. "Come," he whispered in the darkness,
seeking to draw Carla into the hiding place; "come in behind
here. We'll play a joke on your mother." She did not understand, resisting him, her eyes shining in the gloom. "But
why?—Why?" she kept repeating. In the end, however, she
yielded; they went in behind the curtain, flattened themselves in the doorway, and Leo put his arm round the girl's
waist again. "Now you'll see," he murmured; but Carla saw
nothing; she stood erect and rigid, closing her eyes in the
undulating, dust-scented blackness behind the curtain, allowing Leo's hand to wander over her cheeks, her neck. "Now
you'll see," he whispered to her. The curtain quivered from
top to bottom, and she felt the man's lips pressed against her
breast, then creeping awkwardly up to her chin and finally
stopping at her mouth, in a profound but short-lived kiss.
The voices came nearer, and Leo drew himself up. "There
she is," he murmured in the darkness, and he squeezed Carla

[35]

with a confidential, intimate violence and an assurance that had previously been lacking.

The glass door opened; Carla held the curtain a little to one side and peeped out. In the luminous square of the open doorway the figure of her mother, full of highlights and shadows, was expressive of astonishment and incomprehension. "But they're not here," exclaimed the familiar voice; and Lisa, invisible, asked from the corridor, "Wherever can they have got to?"

The question received no reply. The Signora's head, thrust forward, peered about as though to explore the vestibule. Her features, in that semi-darkness, seemed hollowed out, so that the soft, painted face looked like a mask petrified in an expression of pathetic bewilderment. Each wrinkle, the mouth half open and black with make-up, the staring eyes, the whole face seemed to be crying out, "Leo is not there . . . Leo has forsaken me . . . Leo has gone." Carla watched her, half curious and half pitying, divining the fear that trembled behind that mask; and it seemed to her that she saw that same face as it would be in the days to come when her mother knew of the treachery of her lover and her own daughter. The spectacle lasted only an instant; then the head withdrew. "It's strange," the voice could be heard saying, "Merumeci's overcoat is still here, and they're not."

"Perhaps they're in the hall," answered Lisa. And so, amidst wonderments and speculations, they both went away.

"Did you see?" murmured Leo; he bent down again and clasped the girl to his breast. This is the end, she thought once more, putting her mouth to his; she liked this darkness that prevented her from seeing him and thus left her all her illusions, and she liked this intrigue. Then they separated. "We must go now," she whispered, holding the curtain apart with both hands, "we must go, Leo, or they may notice."

He agreed unwillingly, and one behind the other they came out from their hiding-place, like a couple of thieves. The light shone out brilliantly, and they stood looking at each other. "Is my hair untidy?" Carla asked; he shook his head. "And now, what are we going to say to Mom?" she added.

A coarsely mischievous expression lit up the man's red,

excited face, and he slapped his thigh and laughed. "Ah, that was grand," he exclaimed, "splendid . . . What are we going to say to them? Why, that we were here, of course . . . that we were here all the time. . . ."

"No, Leo," said Carla, looking at him doubtfully and joining her hands over her stomach. "Not really?"

"Yes, really," he repeated. "Ah, here she is."

The door opened and Carla's mother reappeared. "Why, they're here!" she exclaimed, turning towards Lisa; "and we've been looking for them all over the house. Where were you?"

Leo made a gesture of surprise. "We were here all the time."

The Signora looked at him as one looks at a poor idiot. "Don't talk nonsense. I came in here a little while ago and there was no one here and it was all dark."

"In that case," answered Leo placidly, taking down his overcoat from the peg, "you evidently suffer from hallucinations. We've been here all the time. Isn't that true, Carla?" he added, turning to the girl.

"Absolutely true," she replied, after a second's hesitation.

There was an ominous silence. The Signora had the impression that everyone was making fun of her, but was quite unable to find any reason for it; she suspected some mysterious purpose, some dark Machiavellian plot, and, irritated but irresolute, was weaving a network of inquisitorial glances between Leo, Carla and Lisa.

"You're mad," she said to him at last. "Five minutes ago there was no one here . . . Lisa was with me, and she is my witness," she added, pointing to her friend.

"Yes, it's true; there was no one here," said the latter calmly.

There was silence again. "And Carla is witness that we *were* here," said Leo, casting a meaning glance at the girl. "That's the absolute truth, isn't it, Carla?"

"Yes, it's true," she admitted in confusion, struck, for the first time, by the incontestable fact that they had indeed been there, in the vestibule, when her mother had come in.

"Very well, then," said her mother bitterly; "very well . . .

[37]

You're right, and it's *I* who am mad, and Lisa too." She paused for a moment. "Leo may allow himself these jokes, if he chooses." Then, turning towards Carla, she burst forth: "That's his affair. But that *you* should start making fun of me —you ought to be ashamed of yourself. A nice sort of respect you have for your mother."

"But it's perfectly true, Mom," Carla protested. The joke was becoming painful to her now, it was penetrating like a thorn into the impatience that possessed her; "we *were* in the vestibule." She wanted to add: "We were behind the curtain, Leo and I, embracing"; and she pictured the scene that would have burst forth like an explosion at these words. But it would have been the last; everything, then, would have been over.

In the meantime Lisa, with an expression of boredom, was saying: "Shall we be going, Merumeci?" And he, ready to leave, was holding out his hand to the Signora. "Think about it upstairs," he could not help saying with a smile, "think about it all night long." To which she replied, with a shrug of the shoulders, "Personally, I sleep, at night." Then she kissed Lisa, murmuring to her: "Well then, remember what I said to you." The girl opened the door, a gust of cold air came into the vestibule, and the two of them went out and disappeared in the darkness.

4

MOTHER AND DAUGHTER went upstairs together. Before they parted the mother—who, offended by the farce in the vestibule, had not spoken a word—asked her daughter what she was doing next day. "Tennis," answered Carla; after which, without kissing, they went each to her own room.

In Carla's room the lamp was lit, for she had forgotten to turn it out, and in that white, glowing light, the furniture and all the other objects seemed to be awaiting her arrival. When she entered she went over and looked at herself in the big wardrobe looking-glass. There was nothing abnormal in her appearance except for the tired, dark-ringed, mysteriously sparkling eyes; blue-black haloes encircled them, and the profound look in them—a look filled with hopes and illusions—troubled her as much as though it had come from some other person. She stayed this way for a moment, leaning with her hands against the glass, then drew back and sat down on the bed. She looked around. The room in many respects was like that of a little girl of three or four years old: the furniture was white, less than the normal size, hygienic, the walls white with blue friezes; a row of neglected, ragged dolls, with crooked heads and turned-up eyes, sat on the little sofa under the window; the fittings were those of her childhood, and her mother, short of money, had been unable to exchange them for something more suitable to her present age; besides, in any case, she had said, what need was there for new furniture? She would be getting married and would be leaving the house. And so Carla had grown up in the narrow framework of her earliest years. And yet the room had not stayed as it was then, bare, infantile; each age had left its trace, in knickknacks and odds and ends; and now it was full, comfortable, intimate, but with a quality of intimacy in itself ambiguous, sometimes feminine (the dressing-table with its faded ribbons, for instance, and its perfumes and powders, creams and make-up, and the two broad pink garters hanging beside the oval mirror), and sometimes merely childish; and its equivocal character was complicated by a flimsy, wholly feminine untidiness, made up of garments thrown over chairs, of open bottles and shoes lying upside down on the floor.

Carla looked at these things. Her contemplation was uninterrupted by thought: there she sat, on her bed, in her room, the light burning, everything in its place as on other evenings —that was all. She began to undress, taking off her shoes, her dress, her stockings. And as she performed these habitual acts she looked furtively around, seeing now the mop-haired head of a doll, now the clothes stand with dresses hanging on it, now the dressing-table, the lamp . . . and that light, that special, quiet, familiar light which, by dint of illuminating them, seemed to be right inside the very objects themselves, and which, together with the carefully closed window veiled by its short, dazzlingly white curtains, gave a pleasing if slightly distressing sense of security. Yes, there was no doubt; she was in her own room, in her own home. It was probable that outside those walls it was night, but she was separated from it by that light, by those objects in such a way that she could ignore it, and could think that she was alone, yes, all alone and out of the world.

She finished undressing and, quite naked, shaking her big, ruffled head, rose and went to the wardrobe to fetch a clean pair of pyjamas. She took those few steps lightly, on the tips of her toes; then, as she stooped down and opened the drawer, noticed that her big breasts moved of their own accord, just there, under her eyes. As she drew herself up again, she caught sight of herself in the mirror. She was struck by the awkward, timid, attitude of her naked body, and then by the disproportion between her too-large head and her too-slender shoulders; it was owing to her hair, perhaps; and she took a mirror from the wardrobe shelf and held it behind the back of her neck. Yes, her hair was too long. I must go to the hairdresser, she thought.

She looked at herself again. Yes . . . her legs were a little crooked—oh, only a very little!—from the knees downwards, and her bust . . . her bust was too low; she lifted it slightly, with her two hands. "It ought to be like that," she thought. She turned her head and tried to make a close inspection of her back; and then, as she gazed over her shoulder and sought to take in, as a whole, this other image of herself, she was assailed by a sense of contrast between the futility of these posturings and the grave events of the past day: Leo had kissed her, she reminded herself, only a few minutes before. She put down the mirror and returned to the bed.

She sat down and stayed, for a moment, quite still, with her eyes fixed on the floor. "A new life really *is* beginning," she said to herself at last. She raised her head, and suddenly it seemed to her that this quiet, innocent, unsuspecting room, these familiar things, partly shabby and partly silly, made up, altogether, a living entity, a single person with a clearly de-fined figure, for whom she was in the process of preparing, secretly and without any fuss, a monstrous betrayal. "In a very short time . . . good-bye for ever," she kept on saying to herself with a joy melancholy and nervous, and as she sat on her bed she waved her hand in farewell to the objects that surrounded her, as though from a departing ship. Vast, crazy, melancholy images passed through her mind, and it seemed to her that a chain of fatality linked all these events together. "Isn't it strange?" she said to herself, "tomorrow I am going to give myself to Leo and thus a new life should begin . . . and it so happens that tomorrow is the day on which I was born." She remembered her mother. And it is with *your* man, she thought, with *your* man, Mom, that I'm going. Even this ignoble coincidence, this rivalry with her mother, pleased her; everything must be impure, dirty, low, there must be neither love nor affection, but only a dark sense of ruin. "I must create a scandalous, impossible situation, full of scenes and hopelessly shameful," she said to herself; "I must ruin myself utterly." She kept her head bent and then, suddenly raising her eyes, caught sight of herself in the wardrobe mirror and, without knowing why, began trembling all over; she wanted to weep and pray, and it seemed to her that these melancholy thoughts had already destroyed her. "Where is my life going?" she kept asking herself, looking down on the floor, "where is it going?"

These grievous words, in the end, held no more meaning for her; and she realized that she was no longer thinking, that she was naked, that she was sitting on the edge of the bed; the lamp was burning, around her the objects in the room were in their usual places; and of the exaltation of a few minutes earlier there remained nothing but empty bitterness. She felt that, by an effort, she had approached the true center of her problem and had then, unaccountably, lost sight of it.

What will happen will happen, she thought. She picked up the pyjamas, idly put them on, slipped under the bedclothes, turned out the light and closed her eyes.

5

No SERVANT slept in Lisa's flat; she did not want one. For indispensable matters such as cooking and cleaning she had the services of an active little woman, the portress of the building, who "came in"—a system which, certainly, was not without inconveniences; but Lisa, whose life was extremely free not to say disorganized, preferred it that way.

That morning she woke late. For some time now she had been coming home after midnight; her sleep was without pleasure, and she rose almost more tired and nervous than the day before. She roused herself with difficulty and looked around without moving or raising her head. A thin, dusty gloom, pierced, like a sieve, by a thousand threads of light, filled the room, and in this half-darkness could be dimly discerned the mute, dead shapes of old pieces of furniture, of silent mirrors, of clothes hung up, and of a dark patch which was the door. The air was heavy with the stuffiness of sleep and with the smell of the furniture; the window was closed. Lisa got out of bed and, pushing back the hair that hung over her damp face, went to the window and opened the shutter. A white daylight invaded the room. She pulled aside the curtain; the window panes were pearled over with moisture, showing that it must be cold outside; and through this thick dew could be dimly seen vague, thin, pure colors—a piece of white, a patch of green, dissolved, as it were, in a pool of water. With a sweep of the hand she tore apart the liquid veil and saw a piece of reddish roof which appeared so dull, so uninteresting, so opaque, that she had no need to look upward to see that the sky was gray. She drew back and took a few steps around the crowded room. The big double bed, of dark, common walnut, full of tumbled white sheets, took up a great deal of space, and was so near the square window that sometimes on winter nights it gave her great pleasure, as she lay under the warm bedclothes, to see only a yard away the stream of rain pouring from the vast torrential night down the window panes. Besides the bed, there were two big wardrobes of the same homely, evil-smelling wood, with immense yellowing mirrors. The room was of moderate size, but, with such furniture, the amount of space left over for moving about was exceedingly small.

She went over to the clothes stand. She was wearing nothing but a transparent nightdress that made the outlying portions of her figure appear even shorter than they really were; her legs were entirely uncovered, right up to the deep fold of flesh that divided the rotundities of her buttocks from her white, hairless thighs; and her muscular breasts, scarcely lower than they had been when she was twenty, were half exposed—two smooth, veined swellings. She caught sight of herself in a looking-glass, half naked, bending well forward as though to hide the dark region of her groin beneath that inadequate veil, and judged she had grown thinner; then she slipped on a dressing-gown and went through into the bathroom.

It was a gray, bare, chilly little room, with dull, painted pipes, a bath of enamelled metal, a solitary, rusty mirror, and damp shadows filling every corner. Lisa turned on the light. It occurred to her that three days had gone by since she had washed herself all over, and that she would have to have a bath; she hesitated: was it really absolutely necessary? She looked at her feet, the toenails were white, and appeared to be clean; no, there was no need, all the more since, if—as was probable—she spent the night with Michele, she would then have to wash thoroughly next day. She made up her mind, went over to a basin fixed to the wall, turned on the taps, waited till it was full; then she took off her dressing-gown, pulled her nightdress down to her waist and washed herself—first her face, puffing and sneezing as she did so, then her neck and armpits, making movements to try and prevent the water trickling down from her breast and shoulders to the lower parts of her body which were still warm from the night. Each time she bent down she felt the nightdress mounting up her back, while a stony chill rose from the tiled floor; at the last moment she could not find the towel, and ran back, blinded and streaming with water and naked as she was, into the bedroom to fetch one.

She dried herself and sat down at the dressing-table. Her toilet was a brief process, for she used no creams or make-up, and all she had to do was to apply a little powder and scent and comb her hair; and finally she turned her back on the mirror and bent down to put on her stockings. Two thoughts were now alternating in her mind—the thought of breakfast and the thought of Michele. She liked good things to eat in the morning with her coffee—little pastries and jam and butter and almond cakes; she was greedy and did not leave the table until she had had more than enough, but today she feared she would have to go hungry. "If Michele comes quite soon," she said to herself, "it's better for him not to find me eating. Never mind . . . another time." She straightened herself up, put on a pair of pink panties, then a very tight brassiere that swathed her bosom like a corset, and meanwhile, to console herself, she allowed her imagination to depict Michele as being madly in love but shy, an inexpert youth to whom she would give herself trembling with joy. A pure love, in fact. After the life I've led, she convinced herself, a little innocence won't do any harm. Sleepless nights, exhausting pleasures, joyless excitements—the foul mist vanished away. Michele was bringing her sunshine, blue sky, frankness, enthusiasm; he would respect her like a goddess, would lay his head upon her knees; she had an insatiable desire for him, and could hardly wait for the moment when she would drink at that fountain of youth, when she would return to a fresh, stammering, modest love such as she had almost forgotten in the last twenty years. Michele was purity itself; she would give herself to the boy without sensuality, almost without ardor; naked, she would dance to meet him, would say to him, "Take me"; their love would be far from ordinary, a love of an old-fashioned kind.

She finished dressing, left the room, crossed the dark passage and went into her light-filled boudoir. This room was all white and pink, the furniture and ceiling were white, the carpets, the upholstery. the sofa, pink. Three big windows, gracefully veiled, diffused a quiet light, and at first sight everything looked pure and innocent; many delicate things could be seen—here a work-box, there a small bookcase full of many-colored books, some sparse flowers on the painted shelves, a few glazed water-colors on the walls—a number of things, in fact, which at first made you think: "What a nice, bright, quiet little place; it must be the abode of some young girl!" But if you looked more carefully you changed your mind, because you then realized that the boudoir was no younger than the rest of the flat; you observed that the paint on the furniture was flaking and yellowed with age, that the upholstery was discolored and in places threadbare, that the sofa cover was torn and the cushions shabby; one more look and you were convinced: holes could be seen in the curtains, the glasses of the water-colors were broken, the books dusty or torn, and there were wide cracks in the ceiling. And if, finally, the mistress of the house was present, there was no need to look any farther, for all this decay leaped to the eye just as though her figure proclaimed it.

Lisa sat down in front of the writing-table and waited; the idea of breakfast now came back to her, and she had a great desire for it but did not know what to do. If only I knew what time he was coming! she thought with annoyance, looking at the watch on her wrist, but in the end she controlled herself and gave up the thought again, returning to her tender, merciless, excited imaginings. I'll make him sit on the sofa, she thought suddenly, and I'll lie down behind him. We'll talk a little. Then I'll begin to whet his curiosity on some risky subject, and I'll look at him. And if he isn't a fool he'll understand. She examined the sofa as if it were some instrument whose quality and efficacy she wished to assess; and said to herself that if all went well she would keep the youth waiting for the delicate pleasure of watching him sigh, and then finally, after a few days, would invite him to dinner and keep him the whole night. And what a dinner that would be! All sorts of tit-bits, and—above all—wine; and she would put on that dress that suited her so well, the blue one, and would adorn herself with those few jewels that she had been able to save from the rapacious hands of her ex-husband. The table should be laid here in the boudoir, for the dining-room was much less intimate—a table for two, full of good things, fish and meat pies and vegetables and sweets— a small table, rich and glittering, for two, just for two, there was no question of a third, however much anyone wanted. Eyes shining with joy and tenderness, she would sit opposite her dear boy—even while she ate she would not stop looking at him; she would pour out wine for him, lots of wine, she would talk to him in a humorous, inquisitive, suggestive, maternal tone; she would find out about his little love affairs, would make him blush; every now and then she would give him a gentle wink, and their feet would touch under the table; and when dinner was over they would clear the table together, laughing, touching each other and knocking against each other out of sheer desire. Then she would undress, would slip on a dressing-gown, and would make Michele put on one of her husband's pairs of pyjamas, which would fit him perfectly since they were of the same height, though the boy was slimmer. Then, sitting on the sofa, she and Michele would know the joy—the maddening, greedy joy—of the prelude to their first night together. And at last they would go together into the bedroom.

Excited by these fantasies, she remained sitting at the desk. She kept her head bent, and from time to time, as if to chase away her thoughts, brushed back her hair, or, still without ceasing to think, twisted her feet and looked at her shoes. The sound of the bell quickened the beating of her heart; she smiled, glanced at herself in a mirror, and went out into the corridor.

[47]

Before opening the door she switched on the light. Michele came in.

"Perhaps I've come too early?" he said, hanging up his coat and hat.

"Of course not." They went through into the boudoir and sat down on the sofa. "Well, how goes it?" asked Lisa. She took up a box of cigarettes and offered it to the boy; he refused and sat there deep in thought, his hands resting on his knees.

"All right," he replied at last; and there was silence.

"If you don't mind," she said, "I'm going to lie down on the sofa. But you . . . you stay there . . . make yourself comfortable." She lifted her legs and stretched herself out against the cushions. Michele saw her white, clumsy thighs and smiled to himself. The idea came to him again: Obviously she wants to excite me. But Lisa did not attract him, not in the very least, and all this was quite uninteresting to him.

She looked at the boy, wondering what she could say to him. Those pretexts towards greater intimacy which a few minutes earlier had seemed so spontaneous, now, in her agitation, escaped her; her mind was blank, her heart in a tumult, and she suddenly recalled, for no apparent reason, the scene of the evening before, the quarrel between Leo and Michele, which at the moment she had found interesting. She hesitated to speak of it again, but was encouraged by the idea of getting back at her old lover by telling the boy—if he did not know it already—of his mother's intrigue; then, by indirect means, she would be able to arrive at a more exciting conversation.

"I bet," she said, looking at him, "I bet you're dying to know why I asked you yesterday evening not to make that apology to Leo."

He turned. It's you who are dying to talk about it, he wanted to answer. But he restrained himself. "I'm not exactly *dying* to know," he said; "but tell me, anyhow."

"I believe I have more right than anyone to open your eyes," she began.

"I don't doubt it."

"One keeps quiet for a long time, one pretends not to see

[48]

. . . but in the end it gets the better of one. What I saw last night revolted me."

"Forgive my asking," said Michele, "but what exactly was it that revolted you?"

"That apology to Leo"; she gazed at him seriously, "and, above all, that it should actually have been your mother who insisted on your humiliating yourself like that."

Ah, now I understand, Michele thought and his face lit up with irony. You want to break the great news to me that my mother has a lover. A sharp feeling of disgust, both with himself and with the woman came over him. "But perhaps it wasn't a humiliation," he added aloud.

"Yes, it was, whichever way you look at it. . . . And doubly so, when you hear what I'm going to tell you."

He looked at her and thought, If I took hold of you now 'round the waist, or pinched your back, you'd soon drop that solemn, secretive air—and how you'd wriggle! . . . "I warn you," he said aloud, and it seemed to him that he was being truly sincere, "that I'm not in the least interested in knowing anything."

"Very well," answered Lisa, not at all disconcerted; "you may be right . . . but I feel I've got to speak . . . you'll thank me later . . . you must know that your mother has committed an error. . . ."

"Only one?"

Of the two alternatives open to her—being annoyed or laughing—Lisa chose the second. "No doubt she's committed thousands," she said, smiling and coming a little closer to the boy, "but this is certainly the biggest."

"One moment," interrupted Michele. "I don't know what you're going to tell me . . . but if, as it seems, it's something serious, I should like to know why you're revealing it to me."

They looked at each other. "Why?" echoed Lisa, slowly dropping her eyes. "Because you interest me very much and I'm very fond of you too, and also, as I said before, because certain kinds of injustice revolt me."

He knew of the ties that had existed between her and Leo. Or rather, he thought, it revolts you that he was taken away from you, eh? But he nodded gravely. "You're right, there's nothing worse than injustice! But come on, tell me, what does this error consist of?"

"Well. . . . Ten years ago your mother first met Leo Merumeci. . . ."

"You don't really mean to tell me," interrupted Michele with a look of assumed horror, "that Leo is my mother's lover!"

They looked at each other. "I'm sorry," said Lisa with pained simplicity, "but that is so."

There was silence. Michele stared at the floor and longed to laugh. His disgust was transformed into a bitter feeling of absurdity.

"And now you can see," went on Lisa, "why, and how much, your mother revolted me when she made you humiliate yourself in front of that man."

He neither moved nor spoke. Again he saw his mother, Leo, and himself in the act of asking Leo's pardon—small, silly figures lost without hope in the greater vastness of life. . . . But these visions did not shock him nor rouse any sort of feeling in him; he wished he could be quite different—indignant, filled with spite and inextinguishable hatred; instead of which he suffered because he was so utterly indifferent.

He watched Lisa as she raised herself to a sitting position beside him. "Come, come," she said, putting a clumsy, consoling hand on his head, "come, come . . . cheer up! I understand how unpleasant it must be to you. . . . One exists with the certainty that a person deserves one's affection, one's esteem, and then . . . there comes a moment when everything collapses around one. But it doesn't matter . . . this is part of your training for life."

He shook his head, biting his lips so as not to laugh; but Lisa imagined that he was overcome by grief. "Not all ill is sent to harm us," she said in an affected, honeyed voice, without interrupting her stroking of the boy's hair. "This will bring us together, won't it? Would you like me to be to you what your mother once was? Tell me, would you like me to be your friend, would you like to take me into your confidence?" She was sincere, but her voice was so flutelike, so artificial, that Michele wanted to clap his hand over her mouth; but he sat quite still, with his head obstinately bent. The vision of himself sitting beside this woman on the edge of the sofa, with a face half contrite and half idiotic, seemed to him so ridiculous that in order not to laugh, there was only one possible thing to be done—to keep perfectly still.

Lisa became even more enthusiastic. "You must come and see me often. We'll have good, long talks. We'll make a great effort to build up a new life, to reorganize things."

He looked at her stealthily. Her face, below the fringe of blonde hair, was red, red and excited. So that's how you begin your organizing, he thought. Then he remembered the relative who was supposed to be coming that morning: why not take the whole business seriously and turn it to good use? Why not keep up the humbug?

He lifted his head. "This has been a hard blow," he declared, like someone who has mastered a great sorrow, "but you're right. . . . I've got to make a new life for myself."

"Certainly you must," Lisa agreed fervently. After which a profound silence followed. Both of them, for different purposes, affected an entranced, inspired fit of abstraction; they sat quite still, side by side, looking at the floor.

A rustling sound; and Michele's arm slipped in behind Lisa's back and around her waist. "No," she said in a clear voice, without moving or turning her head, as if she were replying to some interior question. Michele smiled unwillingly, for he was conscious of a certain troubled stirring within him, and he pulled her more closely to him. "No, no," she repeated in a weaker voice, but she yielded and laid her infatuated head on the boy's shoulder. Then, after a moment of sentimental immobility, he took her by the chin and, in spite of the false, mute protest in her eyes, kissed her on the mouth.

They separated. "How naughty you are!" said Lisa, pathetically, with a half smile of gratitude; "naughty, and audacious too." Michele glanced at her with a cold look in his eyes; then a smile passed over his thin, serious face; he put out his hand and started pinching her in the ribs as hard as he could, under the arm. "Ooh, ooh!" she cried, laughing and opening her mouth wide and wriggling, "ooh, ooh!" She waved her arms and legs; finally she fell off the sofa, and, as her whole body twisted and squirmed, her dress rose up about her belly, and her big thighs, their white smoothness broken by the tautness of their muscles, were exposed to view. Michele relaxed his embrace. Lisa sat down again and pulled her skirt down over her knees.

"Oh, what a bad boy you are!" she cried in a falsetto voice, pressing a hand to her panting bosom. "Oh, what a bad boy!" Michele said nothing but observed her with earnest solemn curiosity. "Now this," she went on, putting her hands on his shoulders, "this is what you ought to do to me—watch." She pursed her lips into the shape of a heart and brought them close to the boy's lips, touched them lightly and then withdrew, her eyes shining with satisfaction. "That's how you ought to do it," she repeated, trying to hide her own excitement.

Michele twisted his lips; then he got up and walked around the boudoir, hands in pockets, looking at the commonplace water-colors hanging on the walls; he was irritated and excited. "Do you like them?" he heard suddenly from behind him. He turned and saw Lisa. "They're just rubbish," he said.

"Well, really," she answered, mortified. "They always seemed to me rather good."

They went back to the sofa. The boy's temples were throbbing, his cheeks burning. All this is degrading, he thought in disgust; but as soon as they had sat down, he threw Lisa back on the cushions as though he wanted to possess her there and then. He saw her glossy eyelids close, her face assume an expression of abandoned ecstasy, half repugnant, half ridiculous; and the impression was so strong that all desire vanished. He kissed her mouth coldly, and then, with a kind of groan, plunged his head down into her lap. In the darkness there, he thought: I want to stay like this until I go away; I don't want to see her any more, or kiss her any more.

He felt caressing fingers touching his hair, stroking it. "What's the matter?" asked the familiar, false voice.

"I was thinking," he replied in a hollow tone, closing his eyes, "what a very slight effort is required to be sincere, and how, instead, one does everything possible to go the other way." He sighed; it seemed to him that he had explained himself clearly. Why do I stay here? he wondered. Why do I tell lies? It would be so easy to tell the truth and go away.

"Yes, that's just what happens," she answered, without ceasing to stroke his hair; "that's perfectly true. But you mustn't have ideas like that any more. You won't need anybody else now; I'm here, and we'll be together . . . and we'll ignore the rest of the world." She uttered these words with a fervency of tone that made the boy shudder. "We'll live far away from all the things you dislike, won't we? Far away from all these miseries. You'll tell me all about your life and your troubles and your unhappiness, and I'll give you all the love I possess, that I've kept in reserve for you. I'll be your companion, shall I?—your faithful, humble companion—oh, yes, very, very humble—who will listen to you in silence and comfort you with her caresses, like this . . . like this. . . ." The hand that moved over the boy's head stiffened; Lisa bent down and wildly kissed his hair and the back of his neck, while her feverish fingers clutched his bowed shoulders and squeezed them nervously. Her heart was trembling. At last I love and am loved, she thought. . . . At last.

Michele did not stir. He had never before seen absurdity confused to such an extent with sincerity, falsity with truth; and a painful embarrassment took possession of him. If she'd only stop talking, he thought. But no, she can't help going on. From moment to moment he was seized by a hysterical longing to tell the truth, his own, real truth, the only possible truth, and then go away; but he was held back by a feeling of compassion; besides, had he not himself first deceived Lisa by embracing her in that way?

"My dear . . . my dear," she went on repeating, her face pressed against his head, "you can't imagine how dear you are to me. The boy wanted to say "You go altogether too far"; but his eyes were filled with darkness, he felt he had never seen the light; and her words, her caresses, her voice, all gave him the sensation of a night unrelieved by hope.

[53]

He raised his head and sat up, rubbing his dazzled eyes. "It's time I went away," he said. "And that relative of yours— when is he coming?"

"I'll go and telephone him," said Lisa, who obviously was not expecting this question. She went out.

He was left alone. He got up, went over to the wall, looked absent-mindedly at one of the water-colors; then, as though absorbed in thought, opened the door slightly. The telephone was there, fixed to the wall at the end of the dark passage, but there was no Lisa: her leaving the room had been a mere pretense, her relative did not exist; she had lied in order to entice him to her flat.

"A pretense," he said to himself, closing the door again carefully. "It's quite right to pretend." He went back to the wall and resumed his contemplation of the water-color, which represented a farmhouse and some haystacks. A slight but wearisome disgust oppressed him, just as when one feels a desire to be sick and tries to restrain it; but the thought, *When all's said and done, she's just like me*, served, in the end, to arouse a measure of compassion in him for that needlessly untruthful figure. We're all the same, he thought. Of all the thousand ways of performing an action, we always, instinctively, choose the worst.

After a moment the door opened and Lisa came back into the room. "I'm so sorry," she said, "he's busy and can't come. . . . But he says tomorrow . . . tomorrow afternoon, if you can." They stood looking at each other; Michele's disgust, and his feeling of pity, were intensified. This is too much, he thought. This is leading me by the nose. And tomorrow it will be the same story over again: come back tomorrow. It seemed to him that if he pretended not to have understood it would establish a kind of complicity between them, a bawdy self-deception that would allow them as they went on waiting for the non-existent relative, to come to an agreement, without too many scruples, on all other points.

"No," he said, "I'm not coming back tomorrow."

"But he's *coming*," she persisted, with a sort of effrontery; "and if you're not here. . . ."

Michele put his hand on her shoulder and looked at her.

"All this is quite ridiculous," he said; "he's not coming. Why not tell the truth?" She was alarmed, he could see, and—which was worse—in order not to meet his eye, she hazarded a wanton, shameless smile, as though she did not at all mind being caught in the act.

"What d'you mean, the truth?" she repeated, without looking at him and without ceasing to smile. "I don't understand you . . . unless anything unforeseen happens, he'll certainly come."

"I looked into the passage," explained Michele calmly. "You didn't telephone . . . and this relative doesn't exist."

There was a moment's silence; then Lisa, taking the easiest line, smiled again and shrugged her shoulders slightly. "And if you looked into the passage, why do you ask me all these questions?"

Michele observed her carefully. Is it really possible, he thought, that she doesn't feel we ought to be on a better footing than *that?* He decided to make another effort. "No," he insisted, "don't take that attitude about it. It's a very serious matter. Why, instead of playing the fool like this, didn't you simply say: 'Come back tomorrow and we'll have tea together?'"

"Yes, I ought to have said that, I know." She spoke without humility, with a kind of impatience. "All the same you'll come, won't you? In any case you needn't worry; even if I didn't speak to my relative, I certainly *will*, as soon as I can."

There now, thought the boy. She thinks that my finding fault with her is owing to my disappointment at not meeting that blasted relative. His expression hardened. "No, I shan't come," he said, "and you needn't speak to anybody." He left her and went out into the passage.

A smell of cooking pervaded the dark, confined space. "You really mean that you won't come?" she asked, half imploring, half incredulous, as she handed him his hat. He looked at her and hesitated. Everything had turned out, in the end, to be useless—both disgust and pity; and the woman remained as firmly fixed in her misconception as before. This sense of the vanity of his efforts hurt him, and the desperate, agonizing boredom that oppressed him made him want to cry out. "What would be the use of coming?" he demanded.

"How d'you mean, what would be the use of it?"

"It wouldn't be any use"—he shook his head—"not the slightest. Since you're like that, there's nothing to be done. You're all like that."

"What d'you mean, like that?" she insisted, blushing in spite of herself.

Mean, sordid. Love, for you, just means going to bed. What I was chiefly thinking about was meeting your relation. This was the answer Michele would have liked to give; instead, he said: "Very well, then. . . . I'll come all the same," and there was a moment's silence. "But before I go," he added, "explain one thing to me. . . . Since you're now sure that I . . . that I love you, and therefore that I shall come back, why did you go on making use of that excuse about your relative, instead of telling me the truth?"

"I disliked the idea of confessing to you," she explained, not without some hesitation, "that I had invented that story, in the first place, in order to get you to come here."

"But there was no need for it, even in the first place," said Michele, looking at her intently.

"No, I know," she admitted, humbly; "you're right. But who is without sin? Besides, that relative of mine really does exist, and he's very rich. Only it's a long time since I've seen him."

"Well, never mind," said Michele. He took her hand. "Till tomorrow, then," he began; but suddenly realized that Lisa was looking at him in a strange manner, with a half timid, half flattering smile. He understood. So be it, then, he thought. He bent down, clasped her to his breast and kissed her on the mouth, then released her and went out. In the doorway he turned to say good-bye, and then saw that Lisa, like a young girl in love for the first time, was hiding modestly, bashfully, behind a coat that hung on a peg in the darkness of the hall, and, with two fingers to her lips, was blowing him a last kiss.

What a sorry farce! he thought; and, without turning back again, went off down the stairs.

6

THAT DAY, the Signora finished dressing extremely late. At midday she was still sitting at her dressing-table, slowly moving the little darkening brush over her swollen eyelids, with many grimaces and the greatest possible care. The moment she woke, the fantasies of jealousy had put her in a bad humor; then suddenly she had remembered that this was Carla's birthday, that she was twenty-four, and a swift, hysterical rush of maternal feeling had flooded her heart. My little Carla, my poor darling little Carla, she thought, almost weeping with tenderness. Really, she's the only person in the world who loves me. She got up and dressed with this thought of Carla and Carla's birthday in her mind; it seemed to her a piteous thing, a touching fact to be wept over, and she had never, during the whole of that time, stopped picturing the presents and the treats that she would shower upon the girl. She hasn't many dresses. I'll give her some. I'll give her four or five. I'll give her a fur coat, too . . . she's wanted one for such a long time. Where the money was coming from for all this generosity, she never stopped to think. And she must find a husband, she went on to herself. Then I shall have nothing more to wish for. And then, as she reflected that her daughter was twenty-four and still unmarried, there swept over her a fury of vituperation against men in general. All these idiotic young men! All they want is to amuse themselves and waste their time, when they ought to be thinking of settling down to family life. But of course Carla would get married. She's good-looking, she thought, counting her daughter's gifts on her fingers. In fact I might say *very* good-looking. She's good, too, with an angelic sort of goodness. Then she's intelligent, cultivated . . . she's had an excellent education. What more can you want? Money—ah, that was it—money was lacking; Carla would go to her husband's house just as she had come into the world, naked, rich only in her virtues; of that there could be no doubt. But was it true, then, that nowadays only rich girls got married? Hadn't there been cases, quite recently, of girls marrying extremely well without a penny of their own? Slightly fortified by this idea, she went out of her bedroom into the anteroom.

A bunch of magnificent roses, together with a box, lay on the table in the middle; there was a note among the flowers. The Signora took it, tore open the envelope and read: "To Carla, my *almost* daughter, with the most affectionate good wishes, Leo." She put the note back among the roses. How delicate he is! she thought, pleased. No other man in his position would know so well how to behave towards his mistress's children. But he eliminates every possible ground for suspicion. He's like a father. She wanted to clap her hands with delight, and if Leo had been present she would have embraced him. Then she opened the box, which contained an embroidered silk handbag with a clasp made of some blue stone; and the mother's joy was complete.

She took the box and the bunch of flowers and ran to Carla's room. "Many happy returns of the day!" she cried to her. "Look what's come for you!" Carla, who was sitting at the table with a book in her hand, got up and read the note without saying a word; Leo's impudence, his complacency in addressing her as "my *almost* daughter," brought back to her mind, in contrast—and so brusquely that it made her shudder—the distressing and, in a sort of way, incestuous quality of her intrigue with him. She looked up; her mother's eyes were shining with joy, and she was smiling with emotion as she clasped the bunch of flowers, in a slightly absurd way, to her bosom. "Very nice of him," said Carla coldly. "And what is there in that box?"

"A handbag," replied her mother enthusiastically, "an extremely smart evening bag for which he must have paid at least five hundred lire. Look!" She opened the box and showed the girl Leo's present. "Isn't it lovely?" she added.

"Very lovely," answered Carla. She put it down on the table and they exchanged a glance.

"And so," her mother said suddenly in a voice full of emotion, "and so my little daughter is twenty-four today. And yet it seems only yesterday that she was just a small child."

"Yes, Mom, it seems so to me too," Carla answered, without a hint of irony. But she would have liked to add: "From today onwards I'm not going to be a child any more."

"You used to play with your dolls," her mother went on. "You used to rock them in their cradle and make signs to me not to talk, and then tell me they were asleep." She stopped half-way through these touching recollections and looked hard at Carla. "Let's hope that some day you may be doing the same thing with dolls of flesh and blood."

"Yes, Mother, let's hope so," answered the girl, embarrassed and at the same time sorry for her mother.

"Truly, Carla," the latter insisted, as though she wished to convince her daughter of some great and profound truth, "there's only one thing I want . . . for you to get married. Then I shall be happy."

Carla smiled. *You?* But should *I* be happy? she wondered. "Yes, indeed," she replied, hanging her head. "But it takes two to get married. . . ."

"He'll turn up all right," exclaimed her mother with complete confidence. "In fact . . . listen. It may seem absurd to you, but I have a kind of presentiment that you'll get married during this next year . . . or get engaged, anyhow. I have this idea. . . . I don't know why; it's one of those things that can't be explained. But you'll see, it will turn out to be true."

Something quite different will turn out to be true, Carla

[59]

wanted to answer, and she thought of her decision to give herself to Leo that very day. Her mother's lack of understanding gave her the painful sensation that they were all of them shrouded with no hope of escape, in some kind of impenetrable darkness. She smiled and answered firmly, "Of course, something's bound to happen."

"I have a presentiment that it will," her mother repeated with conviction. "And these flowers—where shall we put them?"

They put the flowers in a vase and went out of the room. There was little light in the anteroom; the narrow window on the staircase was veiled by a red curtain, and the empty corners were plunged in gloom. They sat down on a sofa. "Tell me," Carla's mother immediately asked, "how did you think Lisa was, last night?"

"How did I think she was? Just as usual."

"Did you think so?" said her mother doubtfully. "I thought she'd got fatter . . . and—I don't know—that she'd aged, too."

"Oh no . . . I don't think so," replied Carla. She had understood what her mother was driving at. It's me you ought to be jealous of, she thought, not Lisa.

"And that frock she was wearing," continued her mother, "I've never seen anything in worse taste. And *she* thought she was wearing something quite remarkable."

"Really," said Carla, "I didn't thing it ugly."

"Hideously ugly," asserted her mother. She remained for a moment with her eyes staring wide open into the void as though she could see the figments of her jealousy taking concrete form in front of her. Then, turning sharply towards her daughter, "Now tell me the truth," she said. "Did you notice how Lisa attached herself to Merumeci?"

Here we are again, thought Carla, and longed to cry out, from sheer boredom *It wasn't Lisa, but me. We were embracing behind the curtain . . . yes, embracing.* But instead she replied: "How d'you mean—*attached* herself?"

"*Attached* herself," repeated the other woman; ". . . and how anxious she was to get him to take her home. D'you know what *I* think?" she added, bending forward, "that she

[60]

would very much like to re-open their old relationship. That's why she was making such languishing eyes at him. . . . But Merumeci has something else to do than think about *her*, poor woman. . . . In any case, if he wanted, he could find a thousand women better than *her* . . . with his looks, and his figure. She's eaten up with envy and hypocrisy; she says one thing to your face, another behind your back. Well, really, I'm kind to everyone, I always find good qualities in everyone, I wouldn't hurt a fly—but that woman, I just cannot bear her."

"But you're a friend of hers."

"Well, what can one do?" said her mother. "One can't always tell the truth to people's faces. Social conventions often oblige one to do exactly the opposite of what one would like. Otherwise I don't know where one would finish up." She reinforced her words with gestures that implied: Make no mistake about it. It really is like that. She raised her eyebrows, she twisted her mouth. But Carla's expression hardened, and she made a great effort not to look at the maternal mask in front of her. *A little more truth*, she wanted to cry out, *might perhaps improve matters*.

"But falsity for falsity's sake," continued her mother, "systematic hypocrisy, such as Lisa goes in for . . . well, that's a thing I can't stand. Anything but that. For instance, I'm sure that it wasn't for *our* sakes that she came here last night! She must have known, somehow or other, that Merumeci was here, and that's why she came in. After all, she had nothing of interest to say, she stopped a very short time, and she just couldn't wait to be gone again."

Carla observed her mother almost with pity. The laborious, painful way in which she dug up these false interpretations always inspired her with a mixture of disgust and compassion. "Really?" she said, just in order to say something.

"Without the slightest doubt," rejoined her mother with assurance. She sat for a moment deep in thought; then, in that clear half-darkness, among the velvet door-curtains, her painted face twisted itself into a grimace of hatred. "Why," she said, "that woman is repulsive to me, even physically. . . . I don't know. She gives the impression of being clammy and

at the same time full of desire, full of heat . . . like a bitch
. . . yes . . . she looks at men with those shining eyes, in an
inviting sort of way . . . as much as to say: come with me.
But, good heavens, if I were a man, I wouldn't want to touch
her even with the tips of my fingers. It would disgust me."

"I assure you, Mom," said Carla, "she doesn't have that
effect on me."

"You don't understand," said her mother. "There are some
things you can't understand. But I, who am a woman of experience, with a knowledge of life, when I see a person of
that type, with those eyes and that figure . . . I can sum her
up in a moment—just like taking a snapshot."

"Well, perhaps so," Carla admitted. They were both silent
for a moment, and there was no sound or movement in the
house. Then, from downstairs, from the far end of the corridor, came the noise of the front door being slammed. "That
must be Merumeci," said the Signora, rising to her feet. "You
go and receive him; I'll come in a minute."

Carla's heart began to beat more rapidly. She went downstairs one step at a time, like someone who feels faint and
goes slowly to avoid falling; she went into the drawing-room,
and, just as her mother had imagined, Leo was there, standing by the window with his back to her.

"Ah, there you are!" He took her by the arm and made
her sit on the sofa.

"Thank you for the present," she said at once. "But why
that note?"

"What note?"

" '*Almost* my daughter,' " she said, her eyes fixed upon
him.

"Oh!" exclaimed Leo, as if he had forgotten it. "Yes, of
course. . . . That was what I wrote . . . almost my daughter
. . . perfectly true."

"Why did you write that?"

A half gratified, half impudent smile lit up the man's face.
"First of all, out of consideration for your mother . . . and
also because I like to imagine that you are my daughter."

She looked at him. How shameful, she was thinking, how
utterly shameful! But her longing for destruction was stronger

[62]

than her disgust. "I—your daughter!" she said with a faint smile. "Really, I never thought of such a thing. What put that idea into your head?"

"Last night," answered Leo quietly, "while we were behind that curtain. At that moment, I don't know why, I remembered seeing you as a little girl, no taller than that, with bare legs and your hair down your back, and I thought: I might easily be her father, and yet in spite of that. . . ."

"In spite of that we love each other, don't we?" Carla concluded, and, looking straight into his eyes: "But don't you feel that those two things are—what shall I say—irreconcilable?"

"Why?" answered Leo, without ceasing to smile, moving his hand across his forehead. "In a general way, perhaps . . . but in each separate case each person acts according to his own feelings."

"But it's against nature!"

Leo laughed at the girl's serious, anxious expression. "Yes, but since you're *not* my daughter, the question doesn't arise." Their eyes met.

"By the way," he added, "before I forget. After lunch make some excuse and go out into the garden . . . in the direction of the shrubbery. . . . I'll join you almost at once. . . . Are we agreed?" She nodded. Leo, satisfied, folded his arms and looked up at the ceiling; he did not intend to touch her, since at any moment he expected the indiscreet arrival of her mother. Rather than be left full of unsatisfied excitement and desire, he thought, it's better to put the whole thing off till later, when there will be nobody there and I can take my time. But whenever he looked at Carla, his face glowed like a lamp; he wanted to seize her, embrace her, possess her there on the sofa, that very moment.

These images of lust increased his resentment against his mistress; he recalled the jealous scene that Mariagrazia had made the night before, and a feeling of irritation, unsoftened by pity, swept over him. "Your mother," he said brusquely to Carla, "is a first-rate goose."

The girl turned and was on the point of answering, but the sound of doors opening and closing prevented her; and then her mother, almost dragging Michele by the hand, came into the room. "Good morning, Merumeci," she cried to her lover. Then, without any transition, she pointed towards her son and went on: "Here's Michele. He says that, if we sell the villa by auction instead of handing it over to you, we could not only pay you but might have a few tens-of-thousands of lire left over for ourselves. Is that true?"

Leo's face darkened. "That's nonsense," he said without moving. "No one will ever offer you more for the villa than the amount I'm giving you."

"But when all's said and done," said Michele, coming forward, "you aren't giving us anything. You're just turning us out, that's all."

"I've already given you a good deal," answered the other, irritated and bored, looking at the window filled with white sky. "But in any case," he added in a resentful voice, "do just as you like. Sell the villa, give it away, as you like. But I warn you that I shan't help you in any way . . . and that the day that sum falls due, it has got to be here, in my hands."

Leo knew the risk he was taking in saying this; supposing they really did put the villa up at auction? In that case its true value would come to light and the whole business, as far as he was concerned, would peter out. But the Signora, who knew nothing about auctions and sales, who had the impression that business was synonymous with swindling, and who, above all, was frightened of being deserted by her lover and would have done anything to ingratiate herself with him, reassured him.

"No," she broke in, "not by auction—certainly not. But surely, Merumeci, you could give us better terms. We could come to some sort of compromise."

"What sort of compromise?" he demanded, without looking at her.

"For instance," she said, with sublime stupidity, "allow us the use of the villa until Michele gets a job and earns some money, and until Carla is married."

Her proposal was greeted with a high, forced, contemptuous laugh. "I should have a long time to wait in that case," said Leo at last, when his false hilarity had died down, "a nice long time. . . ." He looked at Carla and read his own thought in her sad, resigned eyes: Who is going to want to marry *me?* But the feeling he himself derived from the thought was different: there was no pity or melancholy in it, merely vanity and pride at being the controlling destiny in her life.

"What?" asked the Signora, offended. "What do you mean?"

"I don't want to be misunderstood," Leo explained. "I have no doubt that Carla will get married very soon, and I hope so with all my heart. . . . But with regard to Michele, I don't believe he can possibly make any money for many years to come, nor do I think he is on the right road for doing so. On that point, dear Signora, I have my honest doubts."

So far Michele, who had allowed himself most unwillingly to be dragged into this discussion by his mother, had said nothing. But now, hearing himself thus openly accused of idleness and ineptitude, he saw that in spite of all his indifference, he must take action. The moment has come to be indignant, he told himself, and he took a step forward. "I am not the sort of person you think," he said in a completely false tone of voice. "I shall prove by my actions that I am capable of working and earning money like anybody else. You shall see," he went on, secretly wondering at the expression of approbation and pride that filled his mother's face, "that, even without your help, I shall manage to support myself and my family."

"That's perfectly right," exclaimed Mariagrazia. She moved her hand proudly over the head of her son who smiled with pity for her. "Michele will work and get rich," she said, elated at the idea, "we have no need of anyone else."

But Leo was not so stupid. He shrugged his shoulders angrily. "Rubbish," he cried. "One never knows, with Michele, whether a thing's a joke or a serious subject of conversation. You're a buffoon, that's all you are, just a buffoon." He had reached the summit of his indignation. If there was one matter about which he could not bear witticisms to be

[65]

made, it was business; he would have liked to leave them all, there and then, and rush out of the house.

Michele took another step forward. "A buffoon?" Was it, or was it not, a serious insult, an injury to his honor and his reputation, to be thus called a buffoon? To judge by his own unruffled indifference, it was not; if, on the other hand, one thought of the significance of the word and of the far from friendly feeling that had inspired it, then it certainly was. I must act, he thought, with a kind of intoxication. For instance I might hit him. There was not a moment to be lost; Leo was there, only one step away, leaning against the velvet curtain in the embrasure of the window; the cheek that he ought to strike was there in the full light—broad, rubicund, well nourished, well shaved, with plenty of room for his whole hand, so that there was no fear of missing the target . . . and so . . .

"Oh, so I'm a buffoon, am I?" he said in a colorless voice, approaching still nearer; "and don't you think I might possibly take offense at being called that?"

"Take offense as much as you like as far as I'm concerned," replied Leo, with a smile of complete unconcern, but watching him closely.

"Take that, then!" Michele raised his hand; but, with surprising rapidity, his wrist was seized, his gesture thwarted, and, without his even knowing how it happened, he found himself thrust back into the corner of the window; Leo had hold of him by both wrists, and behind him the two women ran up in consternation.

"Oh, so you wanted to hit me, did you?" said the man at last, with a sort of quiet sarcasm. "But you're making a big mistake. The man isn't yet born who'll succeed in doing that." He spoke calmly, but with clenched teeth. And from behind him: "What's the matter? Why . . .?" the Signora was exclaiming. As for Michele, he was chiefly struck, in spite of his own uncomfortable position, by the other man's powerful, assured elegance. His double-breasted jacket of brown cloth fitted smoothly to his torso, his shirt was white and fresh, his starched collar of glossy white linen formed an admirable support for his close-shaven throat, his cigar-brown, yellow-edged tie, neatly knotted, lay tidily in the opening of his waistcoat. All this he observed in a few seconds. Then he raised his eyes and said simply, "Let me go."

"No, my friend," answered the other, "no. I'm not going to let you go, I'm going to talk to you for another half-hour yet." But in the meantime Carla and her mother had intervened. "Let him go, Merumeci," said the girl, putting a hand on her brother's shoulder and looking at her lover. "Surely you can talk to him without holding him like that, can't you?"

The two men separated. "All I've got to say to him," announced Leo sharply, "is that it's time to stop all this nonsense. And, apart from the fact that the whole thing is quite out of the question, this hardly seems to me the best moment for discussing a compromise."

"Of course you're absolutely right," said the Signora, with mealy-mouthed promptness. "But don't take any notice of Michele . . . he doesn't know what he's doing."

You do, I suppose! thought the boy, looking at her. "But in that case why did you drag me into it?" he asked, coming forward.

"And for that reason," went on his mother, disregarding her son's interruption, "if you want to talk about this business, you must do so with me."

"Is that what you want, then?" said Leo, looking from one doubtful face to the other. "Well . . . once and for all, I'll tell you my final terms: I'll leave you the villa until you've found somewhere else to live . . . and then . . . in addition to that . . . I'll give you a certain sum of money . . . let's see . . . thirty thousand lire, for instance."

"Thirty thousand lire?" repeated the Signora, opening her eyes very wide. "What?"

"Let me explain," said Leo. "You maintain that the value of the villa exceeds the amount of the mortgage. I say it doesn't, but in order to prove that I am a true friend to you, I am offering you thirty thousand lire over and above . . . which will make up for . . . I don't know . . . work that may have been carried out in the house recently. Anyhow, the improvements that have been made since the mortgage."

[67]

"But the villa is worth more than that, Merumeci," insisted the Signora, almost mournfully, "it's worth more."

"Well then, you know what I say?" answered Leo calmly. "Sell it to someone else . . . and you'll see that you won't even be able to pay me the thirty thousand lire. In the first place, with the crisis that's going on, it's a bad moment; nobody's buying and everyone is wanting to sell; you've only to look at the back page of any newspaper to see that. . . . Besides, since the villa's outside town, it's going to be difficult to find anyone who wants to come and live up here. But do as you like. Not for anything in the world would I wish to have feelings of remorse for having given you bad advice."

"I should accept Merumeci's terms, Mom," said Carla. "Personally, I can hardly wait to leave the villa and go and live somewhere else, even if we are going to be poor."

Her mother made a gesture of exasperation. "You keep quiet," she said. After which there followed an appalled silence. Mariagrazia saw visions of abject poverty, Carla of the destruction of her old life; Michele saw nothing at all and was the most despairing of the three.

"In any case," added Leo, "we can talk about it again. Come . . . come to my office the day after tomorrow, Signora, and then we can discuss the whole matter at length."

She agreed to this, with a sort of eager, mournful enthusiasm. "The day after tomorrow . . . in the afternoon?"

"Yes, in the afternoon."

For some moments they did not speak; then, at a word of invitation from Mariagrazia, they went, all four of them, from the drawing-room into the dining-room.

The table had been prepared with solemnity and refinement; silver and crystal and all the best family china glittered on the white tablecloth, in the white daylight of the room. The Signora sat down at the head of the table, and, although their places were the same as the night before, directed them to their seats: "Merumeci here, Carla there . . . Michele over there"—whether in order to mark the importance of the celebration or from an old habit of entertaining a larger number of guests on such occasions, it was impossible to say.

"I should have liked," she said, as she began eating, "to have had a proper luncheon, such as *I* understand it, for Carla's birthday today, with all sorts of special things—a real, proper, correct luncheon, in fact. . . . But what can one do? All that is out of the question nowadays . . . I have a cook who, although she is not bad, never reaches the point of being really good. It's no use saying to her, do this and do that . . . true passion is lacking. . . . And when passion is lacking, everything is lacking."

"You're right," approved Michele, with ironical gravity. "That's just it. Without passion one can do nothing. I myself, for instance, although I made a great effort to hit Leo, couldn't manage it, because I lack passion."

"Whatever's that got to do with it?" his mother broke in, growing red in the face with anger. "What's Leo got to do with it? We were talking about the cook. Ah, Michele, you can never get away from yourself. . . . Even on a day like this, your own sister's birthday, when everything else ought to be forgotten and we ought all to be genuinely happy together, you start talking about quarreling and hitting people. Won't you ever learn any better?"

"Let him talk, my dear Signora," put in Leo, without raising his eyes from his plate. "It's all the same to me. I'm not listening."

"All right, Mother, I'll be quiet, I'll be quiet," exclaimed Michele, who saw that he had struck a false note. "Don't worry. I'll be as dumb as a fish. I won't disturb the proceedings any more."

There was silence again. The maid came in and removed the plates, and then the Signora, who had never, for one moment, ceased gazing with inquisitive eyes at her lover, turned to him. "Did you enjoy yourself last night, Merumeci?"

Leo threw a quick glance at the girl, as much as to say: "Here we are again"; but Carla did not respond. She heard him ask: "Where? When?"—and at the same moment felt a foot pressing against hers, under the table. She bit her lip: this shabby duplicity gave her a sense of great bewilderment; she wanted to jump up and cry out the truth.

"Where?" her mother was answering in the meantime; "why . . . with Lisa, of course!"

"Really . . . if you think there's anything very enjoyable about driving somebody home."

"I wouldn't think so, myself," she protested, with a knowing smile. "I'm frankly bored in the company of some people. But you, since you seek that company, it means that you like it."

Leo was on the point of replying when, in his usual inopportune way, Michele broke in. "Oh, Mother," he exclaimed, parodying the words that Mariagrazia had uttered a short time before, "you can never get away from yourself. Even on a day like this, your own sister's—no, excuse me, your own daughter's—birthday, when everything else ought to be forgotten and we ought all to be genuinely happy together, you start talking about Lisa, about driving people home. Won't you ever learn any better?"

This buffoonery made Carla smile against her will and made Leo laugh frankly. "Well done, Michele," cried the latter; but Michele's mother was offended. "What's it got to do with you?" she said turning to her son. "I suppose I may talk to Merumeci as I wish, on such subjects as I choose, without your having to butt in?"

"But on a day like this?"

"What's that got to do with it?" She shrugged her shoulders angrily. "I merely mentioned. In any case," she went on, "let's talk of something else. Only I warn you, Merumeci, that from now onwards you must choose some other place for meeting your mistresses. I don't keep a *maison de rendez-vous* . . . d'you see?"

It was the first time that Mariagrazia had given way to an outburst of such violence; and an unexpected thing happened. Carla, who had always kept quiet during such scenes, began to protest. "There is one thing I should like to know," she began; she made a great effort to keep her words and her tone calm, but the distortion of her childish face, a certain redness in its color, and the look of unaccustomed hardness in her eyes, all betrayed a profound anger. "I should like to know, Mother, whether you realize what you are saying . . . that's all I want to know."

Her mother looked at her as one looks at some strange, living phenomenon. "Ha, this is something new! So I'm no longer free to speak!"

"I should like to know," Carla insisted—and her voice had now become louder, and was shaky, and there was a trembling on her lips, "I should like to know whether all this ought to be allowed?" She bent her big head forward a little and stared her mother in the eyes, in a strange way, from under her lids.

For a moment there was dead silence. The other three looked into each other's faces, astonished and uncomprehending; and perhaps it was only Leo who had, at that moment, some vague perception of Carla's state of mind. In order to look at her mother more closely, she had turned slightly sideways to the table and was sitting huddled in her absurdly high-backed chair, so that her thin shoulders looked narrower, her head larger; she looked as though she were preparing to take a leap. A little fury, he thought, observing her. Now she's going to fling herself upon Mariagrazia and scratch her face. But his catastrophic predictions were not to be realized; all Carla did was to raise her head again. "That's what I want to know," she repeated, "and how we can possibly go on like this, day after day, with this continual irritation, without ever changing or ever getting away from this miserable state of affairs, being satisfied with any stupid thing that comes into our heads, always arguing and quarrelling for the same reasons and never rising above ground-level, not even that much?" She held the palm of her hand just above the table, trembling, her angry eyes filling with tears. "And now," she went on, sitting bolt upright, "I want you to tell me whether all this is a good thing. You don't realize it . . . but you ought to see yourself in a mirror while you're talking and arguing; you'd be ashamed of yourself, and you'd understand the degree of irritation and weariness one can reach, and how much one can long for a new life completely different from this. . . ." She broke off and, rather tearful and red in the face, helped herself, without knowing what she was doing, from the dish the maid handed to her.

Finally, her mother recovered from her astonishment.

"This is the last straw," she exclaimed. "From henceforth, I suppose, I have to ask my daughter's permission before I am allowed to speak? I waited to hear what you said but it seemed to me I must be dreaming. This is indeed the last straw."

"It seems to me," said Michele quietly, "that Carla only just touched upon the truth. All this is more than irritating, it's revolting. But it's no use protesting; better get accustomed to it."

"Don't let's exaggerate," said Leo in a conciliating manner. "Carla didn't mean that."

"Get along with you," the Signora answered him; "I know who I'm dealing with. You know what they are—Carla just as much as Michele? A couple of egoists . . . and that's the truth. A couple of egoists who, if they had their way, would go off and leave me alone."

Her voice was trembling, her lips were trembling: yes, they would all go away, Leo and the others too, and she would really be left alone. Carla looked at her, and now she felt sorry she had spoken; what was the use of it, anyhow? You can't empty the sea with a tumbler. Her mother would remain just as she was, ridiculous, lacking in understanding, lost in her own darkness; not even a miracle could change her. There was nothing to be gained by coming into conflict with her; it was better to act. Really and truly to go away, she thought, looking at Leo's red, unruffled face, this very day, now, and never come back again. But, stifling the disgust she felt, she braced herself for a reconciliation. "Now please, Mom, I didn't mean to offend you," she said mildly. "I only wanted to ask you, since today is my birthday—as you yourself said—to put aside any sort of discussion and . . . and . . ."

"And all to be genuinely happy together," concluded Michele with a grimace.

"Exactly," approved Carla, quite seriously, "to be happy." But when she looked at her mother's silly, discontented, undecided face she felt she wanted to shout: *Be happy about what? About being as we are?* She was silent for a moment, then she added: "Well, Mummy, you're not really offended, are you?"

"I never take offense," answered her mother with dignity.

"Only it did not seem to me that that was the way in which a respectful daughter ought to speak to her mother."

"Of course you're absolutely right, Mom," persisted Carla, more and more mildly, "absolutely right. But now let's forget the whole thing, anyhow for today, and think about something more cheerful."

"You're a sly one," said her mother, half smiling. "All right then, let's forget about it, since today is your birthday. Otherwise, things would have been different."

"That's fine," Carla approved, still keeping her tone of determined serenity. "Thank you, Mom. And now you two, Leo and Michele, tell us something cheerful, so that we can laugh."

"Really, without any notice," said Leo, putting down his fork, "I don't know what I can tell you."

"I," began Michele, "I think I know a really good story. Would you like me to tell it to you?"

"Let's hear it," his mother encouraged him.

"Here it is, then." Michele raised his head and began reciting. "It was Good Friday evening, and the Calabrian brigands were sitting around the fire, when one of them said: 'Come on, Beppe, you know so many stories, tell us a good one.' And Beppe began, in a cavernous voice: 'It was Good Friday evening, and the Calabrian brigands were sitting round the fire, when one of them said: 'Come on, Beppe, you know so many stories, tell us a good one.' And Beppe began, in a cavernous voice: 'It was Good Friday evening . . .' "

"Stop, stop, that's enough," his mother interrupted, laughing; "for goodness' sake. It goes on for ever. We understand."

"The snake that eats its own tail," remarked Leo sententiously.

The maid came into the room with a superb cake on which, in letters of cream, was written: "Good Wishes!" The Signora helped herself first, then Leo, then Carla, and finally Michele.

"So you didn't like my story?" demanded the latter.

"Not in the least," replied his mother, who was eating with a certain unwillingness. "It couldn't have been sillier."

[73]

"Is that the sort of thing you learn at the University?" asked Leo quietly, without raising his eyes from his plate.

Michele looked at him sideways, but did not answer. "There's one other story," he went on; "but I'm afraid that one isn't very likely to please you, either. It's about a middle-aged lady who had a lover."

"But that isn't a funny story," put in Carla hurriedly, looking intently at her brother. "I want something to laugh at."

"That depends," observed Leo. "It might be funny and it might not."

"In any case, Michele," said his mother with dignity, "I don't like your speaking so freely about these things in front of Carla."

Her words almost made Leo smile. Come now, he thought, amused, Carla knows more about it than you do. He sought the girl's foot under the table and pressed it as though inviting her to laugh with him; but, as before, she did not respond to this confidential, collusive contact, for she no longer had any desire to laugh. She looked at her mother's face, which hung like a stupid, vague mask in the white daylight of the room. Oh, to finish with all this as quickly as possible! she thought; to do something that, by tomorrow, will prevent her ever talking like that again! The feeling of impatience that possessed her made her long to make some exaggerated gesture or burst into ironical laughter, so that her mother could no longer have any illusions of any kind on the subject of her innocence.

"What a pity!" Michele was saying meanwhile. "It was a most instructive story. Not a matter for laughter, perhaps, but highly instructive."

After which there was silence again; the maid changed the plates and brought in the fruit. "And so, Carla," said Leo, peeling an apple with meticulous care, "from today a new life ought to begin for you—isn't that so?"

"Let's hope so," answered Carla, with a half sigh. There was one idea which tormented her—when should she give herself to Leo, that night or some other day?

"New in what sense?" asked her mother.

"In all senses, Mom."

"I don't understand you, my dear," said Mariagrazia; "explain yourself, give me an example."

"New . . . what I mean is, less stupid, less superficial, less useless, deeper . . . than the life I lead now." The girl looked at her. "New in the sense of changing completely."

"Carla is right," Leo affirmed. "Every now and then it's a good plan to have a change."

"Do please be quiet," said Carla's mother, troubled. "I don't understand . . . how d'you mean, change your life? One fine morning you get up and say: 'Today I want to change my life'; but how is that possible?"

"One can perform some action," said Carla, keeping her eyes lowered and clenching her teeth with rage, "that transforms one's mode of existence in every way, and for good."

"But, my dear child," replied her mother firmly, "I don't see how a respectable young lady can change her life except by getting married. Then, of course, life really does change. She has the responsibilities of a house, she has to look after her husband . . . and then bring up her children, if there are any. There's a whole mass of things that transforms one's habits radically. Now of course I wish it for you with all my heart—but it seems to me hardly probable that you can get married by tomorrow—and so I don't see how your life can suddenly change, just because you want it to."

"But, Mummy," Carla hazarded, nervously squeezing the handle of the knife she held in her hand, "there are other things besides marriage that might bring changes into a person's existence."

"What, for instance?" enquired Mariagrazia with extreme coldness, cutting a slice from her apple.

Carla looked at her almost with hatred. For instance, becoming Leo's mistress, she wanted to reply; and she pictured to herself, with keen but melancholy pleasure, the astonishment, the indignation, the fear that such words would have aroused. But she contrived, instead, to maintain an air of resigned irony. "Suppose, for instance," she explained in a tone of discouragement, "suppose I met, today, the head of an American film company, and he, struck by my beauty, offered

[75]

me a part in a film . . . my, my life would be changed at once."

Her mother twisted her lips. "You argue like a child. It's no good talking to you."

"Anything is possible," said Leo, anxious to ingratiate himself with the girl.

"What?" said her mother; "possible that my daughter, this very day, might become an actress? Really, Merumeci, you don't know what you're talking about."

"But, joking apart," Carla insisted, "it looks as though we should be leaving the villa in a short time and going to live somewhere else—and trying to live less expensively, too—so won't one's life be forcibly changed, anyhow?"

"Who says we're leaving?" demanded Mariagrazia with a sort of desperate impudence, looking her lover straight in the eye. "Until you've found a husband, we're going to stay here."

Leo stared at her; he turned red with anger, and with difficulty refrained from a violent shrugging of the shoulders. The devil you will! he wanted to shout at her. You'll clear out, and in double quick time too!

"We're going to stay," she repeated with an uncertain smile; "isn't that so, Merumeci?—we're going to stay?"

They all looked at him. Devil take her! he thought; but he answered: "Yes, yes, you're going to stay," being desirous, above all things, not to start a scene and not to spoil things with Carla.

"You see!" exclaimed the Signora in triumph. "I have Merumeci's word. For the moment nothing is going to change."

"Just for the moment . . . yes," murmured Leo, but in such a low voice that nobody heard him. It was then that Carla had her second uncontrollable outburst; the other three saw her go very red in the face and suddenly bang down her fist on the table. "I . . . I don't believe in all this," she said, in a voice so high that it seemed positively shrill. "Do you really want to see me suffocated, Mother? I should prefer ruin—yes, d'you understand?—ruin . . . to all these things. I should prefer to sink right down to the depths. I was saying so just the other day, to Leo—in fact, I can't think of anything else, day and night—and even this morning, as soon as I had got up and looked at myself in the mirror, I said to myself: 'A new year is beginning, for me, which has got to be absolutely different from the last one'—because it's impossible to go on like this . . . it's impossible." Suddenly, from being red in the face she turned pale; she hung her head and began to weep.

The others looked at each other in embarrassment. Carla's mother, in fact, rose to her feet—since evidently these tears seemed to her sincere enough to take away all importance from the accusations that had preceded them—and went over to the girl. "Why in the world are you crying like that, without any reason at all? Come on . . . it's your birthday today . . . you mustn't cry."

Carla did not raise her head, but continued to be shaken by sobs. There was, however, in these blandly consoling words of her mother's, so clear an echo of the times of her childhood, with their puerile troubles and maternal comfortings, that a reluctant feeling of response softened the aridity of her grief. She seemed to see herself again as a small child and was pierced by a sudden regret at having lost that innocence, that irresponsibility; figures and events of those years passed in front of her eyes, through the veil of her tears. A moment went by; and then she was conscious of Leo, in his turn, trying to encourage her. "Come on," he said; "cheer up. . . . What are you crying for?" And then she raised her head again.

"You're right," she said in a firm voice, wiping her eyes; "today is my birthday." She wanted to add something more, but restrained herself. "Why, my goodness!" Leo meanwhile exclaimed, "crying at table!" Her mother was smiling stupidly; and everything was at the same time sweet and bitter.

Only Michele neither moved nor spoke. Hysteria, he thought, seeing his sister burst into tears. If a young man of her own age were in love with her and she with him, she would be calm and happy. He saw no difference between his sister and the other two; all three of them appeared unbearably false and remote. He looked at them. Is it really possible, he asked himself in distress, that this is my whole world, my whole circle of acquaintance? The more he listened to them, the more ridiculous, the more lacking in understanding they seemed to be, stuck fast in their own solitary convictions. Laugh, he thought, I must laugh; but he did not understand why, he did not know whether it was from disgust or pity, as he saw them there, Leo, his mother, Carla, for the thousandth time, changeless and yet so full of faults, sitting around that table. His expression darkened, his eyes closed in weariness. There's some mistake, he kept repeating to himself. "There must be some mistake." And he lowered his head to hide his wet eyelids.

No one saw, no one understood. The fruit had been eaten, and each of them had a champagne glass beside his plate, and Leo was reading the labels of the two bottles of French wine that the maid had just brought in. "This one is good," said the connoisseur at last, "and this one is very good indeed."

"This one first, and the other one later," said the Signora sagely. "You open them, Merumeci."

Leo took the bottle and removed the wire from the cork. "One, two, three," he counted dramatically; and at "three" the cork popped out and Leo—hastily, so as not to spill the froth—poured the wine into the glasses. They rose, all four of them, to their feet beneath the dusty chandelier.

"Your health, Carla," said her mother, in a low, intimate voice as though there were some secret afoot. Glasses clinked; affectionate, and in a way pathetic, calls crossed and re-crossed in every direction—"Mom," "Michele," "Carla," "Signora," "Merumeci"—over the untidy table, among the four bent heads. The crystal of the glasses tinkled, tinkled mournfully each time they knocked together; then they all drank, looking at each other, over the wine, with doubtful eyes.

"It's good," said the Signora at last; "one can tell it's old."

"It's extremely good," agreed Leo. "And now," he added, "I'm going to make a speech . . . a speech that includes you all. But first of all I would beg Michele not to look as if he had been condemned to death: this is not hemlock, it's champagne."

[78]

You're right, thought Michele, I must laugh. And he made such a silly face that he realized what he was doing and smiled.

"That's better," said Leo, who was delighted with his own allusion to Socrates. Then he raised his glass. "To your new life, Carla." He smiled, then went and clinked his glass against the girl's. "I know perfectly well," he went on, looking knowingly at her, "what your great longings are, and what you think about day and night. And so I believe I'm not far wide of the mark in wishing you a happy marriage in every sense of the word, that is, with a man who is rich, handsome and intelligent. Have I guessed right or not?" From behind her glass the Signora joyously nodded; the heroine of the occasion, however, neither answered nor smiled. This suggestive, ironical artificiality on the part of the man gave her a sudden glimpse of the ruin for which she was heading; yet she felt she must allow herself to be dragged down to the lowest depths. She gave him a cold glance of assent and then, not without disgust—for she had never liked this French wine—emptied her glass to the last drop.

"To the health of the Signora," went on Leo. "And, from what I gather, since that seems to be what she desires, let us wish, on her behalf, the exact opposite of what we wish Carla—that nothing may ever change, that everything may stay just as it is, both as regards old habits and also," he added, with inspired cleverness, "old friends." He noticed her smile just as if he had tickled her under the arm. "Here's to old friends!" she cried wildly; then she quickly clinked her glass against that of her lover and drank with enthusiasm.

"And now, Michele, to our friendship," said Leo finally. He drank his wine at one gulp and, going over to the boy, held out his hand. Michele looked up at Leo, who was smiling in an assured, good-natured fashion, he looked at the hand spread out right under his nose—for he was sitting, Leo standing; all he saw of Leo himself was his ample torso and, beyond and above it, the red, paternal smile that meandered foolishly between his heavy cheeks. Refuse, he said to himself, refuse and laugh in his face, and he started to get up, putting down his napkin on the table. Then, as he looked round, he realized that a deep silence had succeeded the laughter, the talk and the toasts; not even the chandelier and the scattered china on the table were more motionless than Carla and his mother. The latter was gazing at him, her head supported on her hands, with eyes both anxious and imperious, while two deep wrinkles furrowed her brow; it was impossible to tell whether she was imploring or commanding him.

His uncomfortable feeling of pity returned. Don't be afraid, he wanted to say. No one is going to touch your man, Mom, no one. His eyes, between Leo and his mother, became fixed, dazzled, distracted by the white light. He was in a dream, a nightmare of indifference.

"Come on . . . come on," he heard Leo say; "give me your hand and everything will be over." He held out his right hand and Leo clasped it. Then, immediately, with a promptitude that seemed to him hardly credible, he found himself in the other man's arms; they embraced and kissed each other.

There was an immediate return to the greatest cheerfulness. "That's splendid!" his mother applauded. "Well done, Michele!" "It can't possibly be," cried Leo, highly delighted, "that there should be disagreements between two good, honest people like Michele and me"—while, privately, he was thinking: And now that we've embraced, will he leave me in peace? It was only the boy who, sitting there at the bottom of the table, hung his head over his plate and appeared to be ashamed, to be regretting that embrace as though it had been an evil deed. At last he raised his eyes; but the other three, now that the obstacle of his hatred had been overcome, were no longer paying any attention to him. They were grouped around the far end of the table, and seemed remote and strange as if seen through glass; they were laughing, drinking . . . and ignoring him.

Leo had taken up the bottle again and was pouring out wine for the two women, for the daughter especially. I shan't recognize myself, he thought, if I fail to make Carla drink at least one of these two bottles. He knew that her getting tipsy would make his conquest easier, and was already imagining the delights of their meeting in the garden; and—

whether owing to the abundant meal he had eaten or to some other cause—he was conscious of a mounting desire that ran all through his body.

"Now remember," he said in a severe tone of voice, raising his glass, "nobody is allowed to leave the table until these two bottles are empty."

"*You* drink them," said the Signora, who was laughing a great deal and, between one burst of laughter and the next, casting pathetic, ardent glances at her lover. "You drink them, or Carla. I really can't."

"All right," he agreed. "Carla and I will drink them. Won't we, Carla?" And he raised his glass again.

The girl looked at him. She did not like this wine, but in her lover's gesture and the glance that accompanied it there was an irresistible, menacing air of command that forced her, in spite of herself, to accept his invitation. "The whole glass," he urged, "right to the last drop." Her mother was laughing, and Carla looked first at Leo, then at her. Get drunk, she thought all of a sudden, feverishly, in terror; those faces opposite her, in the white afternoon light, frightened her, they were the mean, uncomprehending faces of her life. Never to see all this again; then in disgust she lifted her glass, drank, drained it, until she saw it empty. The foaming liquid, faintly sweet, filled her mouth with its pungent taste. She did not swallow it at once, and for a moment felt a desire to spit it out again, right into her lover's face; but she restrained herself, closed her eyelids and listened to the satisfied gurglings in her nauseated throat; then she opened her eyes again, and there was the bottle once more hanging over her glass, and Leo's hand tilting it, and a yellow flood of wine filling the glass again.

Leo was speaking to her mother. "You must drink too," he encouraged her. "You know the saying: 'Fill the glass that's empty, empty the glass that's full, never leave it empty, never leave it full.'"

"Oh, oh," laughed the Signora, delighted at these old-fashioned witticisms.

"*In vino veritas,*" went on Leo. "Drink with me. I'm sure you're already well away after a couple of glasses."

The Signora was offended. "You're quite wrong," she said with dignity. "There are few women who can carry their wine as well as I do." And, to give proof of her prowess, she emptied her glass.

"Well, tell me then," jested Leo, who by this time was completely restored to good humor, holding up two fingers. "How many fingers am I showing?"

"Twenty," replied his mistress, with a burst of laughter.

"Splendid!" For a moment he was silent, looking at the two women, the mother and the daughter. "And now," he added, turning suddenly towards Carla, "now let's drink. Let's drink to the health of your future husband."

"Of course!" cried the Signora, highly delighted, "I'll drink too."

Carla hesitated. Her vision had already begun to be distorted by tipsiness; it was like wearing over-strong spectacles, or looking into an aquarium—objects quivered, joined themselves together and became confused. By the time I've drunk this glass, she thought, I shan't understand a thing. She smiled vaguely, took up the disgusting glassful of wine and drank. She seemed immediately to have taken an immense upward leap into the heaven of intoxication; she was invaded by a feeling of great gaiety, by an urge to talk and to show the others that she was entirely in possession of her senses.

"I don't at all mind drinking the health of my future husband," she said, carefully articulating her syllables, "but who is that husband to be?"

"Only God knows that," said her mother.

"If I didn't by now think of you as a daughter," Leo began, "I should propose myself as a husband. Would you accept me?"

"You!" she cried, pointing one finger at him, "you, my husband! But . . ." She stared at him for a moment: wasn't this her mother's lover? "Really you're too stupid, Leo."

"Oh, as far as that goes," protested her mother, offended, "he's not in the least stupid. I hope you get a husband like him."

"Then you would agree, Carla?" insisted Leo, smiling. "We'd go for our honeymoon to Paris. . . ."

"No . . . I'd rather go to India," the girl broke in, in a mournful voice.

"Paris is far more interesting," said her mother, who had never been there.

"Very well, India then," Leo conceded. "I would give you a car, a house, clothes. Will you marry me, then?"

Carla looked at him. Her ideas were confused by tipsiness: why did Leo talk in that way? Was it perhaps in order to mock at her mother? But in that case one ought to be laughing. "Personally," she answered at length, in an uncertain tone, "I've nothing against it. But you would have to ask Mom's consent."

"How about you, Signora?" asked Leo, still with that quiet, satisfied smile on his face. "Would you accept me as a son-in-law?"

"Let us see," she replied in a facile sort of way, for, partly owing to the wine and partly to excitement, all this appeared to her highly comic. "Let us see . . . Have you a good job?"

"I am employed at the Ministry of Justice and Mercy," answered Leo humbly. "I earn eight hundred lire a month. But my superiors like me . . . I have been promised promotion."

"And how about your family?" said the Signora, trying hard not to laugh.

"I have no family left; I am alone in the world."

"Are you religious?"

"Extremely religious."

"And do you really think," she concluded, "that you will be able to make my daughter happy?"

"I am convinced of it," said Leo, gazing intently at Carla.

"Then get married and God bless you!" cried Mariagrazia, with a burst of laughter.

"Let's get married, Leo!" Carla applauded, but without gaiety.

Leo was laughing too. "I think the general tests have gone well," he said. "Now there's nothing left but to wait for the real husband."

He took the second bottle and refilled Carla's glass. I must make her drink, he repeated to himself; make her mop it up like a sponge. He looked at her. "Now a little toast to the health of the Signora," he proposed. Carla took up her glass with a trembling hand and drank; and then, so suddenly that she was frightened, she realized that she was drunk. Her head was going round, her throat was dry, however wide she opened her eyes she could not manage to see clearly; and one can say that from that moment she lost the exact consciousness of what she was doing. She was no longer capable of seeing or hearing. The glass and silver objects on the table appeared to her so brilliant and precise that her eyes hurt, the faces of her companions so still and hard that they looked like masks; but from time to time this reality was pervaded by a quivering pulsation, outlines became blurred, eyes and mouths spread out like stains on the chalk-like faces, white flashes shook the air. Similarly with her hearing: she would catch the words entire, but however much she turned them this way and that she could not manage to grasp their meaning. And now that I'm drunk, she kept saying to herself, how ever shall I be able to talk to Leo in the garden? This fear obsessed her; she repented bitterly of having drunk so much, and wanted to cry.

Leo, however, was determined that she should go on drinking. As he discoursed with her mother, he pretended to take no notice of the girl and not even to look at her; but in the middle of an anecdote he would turn round, bottle in hand, with an air of hilarity, and pour out more wine. "Come on, Carla . . . keep going," and he would raise his own glass. Carla, staring at him, wanted to ask him why; Leo's motionless face and his hand clutching the bottle, his movements, his words—everything seemed to her to be charged with a cruel fate, uncomprehending and automatic, just as if the man had been a mechanical puppet placed there for the purpose of pouring wine for her, every five minutes, out of the bottle. But she made no protest, overcoming her own disgust, drinking, then putting down the empty glass and gazing at it with drowned, frightened eyes; very soon, she knew, the squat neck of the bottle would appear again and pour out, ruthlessly, a new flood of wine.

At last the second bottle came to an end. "We've drunk it all," said Leo gaily; "well done, Carla!" The girl did not answer; she held her head down, and her hair was hanging over her eyes. "Well?" he insisted, "what's wrong? Perhaps you feel a bit dizzy, do you? Have one," he added, holding out his case; "have a cigarette." And then at once, seeing her light one and smoke it with difficulty: All she needs is a rose at her bosom, he thought. That's all she needs to make her look like one of those night club girls. And it was true. Like a woman in a dance hall in the early morning, Carla was leaning her elbow on the table, her rumpled head in her hand, and staring straight in front of her with the cigarette hanging out of the corner of her mouth; her dress, which had belonged to her mother and was too big and too matronly for her, had slipped off her shoulder and showed the first swelling whiteness of her breast. Acute discomfort oppressed her; she leaned helplessly on the table and felt she was dying.

Mariagrazia looked at her but did not reproach her. "Go into the garden," she advised; "go and get a breath of fresh air . . . it will do you good." These words inspired in Carla, in spite of her drunken state, an acute feeling of sarcasm. What's going to do me good? she felt inclined to reply, meeting Leo there? Of course that will do me good, of course it will. But instead, she said, "Are you quite sure?"—and rose to her feet.

She was immediately aware of how difficult it would be not to fall. The whole room was heaving and quivering, the floor was going up and down beneath her feet like the deck of a ship, the walls were swaying, a picture which at one moment was upright at the next was hanging crooked, a piece of furniture was falling on top of her, and it seemed as though the table, with the three people seated round it, would at any moment touch the ceiling. Someone was looking at her from the far end of the table, with wide-open, tearful eyes and his head supported on his hands: was it Michele? She had no time to discover, but went stumbling out of the room and vanished in the gloom of the corridor.

"She's not accustomed to wine," said her mother, who had followed her with her eyes.

"Well, well," replied Leo, "only someone who, like me, went through the war and drank the *grappa* they make in that part of the country, knows what real drunkenness is." He took the bottle, poured the few remaining drops into Carla's glass. "To our friendship, Michele," he cried, turning towards the boy.

But Michele did not speak, nor did he drink, nor reply to the toast; he sat with his head bowed, overcome by a hateful disgust mingled with regret and humiliation. He was contemplating the memory of himself in Leo's embrace, with his nose against Leo's shoulder and his arms hanging down, moved— yes, really almost moved—in his hopelessly sentimental heart. He savored again the kiss he had received—and the kiss he had given, too . . . oh, what a wonderful moment! And it seemed to him that formidable peals of laughter were reverberating noisily in his ears. Though mocked, he was pleased; yes, that was it; while Leo triumphed, taking the money and his mother as well. And he himself was left empty-handed, satisfied with a toast, with an embrace, mere insubstantial trifles.

Two bottles had been emptied; lighted cigarettes consumed themselves in smoke.

A calm, white light shone through the curtains at the window; and then, obsessed by her jealousy, the Signora returned obstinately to her ancient quarrel. "Why don't you drink to the health of your distant lady friend?" she inquired, and added, in a disagreeable tone of voice: *"Loin de toi, loin de ton coeur."*

Leaning far back in his chair, Leo did not answer, but, weighed down with the processes of digestion, looked at her with expressionless eyes. In the pauses, a heavy silence of repletion yawned. And then, from the pipes of the radiator, came an echoing clang—brooon . . . brooon. . . . Someone down in the basement was poking the furnace fire.

7

CARLA WENT ALONG the corridor and into the vestibule. There hung the curtain behind which she had hidden the evening before, with Leo; and now everything was swaying around her, and she clung to it to avoid falling. Then she went out, down the flight of marble steps. A deathly calm hung heavy upon the garden. Beyond one could see the trunks and the bare branches of the trees, some way off, the forlorn-looking boundary wall, yellowish in color, with big stains of damp on it. There was neither light nor shadow, nor was there any wind; the air was cold and still, and across the gray sky, at a great height, flew a multitude of rooks, now scattering, now closing in again, and softly receding farther and farther into the immensity. From some unseen hiding-place a bird whistled thinly, and it was as though all nature shivered.

Step by step, supporting herself against the wall, she went all around the house. She looked up towards the closed window of the dining-room: what were they doing, those three? Were they still sitting round the table, drinking? Or were they arguing? She picked up a pebble and threw it in front of her, she gathered a flower, she performed several small actions in order to prove to herself that she was not drunk. But, at a certain distance from her, everything became confused. The trees writhed like snakes; everything was shrouded in mist; and also—it was no use trying to deny it—her legs would scarcely support her, and she had the impression that at each step she took, the ground heaved and gave way under her feet.

Behind the house, the garden was less spacious than on the other side, but more overgrown. Big trees grew there, and thick bushes, breast-high. Only one narrow path along the surrounding wall, skirted this mass of unkempt vegetation; but it, too, was so neglected, so grown over with grass and overhung with branches that in places it was difficult to trace its original direction. There was also, at the farthest end of the garden, a small rectangular building, a kind of shed; but from the place where Carla was it was impossible to see it, for it was hidden by the trees.

A green-painted seat stood against the wall of the house; Carla sat on it and took her head between her hands. She was weighed down by a discomfort such as she had never felt before, for her drunkenness instead of diminishing was increasing, and her first sensation of lightness and easiness had been succeeded by giddiness and nausea. The vague heaving and swaying of everything was now becoming unbearable. "Is there no way," she wondered, looking down at the white, ant-like swarming of the gravel, "is there no way of stopping this torture?" There was no answer. Overcome by the contrast between her own ravings and the dumb quietness of nature, and with a vague longing to surrender herself, to merge herself utterly in nature's immobility, she closed her eyes. She did not sleep, she did not think, but stayed this way, with her eyelids tight shut, for about ten minutes. Then she felt a hand touch her shoulders; she re-opened her eyes and saw Leo.

He was carrying his overcoat on his arm, also his hat, and he had a cigarette in his mouth. "What's the matter? Why are you sitting there like that?" he asked. The girl raised her head. "I feel ill," she answered simply.

"Ill, ill?" Leo repeated, with smiling impatience. "Well, get up and walk, and then you won't feel ill. You've only drunk a bit too much."

She rose listlessly to her feet, but immediately clutched at him with both hands. "Hold me up," she besought him; "everything's going round and round." She looked into her lover's face, then dropped her head again and breathed a long sigh.

They took a few steps, going in under the archway of branches and along the damp, enclosed path that ran beside the wall. Every now and then Leo asked the girl, "Are you feeling better?" And she replied, "No."

"Are you feeling better?" "No." The branches of the trees that interlaced above their heads were as still as the patches of gray sky visible between them; a thick layer of black, wet leaves deadened the sound of their footsteps; the silence was profound, not a sound was to be heard. "Are you feeling better, my dear?" Leo asked again. Excited and full of desire, he was considering the most opportune moment to embrace his companion; her body hung languidly upon his arm, her rounded hip pressed against his, and these contacts kindled a flame of lust in him. Keep calm, he thought. In a moment I'll take her into the shed and do what I want with her. Just a little patience.

Carla's eyes wandered hither and thither in the narrow space of the path, full of shadows and untrimmed shrubs. "Why did you make me drink?" she asked at last, in a mournful voice. "Why *did* you drink?" retorted Leo. Questions, always questions. They came to a stop. "I drank," she began volubly, "so that I wouldn't see Mom and you any more . . . or Michele either . . . so that I wouldn't see anybody any more." She lowered her eyes and shook her head. "But if I'd known I was going to feel so sick, I wouldn't have done it."

"Don't let's talk nonsense," cried the man, in such a high voice that he himself was surprised. "You drank because you liked doing it." He saw her smile mysteriously. "Perhaps you think I love you, do you?" she asked in a confidential tone.

They looked at each other—Carla serious, but with the slight madness of intoxication in her shining eyes, Leo half excited, half cynical, and with an expression of agitation.

Then, without warning, he reached down and seized the girl by the hips, roughly. She broke into a strident laugh and started struggling with her arms and shoulders, with drunken movements that were, in a way, indecent. "Leo . . . oh Leo!" she cried between hiccups of laughter, "Leo . . . don't look at me like that! . . . no . . . let me alone!" The low vault of overhanging branches stifled the shrillness of her voice. At intervals, between her turnings and twistings, she saw the man's red face stretched out towards hers; it was full of a cunning, slightly senile sensuality. She herself did not know why she was struggling. At last he got the better of her contortions and clasped her in his arms. For a moment he looked at her, at her terrified eyes, her white face, her half-open mouth; then he stooped and kissed her.

They separated, and went, staggering slightly, farther into the gloom beneath the dead tangle of shrub and tree. But then Carla stopped hesitatingly, and nervously squeezed her companion's arm. "Leo," she murmured, raising a warning, childish finger, "Leo, there's no need . . . there's no need. . . ." Suddenly she was silent, standing there motionless, her attention distracted both from her weeping and from the remark she had made, staring at something in the shadowy path with eyes in which, beneath the veil of tears, there was a curious change of expression.

"Well?" demanded the man; but Carla appeared fascinated by a stone half buried among the dead black leaves on the ground, a round stone as white as an egg; nor could she have spoken if she had wished. The phrase "there's no need" had issued from her mouth almost without her knowledge; besides, the feelings that had inspired it had now vanished, and darkness had returned.

"Come on . . . come on," Leo encouraged her. "What is it there's no need for? No need to drink? . . . Well, I know that . . . But now," he added, pushing her forward, "walk, go on walking a little."

They had reached the end of the garden. The path, here, formed a kind of loop round the side of the shed, which stood against the garden wall; its other wall was entirely hidden by climbing plants, and all that could be seen was the doorway, with a door hanging on rusty hinges.

"Ah . . . and what's this?" asked Leo, as though the sight surprised him.

"The gardener's house."

"The gardener's house? Ha, that's a good one! And is the gardener at home?"

"No."

"The gardener's house" Leo repeated, as though the words pleased him to an extraordinary degree because of some hidden meaning in them. "Come along, let's go and look at it."

Carla laughed, for this seemed quite absurd to her, but she obeyed. The door was open, and when pushed back revealed a single, low-ceilinged room, with a dusty wooden floor; the walls were bare, one corner was occupied by a narrow iron bedstead upon which was a grayish mattress that had burst in several places and showed its woolen stuffing, while in the opposite corner—tripod of a long-abandoned ritual—was a rusty basin on a stand. That was all. Listlessly Carla contemplated these humble objects. Her feeling of nausea had by now become close to intolerable, and she wanted to go back to the house and lie down on the divan in her own room; but, overcome by her drunkenness, she bent her knees and sank down on the bed.

"Why?" she asked, in great distress, "why did you make me drink?" She stared down at the floor-boards, locks of hair falling in front of her eyes, and, in her bewilderment and discomfort, her mouth filled with saliva. Leo sat down beside her. "This is the moment," he was thinking excitedly, and he put his arm round the girl's waist. "Come," he cooed at her; "be reasonable. It was you who drank, of your own free will." Carla shook her head but did not reply. "In any case," he went on, "what does it matter?" He pulled her dress down on to her arm and kissed, respectfully, the bared shoulder. "It'll be better soon."

He could not take his eyes from the small expanse of bare breast that the ample garment left visible. Then suddenly he seized her, threw her back and kept hold of her. There was a struggle; creakings of the bed; vain twistings and turnings.

"Let me go," she murmured at last, and then lay utterly still, exhausted by her effort and by a languor such as she had never known. From the ceiling, at which she stared with wide-open, suffering eyes, she saw, plunging down at her like a meteor, the red face of Leo; his kiss landed on her neck, crept to her cheek, and then stopped at her lips. Carla closed her eyes and reclined her head on her shoulder; indifferent to the soft, moist contact of the man's mouth, all she wanted was to sleep. But a sound of torn-off buttons rolling on the floor, and a series of jolts in the back, caused her to start up again; she reopened her eyes, saw a flaming, excited face bending over her, realized that her shoulders were bare and started struggling, clutching vainly at the edges of her dress as if they were the edge of a precipice. Two violent jerks almost broke her nails. With a concentration that contrasted oddly with the excitement in his face, Leo lifted the girl off the bed for a moment and, not without difficulty, pulled her dress down to her waist; then hurled himself back on her breast and started, with nimble fingers, to free her bare arms from the shoulder-straps of her slip. Frightened, Carla looked at him and, every time she tried to struggle, saw him make gestures like those of a surgeon during an operation, raising his eyebrows, shaking his head, and twisting his mouth as much as to say, "No, my dear . . . don't get excited . . . it's nothing . . . leave it to me." This masterful impersonation and her own languor were of more avail than Leo's exertions; Carla yielded, raising her arms when required, arching her back as much as was necessary, and making no effort to hold on to her slip when Leo carefully pulled it down to her belly. Then, half-naked, she fell back, with eyes closed, on to the mattress; her feeling of nausea was growing stronger and stronger; she no longer had any thought in her mind, but felt she was dying.

Ah, what a lovely little girl! Leo was thinking meanwhile. Her nudity dazzled him, and he did not know where to begin, whether at the delicate, thin, white shoulders or at the youthful breast, of whose tenderness and milky whiteness his greedy, astonished eyes could not have enough.

Ah, what a lovely little girl! And already he was bending

[92]

forward to embrace her when he saw her raise her head with a look of fear in her eyes. She was extremely pale, and from her closed mouth and jerking chin came guttural sounds. He freed himself and drew aside as Carla, overwhelmed, sat up on the bed, her eyes fixed on the washstand in the opposite corner. Leo understood, took up the basin and held it out to her, only just in time; from her open mouth, into the rusty vessel, poured a thick, many-colored, steaming flood. She ceased; then, with a heaving of her disordered vitals, began again. Fuming with rage, he watched her, supporting her forehead. My fault, I must admit, he was thinking. I ought not to have made her drink like that. It was no use pretending now; for that afternoon everything was over, there was nothing to be done. He looked at her and felt himself exploding with anger: there she was, the girl of his dreams, naked, ready to surrender herself; and on her knee she held, not his head, her lover's head, but that dreadful basin at which she was gazing with fascinated eyes. And to think, he kept on musing, to think that if I hadn't made her drink, she would, at this very moment, have been mine.

Her vomiting, in the meantime, was finished, and Carla thrust from her the full basin, which her companion, not without disgust, took and put back on its stand. As he turned, Leo looked at the girl sitting, still uncovered, on the edge of the bed, her head bowed and her arms hanging at her sides, and he was struck by the contrast between the thinness of her body—for her ribs were visible and her shoulders were narrow and sharp—and the abnormal size of her breasts and her head. Not well-made, he thought, to comfort himself. "How d'you feel?" he added aloud.

"Very bad," she answered. She looked down, turning the bitter saliva round and round in her mouth; every now and then her eyes moved to the garments pulled back over her half-naked belly, and she was beginning to feel cold. A hopeless disgust oppressed her. Everything's finished, she thought; and in very truth, as her intuition told her, something had indeed come to an end, without either pleasure or dignity, in that basin; but what exactly it was, she could not have said. Gradually she lifted her head and looked at her lover with eyes full of tears. "And now?" The words came from her mouth almost without her intending them. "Now get dressed and let's go," he replied, with a kind of contained fury; and he got up and began walking up and down on the creaking floor-boards. From time to time he looked at Carla as she dressed herself; he was conscious of returning desire, and more than once asked himself whether it might not have been better to wait a little until her feeling of sickness had vanished, and then renew his assault upon those charming forms; but by this time it was too late, for Carla was ready. It's no good, he thought angrily; the magic has gone out of it . . . there's nothing more to be done today.

He went over to the bed. "And now how do you feel?" he asked.

"Better," the girl answered, "better." She had finished, and she got to her feet; and then, without touching each other, one behind the other, they went out of the shed.

Outside, there was a sound of pattering on the leaves. "Ha, it's raining," exclaimed Leo in surprise. Carla's silence made him uncomfortable, and he tried hard to appear at ease. They took a few steps forward. The air, in the close shelter of the trees, was still and suffocating, the tangled boughs were wrapped in dark shadow, and round each of their footprints, on the slippery ground, there was a ring of water squeezed out of the dead leaves. "It's strange," he went on, "every day the same weather. At dawn it's clear, during the morning it deteriorates, and then it rains from early afternoon till night-time." There was no reply. "We'll meet again this evening, then," he persevered.

Carla stood still and looked at him. Never again, she wanted to say, but was held back by the thought: I must go through with it . . . right to the end . . . right to the point of destruction. She walked on. "Perhaps . . . I don't know," she answered, her head down, without looking at him.

They had come to the end of the path, and they stopped again. "It's all very well," said Leo, with a silly smile, grasping her by the arm, "but even when you feel ill you're a lovely little girl." They looked at each other. If only I could love him, thought Carla, observing the man's red, inexpres-

sive face. She still felt the remains of her drunkenness, her
head ached, and she had a great longing for repose and affection; but Leo now gave her a little slap on the cheek.
"Silly little thing," he kept on saying, "silly little thing, you
insist on drinking and then you feel ill . . . you little silly . . .
very, very silly . . ." Then he pulled her to him. "Give me a
kiss and we won't say any more about it." They kissed, and
then separated; and then Carla came out from the sheltered
path and ran off in the rain and disappeared behind the corner
of the house.

What a nasty day, thought Leo, as he too went on his way;
what a stupid day! It was raining steadily now from a lofty
sky; the garden was already soaking wet, and the uninterrupted liquid rustling of water drowned all other sounds. Leo
went off in a discontented frame of mind; not merely had
Carla's birthday cost him, between flowers and a present,
about five hundred lire, but also, thanks to that treacherous
wine, the adventure had come to an end in a way both ridiculous and disgusting, one hardly knew which. Carla wants it
all right, he said to himself angrily; there wasn't even any
need to make her drunk. But now we've got to start all over
again. It was only when he found himself in the street and
wondered which way to go that he remembered that Lisa
had invited him, the night before, to go and see her that day.

At first the idea of going back to his old sweetheart seemed
to him absurd; he did not like retracing his steps over roads
he had already travelled, and such a visit appeared to him
like yesterday's warmed-up soup. But, on the other hand, the
desire Carla had aroused in him had failed to find relief.

If I don't get satisfied today, he said to himself as he walked
along in the rain through the broad, empty streets of this
wealthy suburb, I shall burst. The image of Carla, naked and
in tears, stayed in front of his eyes—and in so persistent a
manner that he made a movement with his hand as if to chase
it away. All right then, he decided at last, let's go there.
After all, Lisa's a woman too.

This decision put wings on his feet. He called a taxi; "Via
Boezio," he commanded as he threw himself in and sat down;
and the car started. Leo lit a cigarette. It will be the finest

day of her life, he said to himself; and he imagined that the
moment she saw him, Lisa would throw herself at him, her
arms around his neck. Last night she made a bit of a fuss. She
wanted to send me off with a flea in my ear; but of course
even she has her feminine pride. But today . . . today she
won't need so much asking. The movement of the taxi shook
him this way and that. He felt that by visiting Lisa in this
way, he was being generous, was at the same time benefiting
himself and doing a good deed. It will be the finest day of her
life, he repeated. I shall be giving her something she's never
dared hope for, and at the same time shall be making the best
of this stupid day. He threw his cigarette out of the window.
Now, its wheels slipping softly on the wet asphalt, the taxi
was turning into a deserted street with plane-trees on each
side. Leo sat with his money in his hand. When the taxi
stopped, he got out, stood bent in the rain as he paid the
driver, then disappeared hurriedly into the porch.

He went slowly up the stairs, recalling with complacency,
but without melancholy, how many times he had mounted
them ten years before.

There's no denying it, he thought without even attempting
to explain the meaning, ten years are ten years. He rang the
bell, the door was opened, he went in. He found everything
just as before, so much so that he had the impression, for a
moment, that he was not his present-day self but the man he
had once been; everything was in its place, the cupboards in
the dark passage, the tinkling glass door of the boudoir at
the far end, and also—yes, there they were—the same lowered
curtain, the same carpets. He sat down in one of the creaking
armchairs and lit a cigarette.

After a moment Lisa came in. "Oh, it's you!" she said carelessly. Then she sat down and looked at him as if to ask the
reason of his visit.

"Weren't you expecting me?" said Leo, surprised—for he
was convinced that he was anxiously awaited. Last night you
made me think quite the opposite."

"One says all sorts of things," she began, pulling her skirt
down over her knees; "especially at night, when one can't
see people."

[96]

She's cunning, thought Leo, she wants to be entreated. He moved his chair close to Lisa's, and then, bending forward, said: "But I myself am convinced that you were speaking seriously."

"Suppose I'd changed my mind?" she retorted vivaciously. Her weakness of the night before now appeared to her in its true light, not as a return of love for Leo but due to a momentary bewilderment and to ignorance of her own feeling for Michele. "A great many things," she went on seriously, "can happen between yesterday and today."

Leo looked closely at her, his eyes moving first to her face, then to her body, to the white swelling where her breast began, to the small expanse of bare shoulder which, in the dreary half-light of the room, looked fresher and cleaner and more shapely than it really was. She's trying to tempt me, he thought. Well, well, well. . . . She's as cunning as a vixen. He stretched out his arm. "D'you know that you've improved in looks in the most extraordinary way?" he said.

"Ah! You mean I was ugly before?" she exclaimed, with instinctive coquettishness. But she at once repented this moment of weakness. I must get rid of him, she thought, I must show him that he's made a mistake. Then, as she looked at Leo, she saw how red in the face he was, how excited, how sure of his conquest; one had only to watch the way in which he reached forward in his low armchair, with his chest puffed out to bursting-point and his eyes shining with desire and trying to be full of expression and passion both at the same time; and there came over her such a strong feeling of resentment, mingled with the pride of victory ("Now I love and am loved," she wanted to shout at him), that she suddenly saw it would be much more amusing and much cleverer to make him think he was desired and loved, and then undeceive him all at once; in a word, to make a mock of him.

"You've always been beautiful," Leo was saying, "but now you're even more beautiful than usual."

"But you've got Mariagrazia," protested Lisa, putting her plan into effect, "what d'you want to bother with me for?"

"It's all over between me and that woman . . . completely

over . . . whereas you've begun to interest me again, as you used to do."

"Thank you very much indeed."

"A misunderstanding," he went on, "has kept us apart until now . . . just a misunderstanding. You know how it is? One often makes mistakes . . . and I made a mistake about you, I recognize that now. But I've come today to say to you: let's forget the past and be reconciled."

He paused and held out his hand to Lisa.

She looked at his face, then at his hand. "But how d'you mean, be reconciled? We've never been enemies."

"No, really . . . this won't do," protested Leo. "Let me say at once, it won't do. For Heaven's sake don't pretend you don't understand, don't pretend—forgive my saying so—to be stupid. You understand perfectly well what I'm driving at. I spoke quite clearly. It's a question of forgetting the past, of being reconciled, and also—why not? I speak for myself, anyhow—of starting again from the beginning. . . . As you see, *I'm* not confusing the issue. I'm saying what I think, without using any roundabout expressions. And now it's up to you to answer."

"But . . . I don't know," she began, pretending to be full of doubts.

"What d'you mean, you don't know? Come on, pull yourself together."

"Well," concluded Lisa, "let's certainly be reconciled, if you like. As for beginning all over again—we'll have to see about that."

Now the worst is over, thought Leo, well pleased. She's not in the least stupid. She's understood everything. He bent down and warmly kissed her hand, then lifted his head again. "What I like most of all in you," he said, "is your straightforwardness . . . roundabout methods aren't necessary with you . . . one isn't misunderstood. . . ."

"The reason for that," she replied, stressing the words by a tone of voice that was full of hidden meanings, "is that I can always make a timely guess at other people's intentions."

"Ah, that's splendid!" exclaimed Leo, once more moving

his chair closer to hers; "tell me then, for instance—what d'you think *my* intentions are, now?"

"Your intentions, now?" She looked at him; these conversational snares, this ritual, as it were, consisting of questions and answers, with the same end always in view, now—though in the past she herself had made excessive use of it—inspired her with a kind of haughty disgust. It's over and done with . . . all that's over and done with, she thought. Now I love and am loved. But she intended to carry her own pretense through to the end. "Your intentions, now?" It certainly wouldn't be difficult to say what *they* are."

"Well then, if you know," insisted the man, bursting with curiosity, "tell me."

"Well," she began, modestly and with half-malicious, half-reticent hesitations that were extremely effective, "if you really want to know . . . it seems to me that you have intentions which are—what shall I say?—warlike."

"What d'you mean by that?" demanded Leo, bending so far forward that his chin almost touched Lisa's bare shoulder.

She looked into his face. What I mean by that, she wanted to reply, irritated by that red face reaching out towards her own, is that it's no use your bothering yourself. I love Michele. Michele is my lover. But she restrained herself. "Be careful," she warned him in a bitter-sweet tone of voice; "if you bend forward like that you may easily fall."

Leo was too excited to listen to what she was saying. "What?" he asked, stupidly.

"You may easily fall," repeated Lisa, "or hurt yourself."

"In any case," he answered without raising his head, speaking in a slow, pig-headed sort of way, "my intentions are perfectly simple. You get dressed now and we have tea together . . . at my flat, if you like—why not? Then we dine and go to a show, and finally I bring you back home."

There was a moment's silence. Lisa appeared to be very hesitant. "I would come," she said at last; "only how am I to know that you really love me and that this isn't just a passing caprice, after which you'll go back to Mariagrazia?"

"But it isn't," he objected, still keeping his head lowered and speaking with the same obstinacy—an obstinacy made up of repressed desire and impatience. "You're wrong. I've already told you, and I tell you again—I shall not go back to Mariagrazia, because everything is over between her and me, and has been for a long time. I went on with her as long as I could. It was one of those relationships that drag on and on for ever, partly from habit, partly for other reasons."

"Practical reasons?" suggested Lisa.

"Practical, indeed! But, to cut it short," Leo at last raised his eyes and looked at her, "don't bring in Mariagrazia who has nothing at all to do with it. Instead of that, give me an answer."

"What about?"

"Oh, really!" said Leo, with a kind of lightness in his tone, and at the same time, as if with the intention of rearranging the edge of her dress, putting his hand on Lisa's shoulder; "I've already said . . . Will you come out with me today or not?"

She hesitated; was she now forced to tell him the truth? But she was saved from it by the hand which now, as if by chance, was feeling her neck. "No," she protested, "leave me alone. There's nothing I dislike more than being touched on the neck."

"Once upon a time it used to give you great pleasure," answered Leo slowly, gazing at her and bringing his face close to Lisa's.

"Yes . . . but I'm not the same person I used to be," she said hurriedly, striving to resist the attraction of that hand. "Leave me alone."

"So that's how it is?" Brusquely Leo rose to his feet, bent over her, pulled her head back by the hair and attempted to kiss her; but Lisa, just in time, managed to put her hand in front of her mouth. "Come on, don't be disagreeable," said Leo commandingly, and there was in his eyes, and in the way in which he tried to remove the obstacle of her hand, so great an assurance that he would win in the end, so obvious a skepticism with regard to the seriousness of her resistance, that Lisa felt herself invaded by blind fury. "Leave me alone, I say," she exclaimed in a determined voice, her eyes flashing with anger. But the man took advantage of this to gain possession of her unwilling lips. For a moment she submitted to his kiss, twisting and struggling in vain to free herself, then, in the end, managed by means of a violent wrench to rise to her feet; the shock was such that Leo lost his balance and fell backwards into his armchair.

He got up and nervously rearranged his disordered jacket. "Lisa," he said, "don't let's play the fool. Haven't we decided to be friends again? What sort of behavior is this?"

She pointed theatrically towards the door. "Go away," she commanded.

"But—what d'you mean?" began Leo, flying into a rage.

"I don't love you, I've never loved you," cried Lisa, stooping and hissing the words into his face. "I let you believe it today, just for a moment, so that I might have the fun of hearing all the rubbish you would say to me. And now go away."

He stood for a moment motionless, astonished. Then, suddenly, he passed from stupor to an outburst of vindictive, obstinate rage. "Ah, I see," he shouted, "that's how it is. I've got to go away, have I? After having danced for your amusement. Well, I'm *not* going away." He hesitated, seeking vainly for some punishment that would fit Lisa's offense: should he smash a piece of her furniture, or some of her china? Should he slap her face?

"I shan't go away until I've kissed you." He threw his chair aside and started to seize Lisa in his arms; in his rage, the intended kiss amounted, actually, to possession, and he thought confusedly that he would throw her down on the floor and take her, there and then, on the carpet. But Lisa avoided him and took refuge behind an armchair. For one moment they stood face to face, both of them bending forward and clinging to the chair, watching each other closely and each trying hard to guess what the other's next movement would be. "Go away," she said at last, panting, her hair disordered, frightened by the brutality of the man's swollen face so close to her own. And then, with a kind of rough cunning, Leo put out his hand and seized her brusquely by the hair; he pushed the chair away and snatched her into his arms.

For a few seconds they wrestled together, Leo trying to frustrate Lisa's movements while she struggled to escape from his embrace. At length she succeeded, and took refuge against the door.

"Go away," she commanded again, her voice breaking; "go away or I shall call for help." She was red in the face, her hair was ruffled, she was panting; her dress was unbuttoned on one shoulder; she stood with her hands pressed back against the door and her bosom thrust out. "Go away," she repeated; but now someone in the passage outside was pushing against the door and trying to come in.

"It's all right, Maria," she cried without turning; "I don't need you."

"Open the door," commanded a male voice from outside. "It's not Maria . . . open the door." Automatically Lisa drew aside; the door opened and Michele walked in.

He held his hat in his hand, and he still wore his green, dripping waterproof. He looked at Lisa, panting and dishevelled, at Leo, red in the face, and the true nature of the scene focused itself in his mind. Leo came, he thought, to try and renew their old relationship, and Lisa turned him down. But he did not act on this thought, for it seemed to him, in a confused way that he ought to take advantage of the occasion to break with Lisa once and for all; besides, wasn't that attitude *de rigueur* in similar circumstances?

"Excuse me," he said in a toneless voice that he strove to make ironical; "the fault is entirely mine. I had decided never to come here again and I came. I have disturbed you. Excuse me." He made a stiff, ridiculous bow, turned on his heel and vanished; the door closed.

This springless jack-in-the-box that had popped out of the darkness of the passage and immediately popped back again had calmed Leo down; he smiled. "Is *that* your love-affair, Lisa?" he asked.

Absorbed in her own feelings of astonishment, she nodded gloomily. Then, suddenly, as if the thought of Michele having left, perhaps for ever, wiithout saying good-bye, had become unbearable to her, she rushed to the window and threw it wide open.

[102]

The flat was on the first floor, the windows low down. She put her head out and looked up and down the street. It was wet and empty, the air was cold and it was raining, and a big, leafless plane-tree right in front of the window blocked the view of the sky; but a few yards away to the left someone wearing a green, belted waterproof was walking quietly away, along the wall. "Michele!" she called, leaning out, "Michele!" She saw him turn slightly, look at her curiously, and then continue on his way. "Michele!" she cried, louder; and this time, without turning, without stopping, the boy waved his hand. He was some distance away by now, down there on the gleaming pavement; he was walking at a good pace, and would soon be turning out of the street; Lisa, therefore, saw that it was useless to persist, and turned back into the room.

"He'll come back, don't worry," said Leo, with false good humor, as he stood in the middle of the room; "I know him . . . he's not the kind of person to take things very seriously. He'll come back, you can be sure of that."

His voice was a provocation, an outrage, a cruel insult; and, in an extremely dignified manner, Lisa walked over and pressed a bell on the opposite wall. A moment passed, and then the maid appeared.

"Maria, will you please show the gentleman out?" It was the end, the utterly commonplace, ridiculous end; it was only two steps from the sitting-room to the door. The gentleman went off, muttering in an ignoble fashion. "I'm going, Lisa. . . . I'm going. . . . Give Michele my greetings." The maid did not understand and looked stupidly first at the man, then at Lisa; but Leo did not wait for her to show him the way, he took his hat and coat and went out by himself.

He felt inwardly refreshed by the rain. He put up his umbrella and walked along almost without a thought in his head. It might, or might not, have come off, he said comfortingly to himself at one moment, and it didn't. And then again, serenely: I've learned a lesson today—that's a chord it's better not to strike. After which he thought about nothing at all, but lit a cigarette and, taking care not to step in the puddles, walked along at his usual pace, which was neither slow nor hurried.

When he reached the end of the street he came out into a large and rainy square with neither monuments nor gardens in it. In the corner, underneath the post that marked the streetcar stop was a small group of waiting people; and as he approached he recognized Michele leaning against the post. "Ah, you're still here," he said to him, without a shadow of ill-will.

"Yes," answered the boy, raising towards him a pair of bored-looking eyes, "I'm waiting." There was a moment's silence.

"Well then," said Leo, "since I'm going home, let me give you a lift in my taxi. Taxi!"

Michele accepted. What's all this about? he thought, as he threw himself down beside Leo inside the cab.

For a minute or two they did not speak. Then, at last: "May I ask," said Leo, "why you went away just now? Didn't you know that the one thing she wanted was for you to stay?"

Michele did not answer at once; he was looking out of the window at the wet house fronts. "Yes, I know," he said at last.

"Well then . . . why didn't you stay?"

"Why? Because I don't love her."

This answer made Leo smile. "But, really," he began, "do you think that one should only go with a woman when one loves her?"

"That's what I think," replied Michele, without turning his head.

"Oh well, then. . . ." Leo murmured, a little disconcerted. "But I myself, for instance," he went on calmly, "I've had plenty of women I never loved. Lisa herself, for one. And in spite of that I've never had anything to be sorry for. I've amused myself as well as anyone."

"I don't doubt it," said Michele, with clenched teeth. God blast you! he would have liked to say, d'you think everyone in the world is like *you?*

"Apart from that, I must say," went on Leo, "when I see

a boy like you, who doesn't know many people and hasn't much in the way of resources, turning up his nose at a woman like Lisa, who—whatever she may be—is certainly not to be despised—well, it seems to me as if the world had turned upside down."

"Let it turn upside down!" muttered Michele, but the man did not hear.

"As far as I'm concerned, you can do as you like," concluded Leo. He lit a cigarette and wrapped his overcoat closely round him.

Michele looked at him. "According to you, then," he said, "I ought not to give up Lisa?"

"Of course not . . . certainly not," Leo approved, taking the cigarette from his mouth. "In the first place because Lisa is really not to be sniffed at. I was looking at her today . . . she's plump but she's firm; she has a bosom . . ." he went on, with a sly wink in the direction of the disgusted Michele, "and a pair of hips! Besides, my dear boy, she's a woman who can provide far greater satisfactions than one of the usual rose-watery young ladies. She's full of temperament . . . a real woman. And, in the second place, where are you going to find a mistress nowadays who can receive you in her own home? That, for you who can't afford a room or a little flat, is a great convenience; you come and go, in and out, and no one says a word to you; it's just as if you were in your own home, and you don't have to worry about it. Otherwise, especially at your age, you always end up by taking your girl-friend to some horrible place—some restaurant or hotel or somewhere—places that take away all appetite even to think of them. And if to all this you add that Lisa won't cost you a penny, literally not a penny—well, really, I don't know what more one could desire."

No indeed, repeated the boy to himself with a certain sadness. What more could one desire? He did not speak, but sat bending slightly forward, looking now at the other man, now at the street. It was already twilight, but the lamps were not yet lit; a damp gloom had invaded the crowded street so that you could not see the far end of it, and people, umbrellas, vehicles, everything at a little distance was merged into the same rainy remoteness in which the yellow lights of trolleys and cars passed hither and thither, swift and isolated. "And what am I going to do now?" wondered the boy. Every time he contemplated the ceaseless movement and agitation of life, his own inertia struck terror into him.

"Never mind, my dear boy," he heard Leo saying; "don't think so much about it. The thing is much simpler than you imagine. The one thing Lisa's waiting for is you. Go back there this evening and she'll welcome you with open arms."

He turned. "And so I've got to pretend to love her?" he began.

"But why pretend?" broke in Leo; "who's forcing you to do that? Don't take it all so seriously. The main point is that she's ready to go to bed with you. Accept the situation and be satisfied."

Thoughtfully, Michele turned to look at the street. "Will you stop in the square?" he said; "I'll get out there." A moment's silence followed. "Supposing," he went on at last, "supposing someone has offended you in some way . . . someone you don't really dislike—in fact, in spite of what he has done, you can't hate him. Would you, in that case, pretend to get angry and give him a slap in the face—or not?"

"That depends on his offense," replied Leo.

"The worst that there can be."

"But in that case," Leo objected, "it would be impossible for me to go on liking him, or for the affair not to matter to me."

"But just supposing."

"Well then, I should certainly slap his face for him," answered Leo without hesitating. The taxi stopped in the square. But before Michele got out Leo took hold of him by the sleeve. "Take my advice," he said, with a wink and an expressive movement of the hand, "Lisa . . . get on with it!" After which he threw himself back in his seat, shouted his address to the driver, and the taxi moved away.

In five minutes he was at home. He went into his study, an almost bare room with a high dado of brown panelling, bookshelves and an American desk, and sat down. The gloom of the rainy twilight invested these commonplace pieces of furniture, these practical objects, with an unbearable look of dullness, of precariousness; it was the worst moment of the day, for the whiteness of afternoon was gone and the blackness of night not yet come, the daylight was so feeble that it was impossible to see and the light of a lamp unpleasantly strong in that gray dusk. But Leo had no difficulty in overcoming any possible discomfort; he turned on the light, read over a business letter and prepared to write an answer to it. At that moment the telephone bell rang.

Without putting down his pen he took up the receiver and put it to his ear. "Who is that?" asked a feminine voice. The voice of Mariagrazia, thought Leo. "31, 496," he replied. "Am I speaking to Signor Merumeci?" the voice went on. "Yes." "This is Mariagrazia. Carla suggests going to dance at the Ritz . . . would you like to come with us?" "All right. I'll be with you in about an hour," he said. "By the way," she went on, "where are we going to meet?" But Leo had realized that this was the beginning of one of her usual interminable conversations. "We'll see," he replied, and hastily hung up the receiver.

After this he finished his letter and then, slowly, wrote another. Of business, in the proper sense of the word, he had none; he did not work, his activities being limited to the management of his property, which consisted of a few houses, and to a little cautious speculation on the stock exchange. Yet his wealth increased regularly each year, for he spent only three quarters of his income and devoted the rest to the acquisition of more house property. He now closed his letter, lit a cigarette and went into his bedroom; he had less than an hour to shave, dress, and get to the Ardengos' house. He washed and shaved with the minutest care, and started to dress. Clothes, suits of the finest quality, gave him immense pleasure; and the wearing of such clothes was one of his favorite hobbies. He put on a white silk shirt and a black and silver tie, socks of red and gray wool, and finally, not without considerable contortions, a suit of blue herring-bone cloth of truly remarkable cut. He stood admiring himself in the wardrobe mirror, and—whether it was that the subdued light in the room transformed and rejuvenated him, or that his beautiful clothes had quite gone to his head—came to the conclusion that there was a fine, noble look about him, a look of dignified melancholy. He glanced at his watch; three quarters of an hour had already passed, and he went out hurriedly, rushed to the garage, took out his car; ten minutes later he was ringing at the Ardengos' door.

In the drawing-room only one lamp was burning, beside which Leo found Carla sitting motionless. She was ready to go out; she was wearing a light, peach-colored dress, her face was powdered and made up, and her hair curled. "Mom will be here in a moment," she said.

"Good," began Leo, sitting down also, and rubbing his hands together vigorously. "And you . . . how are you?"

"All right." There was silence; Leo took the girl's hand and kissed it. "Well," he said; "what are we going to do?"

"We're going to dance," she answered dreamily. "And you'll dine with us this evening, won't you?"

"I think perhaps I won't dine with you," Leo replied, "but I'll certainly come in after dinner."

There was a sound of doors opening and shutting, and the girl quickly withdrew her hand. Michele came in. "How wonderful you look!" he cried, with forced gaiety. "Good evening, Leo. Well, and what are you doing here, you rich, fortunate, beautifully dressed people?"

"We're going to dance," answered Carla, with the same expression and voice as before.

"To dance?" Michele sat down. "In that case I'll come too. May I, Carla?"

"It's Leo who's doing the inviting," she said, looking at her lover.

Leo raised his head. I haven't really invited anybody, he would have liked to answer.

"Why, Leo," Michele was protesting, "I can still afford to pay for tea!" Carla looked again at Leo.

"Never mind about that," the latter hastened to reply. "I'm the host and of course I'll pay for everything."

For a moment all three were silent. "Well then, Michele," concluded his sister; "you can come on condition you go and change your clothes."

"Yes, of course . . . of course." The boy bent down to look: he was, indeed, incredibly dirty, his shoes covered with mud and his trousers splashed right up to the knee and wrinkled from the rain. "You're right," he said, and got up from his chair. "A thousand thanks, my most generous friend," he said to Leo, "I'll go and get cleaned up." He bowed and left the room.

"I feel sad," said Carla, before the door was closed.

"Why?"

"Goodness knows." She looked towards the black window panes, upon which trembling gleams of light showed that rain was still falling. "Perhaps it's the weather." Her big head drooped mournfully towards her companion, who took hold of her by the hair and kissed her. "You must dance with me," she said with a cool lack of modesty, after the kiss, "with me, all the time. You can leave Mom to sit still . . . or she can dance with the others, or with Michele, if it comes to that." She laughed drily, and felt that she was truly a year older. It's the end, she said to herself.

They kissed again, and then Leo said, deliberately: "Then you'll come and see me this evening, won't you, Carla?"

She turned pale. "What d'you mean?"

"At my flat," explained Leo, looking her straight in the eyes. He saw her hesitate, then bend her head as if she wanted to look for something that had fallen on the carpet.

"No . . . that's impossible," she said at last.

"Why impossible?" Leo insisted. "You promised me. You *must* come."

"No . . . no," she shook her head; "that's impossible." For a moment they did not speak; Leo looked at the girl, and the sight of her breasts, swathed in the stuff of her dress, excited him, so that an unaccustomed heat glowed in his cheeks. What a mistress she'll make! he thought, what material! what a mistress! The desire he felt for her made him clench his teeth, and he seized her around the waist. "Carla, you *must* come. It's absolutely necessary. If you don't come, then . . ." he hesitated, searching for the support of some pretext or other. He suddenly recalled the distaste she felt for her present existence, her desire for a new life. "Then,"

[109]

he concluded modestly, "how will you manage to make yourself a new life?"

She looked at him. He only wants to amuse himself with me, she thought, with a sharp sense of reality, but he's right. And what about my new life? She realized that in order to change, she would first have, pitilessly, to destroy; but this nocturnal surrender, in a distant house, repelled and frightened her. "I'll come in the daytime," she proposed with false simplicity; "one of these days . . . shall I? We'll have tea together . . . we'll have a good talk . . . is that all right?"

"I don't want tea. I want *you*," said Leo; but he returned immediately to a more effective tone of seriousness: "No, my love, either tonight or nothing."

"But please, Leo," she implored.

"I'll wait for you in the street with the car," went on her lover, "and I'll bring you home again before morning." He paused and looked at her for a moment. "And you'll see, you'll dislike it so little that you'll come back every night."

"No," she said, with a sort of terror; "no." After all, she thought, it will have to be made clear. It will be necessary to say everything. She looked at the man, and now, suddenly, because of the distress she was feeling, she wanted to cry out. Every night, she repeated to herself. What does it mean? How have I reached this point?

"I know you'll come," said Leo, and seized her almost roughly in his arms. "Tell me—you *will* come, won't you?"

She clung to a last excuse. "It's only two days since . . . since we've loved each other. Why not wait a little? Don't you know that every woman has her pride?"

"My dear," he answered hastily, "I understand . . . and that means that I shall expect you, without fail, this evening; that's agreed, isn't it?"

She still hesitated, looking askance from under the little hat she was wearing. "I'll tell you later, while we're dancing," she answered at last. "Yes," she added as though to convince herself, "I'll certainly tell you while we're dancing."

God be thanked, thought Leo. He embraced her. "And now the only thing that remains is to—to go and dance," he said gaily. He took her by the hips and, bringing his own passionate face close to the frightened, made-up face of the girl, "D'you know what you are?" he said; "you're a love . . . yes, a love of a little girl."

There was a sound at the door. "Shall we go, then, Merumeci?" said the Signora, coming into the room.

Leo rose to his feet. "All right," he replied hurriedly; "let's go." Carla also rose and went towards her mother. "Why aren't you taking the bag that Merumeci gave you?" asked Mariagrazia, examining her daughter from head to foot; "it would go marvellously well with that dress."

"I'll go and get it," said Carla; and went out.

She went hastily upstairs and ran to her room. The bag was lying on the chest of drawers; extremely elegant it was, in the most exquisite taste, and as she took it up it suddenly occurred to her that this might well be the first of a long series of presents. This idea struck her with such force that she remained standing there in front of the looking-glass, gazing at herself; and she seemed to see herself sitting on Leo's knee, giving him a pat on the cheek or leaning her head affectionately against his chest, and asking him in a low voice for the money for some little dress she wanted; or she would be going with her lover to some famous dressmaker, or to order three or four of those hats from Paris, the latest thing that season, that she liked so much. All this, indeed, was highly attractive, as it was, also, to be the owner of a car, of a house, of jewels, and to travel and see other peoples and countries—in fact, to know no limits to her own activities and her own desires; extremely attractive; and already, in spite of herself, she was smiling, when suddenly, going closer to the mirror, she noticed a red, round mark on her neck. At first she did not understand what it was; she rubbed it with her fingers, examined it again. Then finally she remembered that Leo, in the drawing-room a short while before, had kissed her on the neck. An absurd fear came over her that her mother might notice it; she took her powder-box and powdered the place thickly, and then, while she was twisting this way and that in front of the mirror to see if the guilty redness had vanished, Leo's imperious invitation to her to go that night to his flat, and the presents and clothes she had dreamed of, appeared to her all bound together in one single, inexorable association. My God, is *that* my new life? she asked herself, with a superficial, conventional sort of fear, not being yet conscious enough of her own feeling to be really frightened. Is it to be *that?* But in any case she had no time, now, to go deeply into the matter; out of the darkness, from the garden below, came the strident sound of the car horn, warning her that it was time to go.

She put out the light, and rushed downstairs, tortured, in the midst of these practical acts—even though no precise thought took shape in her mind—by an acute feeling of sadness, a violent longing to weep, that twisted her face into a ridiculous grimace. The corridor was dark; she felt her way into the vestibule, opened the door, and was greeted by the boisterous clamor of her mother, Leo and Michele, who were waiting in the car. The open space in front of the house was enveloped in thick darkness, it was raining noiselessly, and there was nothing to be seen except a few gleaming reflections, here and there, from the car, and its yellow, lit-up windows, from behind which the pink, joyful, satisfied faces of the three people inside the padded box watched her arrival with curiosity. It was a matter of a moment; and then Carla jumped in and dropped into the seat beside her lover; and the car moved off.

Not one of the four spoke a word the whole way. Leo drove the big car skillfully in the confusion of the crowded streets; Carla, sitting motionless beside him, gazed dreamily at the moving traffic, where, beyond the glossy hood of the car, between two black processions of umbrellas beneath the rain, red-lamped vehicles darted hither and thither in a way that appeared crazy. Her mother, too, looked out of the window, but not so much in order to see as to be seen: the big, luxurious car gave her a feeling of happiness and wealth, and every time some humble or common head emerged from the gloomy turmoil of the street and was carried along past her eyes by the current of humanity, she felt like hurling a sneer of contempt into the unknown person's face, as much as to say: "You, you ugly half-wit, you have to walk, and quite right too, it's all you deserve. . . . But I, on the other hand, I, quite rightly, loll upon cushions as I cleave my way through the common herd."

Michele was the only one who did not look out into the street, for he was more interested in what the car carried within its sumptuous box; indeed it seemed to him that there was nothing else to look at. Darkness hid the faces of his three companions, but each time the car passed underneath a lamp-post, a vivid light illuminated, for a moment, the still, seated figures. Then his mother's face would become visible, with its weak but deep-cut features, its eyes full of vanity; Carla's, the spell-bound, childish face of a little girl going to a party; and Leo's, in profile, red, well-proportioned, rather hard, like some inexplicable, frightening object revealed, for one instant, by a flash of lightning. Each time Michele saw them, he was astonished that he himself should be in their company. Why these people, he thought, rather than others? These figures were more than ever foreign to him, so that he almost did not recognize them; and it seemed to him that a blue-eyed blonde in place of Carla, a tall, thin woman in place of his mother, and a small, nervous man in place of Leo, would have made no difference to his life. Yet there they were, in the darkness, motionless, each jolt of the car causing them to knock against each other like lifeless marionettes: and it seemed to him that there could be nothing more distressing than to see them so remote, so detached, so hopelessly alone.

They arrived: four black rows of cars filled the dark space in front of the hotel. There were cars of every sort and size, and their drivers, clothed from head to foot in shiny rain-coats, talked and smoked in little groups. And, in luminous contrast with the gloom of the winter evening, the entrance of the Ritz shone out with a luxurious, hospitable light. The revolving door of wood and glass, with its familiar sound, introduced them one after the other into a hall full of men-servants and pages; then, passing by way of a cloakroom overflowing with numbered overcoats, they went through a series of empty, gilded reception-rooms and finally reached the ballroom. There, sitting at a little table by the door, was a man selling tickets; Leo paid, and they went in.

It was already late, and a large crowd filled the long, low

room. The tables were arranged along the walls, in the middle people were dancing, and at the far end, from a kind of gallery overhung by two palm-trees, an American Negro band was playing dance music.

"What a crowd!" said the Signora admiringly but pessimistically, throwing a dignified glance round the room. "You see, Carla, we shall never find a place."

In spite of these forebodings, they found a small table in a corner; they sat down, and the Signora divested herself of her cloak. "You know," she said, looking about the room and turning towards her three companions, "there are quantities of people we know here. Look, Carla . . . the Valentinis."

"And the Santandreas, Mom."

"And the Contris," added her mother. She bent forward a little, and went on in a lower voice: "Talking of the Santandreas—you know they went for their honeymoon two months ago to Paris? In the same sleeping-car there were the bridegroom, the bride, and the bride's boy-friend . . . what's his name? You know. . . ."

"Giorgetti," said Carla.

"Yes, of course, Giorgetti, that's it. Just imagine! Really it seems hardly possible!"

The music stopped, and after some vain applause the dancers went back to their places; at once the buzz of conversation became louder. The Signora turned towards her lover. "How would it be," she proposed, "if we went to the theatre this evening to see that French company? I have a box for a second performance, either this evening or the day after tomorrow."

"This evening I can't," said Leo, looking closely at the girl. "I have an appointment at eleven that I can't cut."

"An appointment at eleven o'clock in the evening!" echoed the Signora, half sarcastic and half confidential. "Tell us, Merumeci, is it male or female?"

Leo hesitated; should he arouse the Signora's jealousy or not? "Female, of course," he answered finally; "but I didn't explain myself very well. It's not so much an appointment as a visit . . . a cold supper . . . at the house of a lady who's entertaining some friends."

"And who is this lady, if I may ask?" asked the Signora, now thoroughly irritated, in a hard voice. Leo was disconcerted; he had not foreseen this indiscretion, and he searched and searched for the name of someone the Signora did not know. "Miss Smithson," he announced at last. "You know, the artist."

"Ah yes indeed!" exclaimed the Signora, in bitter triumph. "Miss Smithson. What a pity, really, *what* a pity, that just the day before yesterday I happened to go to my milliner, and my milliner showed me a hat that Miss Smithson had ordered to be sent to her at Milan! . . . Yes, indeed, because your artist friend has already been in Milan for five days."

"What d'you mean, in Milan?" repeated Leo, astonished.

"Why, yes," put in Michele; "didn't you know? They put forward the date of the Private View of her show."

"Go and keep your appointment with Miss Smithson, then"—the Signora wore a poisonous smile on her face—"go, by all means; but I'm afraid that, even if you catch a train at once—or even an airplane—you won't get there in time." She paused for a moment, and Leo did not answer; Carla, almost frightened, was observing her mother closely. "My dear man," the latter went on, "that sort of lie is easily seen through. And now, would you like me to tell you who this famous lady is that you're going to visit? Not an honest woman, certainly; you can't know any like that. Some low female, no doubt—some *cocotte* of the worst kind."

Carla's pallor was now so pronounced that Leo feared for a moment to see her faint or burst into hysterical weeping; but this did not happen. "Mother, don't shout so loud," said the girl in a quiet voice; "someone might easily hear."

There were three loud taps from the conductor's baton, and the music began again. "Well, Leo," she added; "shall we dance?"

They walked towards the dance floor one behind the other, through the people sitting at the tables. The pallor that Leo had noticed did not leave Carla's cheeks as she advanced through the chattering crowd, and there was a kind of stiff dignity in her expression; but, while still among the crowd, and before giving her hand to her companion, she threw back her head and said firmly—almost, he thought, with clenched teeth: "It's understood, Leo, that I'm coming to you this evening. You can expect me without fail."

"Seriously?"

"Perfectly seriously." Her voice had already changed; it was no longer firm, but trembling, and it seemed as though both breath and confidence had deserted her. "But now," she added, "don't talk to me any more. I just want to dance."

As they danced, Leo supported the girl's waist with all the strength of his arm; a lightness, and unaccustomed eagerness lent wings to his feet, and, although the space was small and the crowd dense, he strove to execute the most difficult steps. Now I've got you, he was thinking, this time I've got you. There was a sense of melancholy confusion, however, in the girl's heart: she danced unwillingly, she longed to get out of the crowd and sit down by herself in some corner and close her eyes. The merry-go-round of dancers rotated in continuous movement before her eyes—faces of men, of women, expressionless, serious, smiling; the music was triumphant, victorious, but not without a little trembling chord of sadness in it—very ordinary, really—which came back insistently from time to time. The sight and sound of faces and music made her head swim.

The dance was finished now, and the couples were returning to their places; Michele and his mother were also returning, in the midst of a fierce quarrel. "Never again shall I dance with you," repeated Mariagrazia in indignation.

"What's all this about?" demanded Leo, authoritatively.

"Never again," she went on. "Just imagine—everybody was looking at us. What on earth must they have thought? It was terrible. He danced like a . . . like a . . ."—she searched for a comparison and, in the confusion of her anger, could not find one—"like a thief."

"What! Really!" exclaimed Leo, in astonishment.

"Like an ill-mannered lout," she corrected herself with dignity.

"Please tell me," said the boy, making an effort to smile,

"please tell me how thieves dance? And, in the present company, who is the thief, I, or somebody else?"

"Oh, be quiet," she implored, looking round.

"No, I won't," persisted Michele. "In any case, *I* dance more like the victim of a thief, relieved of all earthly incumbrances, of all passion and delight. If you want to know how thieves dance, you'll have to try someone else. Certainly you will," he concluded, staring hard at Leo, "someone else."

For a moment Leo, sitting motionless between the two anxious women, did not say a word. Then he smiled. "I really believe," he said, rising to his feet, "that something must have happened to you, Michele. And therefore I think it would be better if you went away . . . unless you want *me* to go."

"Yes, Michele, go away," implored his mother.

Michele looked at her. "And so," he burst forth, "you prefer to send away your own son rather than an outsider like Leo?"

"But after all—it was Leo who invited us!"

There was no reply to that. She's right, thought Michele, it was Leo who paid. He stared straight ahead at the big, low room with its deafening buzz of conversation, at all the groups of people, the women with painted faces and crossed legs exposed to view, the men sitting in self-possessed attitudes with cigarettes in their mouths, at all the groups of people eating, drinking, talking in a nonchalant manner; at the Negroes tuning their instruments across the floor under the palm-trees. No; there was no reply. "You're right," he said finally; "I'll go. Amuse yourself. The thief is going away." And he went.

Outside, it was still raining. *Thief, thief*, Michele repeated to himself, almost without resentment, and with a kind of false exaltation. He tried to rob me of Lisa too. Who is the thief, anyhow? But, a few minutes later, he was forced to recognize, to his own astonishment, that he was not in the least angry; he was, on the other hand, perfectly calm. No action on Leo's part, however villainous, was capable of shaking his indifference; after a sham outburst of hatred, he always ended by

[117]

finding himself as he was now, somewhat dazed and light-headed, his mind empty.

The pavements were crowded, the streets crammed with vehicles, for it was the busiest moment of the afternoon. With no umbrella against the rain, Michele walked slowly along as though it were a day of sunshine, looking idly at the shop windows, at the women, at the electric signs hanging in the darkness. But however hard he tried he could not manage to take any interest in the well-known spectacle of the street; the anguish that had taken possession of him, for no particular reason, as he walked away through the empty reception-rooms of the hotel, did not leave him; the image of himself as he really was and as he could not forget that he was, pursued him. He seemed to have a clear vision of himself—alone, wretched, indifferent.

He felt a sudden desire to go into a cinema. There was a very luxurious one in that same street, which displayed, at its marble doorway, a kind of luminous, continually-revolving whirligig. Michele went up to it and looked at the photographs; but they were of some bit of Chinese nonsense made in America—altogether too stupid: so he lit a cigarette and continued his drifting progress in the rain, through the crowd. Then he threw away the cigarette. There was nothing to be done.

But his anguish was increasing; of that there could be no doubt. He already knew the course it would take: first the vague uncertainty, the lack of confidence, the sense of emptiness, the need to busy himself with something, to find some passionate interest; then, very gradually, the dry feeling in the throat, the bitter taste in the mouth, the wide, staring eyes, the insistent recurrence of certain absurd phrases in his vacant mind, a state, in fact, of furious and disillusioned despair. Of this state of anguish Michele had a most painful dread: he longed not to think about it, but to live, like everybody else, from minute to minute, with no anxieties, at peace with himself and with others. Oh, to be an imbecile! he sighed sometimes; but, when he least expected it, a word, an image, a thought would bring him back again to the eternal question; and then his listlessness would go to the winds. All efforts to recapture it would be vain, and he would be forced to think.

That day, as he walked slowly along the crowded pavements, he was struck, as he looked down at the hundreds of feet trampling in the slush, by the vanity of his own movements. All these people, he thought, know where they're going and what they want, they have a purpose in life and that's why they hurry and torment themselves, and are sad or happy. They have something to live for, whereas I . . . I have nothing. . . . I have no purpose. If I don't walk, I sit: it makes no difference. He kept his eyes fixed on the ground: yes, there truly was, in all those feet trampling the mire in front of him, an assurance, a confidence that he did not possess; he looked, and the disgust that he felt with himself increased still further. Wherever he was, he was the same—idle, indifferent; this rain-soaked street was his own life, which he traversed without faith and without enthusiasm, his eyes dazzled by the deceptive splendors of the advertising signs. How long is this going on? he wondered. He looked upwards; the silly revolving signs were there in the black darkness above, one recommending a toothpaste, another a shoe-polish. He lowered his eyes again; the movement of his feet continued steadily, the slush squelched from under his heels, the crowd walked. And where am *I* going? he asked himself again. He slipped one finger round under his collar. What am I? Why don't I run, why don't I hurry along like all these people? Why not be a man of instinct, a sincere human being? Why not have faith? His distress oppressed him; he wanted to stop one of the passers-by, take him by the coat collar, ask him where he was going, why he was hurrying like that; he wanted to have some kind of purpose, even an illusory one, instead of trudging along like this, from street to street, among people who really had a purpose. Where am I going? Once upon a time, it appeared, men used to know their paths in life from the first to the last step; but now it was not so; now one's head was in a bag, one was in the dark, one was blind. And yet one still had to go somewhere; but where? Michele thought he would go home.

A sudden haste came upon him. But the street was crammed

[119]

with vehicles which—since there were too many of them—were compelled to move very slowly along beside the pavements; it was impossible to cross. In the diagonal rain, between the dark or illuminated façades of the houses, the two opposing files of cars, one going up and the other down, were waiting to free themselves and leap forward; and he too waited. Then, among all the others, he noticed one car that was larger and more luxurious than the rest; inside it sat a man leaning stiffly back, with his head in shadow, and across his chest lay an arm, a woman's arm. You could see that she was sitting beside him and had fallen across his knees with her hand clasping him round the shoulders, as though in supplication. yet not daring to look him in the face. The motionless man, the clinging woman, were presented for one moment to Michele's eyes in the white light of the street-lamps; then the car moved on, gliding like a whale in among the other vehicles, and all Michele could see of it was the little red light above the number-plate, looking like an advertisement. Then this last sign vanished.

The brief vision he had seen left him with an intolerable nervous depression. He did not know the man and woman, they were evidently people of a completely different world from his, possibly foreigners; and yet it seemed to him that the scene had been produced from his own mind and was one of his own anxious imaginings, brought to life and displayed before his eyes by some superior power. That was his own proper world, a world in which people suffered genuinely, where you might cling to shoulders that were bereft of pity, might supplicate in vain—not this limbo full of absurd bickerings and false sentiments, in which the distorted, unreal figures of his mother, of Lisa, Carla, Leo and all the people he knew, vainly agitated themselves. He could have truly hated that man, have truly loved that woman; but he knew that it was useless even to hope, for the promised land was forbidden to him and he would never reach it.

A policeman had now held up the interminable traffic and Michele was able to cross. Half-way across the street he felt a kind of dizziness, an intolerable discomfort; so he took off his hat and let the rain fall on his bare head.

He could not have explained the true nature of his feeling, for a great number of undefined longings were fermenting in his soul, and the torment of thought inflicted a suffering that was also physical. An empty taxi went past close to him; he jumped in, gave the address of his home; but the memory of those two haunted him, the man and the woman clinging to him in the luxurious car. I wish I knew where they'd gone, he thought, almost seriously. I could give the driver their address, and go and see them, and beseech them to take me with them. These absurdities and the images that accompanied them calmed him down a little; but at each jolt in the road he seemed to be awakened from some unattainable dream, and he realized with bitterness that such vain fancies would not alter, even in the slightest degree, the reality of the world in which he lived.

In five minutes he was home; he hurried across the front garden, in rain even heavier than before, and went into the dark hall. The corridor too was plunged in gloom; he put down his hat and coat on a chair and, without turning on the lights, felt his way towards the stairs. But as he went past the drawing-room door he noticed that a little light was showing through the key-hole, and he heard music, dance-music, in fact—the same, it seemed to him, that he had heard a few minutes before in the hotel ballroom. This is a kind of persecution, he said to himself; and he opened the door and went in. The part of the room which was usually devoted to conversation was in darkness, but the other part, beyond the arch and its two pillars, was lit up, and somebody was playing the piano. He walked forward, and the person who was bending over the keyboard then turned and looked at him: it was Lisa.

She's come here to explain things to me, thought Michele, bored. As if I hadn't already understood the whole situation. He sat down in an armchair, away from the light. "We went to the Ritz," he said calmly; "but it was really too dull and I came away. Also—just imagine!—I had a quarrel with Leo."

She looked at him with curiosity. "Ah! did you really?" she asked, getting up and coming over to him. She sat down in front of him, as close as she could. "And what was the reason?" she added, in a hesitating but confidential manner. "Perhaps it was about me?"

Michele glanced at her questioning face and had a great desire to laugh. "My poor Lisa," he wanted to say to her; "what must I do to convince you that I don't love you?" But, out of pity for her, he restrained himself. "No," he answered shortly; "not about you, about business matters, my mother's business matters."

"Ah, I see," said Lisa, rather disappointed. She gazed insistently, passionately, at the boy, and was tormented by a desire to justify herself, to explain what had really happened. After that, everything will be clear, she was thinking, and he'll put his head on my knee, as he did this morning. These thoughts absorbed her, and time was passing, but she could not think of any pretext for mentioning the subject that lay so close to her heart.

Then their eyes met. "I said that," began Lisa, "because I think you have every reason to be angry with me and with Leo."

"Why? I've no reason to be angry with either of you," Michele answered, observing her attentively. Don't you believe it? he longed to add.

"I understand you," went on Lisa, "Oh! indeed I understand you. And that's why I feel that I owe you an explanation."

Michele neither spoke nor moved. I must give her the impression that I'm far removed from all these arguments of hers . . . that I don't know anything about them.

"First and foremost"—Lisa bent forward and looked the boy in the eyes—"if you think there's anything between me and that man, I assure you you're quite wrong. There was once—I must tell you now, it's no use trying to hide it from you—there was once a . . . a relationship. He loved me." Lisa made a slight gesture to show that it was a question of digging up the distant past. "I was young, and at that moment I was in need of help; so—partly because of his persistence, partly because of my own situation at that time—I ended by giving in to him. . . ."

[122]

"I've been told that you're still a married woman," interrupted Michele, almost without meaning to.

"My husband ran away," replied Lisa, with extreme simplicity, "a year after our wedding, taking all my jewelry with him." She remained for a moment deep in thought, but without any sign of sadness or embarrassment, like someone who is making an effort to take up the thread of a conversation after some quite insignificant interruption.

"I gave in to him," she began again, after a short pause, "and the thing dragged on for a few years—three years, to be exact—until one fine day I realized that I didn't love him, that I had never loved him, and so we parted."

Wasn't it really that he left you for my mother? Michele wanted to ask. But he forebore; what was the use of it?

"And we didn't see each other any more, except occasionally at your house, until . . . until today, when he came to see me with goodness knows what intentions. Perhaps he thought he could begin the whole thing over again." She laughed, to indicate the complete absurdity of Leo's hopes. "As if I could forget his conduct towards myself, and—apart from that—as if I had no other friends but him, and he had only to come to me in order to obtain everything. I was just in the act of turning him out when you arrived. That is the truth, believe me; I can swear to it on all that I hold most sacred."

Lisa paused and looked at the boy with an expression that was both imploring and doubtful. He, for his part, had lowered his head and sat staring at his hands.

"Yes, of course," he said finally, showing a pair of uncomprehending eyes and a preoccupied face.

Of course what? What did "of course" mean? Did it mean: "Of course you didn't betray me?" Or did it mean: "Of course you *did* betray me?" The words increased the confusion in her mind. Bending forward, still filled with emotion from the speech she had just made, she gazed at Michele as though she expected to find in his face the explanation of his reply; but the boy displayed the most unruffled indifference, and there was a sort of hardness in his eyes; he looked as if he had never spoken.

Disappointed, Lisa sat back in her chair; all sorts of apprehensions jarred in her mind. He doesn't believe me, she was thinking, and was almost wringing her hands with pain. And yet it's true. A few moments passed in this way, in an embarrassing silence; then she burst out laughing.

"Poor Leo!" she exclaimed; "it's not been a good day for him. He's quarrelled both with me and with you . . . not to mention your mother, which is the normal thing. He's had no success at all!"

Her laughter was nervous, artificial; and between one trill and the next she observed Michele and saw that his bewilderment had redoubled. She went on laughing; the drawing-room was half in darkness, the two little lamps on the piano, screwed into two sham snuffed-out candles, shone on the glossy, oblong lid and looked like two tapers on a bier; still she laughed, until her laugh died in her throat at the sight of Michele's motionless and—yes, indeed it was—vaguely pitying face in front of her. The expression she saw there signified clearly: I happen to find myself in the company of a mad-woman; I must listen to her, approve all she says, and make a special effort not to irritate her. And nothing could have been more agonizing to her, in her desire for understanding and her hunger for passion, than this deliberate coldness. Then Michele spoke.

"Certainly," he said, "things might have gone better for him."

This reply destroyed Lisa's last illusions, and a bitter, passionate discouragement took possession of her. He's avenging himself, she thought. He thinks I've betrayed him and he won't even listen to me, and he answers me as if I were an idiot.

Michele was there, right in front of her, there could be no doubt of it. The purity and sincerity she had wished to rediscover were still there, in his eyes and on his brow; his passion was real, it truly existed; and it seemed to her that, if only she could find the right words, she could surely convince him.

"Look, Michele," she begged, bending forward again, as before. "It's not my fault that you found me with Leo—he just arrived. Besides, how could you believe, after what happened between you and me this morning, that I could, on the very same afternoon, accept this man's advances without more ado? And look—it would anyhow be absolutely impossible for me to love Leo: he's coarse, he's unimaginative. You judge me wrongly; you must revise your opinion. You think I'm frivolous and—what shall I say?—facile; but I assure you it isn't true. I'm quite a different sort of person. I need something more than that—ah, if you only knew how much I've thought about it!—something that isn't merely outward appearance, that isn't just the material body, but also . . ." She stopped suddenly, gazing at Michele. "And in you, you see," she added in a lower voice, speaking more slowly and bringing her face close to the boy's, "in you that thing exists, and that's why I value you and love you."

This is what's called plain speaking, thought Michele. He did not answer, but drew his head back a little, more in embarrassment than repugnance, and observed Lisa. The whole of the upper part of her body was thrust forward from the low armchair in which she sat, and appeared, thus bent, to be bursting out of her tight-fitting dress, while her short skirt, pulled up at the back, disclosed a large feminine thigh encircled by a pink garter. He was struck by this last detail. She's certainly not to be despised, he thought, Leo is right. But all at once, partly because of the feeling of artificiality inspired in him by the previous conversation, partly because of the baseness of this thought that flashed through his mind, he was filled with a digust so violent that it made his lips tremble. Not *that*, he thought, "no, not that. He lowered his eyes and drew back even further.

"No, don't look at me like that," she exclaimed even before he had spoken, frightened at seeing him stiffen up again just as before, after his brief, favorable agitation at the sight of her nudity. "Please don't be like that. Don't be so reserved. Do please answer me. Tell me seriously what you're thinking about."

Silence ensued, and, for the first time since Michele had come in, he heard the rustling of the rain against the closed shutters. He remembered Leo and the two women whom he had left behind at the hotel.

"What I'm thinking about?" he repeated at length, without a hint of irony. "I'm thinking that they haven't come home yet, I'm thinking that it's bad weather—that's what I'm thinking about. . . ."

There was silence. She was still in the same position, doubled up in her chair; there was nothing to be said, every attempt had failed, hopelessly. . . . She looked at Michele's shoes and it seemed to her that her mind was failing. It would have been better, she surprised herself thinking, if I had not turned Leo down. At least I should have had *him*, now.

The gloom inside the room was, in the meantime, increasing; it was engulfing the walls and the furniture, was growing steadily thicker, descending upon the two who sat there and deepening the darkness all around them; until a kind of cavern was created, hewn roughly out of the blackness, low-vaulted, sooty-ceilinged, a cavern of feeble light. Huddled in this dying halo, the two black figures kept watch over the bier upon which the tapers flickered, flickered and grew red, flickered and grew dark, and finally went out.

"And now what's the matter?" demanded Lisa, in a discouraged voice, out of the night.

"There's nothing wrong," came the answer; "the electric current has failed because of the bad weather. We must wait."

Silence again; darkness, and the rustle of the rain; and then Michele felt a hand on his, and smiled, but without pity. Now is the moment, he thought, the moment to forgive, and to forget, and to abandon oneself to sentiment in this propitious darkness.

But his imagination, oppressed, recoiled from sarcasm, and derived, from the caress of those fingers, a pretext for fantasies of passion. He imagined himself seeking Lisa in the blackness, pressing her, at last, to his breast with a genuine, decisive kiss. For a moment he struggled against this weakness. Images passed in front of his eyes that saw only darkness—the image of Lisa or, to be more precise, the memory of that exposed leg upon which all his desires were fixed, and that other image of the man and woman in the motor-car. Why isn't Lisa that woman? he thought. Why am I not that man? The sound of the falling rain was against the walls of the villa, the darkness was complete, the stupid, eager hand never ceased its warm caressing, and Michele did not dare to thrust it away and lose it; he was counting the seconds and thinking that he would wait one minute for the light that would tear them apart. O hand, he implored, trying hard to smile, wait just a little longer . . . long enough, anyhow, to save appearances. But the light did not come; the minute passed; and then, albeit realizing the absurd weakness of his action, the boy stooped and kissed the hand.

That's the end of everything, he thought the next moment, half pleased and half disgusted. Now I must pull her on to my knee and kiss her on the mouth. And he was on the point of carrying out his intention when there was a sound of voices and laughter from the corridor. The drawing-room door opened; the trembling gleam of a candle pierced the darkness and made the whole room quiver; gigantic shadows leapt up against the ceiling, alternating with splashes of brilliant light. Followed by Leo and Carla, his mother came in.

They came forward with short steps, obviously trying hard to distinguish the two seated figures. Leo was holding the candle, and his red face, all bedewed with light, could be seen clearly; the mother and daughter were one on each side of him, and were only half illuminated. They walked hesitatingly, followed by their own enormous shadows on the walls and ceiling.

"Ah! it's you!" exclaimed the Signora at last, recognizing Lisa.

"It's you again!" said Carla in her turn. "Is it very long since the lights went off? We danced and enjoyed ourselves. And—just imagine!—Leo made Mom dance the Charleston!"

"And how well she did it!" said Leo, coming forward.

"Oh, Merumeci, don't speak to me of that Charleston," sighed the Signora. She sat down, and seemed very tired. "Just fancy," she went on, turning to Lisa. "All of a sudden he held me away from him and started kicking his legs about, and he said to me: 'Do as I'm doing.' At first I wouldn't; then I started imitating him, and in five minutes I was able to dance it better than all the other women in the room. . . . It's not in the least difficult, your Charleston."

"Come, come. It can't quite be said that you really know how to dance it," Carla observed.

"What d'you mean, I don't know how to?" protested her mother, offended. "Look, I'll do it again for you this minute. . . . It's perfectly easy."

"But, Mom," insisted Carla, "it can't be learned in such a short time as that."

"Oh, can't it?" replied her mother, rising to her feet in high irritation. "Well, I'd just like to show you . . . if it's only to prove to you that I'm not in the habit of telling lies, like you." She took off her cloak and put it on a chair. "Now, Lisa, please, will you play a Charleston?" she went on, turning towards her friend. "You'll find one in that pile of dance music on top of the piano."

Lisa rose and Leo followed her, holding the candle. "What would you like?" she said, turning over the music by the flickering candlelight. "*On the Transatlantic Liner? A Night in New York?*"

"That's it . . . *A Night in New York,*" the Signora approved.

Lisa sat down at the piano and prepared to start playing, while Leo stood beside her and held the light for her. Deep in shadow beside the opposite wall, Michele and Carla, motionless and silent, watched.

The facile, discordant tune echoed in the stillness. "Come on!" Leo encouraged her. Looking carefully at her feet, the Signora started to dance. The candlelight fell unbecomingly upon her painted, flushed face, furrowed with soft wrinkles; the dress she wore was close fitting, and at each jerky movement her breast and hips strained at the glossy material. She threw her legs first this way and then that, striving to keep time to the music and to hold her knees well together, but it was clear that she must have forgotten Leo's lesson, for she stopped and looked at her lover with a disappointed expression.

"I don't know. . . . This isn't the tune we danced to at the hotel," she said, "I don't know how to dance it to *this* tune."

"You see, Mom," said Carla, coming forward out of the shadow; "I was quite right."

"Oh no, indeed you weren't." In the light of the candle her mother's face wore an expression of lively displeasure. "The tune wasn't the same."

"You chose it yourself," observed Lisa, turning round from the piano.

Leo stepped forward with the candle into the irritated, disconcerted circle formed by the other three. "Never mind, never mind," he kept saying conciliatingly. "Some other time. . . ."

All five of them were silent for a moment, looking at each other. The rain was falling more heavily now; its ceaseless pattering sound was mingled with violent gusts of wind against the vibrating shutters. Then at last Carla spoke. "We must go and change," she said. "It's almost dinner-time."

"You'll stay and dine with us, won't you, Merumeci?" said the Signora, who wanted at all costs to wrest an appointment out of her lover for the next day.

"No. . . . I mean, yes . . ." answered Leo.

They went off hesitatingly, one after the other, towards the door. The Signora was holding the candle now and saying in a sprightly way, "Whoever loves me, follow me." Carla laughed. But before leaving the room Leo went over to Michele, who was still sitting down. "Well," he asked him, "did you do as I told you? Remember, Lisa is not to be sniffed at; she's fat but expert." After which—not without a sly wink at the silent, indifferent boy—he joined the others. The candle threw one last gleam under the cross-beam of the doorway and was then engulfed in the blackness of the corridor; their voices could still be heard, among them that of the Signora saying: "Carla, open the door." Michele, who had not moved from his armchair, was left in darkness.

They all went upstairs together, stumbling against each other and chattering. In the anteroom on the floor above, Carla found two more candles in a drawer; her mother took them and dragged Lisa off with her to show her a new dress. "A gold collar," she kept on repeating. "You must see. It's the very latest fashion." Leo and Carla stayed in the anteroom.

They stood looking at one another. A solemn, heavy excitement was discernible in the man's inexpressive eyes. He had put down the candle on the table and, with rough-skinned fingers, was tormenting Carla's hand—a hand that pleased him very much because it was white, cool and lean; he was looking up at Carla with a sly, penetrating expression, and his imagination was dwelling upon thoughts of the indecent caresses which that cold hand would know very well how to perform, naturally, and yet not without astonishment. The type of hand, he was thinking, so delicate that it seems like a flower, yet capable of anything in the cause of enjoyment. The more he thought about it, the more excited he became; and finally his expression hardened, he let go of her hand and seized Carla around the waist. The girl, evidently, must have been thinking of something quite different. "No, Leo . . . no, do be careful," she murmured in a low voice, defending herself; she looked around with frightened eyes; then, finally, yielded to him. It was at that moment that Lisa came in.

She saw, in the middle of the anteroom, the two embracing figures, and around them, five doors with velvet curtains. She took a step backwards and hid herself. When she looked again, scarcely parting the curtains behind which she stood, peering from the shadow in which she was plunged by the candle on the table, she saw the two heads still united, bending this way and that as they kissed, and their two shadows leaping, in the utter silence, right up to the ceiling. Her mind was empty of thought and her heart beating fast; she left off peeping for a moment and stood undecided and frightened in the darkness, between the door and the curtain; then looked again, cautiously: the two figures had separated, and were now talking.

"It seemed to me," said Leo, "that that curtain moved."

"Spirit!" he added, laughing, "if you are there, knock once. If you are not there, knock twice." And he gave a parody of people at a spiritualistic séance. Carla, seeing the wrinkles of laughter on his half-illuminated face, laughed too, unwillingly; and Lisa, standing there behind the curtain, was longing really to knock, in order to see them leap into the air in terror, with red faces and fear in their eyes.

[130]

"Sit down here," the man was saying, "sit here, on my knee."

"But Leo!" the girl implored him; "Leo . . . suppose someone were to come!"

"No fear of that." There was a rustling sound; Lisa opened her eyes wide; no, she was not dreaming, Carla was sitting there on the man's knee with her head against his, sitting stiffly, and then . . . why, yes, he was kissing her neck.

"And now, Carla," said Leo gaily, "if you're there, give me a kiss. If you're not, give me two." There was silence; Carla's big, dark head drooped mournfully, then suddenly started back. "No, Leo," she said, "no . . . not that." She twisted away from him as the gigantic shadows swayed; then stopped still. The candle cast gleams of light, now longer, now shorter; the two figures, absorbed, with bent heads, now neither moved nor spoke; the only sound to be heard was the faint creaking, at intervals, of the divan. Then Lisa went noiselessly back into the Signora's room.

Her initial astonishment had been succeeded by a vindictive joy. Now I shall take Mariagrazia by the arm, she decided, and show her what her dear Leo is up to. But the sight of the Signora, as she came back into the room, for some reason disarmed her.

She found her walking up and down, candle in hand, closely and conceitedly inspecting, in the mirror, the effect of her new dress.

"What d'you think of it?" she inquired. She was much preoccupied with a fault she had discovered above the belt, a fold in the wrong place. "I'll put a piece of ribbon there," she said; "or . . . or perhaps . . . but Lisa, help me a moment." She turned around, and around again, dissatisfied; but Lisa had sat down in a dark corner, and now, for a reason she could not explain, the memory of what she had seen made her heart ache, and she closed her eyes.

"I don't know," she said vaguely.

"What d'you mean, you don't know?" repeated the other woman in perplexity, gazing at herself in the glass. "Here I am, worried to death, and you answer me: I don't know. What *do* you know, then?"

[131]

I know plenty of things, Lisa would have liked to reply. But now she had no more wish to disclose the unexpected secret; she was withheld from doing so by a special kind of restraining influence—that of her own dignity, in fact. For she did not wish it to be thought that, in revealing Leo's new intrigue, she was acting out of a paltry desire for vengeance as a betrayed mistress, instead of from the disgust she felt and the affection she bore towards Carla. For this reason she was silent.

"How about putting a gold rose there?" the Signora was asking; and the candle she held in her hand threw gleams of anxiety on to her face.

"Yes, of course," Lisa approved vaguely; but she was seeing those two closely joined heads again, and the sight gave her pain, and it was the first time this had happened to her; it gave her pain, like something that is sad and haunting.

"And how about a belt?" the Signora went on persistently; "what d'you think about a narrow gold belt?" She continued to look at herself and now seemed more satisfied. "It's a perfectly lovely frock," she added, "but that little crease . . . that wretched crease." A look of doubt passed over her face in the candlelight. "I wonder if there's something disarranged underneath?" she suggested, and, putting down the candle on the floor, lifted up her clothes with both hands and fumbled amongst the light undergarments that she wore next to her skin. The candle darted and flickered, and little black coils of smoke twisted about in the air, while Lisa, sitting in her dark corner, neither moved nor spoke; her eyes travelled back and forth from the big bare legs of the Signora to the door behind which, in the anteroom, Leo and Carla were embracing. A feeling of disgust oppressed her—another sensation new to her; a clear-sighted disgust which dwelt upon the girl's youthfulness and coldly foresaw the ruin that this intrigue would bring with it. Indignation she did not feel, nor surprise either—oh no, not after the life she herself had led; but rather—yes, that was it—a sort of compassion, of a not very precise kind, that embraced the Signora, Leo, Carla, the whole lot of them, herself included. The novelty of these feelings was almost frightening to her; she was extremely tired;

and finally there came over her a hysterical longing to get away, to think over in solitude all the things that had happened that day.

She rose to her feet. "I'm going home," she said.

The Signora, who had taken off her dress, came over to her in slip and panties. "Already?" she exclaimed; but she did not detain her, and, having first embraced her, followed her with the candle to the door. "And this evening, what are you doing?" she asked when they reached it.

"I'm going to bed," replied Lisa, with perfect simplicity. She saw the other woman look at her as if she did not believe her. "Good-bye, then," she said, and, being careful to bang the door to warn the two lovers outside, she left the room.

Carla at once got up from the divan and came over to meet her. "I'll come down with you," she said, "and you, Leo, must stay in the dark for five minutes." The light of the candle fell full on her round face; and Lisa noticed that her eyes were tired and lusterless and her cheeks paler than usual. She felt a sudden desire to speak, to tell what she had seen; but the girl had already turned her back and started off down the stairs.

All the way down, at each step, Lisa was tormented by the thought: Ought I to speak or not? She looked at Carla's almost childish cheeks, at her big head, and her feeling of pity increased. It's all Mariagrazia's fault, she thought, that this poor little thing now finds herself in such a situation. They had reached the hall; should she speak or not? Lisa had never known a hesitation so disconcerting, nor had she ever been so acutely conscious of this feeling, so new to her—this feeling of pity. It's not her fault, she kept saying to herself; and she would have liked to make some gesture or other, to give the girl some kind of a look, which, without a word, would penetrate straight to the heart of her shameful secret. But she was incapable of it.

She put on her hat in front of the looking-glass in the corridor, by the light of the candle Carla held up for her; and all the time she was examining the girl closely. "What's the matter with you?" she asked her, "you don't seem to be your usual self."

"The matter?" Carla appeared to be astonished. "Why, nothing."

"D'you know you look pale?" went on Lisa. "I think you overtire yourself."

There was no answer; should she speak or not? She put on her coat and, when she was ready to go out, took Carla's hand. They looked into each other's faces; but the girl could not sustain her friend's probing glance, and lowered her eyes.

"Carla," said the older woman suddenly, in a voice that showed her emotion, "you're changed. What's happened to you?"

"Why . . . nothing."

Lisa, disconcerted, could not make up her mind to go. "Kiss me then," she said brusquely. They embraced; but, as she kissed those cold and somehow insensitive cheeks, Lisa felt terribly dissatisfied. "That wasn't the right way," she kept saying to herself regretfully; "that wasn't the way I ought to have spoken." They went on into the vestibule. "Remember," Lisa added in some embarrassment, "remember that if anything goes wrong, if you have any . . . any troubles, come and see me. Don't hide anything from me."

"Of course, of course," said Carla, almost as if she were ashamed. Lisa went out and the door closed behind her.

Thoughtfully the girl went up again to the first floor; she had found Lisa's remarks alarming. Could she have noticed anything? she wondered; but, the more she thought about it, the more impossible the idea seemed to be: her intrigue with Leo had only been going on for one day, and Lisa had only been casually and briefly in the house. . . . No, it was impossible . . . unless . . . unless perhaps she had suspected something from her and Leo's inexplicable absence from the vestibule, the evening before. But in any case, now, even if she has guessed something, it's too late, she concluded, not knowing whether she was glad or sorry. This evening I'm going to Leo's flat.

She went slowly upstairs, the trembling light from the candle in her hand following her and casting on the wall a grotesque shadow of her with an enormous head. And so I'm going to meet my new life, she thought. She would have liked to feel perfectly calm, but she could not manage it; her heart failed her—useless to deny it—and a feeling of anguish and uncertainty oppressed her. I hope these hours will pass quickly, she thought, heaving a deep, childish sigh. I hope the night will pass quickly. That's all I want.

And in the dark anteroom the gleam of her candle showed her Leo lying back in an armchair. She put the candlestick on the table and sat down beside him. "What a bore, isn't it?—that the light doesn't come on," she began, mainly in order to say something. The man did not answer, but took her hands in his.

"Well, you'll come this evening?" he asked. But Carla had not time to reply; the curtains of one of the five doors were thrown apart and Mariagrazia appeared.

She brought her own candle with her. She had wrapped herself in a great black shawl, and the light on her face showed a malignant expression there. "Lisa has gone away," she said to her lover, without sitting down. "I daresay you, Merumeci, would have preferred me to invite her to dinner, wouldn't you? However, one can't always have everything one wants. And, as it is, your dear friend will have plenty of time to prepare herself for your visit . . . your nocturnal visit." She stressed the word "nocturnal" with a repressed laugh, and without waiting for an answer went off down the stairs.

"Where are you going, Mother?" cried Carla, getting up.

"I think it's dinner-time," her mother replied without turning, going very slowly downstairs one step at a time, holding up the light in one hand and leaning with the other on the wooden banisters. "But, Merumeci, if you want to run after Lisa, don't stand on ceremony. It's all the same to me."

The gleam of light disappeared and darkness returned. Her last words died away at the far end of the landing, beyond the corner of the narrow staircase.

Carla, who had been following the descending figure with her eyes, now turned back towards her companion.

"It's no good," said Leo from his armchair. "Your mother will never change. When once she gets an idea into her head, nothing will get it out again." With a resigned gesture, he

[135]

fell silent, and for a moment or two they did not speak. Carla looked at him with a worried, almost frightened expression.

"D'you know what I think?" she began at last. "That Lisa has guessed something."

"How can she have done that?"

"I don't know. But from the way she spoke to me . . ."

Leo waved his hand contemptuously. "As far as I'm concerned," he said, "she can guess what she likes"; and he tried, with a rapid movement, to pull the girl towards him. But, for no reason at all, she resisted. "No, that's enough for now," she protested, pushing with both hands against his shoulders.

"Come on," he besought her, bending towards her, with an excited face, out of the gloom, and trying hard to keep hold of her by the hips. "What's wrong? Just for a moment, as you did before."

"No." She struggled with unaccustomed violence, her eyes full of anger. Then suddenly she knocked against the table and the candle perched on its edge fell to the floor and went out. Profound darkness ensued, and then—after the sound of a headlong, tumultuous rush downstairs—complete silence.

What an odd girl! thought Leo, left alone in the dark. First she wants to be undressed, and five minutes later she doesn't even let you kiss her on the brow. He was not irritated but only slightly surprised; his desire, by now, was subsiding. Peering about in the surrounding gloom, he felt in his pockets for a box of matches, then lit one; stooping down, he picked up the candle and held the match to it. And now, he thought, let's go and eat. He got up, but after he had taken a few steps remembered suddenly that he had forgotten to tell Carla at what time, and by what means, they were to meet that night and go to his flat.

He went back to the table, put down the candle, and, with methodical slowness, in that uncertain light, wrote a note on a visiting card that he took from his wallet, using his big gold fountain pen. "I shall be waiting for you with the car in an hour's time, at the garden gate." To be given to her when I leave, he thought; after which, well satisfied, he took up the candle again and went downstairs.

There was only one candle burning on the dinner-table.

[136]

The room was in almost complete darkness; of Michele, Carla and their mother, who were already sitting in their places, there was nothing to be seen but their dimly lit faces. The new arrival sat down in his turn and silently began eating. The first course was consumed without anyone saying a word; all four of them stared at the flickering light of the candles, there was not a sound, and each one had a fixed thought in mind of an agitating, anxious kind. But, of all of them, there was no doubt that the most absorbed, the most preoccupied, was the Signora; she leaned her chin on her joined hands, two sharp furrows ran down from the corners of her mouth, and she stared with tearful eyes at the silent swaying movements of the two candle flames.

Finally she made up her mind to glance at her lover; and a look of bitter suffering, and fierce sarcasm, became visible in the strained expression of her face.

"I should very much like to know," she began in a sulky tone of voice, addressing all three of them indiscriminately, "why there have to be such untruthful people in the world. Yes, that's what I should like to know. It's all very well to do certain things—I admit that people must do them if they want to—but then to conceal them, to lie about them, to distort the truth,—that's what makes me really angry."

There was silence; no one wished to assume the responsibility of encouraging her along this road by some incautious reply. She looked at them one after the other, as though spurring them on to speak, but Leo and Carla lowered their eyes, and Michele turned his elsewhere. So, after this indirect attack, she decided on a direct one. "You, for instance," she added, turning towards her lover, "are perfectly at liberty to have an engagement after dinner; nobody's trying to prevent it, even if leaving the house to which you've been invited the very moment you've finished eating is a piece of gross bad manners. But why, instead of telling the truth, invent a whole lot of nonsense—which of course gets the reception it deserves—about going to see Miss Smithson, who happens to be at Milan? Do please tell me—who made you do it? Who asked you to tell such a lot of stupid lies? It was not only a lie, but an insult to me, as if I was such a fool that I couldn't understand certain things. Whereas it would have been so much simpler to tell the truth: 'You know, my dear Signora, I shall have to leave you at such and such a time because I'm going to see . . . to see such and such a person." I should have answered: 'of course, go wherever you like. Go to the devil if it gives you any pleasure.' And that would have been the end of it."

She paused, waving away the dish that the maid was handing to her out of the darkness; she was in a state of extreme excitement, her hands were trembling, and she was automatically taking up and replacing knives and forks and glasses.

"Well, say something!" she cried, seeing that Leo could not make up his mind to speak. "Speak! Spit it out—this famous truth—for once!"

Leo glanced at her sideways; this persistence was beginning to annoy him. She deserves to have her face slapped for two hours without stopping, he thought, observing with hatred that mature and stupid countenance. At least two hours. But he helped himself from the dish and answered between his teeth: "I've nothing to say."

Nothing could have been more exasperating to the Signora than these indifferent words. "What d'you mean?" she exclaimed; "I accuse you, with justice, of lying, and you not merely refuse to give any reason for your behavior, but also answer me rudely, as if . . . as if it was I who was in the wrong. If you want to know what *that* is—it's pure insolence."

Ordinarily Leo never replied to his mistress's reproofs; but this time—whether it was that the physical excitement the girl had aroused in him had provoked in him an unaccustomed nervous impatience, or whether her insults had really wounded him—this time he took offense. "Listen here," he said roughly, turning abruptly from the dish the maid was handing to him, "stop that, once and for all. Otherwise I really *shall* be forced to answer you rudely. Enough is as good as a feast."

He paused, and for a moment stared at her with such a hard, ugly, ruthless look on his face that the unfortunate woman could scarcely breathe. The light and shadow that the two candles cast all around with each darting movement of their flames emphasized the expression of rage in the set of his jaws, in which the twitching of impatient nerves could be seen beneath the red, shaven skin; the corners of the eyes that were staring in such irritation at the Signora assumed brutal lines of sensual fatigue; the violent, contemptuous grimace of the mouth, as if he were with difficulty restraining himself from cursing at her, was underscored by a cone of shadow that half covered his chin. Mariagrazia, tearful, frightened, interrupted in the midst of her burst of loquacious indignation, gazed at that pitiless face, at that species of catapult that was striking her full in the face, and trembled all over; her heart was overwhelmed by an acute feeling of unhappiness, of the utter lack of kindness or love, which suffocated her. Don't look at me like that, she wanted to cry out, and then to cover her face with her hands; but instead she sat motionless, terrified. I love him . . . and he answers me like that! the words kept running, with a forlorn sound, in her empty head.

Then she saw Leo turn and quietly take from the big dish two slices of meat and some vegetables. There was nothing more to be said; the situation was hopeless; her eyes filling with tears, she put down her napkin on the table and rose wearily to her feet.

"I don't want anything to eat," she said; "but the rest of you, go on." And, almost at a run, tripping slightly over the carpet, she went out of the room.

Silence followed this unexpected departure. Leo, who had already taken up his knife and fork, sat there with the two implements in his hands and an astonished face turned towards the shadow by the door through which the Signora had disappeared; Carla also peered wide-eyed in the same direction. Then Michele, who had been the least surprised of the three, turned towards Leo.

"You oughtn't to have answered like that," he said, without any annoyance, in the tone of one who is merely very bored. "You know how impulsive she is. Now we shall have endless trouble."

"And who failed to answer her at all?" replied Leo forcibly. "If her nerves are in a bad state she must look after them. Now one won't ever be able to say anything again."

"You talk too much, anyway, you two," and Michele looked the other man straight in the eyes. "Far too much."

"Nonsense," grumbled the other, with a shrug of the shoulders. "Your mother certainly does talk too much, but I. . . ." He paused a moment, looking now at his plate where the appetizing food was growing cold, and then at the door by which the Signora had gone out. "And now," he went on, "what does one do? She certainly won't want to have nothing to eat." There was a moment's silence, then Carla put down her napkin on the table.

"Michele's right," she said to Leo. "You ought not to have treated Mom like that. We know she has her failings, but after all she's a woman. You behaved badly. She got up and stood for a moment in thought; the things she was going to do repelled her and filled her with a kind of impatient wretchedness. "I'm going to see if she'll come back," she said finally, and moving her chair aside she went out.

In the corridor the darkness was complete, and she felt her way along the wall. "I ought to have brought the candle," she thought. She remembered that after another scene of this kind, her mother had gone and taken refuge in the drawing-room. She took a few steps farther, and then tripped so heavily over the carpet that she almost fell to the floor, and was filled with irritation against Mariagrazia, who, though middle-aged, was so absurdly childish. All this has got to come to an end, she thought, clenching her teeth, as she put her hand on the handle of the drawing-room door. This very evening I'm going to Leo's flat, and all this *will* come to an end. It seemed to her that the darkness that filled her eyes had somehow penetrated into her soul. Now I've got to hunt for that fool of a woman who happens to be my mother, she told herself. She felt quite pitiless, and in spite of that profoundly grieved by her own pitilessness. She bit her lips and went into the room.

As she had foreseen, her mother had crept into a corner of the drawing-room; she could hear in the pitch darkness someone not very far away, weeping and sighing and punctuating these sounds with an occasional nose-blowing. Carla's irritation gave place to a milder sentiment.

"Mom, where are you?" she called out clearly, advancing into the gloom with outstretched arms.

There was no answer. Finally, after knocking more than once into pieces of furniture, she touched her mother's shoulder; the latter, as far as Carla could tell, must be sitting on the sofa in the corner.

"What are you doing here?" she asked, shaking her slightly and looking up towards the invisible ceiling, just as though there were no darkness and she did not wish to see her mother weeping. "Come back . . . come along." The back underneath her hand shook.

"You have dinner without me. I'm not coming," answered the voice of Mariagrazia.

Carla sighed, half in impatience, half in sadness, then walked around the sofa and sat down beside her mother. "Come on, come along," she repeated, putting her two hands on the weeping woman's shoulders. "I can assure you, Mom, Leo had no intention of . . . that he's the first to be sorry for what happened."

"Oh my God, how unhappy I am!" was the only reply; her mother's voice was plaintive, with a childish bitterness in it. "How unhappy I am!"

Carla shuddered. "Come along, Mom," she repeated, her voice growing less assured.

The sofa creaked, two arms were thrown round the girl's neck, and she felt her mother's damp cheek pressed against her own.

"Do you really think," demanded the tearful voice, "tell me, do you really think that he's fallen in love again with that woman?"

"Why—who?" asked Carla, disturbed. She felt the soft, panting breast, against her arm, and did not know what to do; she was repelled at being forced to comfort her own mother. If only she would stop crying, she kept thinking.

"Lisa, of course," insisted the sobbing voice. "Didn't you

see, last night, that they went off together? I'm sure, I'm sure they've fallen in love again. Oh, how unhappy I am!"

It's *me* he loves, Carla wanted to answer. But was it really true? She was filled with sudden disgust at what was going on around her. "What harm have *I* ever done him?" she heard Mariagrazia's voice lamenting,"—to deserve all this? I've sacrificed my whole life for him . . . and now, you see how he treats me." Carla wished she were a thousand miles away. "I don't know anything about it," she said at last, and she was about to free herself from her mother's arms, when, at the far end of the room, quietly—just as though someone had pressed the switch—the two little lamps on the piano came on.

Darkness fled, and immediately, with an instinctive movement, the Signora separated herself from her daughter, stooped down and blew her nose. Carla rose to her feet.

"Is my hair untidy?" asked Mariagrazia, also rising. "Is my face very red?"

The girl looked at her. Her mother's cheeks were marked with pale streaks, her hair was ruffled, her nose was red and her eyes looked very small, as if she were suffering from a bad cold. "No, no . . . you're perfectly all right."

They went out of the drawing-room; the corridor, too, was lit up. Mariagrazia went to one of the round mirrors and tidied herself as best she could; then, Carla in front and her mother following, they went back into the dining-room.

Here too the light was on again, and Leo and Michele, sitting opposite each other, were quietly talking.

"In business," the former was saying, "it's difficult to be successful. The man who doesn't understand about it always puts his money into the hands of the man who does." But, as soon as he saw the two women, he took no further notice of the boy. "We're friends then, aren't we, Signora?" he said, rising and going to meet Mariagrazia.

"Up to a point, yes," replied the Signora, with ostentatious coldness. She went back to her place and sat down.

The rest of the meal was silent; they all had thoughts that dominated them, and no one spoke. She can go to the devil, Leo said to himself, disconcerted, as he looked at Mariagrazia. Although her demeanor was a matter of indifference to him, this unaccustomed rancor boded no good. As for her, she was searching for some means of avenging herself upon Leo, for the pain, having vanished, had left behind it an arid resentment. He's counting on my handing the villa over direct to him, she thought, triumphantly, but I shall put it up to auction. She did not know what real advantage there might be in such a venture, nor did she know the value of the villa, but she imagined vaguely that, apart from the annoyance it would give her lover, she would derive a few thousand more lire from selling it in this way. Carla was thinking of the coming night, and was possessed by an extraordinary agitation. Did I really promise him? she asked herself. Is it really tonight that I've got to go there? As for Michele, he was tormented by an acute sense of discomfort, feeling that his behavior during the argument between his mother and Leo had been of an unparalleled indifference. Another good opportunity lost, he said to himself, for picking a quarrel with him, for breaking with him altogether.

8

At last they left the dining-room, walking with leisurely steps, lighting cigarettes, casting hasty glances at themselves in the corridor mirrors, and went into the drawing-room.

"This evening," Leo said, sitting down on the sofa beside Mariagrazia, "I feel like listening to some good classical music. Come on, Carla," he added, turning towards the girl, "play us whatever you like, Beethoven or Chopin, provided it belongs to the good old days when there was no jazz to give people headaches." He smiled cordially and crossed his legs.

"Yes, Carla," encouraged her mother, delighted with the idea of being able to take advantage of the music to talk more freely with her lover, "yes, do play us something. For instance . . . that fugue. Whose was it? Ah yes, Bach . . . the one you played so well."

Michele, too, was immensely pleased at the idea of some music. He was feeling tired and irritated, and the conventional picture of melody's gentle river in which one might plunge and forget had never seemed so true to him as it did now. Music, he thought, half closing his eyes, and to hell with all these mean squabbles! Some real music.

"It's a long time since I played," Carla warned them, "you mustn't be too severe." She went to the piano, opened it, looked through a few pieces of music, and finally announced: "A Bach fugue."

The first chords sounded. Michele half closed his eyes and prepared to listen; his loneliness, his conversations with Lisa, had made him conscious of a great need for companionship and love, an intense hope that he might find, among all the people in the world, some woman whom he could love sincerely, without irony and without resignation. A true woman, he thought, a pure woman, neither false nor stupid nor corrupt. If I could only find her, it would straighten everything out. At the moment he was failing to find her, indeed he did not even know where to look for her; but he had her image in his mind, half ideal and half material, mingling confusedly with the other figures of that fantastic world, that world governed by instinct and sincerity in which he longed to live. The music would help him to reconstruct that beloved image, and indeed, thanks to his own exaltation and desire rather than to the music itself, the image now began to take shape, from the very first notes, right between himself and Carla. It was that of a young girl, as he surmised from the slimness of her body, from her eyes, from her whole bearing—extremely lovely, no doubt about that—and she was turning away from him and yet observing him intently, without flattery, without a shadow of lasciviousness—oh no indeed, he could have sworn that—but with the frank, surprised curiosity with which children look at others of their own age. "My companion," he thought; and already certain gestures, a kind of embrace, a smile, a movement of the hand, things happening, walks, conversations, were taking shape to and passing across the wishful heavens of his imagination, when a sound of animated but subdued chattering broke the illusion and brought him back to reality.

It was his mother, now carrying into effect her plan of taking advantage of the music to talk to Leo.

"If you want to, Merumeci," she was urging, looking with a poisonous expression at her inattentive lover, "you can go now to that reception of yours. There's no need for you to bore yourself with listening to music here. No one's keeping you. Do go. Go where they're expecting you."

[145]

Leo stared at her. He had no wish to quarrel; he nodded in Carla's direction, as much as to say: "Not now . . . now we're listening to Bach."

"Please go," she insisted. "You're bored here . . . don't say you're not. Why, I saw you yawning. We bore you; on the other hand we can't start dancing in order to amuse you. So you'd better go to a place where you'll be welcomed with open arms, and where there won't be anyone playing the piano, or anyone to disturb you. Do please go." She went on talking and never ceased smiling in a stupid sort of way, seized, at the mere thought of Lisa, by an almost delirious excess of jealousy.

"Besides," she went on, "it would be extremely bad manners to cut Miss Smithson's reception. There'll be all sorts of people there. . . . I expect she's engaged a special train to take her guests to Milan."

Leo would have given anything to be rid of this annoyance. He shook the ash from his cigar and turned calmly towards the Signora.

"If I told a lie," he said, "it was merely out of regard for you, so as not to let you think that I found it boring at your house. The truth of the matter is that I'm not going to any reception this evening, but am going home to bed. I've been up very late for several nights, and I feel tired. This evening I want to go to bed early."

"As yes, I see," she exclaimed, with the expression of one who is not easily taken in. "So you want to go to bed. You're sleepy, you've been up late every night—yes, of course, one can see that you can hardly stand up, that you're almost asleep already. Poor man, if you knew how sorry I feel for you!"

"I don't need anyone to be sorry for me," replied Leo, becoming irritated in spite of himself.

"But don't you realize that you're telling a string of lies, one after another?" Mariagrazia demanded sharply. "First it was Miss Smithson, now it's fatigue. You ought to be ashamed of yourself."

"I'm not ashamed of myself—why should I be?"

"Oh, be quiet, please, please."

[146]

Leo shrugged his shoulders and said nothing. Michele from his armchair observed them with disgust. Blast them! he thought. One can't even listen to music. They've always got one of their miserable arguments going on. The image of his beloved had vanished. A jumble of meaningless notes—that was all the music was now; his mother and Leo had won.

"Go to bed, eh?" went on the Signora, speaking into Leo's ear; "Go to bed—that's it, is it? But I want to tell you this—I know all about it, d'you see? Everything! Since last night and this evening, I know everything!"

"On the other hand, you know nothing at all," Leo burst out, without turning, and he blew a cloud of smoke in front of him. Carla was sitting with her full, fleshy back turned towards him. What a night! he was thinking, what a night it will be! Only an hour or two more, yet to me it seems an eternity. His fixed, motionless gaze ignored her mother, Michele, all the rest of the room. Desire gave him visions—of Carla sitting entirely naked on that same narrow stool, in front of the piano; he seemed to see her white back with the curved furrow running down the middle of it, her broad, rounded hips, and—now that she was turning round—her two breasts as well. But the music was finished and reality returned. Applauded by an unusually affectionate Michele, the girl was the first to speak.

"Did you like it?" she asked.

"Very much indeed," said Leo. "Play it again, Carla."

"No, Carla," put in her mother, "no, don't go on playing. Merumeci is not only bored but is dying to go away. He can barely keep awake, he wants to go to bed. So why keep him any longer?" And to her lover: "Go on," she insisted obstinately, pulling him by the sleeve, "go on, go home to bed."

Leo pulled his arm away, with an unwilling smile; he felt a great desire to give this relentless woman two solemn slaps in the face. For a moment Carla looked at the two of them. Is it really tonight that I'm to go to his flat? she wondered. It seemed strange; now she was sitting at the piano, and in two hours' time she would be in her lover's bedroom. But she had divined his violent impatience, and, partly in order to put off the final moment of her surrender as long as possible, partly from a last shred of coquetry, decided to go on playing.

"Very well," she said firmly. "Leo shall not go away but shall continue to be bored for another ten minutes. Won't you, Leo?" She opened a big volume of music and began playing again, with an attentive and preoccupied expression.

Oh, the little witch, thought Leo. She wants to see me die of impatience. She wants to see me in my death agonies. By this time music, conversation, silence, everything had become an intolerable bore to him; he was devoured by lust, and had only desire—to carry Carla home with him and possess her. God knows how long this is going to last, he thought, as he listened in a rage to the first chords of the music, ten minutes? A quarter of an hour? Devil take it—why in the world did I have the brilliant idea of making her play?

But the Signora had not admitted defeat. She touched his shoulder. "Tomorrow morning," she said with a charming smile, as if she were continuing a conversation, "I shall go to my lawyer and give him authority to put up the villa for auction."

If a brick had dropped from the ceiling and fallen on Leo's head, he would not have been so unpleasantly surprised as he was at hearing these words. His face went red, then purple, he clenched his teeth, and brief phrases flashed through his mind. This is the last straw—and on this particular evening, too! God blast her! Such things only happen to *me*. Then he turned right towards the Signora. "You're not going to do that," he commanded her angrily, pressing his fists, in an instinctive gesture, hard against his chest.

Now they've got each other by the hair, thought Michele, in disgust, as he watched them.

"I shall certainly do it," she answered, with studied calmness, "and I shall do it tomorrow."

"It's utter madness . . . began Leo. He seized one of her hands and pressed it against the sofa. "You mean to sell the villa by auction and so lose fifty per cent! And you come and tell me so this evening!" This particular evening, he repeated to himself with a furious glance in the direction of Carla. "Now—when the contract's all ready drawn up and only waiting to be signed. This . . . this is what's called stark, staring madness."

"Call it what you like," replied the Signora, to whom it seemed a little unreal to be putting on the airs of a calm, fearless saint, "but tomorrow morning, the first thing I do will be to go to my lawyer."

Leo looked at her; to the irritation of unsatisfied sensuality this new embarrassment was now added. His natural instinct was to jump on top of the woman, give her a good hiding— yes, even throttle her; but he managed to restrain himself.

"But you're not speaking seriously," he insisted. "Think it over."

"I've already thought it over."

"Now look, Mariagrazia," began Leo, "don't be so obstinate and perverse. In business one ought never to act impulsively. Now, how would it be . . . shall we meet tomorrow afternoon?"

"It's no good," she answered, with less firmness than before. "I think it's better for me to go and see my lawyer."

You hideous fool! Leo wanted to shout at her. But, instead, he clasped his hands together. "Mariagrazia," he implored, "an auction is a risk; your lawyer may be a cheat— the world is full of them; you're a woman, and it would be easy to deceive you in things you don't understand."

"D'you think so?" she asked, with a doubtful smile.

"I'm sure of it. It's understood, then—I'll expect you tomorrow at four."

She looked coquettishly this way and that, and her middle-aged heart trembled. Do you love me? she longed to ask him. "Tomorrow . . ." she said instead, "no, I can't tomorrow."

"The day after, then."

"Wait a moment," she whispered, looking up in the air as though she were trying to remember something. "Yes, I have an engagement, but I'll put it off. Very well, I'll come. But don't imagine," she added, with a brilliant, flattering smile, "that you'll be able to convince me." She paused, hesitated, and at last took her lover's hand. She was on the point of asking him in a low voice, "And you do love me a little, don't you?"—when the music stopped abruptly and Carla turned round.

"It's no use my playing," she said calmly. "Everyone's talking and chattering. Really it would be better to go to bed."

The Signora quickly detached herself from her lover and looked at her daughter with a disconcerted expression.

"If you want to talk," went on the girl, "don't ask me to play." There was silence.

"We were commenting on your performance," answered Leo finally. "You play well, Carla; go on, do please go on."

This fresh lie was the signal for a kind of rebellion—as though they had all been suddenly aroused from their long torpor. The first outburst came from Michele, who, up till now, had endured his mother's and Leo's conversation in silence. Partly from rage and partly from an instinctive need for action, he seized the newspaper which was spread out on his knee and hurled it violently to the floor.

"There's not a word of truth in it," he cried, looking at Leo. "It's a barefaced lie. You were thinking just as much about the music as I was about . . . about going into the Church. You were talking about business, about lawyers"— he managed, with an effort, to laugh—"and about other things too."

There was silence again. "There!" cried Carla suddenly, clapping her hands together; "there! That's the truth. We can breathe at last."

It was as though somebody had thrown the window wide open and the cold night air had come pouring into the room. For a moment they stared at each other, in stupefied surprise. The first to recover was Leo.

"You're wrong," he said severely to Michele. "Obviously you didn't hear properly."

Such a brazen lie produced a high, disagreeable laugh from the boy. "Ha, ha!" he laughed, throwing himself back in his chair, "that's a good one!" Then he stopped laughing. "Liar!" he said sharply.

They stared at each other. Carla held her breath. Her mother turned pale.

[150]

"My God!" cried Leo, striking his fist on the table, "this is too much." But he did not get up, he remained seated, gazing at the boy with a searching look in his eyes. "I didn't know you were so quarrelsome," he added, and after a moment, "And if you go on like this I shall be forced to box your ears for you." He proffered this last remark in the silliest and most solemn way; and it seemed to Michele that Leo's threat, which had started so proudly, had grown steadily feebler as it progressed, till it ended up in the flat vulgarity of a box on the ears. In reaction to this, his own feeling diminished; there was nothing to be done. No use to throw down the challenging glove, nor make a parade of offended honor; it provided too little concealment for the threatened part, the ears.

"Box my ears, box *my* ears? Mine? Mine?" Each "mine" gave him a further thrust towards action, but he felt cold and indifferent. False were the words that issued from his mouth, false the voice that spoke them. What had become of his fervor? Of his indignation? They had vanished; perhaps they did not exist.

On the table, among the flowers, the little cups and the coffee-pot, lay a marble ash-tray, of white, gray-veined alabaster. With the movement of a sleep-walker he put out his hand, took hold of it, threw it feebly. He saw his mother clasp her hands together, heard her scream. Leo shouted, "This is madness!" Carla was thrown into agitation. He realized that the piece of marble had missed its target, and, instead of striking Leo, had struck his mother—on the head? No, no, on the shoulder.

He got up and walked awkwardly over to the sofa on which his victim lay. With an indeterminate expression on her face, his mother—for some unexplained reason—kept her eyes tight shut and sighed at intervals; but it was quite clear that she was suffering no pain whatever and that her swooning condition was entirely a product of her own imagination.

Michele bent over her, together with the other two. In spite of the fact that the sight ought to have been painful to him, he felt no remorse at all—in fact, he could not manage to repress the feeling that the whole scene was ridiculous. In

vain he said to himself: It's my mother. . . . I've hit her. . . .
She might have been killed. In vain he tried to arouse in
himself a little pity and affection for that motionless, misguided figure, but his heart remained unmoved. His mother,
without changing her position or opening her eyes, now
raised a languid arm and pulled aside with her fingers the
garments covering the shoulder that had been struck; her
bare, plump shoulder became visible, but there was no sign
of injury or bruise or redness—nothing. But her fingers, as if
unsatisfied, continued to pull down her dress, baring one
arm, revealing the armpit. Her fingers, moving over her
bosom—which became more and more exposed and progres-
sively whiter, until the beginnings of the breasts were revealed—seemed to be immodestly pursuing some aim quite
different from that of displaying her wounds, seemed, for
example, to be bent on undressing her.

This soft abandonment was aimed at her lover; romantic
pity must be made to gush from his relenting heart. He will
see me wounded, fainting, with bared breast, was the thought
in Mariagrazia's mind; he will remember that I threw myself
in front of him, that I received the blow of the ash-tray, and
he won't be able to help feeling a deep and grateful tenderness towards me. Her deluded imagination pictured Leo taking her in his arms, gently shaking her, calling her by name,
becoming, at last, seriously concerned at her failure to revive.
And then, finally, very slowly she would come to herself,
would open her eyes again; and her first glances would be
for her lover, for him her first smile. But none of this happened, Leo neither took her in his arms nor called her by
name.

"Perhaps it would be best if I went outside," he said to
Carla, paying no attention to Mariagrazia. It was as if the
Signora had received a splash of cold water right on the
shoulder that she had laid bare for her lover's benefit; she
opened her eyes, she sat up and looked round: there was
Michele observing her with mocking eyes, as if his remorse
were mingled with some other sentiment; there was Carla,
striving to rearrange her mother's clothes. But Leo? Where

was Leo? Not at her side: he had picked up the ash-tray and was trying its weight, then he turned abruptly to Michele.

"Well done!" he said, in ironical encouragement, "well done . . . very well done!"

Michele shrugged his shoulders and looked at him. "Certainly . . . very well done, in fact," he said slowly and calmly. Then, from behind Leo's back, rose the voice of the Signora, sharp and familiar.

"For heaven's sake, Merumeci," she begged, "for heaven's sake don't start again. Don't touch him. Don't speak to him. Don't even look at him. . . ." Apparently she had reached the extreme limit of patience and reason, beyond which lies only madness.

The boy took refuge near the window. The rain was still falling, and it rustled against the shutters and in the trees of the garden; it was raining quietly upon the houses and the empty streets. There must be many people, he thought, listening, as he was, behind closed windows, their hearts filled with the same anguish as his, as they turned their backs to the warm intimacy of the rooms behind them. It's useless, he kept on thinking, his fingers touching the edges of the window, it's useless. This isn't my life. He recalled the scene of the ash-tray, of his mother's ridiculous swooning, of his own indifference. Everything here is comic, artificial; there's no sincerity in it. I wasn't made for this sort of life. The man whom he ought to hate, Leo, was not hateful enough; the woman whom he ought to love, Lisa, was false, and masked her all-too-simple wishes behind unbearable sentimentalities so that it was impossible to love her. He had the impression that he was turning his back, not on the drawing-room of his home, but on an empty, dark abyss. This is not my life, he told himself with conviction, but what then?

Behind him the door closed. He turned, and the drawing-room was empty; both mother and daughter had gone to accompany their guest to the front door; the lamp shone on the motionless circle of deserted armchairs.

"He's only a boy," said the Signora to Leo, in the vestibule. "One mustn't take him seriously. He doesn't know what he's doing."

A contrite expression on her face, she took down Leo's hat from its hook and handed it to him. "He didn't do *me* any harm," said Leo cheerfully, wrapping a woolen scarf round his neck. "I'm only sorry on your account, that the projectile in question should have landed on your shoulder." He gave a cold, artificial, but charming laugh, then glanced at Carla, as though asking for her approval, and finally turned and slipped into his overcoat.

"He's only a boy," repeated the Signora mechanically as she helped him. She was terrified by the thought that Leo might take advantage of her son's imprudence to break off relations with her. "And you can be sure," she added, in a tone at the same time humble and authoritative, "that nothing like this will ever happen again. Leave it to me to talk to Michele. And if there's any need," she went on, irresolutely, "I shall act."

There was silence. "Never mind," said Carla, who was leaning against the door and looking intently at her mother, "don't worry. I'm sure," she went on, looking down and smiling, "that Leo himself has already forgotten it."

"Yes, of course," said Leo; "there are plenty of things more important." He kissed the hand of the Signora, who was still not reassured. "See you again soon," he said to Carla, staring her straight in the eyes; she grew pale, and with a slow, resigned movement turned the handle of the door.

The door flew open violently, banging against the wall, as though someone anxious to enter had pushed against it from outside with all his strength. "Ugh, how cold and damp!" cried the Signora. As if in answer, a wild gust of wind swept into the room; rain poured furiously on to the glossy tiles; the lamp swayed; a light overcoat of Michele's hanging on the coat-stand struck Leo several times in the face with its flapping sleeves; and the two women's skirts were lifted like balloons, rising and then clinging about their legs.

"Shut the door, shut the door!" cried the Signora, seizing hold of the door with both hands and leaning forward in a ridiculous way with her feet close together for fear of getting wet. Carla, like a wading bird, hopped about cautiously on the flooded floor. "Shut the door," repeated the Signora.

But no one moved to obey, they were all gazing in astonishment at this violent, insubstantial force that roared and groaned and screeched and wept upon the empty threshold; and finally the other door of the vestibule flew open. A kind of whirlpool was thus formed which, after rushing through the corridor, plunged into the house; all the doors could be heard banging with a strange clatter different from that of a door being slammed by an angry or inattentive hand, a clatter in which the voices of the wind were mingled with loud thuds, and with pauses that seemed to be preparing for a final crash, the loudest of all. The bare, lofty rooms echoed; the whole villa trembled as though it were bound to detach itself from the ground and, spinning on its own axis like a crazy top, to fly rapidly away on a phosphorescent cloud-peak.

"And now," Leo asked the Signora, seeing her, after many efforts, shut the door, "what do we do now?"

"We must wait," was the reply. All three were silent, Mariagrazia gazing at her lover with bitter, disenchanted eyes. Such haste she found most upsetting. Soon Leo would be gone, would disappear into the rainy night, leaving her to her cold house, to her empty bed; he would go to some other place, to Lisa's flat, for instance—yes, of course, to Lisa's, where he had been so long awaited. And how they would enjoy themselves that night, the two of them, and how they would laugh at her!

She made a last attempt; she pricked up her ears, assuming the strained expression of someone listening intently. "It seems to me," she said, "there is something banging in the drawing-room. Do go, Carla," she added impatiently, "do go and see." All three listened carefully; it seemed as if the Signora wished to create, by imperious gesticulation, the clatter of banging doors which the now silent house denied to her.

"I don't think so," said Carla, after a moment or two. "I can hear nothing . . . absolutely nothing."

"I tell you there *is* something," insisted her mother, anxious and stubborn. "Listen," she went on, amid the most complete silence, "can't you hear something banging?"

Leo laughed. "No," he said quietly, diverted by her stu-

pidity, "no, no. There's nothing banging." He saw with renewed pleasure the expression of pain in her eyes. "An illusion," he concluded, taking up his hat again, "an illusion, my
dear Signora."

"Are you going?" she asked.

"Certainly. It's high time."

"But . . . but isn't it raining too hard?" she insisted despairingly, placing herself between her lover and the door.
"Wouldn't it be better for you to wait a little longer?"

"It's raining," said Leo, buttoning up his coat, "in the same
way that the doors are banging." He kissed the hand of the
humiliated woman, fumbled in one pocket for the gloves that
were in the other, went over to the door and opened it,
holding it back with one hand against the wind. "See you
soon, Carla," he said to the girl as he clasped the hand she
held out to him, smiled and went out.

The two women returned to the hall. The Signora was
shivering. "How cold it is! Ugh, how cold it is!" she kept
on saying. The tired muscles of her face were sagging, she
had gone all to pieces and her dazed glances moved hap-
hazardly from one object to another, faltering and wavering;
there was a look of barren nakedness on her paint-worn face;
her mouth was faintly trembling. "I'm going to bed," she
said, as she went slowly upstairs beside the wooden balus-
trade. "I'm going to bed. Goodnight." Her shadow rose up
to the ceiling, paused on the landing, moved across the wall
in crooked jerks and disappeared.

Carla was left alone in the hall. She went over to the lamp.
Something was rustling slightly in her closed fist—Leo's note,
which her hesitant fingers had retained after her admirer's
prolonged handclasp.

The note was brief. "I shall be waiting for you with the
car in an hour's time, at the garden gate. Leo."

Disconcerted, she started upstairs. *In an hour's time*, she
repeated to herself, *in an hour's time I leave the house*. Step
by step she reached the narrow landing and looked upwards:
the anteroom, in which an armchair and a corner of the sofa
were visible, was empty, and a calm, domestic silence reigned
in its shadowy, enclosed space. In an hour's time, without

doubt, both Michele and her mother would be plunged in sleep. She reached the top of the stairs, went straight to the door of her own room at the end of the dark passage, and as she entered, was at once struck by its look of intimacy and warmth. Everything was in its place, the lamp with its pink shade was burning, her pale blue muslin nightdress laid out on the bed, the sheets folded back; everything invited repose. She had only to undress, creep under the bedclothes, and go to sleep.

Whether it was the sight of the bed, together with the sound of the torrential downpour against the shutters, that overwhelmed her with a great desire for rest and security, or whether it was really the fatigues of the day—anyhow it is certain that she was suddenly assailed by so persuasive a feeling of cowardice, so strong a repugnance for the adventure that faced her, that she was afraid of herself. How about it? she thought. To go to sleep, have a good rest—that's all right. But what then? Tomorrow morning I shall be right back at the beginning again. And then how shall I ever be able to achieve a new life?

She went over to the wardrobe mirror and looked at herself, first closely, then from farther away. Her face was flushed up to her sparkling eyes, but when she looked closely she discovered, between that hectic redness and her eyes, a dark, deeply marked circle that disturbed her like a guilty thought; when she looked from farther away, on the other hand, there was nothing to be seen but a girl dressed for a party, her hands clasped in front of her, her big head a little on one side, with sad eyes and an embarrassed smile. That was all; she would have liked to penetrate the mystery of this image of herself, but was unable to do so.

She took a few steps about the room, then sat down on the bed. A slight anxiety confused her thinking; she felt fully prepared, curious and impatient, as though she was visiting and was walking up and down and looking about her as she awaited the smiling entry of the mistress of the house; but that was all. She sat with her legs crossed, her head bowed, and had the impression that she was meditating profoundly.

She got up and examined herself in the wardrobe mirror again, and realized that she was unable to think at all.

She stayed like this for some minutes. There was no question now of sleeping; she admitted to herself, vaguely, that she was going to give herself that night to Leo, but she did not know when, and it seemed to her that the moment was still, luckily, a long way off. How it's raining! she thought at intervals when the rustling noise of the falling water became louder; but it never occurred to her that she would have to go out into that darkness, would have to face that rain in order to meet her lover. A languid numbness took possession of her, and slowly and with no feeling of sadness, she took her head between her hands and let herself fall back on the bed.

In that position she could see nothing but the brightly lit ceiling; and the only sounds that came to her ears were those of the stormy night outside. Presently—and not without saying to herself again that, sooner or later, she would have to get up and go out—she closed her eyes and abandoned herself to a kind of torpor, full of fear and mistrust; but the torpor turned to drowsiness, and without realizing it she fell asleep.

It was an empty sleep, black as pitch, and there can be no doubt that it was an important factor in her lapses of memory and confusions that night. The absence of dreams clearly deceived the sleeping girl as to the length of her slumber; she woke suddenly and for no reason, and lay frozen by a terrible fear, so that she could scarcely breathe when she realized that she had been asleep. I've been asleep, she thought, and then sat up on the bed in terror and looked around the quiet, lamp-lit room. Goodness knows what time it is . . . two or three o'clock, and Leo will have gone away—he will have waited and then gone. For a moment she nearly burst into tears from regret and despair. "I've been asleep," she repeated aloud, holding her head in her hands and gazing in the mirror at her own image, with its untidy hair and frightened eyes. "I've been asleep!"

She jumped up and rushed to the clock on the chest-of-drawers: only three quarters of an hour had passed, and the hands pointed to a quarter to twelve. This seemed impossible;

she thought that the clock must have stopped, and held it up close to her ear; it was going; it was true, then, and she could still go and meet Leo. She felt almost disappointed; she put the clock down again.

But now another doubt came into her mind. How, exactly, and when was she to meet her lover? She remembered the words "in an hour's time"; nor had she forgotten the detail of the car that would be waiting at the garden gate; but she was not absolutely sure. The note, she thought all at once, where's the note?

She looked all round in search of it; she saw nothing. She looked among the trifles on the chest-of-drawers—nothing; she went to the bed, shook it and turned the pillow upside down—nothing. She was possessed by an unreasoning haste and anxiety; where could that note be? She rushed about the room, throwing objects and clothes in all directions, pulling out drawers. Finally she stopped in the middle of the room. *Now, let's see. I read it down in the hall, but I had it in my hand when I came in, therefore it must be here.* Keep calm; it must be here. As though she were trying to catch some small, agile creature such as a mouse or a butterfly, very cautiously, very carefully she hunted, stooping down, searching under pieces of furniture, twisting so as not to dirty her dress, flattening her forehead and cheeks against the dusty floor, straining her eyes in dark corners. Each time she stood upright she was conscious of a nervous weariness through all her limbs; she half-closed her eyes and, stood still, with her hands spread out in a forlorn gesture. She had an obscure feeling that she was expiating some forgotten fault by means of this melancholy search. Each time she bent down, she felt she would like to break and to lie there on the floor like some object that has fallen and been smashed to pieces.

She hunted with childish scrupulousness in the most absurd places—in her work-basket, her powder-box. She found nothing, and sat down, astonished and feeble. What kind of missive could this be that disappeared as soon as read? A feeling of fabulous, dreamlike unreality imbued her recollections with the kind of impalpable atmosphere that causes one to think, with regard to certain words and certain rapid unusual acts: Did these things really happen, or did I imagine them or dream them or fabricate them? The handclasp, the piece of paper had interrupted the continuity of habit for one single instant, then everything had returned to what it was before; and now, in her confusion, Carla longed to see Leo's missive again. The thing she lacked was not the recollection—even if vague—of having received the note, but the certain, clear knowledge of what it contained; she had touched it, had seen it and read it, but had not had time to convince herself of it, and now she doubted it.

And what was written in it? One hour, or more, or less? Tonight or the next night? Wasn't it too late by now? And wasn't it raining too hard? And would it not be better to go to bed and sleep, and begin her usual life again next morning? As she sat there motionless, bending forward, time passed her by; it seemed to her that because of her doubts, she was destroying herself with her own hands, was killing herself.

She started at the shrill strokes of the clock as it struck midnight, and her first practical thought came to her. I'll go; if he's not there it will mean that I've been dreaming. She looked at the face of the clock and calculated that Leo must already have been waiting for a quarter of an hour. She ran across to the window, glued her face to the black panes to see if it was still raining, listened, looked, but could see nothing. The night was unwilling to reveal itself, and at her back, with inexorable irony, the bedroom displayed, in opposition, its delusive whiteness, its uncaring lamplight. "Whether it's raining or not," she mumbled in a mad hurry, "let's put on a raincoat." Rushing to the cupboard, she pulled it out and put it on in front of the mirror; stooped down and adjusted her slackened garters; powdered her face, put a little red on her lips, combed her hair; jammed on the back of her head the first hat she saw—like an American girl, she thought, seeing her rounded forehead with curls escaping from under the narrow brim. She searched and searched—*those blasted gloves!* She no longer thought, she lived: a mechanical haste had abolished all trace of humanity from her. She rushed again to the clock, with the same bustling haste that—in the midst of doing her hair, putting on her stockings, waving her bare arms as she dressed for some party—made her cry to the maid, "We must hurry . . . it's late . . . it's late." Ten minutes past, already, she thought. *Quickly . . . quickly.* She opened the door, and checking her speed with sudden cunning, went down the corridor on tiptoe.

In the empty anteroom the lights were on and everything—armchairs and sofa—in its place. Noiselessly Carla took the house-keys from the table drawer, and, with every precaution, leaning against the wall and then the banisters, went down the narrow stairs. The wooden steps creaked beneath her feet, and the second flight, just visible to her as she came to the landing, was almost entirely in the dark; it was barely possible to see the brown carpet that wound down it like a snake. The hall was completely dark. She switched on the light, walked along the passage between the two rows of mirrors, took her umbrella from the stand in the vestibule and went out.

The night was black and damp, and from every side came the monotonous sound of the downpour. Carla went down the marble steps from the front door and opened her umbrella with a gesture of familiarity which astonished her; she felt that in certain highly unusual circumstances everything ought to be done in a quite unusual manner.

She was not endowing her flight with all the melancholy, shameful importance that other people in her place would have given to it. Here she was, leaving the house, crossing the drive, bending under her umbrella in an effort not to wet her face in the streaming rain, trying to avoid the puddles—now she was crossing the garden at this late hour without the fear or the surprise, without even the immense, adventurous sadness, that should accompany all grave actions. The wet gravel scrunched under her feet, and she listened to the sound with pleasure. And that was all.

She looked up and saw the black patch formed by the gate, its two white pillars, and the dark foliage of a tall tree bent beneath the rain. Opening the gate, she went into the street, turning her eyes in the opposite direction to where Leo was waiting. "He's not there," she thought, disappointed, observing the quiet light that fell from the street-lamp on to the wet, empty roadway; but already her lover's car was moving up behind her—less rapidly, however, than the sudden ray of light that flashed out as the two headlamps were turned on.

Farewell streets, farewell deserted quarter over which the rain marches like an army, farewell villas sleeping in damp gardens, long tree-lined avenues, storm-swept parks! Farewell to this exalted, wealthy part of the city! Carla, motionless in her seat at Leo's side, gazed at the violent rain streaming down the windshield, at all the lights of the city, the display signs and street-lamps, trickling confusedly down the glass in intermittent waves. Streets succeeded streets; she watched them curving away, flowing into each other, turning and twisting in the space beyond the hood of the car. As the car jolted along, black façades detached themselves from the darkness, sailed past, vanished like the sides of ocean liners making their way with difficulty through heaving billows. Black groups of people, illuminated doorways, lamp-posts—all showed themselves for an instant as they drove past, then disappeared, swallowed up forever in the darkness.

Motionless, spell-bound, Carla looked at Leo, at his hands on the wheel, at his calm, reflective way of driving. These details fascinated her; but her mind was empty. And when after ten minutes the car suddenly stopped and the thought, *we've arrived*, flashed upon her, the effect was such that she caught her breath.

Leo got out and told her to wait. She watched him through the wet glass as he opened something dark which looked like a gate and vanished into the blackness of the garden. "He's got to put the car away," she thought, and the sound of a sliding door being opened came to her through the rain. Then the man's figure reappeared, he got into the car and without taking the slightest notice of her drove it inside the dark cave of the garage. There was a smell of gasoline and oily steel, a small red lamp in a corner; they got out and Leo pulled down the sliding door and very carefully secured the padlock.

A circular lamp to their right lit up the door of the building, with its four marble steps and its closed double door. Leo opened it and led Carla into the entrance hall. In contrast with the dark, soaking garden, everything here was brightly colored and shining. A wrought-iron lantern hung from the ceiling, the walls were whitewashed, with a yellow dado, green palms rose up in the corners; everything was new. At the far side the elevator hung in its cage, but they chose the stairs.

On the first landing the noise of a phonograph, scarcely deadened by an intervening door, rang out among the glossy tiled walls, accompanied by a confused clatter of voices and feet, friendly and cheerful.

"They're dancing," remarked Carla with a forced smile, leaning against the banisters. "Who are they?"

Leo stooped and examined the brass plate on the door. "It appears to be," he said, "Doctor Innamorati, who," he added, partly to amuse Carla, partly to cheat his own impatience, "is at home with his charming wife and young sons and daughters, in order to receive, in a worthy manner, a select company of friends and ladies of the best society." He laughed and took Carla's arm. "Come on," he said. "One more flight of stairs and we're there."

They continued on their way, the music of the phonograph echoing distantly but noisily up the empty, white, brightly lit staircase. In the intervals there was complete silence. One could imagine the small drawing-room, the dancers standing still under the burning chandelier, the laughter, the movement, and in the corners, beside the windows, behind the curtains, the compliments. At the second floor they went in.

In the hall Leo took off his hat and coat and helped Carla out of her raincoat. The hall was spacious and white, and three doors opened from it; opposite the front door was a large, dark, square window which evidently looked over an inner courtyard. They went through into the sitting-room. "Let's sit here," said Leo, pointing to a big leather divan full of cushions. They sat down; a red-shaded lamp on a small table threw its light upon them as far up as their chests, while their heads and the remainder of the room remained in semi-darkness. For a moment they sat without moving or speaking; Carla was looking around without curiosity, her eyes resting first on a bottle of liqueur on the little table, then on the walls, not so much observing as anxiously awaiting a word or a gesture. Leo was admiring Carla.

"Well, my dear," he began at last, "what's the matter? Why don't you say something, or even look at me? Come on, cheer up and tell me what you're thinking about, and if there's anything you want, don't hesitate to tell me. Ask for anything you like, just as if you were in your own home." He put out his hand and gently stroked the girl's serious face. "You're not sorry," he added, without the faintest embarrassment, "that you came?"

She turned her head. "No," she answered, "no, I'm . . . very glad. . . . Only, you know what I mean? I must . . . I must get accustomed to it."

"Yes, yes, get accustomed to it," said Leo with assurance. He moved nearer to Carla. Hell! he thought, troubled and excited, what a bore these preliminaries are! He put his arm around her waist; but the girl did not appear to notice.

"What a pretty dress you've got on," began Leo, in a subdued, caressing voice. "Who made it for you? What a pretty baby you are. You'll see how well we get on together. You'll be my baby, the only baby in my life, my lovely baby."

He paused, and ran his lips quickly over Carla's hand and up her bare arm; then, stopping for a moment at her neck, pulled her big, solemn head towards him. They kissed, then separated again.

"Come and sit on my knee," he invited her. Carla, docile, obeyed, and as she settled herself her dress was caught up round her legs, but she made no attempt to pull it down again. This carelessness on her part convinced Leo of the security of his conquest.

"What room is that in there?" asked the girl, pointing to the other door leading from the sitting-room.

"The bedroom," replied her lover, watching her closely; and after a moment, embracing her again, he said in a persuasive tone. "But don't worry about that. Listen . . . tell me . . . d'you love me?"

"And how about you?" she asked in a faint whisper, looking at him with serious eyes.

"Me? What's that got to do with it? Of course I love you, otherwise I shouldn't have done what I have done. Certainly I love my little Carla, my funny baby, my sweet little Carla." Leo thrust his fingers into the girl's hair and disarranged it. "I love her very much indeed, and woe betide anyone who tries to take her away from me. And I desire her too, of course I do . . . the whole of her . . . I want these lips, and these cheeks, and these lovely arms, and these lovely shoulders, and this body of hers, so feminine, so delicious, so full of fascination and sweetness that . . . that . . . that it'll drive me mad," he burst out finally. Seized by frenzy, he threw himself upon Carla, hugged her with all his might, and fell with her onto the divan; the dispassionate lamplight fell on his back where the jacket was pulled tight over the straining shoulders, and on Carla's pink-stockinged legs. They stayed like this for some moments, while confused words of tenderness issuing from Leo's lips mingled with the throes of his desire. Carla was silent. Her attitude to these transports was docile but not resigned, her ideas were not as lucid as she had expected, her cheeks began to burn with a shameful, agitating excitement; in fact—it was useless to deny it—these caresses did not leave her entirely indifferent, and a certain pleasure, all the more acute for its apparent absurdity, started to dim the clarity of her consciousness. I should like to know, she thought, between the instinctive shivers that her lover's violent, licentious embraces forced from her, what on earth I'm doing. Never before had this love affair appeared to her in such a commonplace, unpardonable, ruinous light. A new life, she thought again, feebly; and then closed her eyes.

But Leo did not allow his sensual excitement to go beyond a certain limit. The moment he saw Carla relax with closed eyes and a face as white as wax against the dark background of the divan, he said to himself: *No. Not here. In the other room. Here it's too uncomfortable!* He raised himself up, and made the girl rise too; and for a moment they sat quite still, panting, without speaking. The light of the lamp left Leo in shadow, as he leaned far back on the divan, but fell full on Carla; and she was no longer the young lady of a few minutes before. Her hair was ruffled and one lock of it fell down in front of her eyes, her face was red, solemn and troubled-looking, and one of the two shoulder-straps of her dress had been broken during the embrace and now hung in two pieces, one on her breast and one down her back, displaying her white, naked shoulder. And then, as she gazed, self-absorbed, in front of her, Leo noticed a strange thing: something that looked very like a little scroll of paper folded in four filled the hollow space under her dress between her breasts, and stretched the red silk of the dress into two or three sharp points. He smiled, put out his hand and touched it.

"What's this?" he asked, without any particular purpose, out of pure curiosity.

Carla turned a frightened face towards him. "Why, what d'you mean?"

"This . . . this piece of paper that you guard so jealously in your bosom," insisted Leo, with an almost paternal smile.

She lowered her head, raised her hand to her breast. Yes, there was no doubt, her lover was right, there was something hidden there, between her slip and her skin, something which seemed to be a piece of paper, only she could not remember having put it there, nor could she think what it could possibly be. She raised her eyes and cast a disconcerted glance at her lover.

"That's the place where all little girls keep their secrets," said Leo, in whom the idea of such a hiding-place aroused feelings of tenderness and excitement. "Let's see, Carla; let me look at this secret of yours." He put out his hand.

"No, I won't allow you to," she cried suddenly, without knowing why she did so, and covered herself with her hands.

Leo's smile vanished. "All right," he said, watching the girl closely. "I'll allow you not to allow me. But do pull out this treasure . . . and read it aloud."

There was silence. Carla looked at him, puzzled and irresolute, guessing that this matter of the piece of paper was beginning to irritate him; she could tell that from his eyes, which had grown hard. And it was in vain that she racked her brain to imagine what this piece of paper, which she was feeling with curious fingers, might contain. But she did not pull it out, partly from a gloomy sense of honor (supposing it really was some secret that she could not confide to anyone), and partly with a vague intention of seeing how Leo would act when pricked by jealousy.

"And supposing," she said finally, in a challenging tone, placing her hands on her knees, "supposing I don't want to show you this letter?"

"Ah! it's a letter, is it?" exclaimed Leo, interested and already disquieted. "And who is it from, if you don't mind my asking—from what person so important to you that you keep it there, in that particular place, and that you can't leave it at home?"

She looked at him through lowered eyelashes, her big untidy head on her bare shoulder. "Ah," she replied with a capricious air, looking up at the ceiling and quietly drumming her fingers on her knees. "I'm not going to tell you."

She's perfectly capable, thought Leo, now extremely irritated, she's perfectly capable of having someone else: perfectly capable of it. He raised himself slowly from the divan.

"Listen, Carla," he said, stressing his words and fixing two imperious inquisitorial eyes upon her; "I wish absolutely to know who that letter is from."

She gave a slight laugh, amused by this show of jealousy, but she did not modify her scornful attitude. "Guess," she said.

"A man?" asked Leo.

"Certainly," she said in a teasing voice; "certainly—unless it's a woman." To thwart some sudden movement on his part she kept her hand on her breast. She looked up, with half-closed eyes towards the shadowy ceiling, she felt tired, and longed to bow her head over this secret that did not exist and go to sleep.

"I understand," said Leo, with a forced smile. "I understand . . . some fellow who's in love with you . . . some boy or other. . . ."

"Not at all," she replied, without lowering her head, "a

man." She watched Leo's vague, broad shadow on the wall opposite, moving this way and that as if he were preparing to jump on top of her.

"A man," she repeated, more wearily than before, and without ceasing the drumming of her fingers "and if you only knew," she added, moved by a sadness without reason, "if you only knew how I love him!" Her eyes were half closed and full of tears, her heart was throbbing. And yet, she said to herself coldly, this man doesn't exist.

"A man! I congratulate you." Leo was now really annoyed. The idea of her non-existent purity, of the conquest that someone else had made, exasperated him. The chaste, childish Carla of his desire yielded place to a young lady who was expert in love, who did not fear to visit men in their own homes; the pleasant excitement, the perfume, the charm of the idyll vanished; and his *amour-propre* as a seducer was left empty-handed in front of an open door.

"It's my own fault," he added with conviction, "it ought to have occurred to me that it wasn't the first time."

"The first time of what?" she asked, instantly turning.

"The first time that . . . you know what I mean . . . that you pay visits, that you go to somebody's house."

A bright flush rose to Carla's cheeks, and she looked at her lover, torn between the desire to protest and tell him the foolish truth, and that of continuing the fiction she had begun. But in the end she took the second course.

"Supposing that was true?" she said, looking him in the eyes.

"Ah, so it's true, is it?" For a moment Leo clenched both his teeth and his fists, then he controlled himself and spoke in a voice shrill with sarcasm. "Ah, you purest of pure virgins, so you have a lover?"

"Yes," she confessed, blushing again. His irony and his tone of voice wounded her, never before had she felt so great a need for kindness.

"But that's splendid, that's wonderful," Leo said slowly. He looked Carla in the eyes and went on, as if speaking to himself. "Of course one sees now. Like mother, like daughter." Then his eyes went bloodshot with a sudden red fury;

he seized the girl by the arm. "You know what you are? A
. . . a . . ."—in his rage he was unable to find the right word
and he stammered—"a shameless . . . and in spite of that you
came here to *my* flat, too?"

"That's a different thing," said Carla calmly.

"What a piece of goods! How revolting! And to think
she's barely twenty-four," Leo went on to himself, looking
at the girl. "And may one at least know who this gentleman
is?" he asked.

"He's a tall man," she said, making an effort to give concrete form to the misty ideal image after which her soul
yearned. "He has chestnut brown hair . . . a fine, calm brow
and an oval face . . . he's not at all florid, rather pale in fact
. . . he has long, slim hands."

"It's Santoro!" exclaimed Leo, choosing the first of Carla's
friends that seemed to him to have some resemblance to the
portrait she was painting.

"No, it's not him." Carla was looking straight in front of
herself. Would to God he existed! she was thinking, I
shouldn't be here now. She was silent for a moment.

"He loves me very much and I love him very much," she
continued, with a simple, easy sweetness which charmed and
surprised her, for now she did not even seem to be lying.
"We met two years ago . . . and we've gone on seeing each
other all the time since then. He's not like you. He's . . . he's
most unusually good and kind—I mean he understands me
even before I speak, and I can confide everything to him
that's in my mind, whatever it is, and he talks to me in a way
nobody else does, and he takes me in his arms and . . . and
. . ." Her voice trembled, her eyes filled with tears; at that
moment she herself was convinced of the truth of what she
was saying, and she almost seemed to see, there in front of
her, in the flesh, this creature of her imagination. "And he
really is different from everyone else, and he's the only person who ever really loved me," she concluded, moved, and
a little astonished too, by her own invention.

"What's his name?" said Leo, not in the least impressed by
her tone or her words. "May one know his name?"

Carla shook her head. "His name—no."

There was a moment's silence while they looked at each other. Then: "Give me that letter," he commanded, in a peremptory manner.

Troubled, she covered her breast with her hands. "Why, Leo?" she began, in an imploring voice.

"The letter—out with it!" All of a sudden he seized the girl by the waist and tried forcibly to thrust his hand into the hiding-place. But Carla wriggled away from him and freed herself, and, disheveled, ran across to the opposite wall.

"Don't you know that no one ever gains anything by violence?" she cried, and, opening the bedroom door, disappeared.

Leo, seized by a limitless rage, hurled himself against the closed door, but Carla had turned the key and he could not get in. "Open the door," he shouted with fury, banging against it with his fists. "Open it, you fool!" There was no answer.

It occurred to him that he could get into the bedroom by way of the bathroom. He ran through the hall into the bathroom; everything there was in place, and nickeled pipes and glossy porcelain tiles gleamed in the semi-darkness. He noticed with pleasure that the green glass door was half open, but at first he could not see Carla; the light was out, and the room was filled with transparent gloom. Can she have thrown herself out of the window? he wondered for a second as he felt his way forward. He turned on the light and found the room was empty. Devil take her; where in the world can she have hidden herself? he wondered, and was on the point of going out again and searching for the fugitive in the other rooms of the flat when he saw her standing there, squeezed into the space behind the bathroom door.

He walked straight over to her, took hold of her by the arm and pulled her out of her hiding-place with some violence, as one might do with a boisterous child. "Out with that letter!" he commanded severely, holding her tight.

They stood looking at each other. The girl was now frightened and humiliated at the thought that her lover would discover how she had been lying; she realized that the piece of paper could not be of any importance, that it could only be a note of invitation or something equally stupid; and she suffered at the idea of being compelled to confess to Leo that her dreams had no reality.

She made one last attempt to protest. "This isn't right, Leo. . . ." She began querulously; I . . ."

"The letter!" demanded the man.

She saw it was useless to object. "So be it!" she said to herself, resigned and at the same time curious to see what the letter might contain. She thrust her hand into her bosom, pulled out the piece of paper, and handed it to Leo. "There it is!"

Leo took it, but before examining it he looked at the girl. And then, as though a sudden and insuperable shame overwhelmed her, her face crumpled up and she turned to the bed and threw herself down upon it, hiding her face in her hands. It was no more than a gesture, unaccompanied by thought or any real feeling; she herself was not deceived as to its significance. Hearing the man laugh, she raised her head again.

"But it's *my* note," he cried, going over to her, "my own note that I gave you today."

She was not surprised. This affair of the letter was ridiculous, for no one could have written to her, no one loved her. But, in spite of that, it seemed to her cruelly unjust that it should be so, unjust that a miracle should not have occurred (why could not her great longing for it have changed that stupid note into a love letter?), unjust that there should be this painfully precise reality. She turned pale. "Yes, of course, your note," she said, with a feeling of bitter, inexorable disappointment. "What did you expect?"

"Then, in that case," he went on, coming close to her and sitting down beside her on the bed, "in that case *I* am that man . . . with chestnut-brown hair and a calm brow . . . it's *me* that you love."

She gave him a lingering glance, as though she were trying to discover, in that red, complacent face, the image she had dreamed of. "But . . . but . . ." she said, hesitating and looking down, with the consciousness that she was beginning to lie all over again; "hadn't you understood that yet?"

For the first time since Carla had known him, Leo gave a

fresh, almost youthful, spontaneous laugh. "No, I hadn't," he cried; and he put his arm around her waist.

"Pretend I never said what I did say," he told her. "Pretend I never said any of it." He stooped and kissed her shoulders, her neck, her cheeks, her breast. Her body began to excite him again; with illusion restored, desire was restored also. "My little liar," he repeated; "my naughty baby who tells lies. . . ."

These amorous outpourings did not last more than a minute. He rose, awkwardly, from the bed. "Well, what about it?" he asked, half serious, half facetious, not troubling to smooth back his untidy hair which made him look slightly drunk—or perhaps merely clumsy. "Don't you think it's about time to go to bed? I'm sleepy . . . terribly sleepy."

Carla smiled with an effort and nodded timidly.

"Well, come on then," he said; "here are some pyjamas." He pointed to some broad-striped garments lying at the head of the bed. "You'll find anything you need there in the cupboard. Get undressed and into bed and I'll be with you in a moment." He smiled at her again, full of confidence now, patted her on the shoulder and went into the bathroom.

9

THE WIDE, low bed occupied an inside corner of the room. She lay down on it and looked around. In the gloom, unbroken by the single lamp that burned at the head of the bed, she could see two wardrobes with shining mirrors, one to the right of the sitting-room door, the other on the opposite side. There was nothing else. The window took up the whole of the wall opposite her; it was low, oblong, with small panes, and had short white curtains; underneath it was the radiator, hidden by a grating. The shutters were closed, the sitting-room door was closed, as was the bathroom door, which she saw sideways, with its glass panels softly lit like the sides of an aquarium when the sun strikes upon them. She looked down at the big white, hairy bearskin that lay at her feet; it had yellow celluloid eyes and a wide-open mouth full of sharp teeth; the flattened skin of its short paws and exiguous tail gave the impression of having been ironed out by a gigantic roller which had left intact nothing but the ferocious head. She got up and automatically took a few steps around the room, touching the radiator, which was warm, pushing aside a curtain. Behind the luminous panes of the bathroom door she could see her lover's shadow passing back and forth, could hear the gush of water from a tap and other sounds. Then—but not before she had examined her own dishevelled, frightened figure in the dark looking-glasses of the two wardrobes—she went back to the bed and began undressing.

The unaccustomed actions that she was performing absorbed her completely, inducing a dreamlike wonder. The thing that made the deepest impression on her was the fact of not being in her own home, of finding herself in this room at that hour of the night. She took off her torn dress and laid it on the low armchair at the foot of the bed; then her stockings, and contemplated, for a moment, her bare legs; her slip and her drawers; then she hesitated: should she take off her slip as well? She considered the matter; yes, certainly, of course it was necessary, so she slipped out of it and threw it on top of her other clothes. She felt naked underneath the cold sheets, and huddled against the wall, one hand between her legs and the other on her breast. As for the pyjamas with the broad stripes, they made her think of of a convict's uniform, and she had thrown them on the floor. It had occurred to her that possibly her mother had worn them.

Gradually her glowing body warmed the sheets. She had the feeling that this warmth had loosened the knot of fear and astonishment which until that moment had constrained her heart; she felt lonely, she was conscious of a great tenderness, an indulgent pity for herself, and she made an effort to gather herself together, to roll herself up in a ball as much as she could, until her lips actually touched her rounded knees. She was moved by their healthy, sensual smell, and kissed them several times, passionately. "Poor dear . . . poor little thing . . ." she repeated as she caressed herself. Her eyes filled with tears; she would have liked to lay her head on her own buxom bosom and weep there, as though on the bosom of a mother. Then, gazing intently at the dimly lit wall, she listened to the familiar sounds that came to her and made it clear, without any doubt, where she was—the rustling of the rain still falling, the sound of someone moving in the bathroom, of water running; and when she moved, the bed gave softly beneath her with a dull and distant murmur—was it that it retained a memory of something, or was it simply because of the springiness of the mattress? It was not like her own bed at home, hard and narrow, nor like those strange beds into which one tumbles after a long journey, beds in which one feels too low or too high and in which sleep is unsatisfactory. No, this was a comfortable bed, extremely soft, full of kind attentiveness and solicitude, only her body was afraid of it, and she huddled to one side, trembling, and put out a hesitating hand to feel the immense, cold space that stretched away behind her, a Siberia of linen, uninhabited and hostile. It was a disagreeable sensation, like walking along a dark road knowing that there is someone just behind.

She closed her tired eyes; it was barely a minute, yet it seemed to her an hour, that she had been in this bed. Why doesn't Leo come? she suddenly wondered. This thought brought others in its train. I shan't turn around until he's turned out the light, she mused, but with no hatred in her mind. I don't want to see him.

She shivered. This is the end, she thought, vaguely and without conviction. From the desire for destruction that had led her as far as this bed there was now born in her a longing for the darkness in which she would cling to her lover. She imagined, not without a certain thrill—whether from an instinctive desire for enjoyment or because of her established plan of complete self-degradation, she did not know—that she would throw herself, in the blackness, in the promiscuity of night, into all those bestial profligacies whose existence she had long suspected without having any knowledge of them whatsoever. But these excited fantasies did not distract her from her prolonged expectation. "Why doesn't Leo come?" And then, exhausted by the exertions of sensuality, she would fall asleep beside her lover. This idea pleased her, and she was thinking that it must be at the same time both sweet and melancholy to sleep with a companion, side by side, or, even better, in each other's arms, naked, closely entwined, in the night; and she was feeling almost affectionate towards Leo, and imagining that she would not move, would even hold her breath for fear of awaking him . . . when the bathroom door opened, with a sound of tinkling glass.

This sudden but familiar sound was as pleasing to her at that moment as a friendly presence in some unknown or alarming place; with that same sound and in that same way glass doors opened all over the world, in her own home as elsewhere. She immediately forgot her whole program, opened her eyes wide, saw on the wall the man's broad shadow, turned around: her lover was bending over her. She scarcely had time to observe that he was not wearing pyjamas but a kind of light dressing-gown, and that he had shaved carefully and powdered his chin and combed his hair; then, with a simple movement, without relaxing the hard, absent-minded expression on his face, he raised the bedclothes and slipped in beside her.

10

Leo was the first to fall asleep; Carla's unexpected, if inexpert, licentiousness had worn him out. After the last embrace as they lay motionless for a few moments, their moist limbs entwined, their eyes half closed, their heads close together on the pillow in a kind of exhausted drowsiness, the girl felt her lover gradually withdraw his arm from her waist, disentangle his legs from hers and turn towards the wall. What about tomorrow morning? she wondered confusedly, listening to the quiet breathing of the sleeper, what about tomorrow morning? She felt extremely tired, it seemed an age that she had been immersed in the thick darkness of this room, her head ached, she did not dare to move. And then, although she still had the clear sensation of a bare body against hers, of sheets full of a special kind of warmth which was entirely new to her, of an indefinable atmosphere which not even for an instant allowed her to forget the house and the room where she was—suddenly all these extraordinary things ceased to astonish her, and it was as if she had in one quick moment become accustomed and hardened to them. She turned over, pulled the bedclothes around her and fell asleep.

She had a strange dream. The imaginary lover whom she had managed to describe so well to Leo was in front of her.

He was tall—perhaps because he was standing while she was lying down—with a noble brow and eyes full of serenity and indulgence. He stood very erect, was carelessly dressed, and gazed at her with wondering intentness, as though he had just come into the room and found her, lying there naked on the bed, her virgin body deflowered and—yes, indeed—sullied here and there, on the breast, the belly, the arms, by Leo's recent transports of desire. She was unable to see herself, and remained lying flat, but she realized from the man's glances that there were marks and stains upon her limbs, and that she was changed, even for him, a stranger, from the Carla she had been before this intrigue. And so they remained, looking at each other, without moving; but in the end the sight of that calm, severe, intent face, the torment of those eyes upon her deflowered body (and the worst of it was that she could not see herself) became intolerable to her, and with an instinctive gesture she covered her face with her arm and wanted to cry. But here was another disagreeable surprise, her eyes remained dry, however hard she tried the tears would not come, she could no longer weep. She was pierced by an immense sorrow, a bitter regret—of what, she did not know; she moaned and screamed (or so she thought in the confusion of her dream), and, though she still lay flat on her back (another torment: the feeling of being nailed down to the bed, of not being able to rise or move), she twisted her bosom and her bare hips this way and that. At intervals, while she writhed spasmodically like a butterfly transfixed, she could see the calm head far away in the distance, the eyes that never ceased looking at her, the pure forehead. "Oh, to weep . . . to weep," she kept repeating to herself, and made every possible effort to wet her arid lids with at least one tear. Her grief could not be expressed, but remained an enormous weight upon her heart, suffocating her; and at last she could bear it no more and stretched out her arms, frantically, towards that distant head. She called the man by the sweetest possible names, names new and spontaneous that moved her profoundly, and she promised to love him all her life, forever (this sense of eternity filled her with a great inexplicable bitterness), but it was in vain, for the man disappeared and

[178]

she herself fell back into darkness. Then there was a burst of sound, steadily increasing in volume, the sound of a single syllable, gloomy as the tolling of a bell: "San . . . San . . . San . . . San . . ." which filled her heart with ghastly confusion and fear; and finally, at the complete name of "Santoro," she awoke.

The blackness in which she had fallen asleep still enveloped her; her whole body was bathed in sweat, and she felt on her left side a region of dampness and burning heat. *Where am I?* she asked herself in terror. Her bewilderment lasted only a moment, for she remembered all that had happened and realized that her sensation of heat came from Leo's bare side touching her own. Feeling that she was suffocating she threw the bedclothes off her chest and drew out her arms; the freedom and freshness gave her great relief. She opened her eyes completely, for now, either from fear of another nightmare or from the nervous exasperation that possessed her, she had no more wish to sleep; she began to recall all that had occurred since the beginning of that night.

The recollection of these happenings came back to her bit by bit. Now she remembered herself in the car as it moved, in the rain, through the streets of the city, now she was in the sitting-room, on her lover's knee, simultaneously there appeared to her the image of Leo in the act of getting into the bed where she was waiting for him, and another picture, stranger and more disturbing, of the two of them, standing naked side by side in the blinding light of the bathroom with its white-tiled walls, dazed and sleepy as they waited for hot water with which to wash themselves. These memories, although so recent, appeared remote and detached from her own self, they did not belong to her nor did she explain them to herself, and they seemed full of an inadmissible unreality. But there was no doubt that she had lived these events, which were so close to her that the figures moving through them appeared to her life-sized. She had merely to put out her hand under the sheets to touch the naked body of her sleeping lover, or to turn on the light, in order to convince herself that she was truly in Leo's room and not her own. Far away from home she concluded with a feeling of perturbation, here . . .

in my lover's bed. But if the recollection of the more normal events of the night astonished her, there were other memories, of things that she had not foreseen and had never had any knowledge of, which overwhelmed her, and she could not have enough of analyzing them, going back again and again to reconstruct them, and enjoying the taste of them all over again . . . the precise memory, for instance, of one or two clear-sighted moments when (the light still being on) she had caught a surprised glimpse of certain attitudes in which she and her lover had found themselves, attitudes so monstrously immodest that they were indelibly imprinted upon her mind.

Because of the darkness that enveloped her or because of a real sense of fear and uncertainty, these recollections began to weary her, and they no longer sufficed to distract her from the consciousness of her present circumstances. What is going to happen to me? she thought. She felt terribly lonely —yes, that was it—as she lay there on her back, in that bed, left to her solitary thoughts, to her fears, her weaknesses; the darkness of night filled her wide-open eyes, and her lover did not caress her brow, or push back her untidy hair, or share her anguished wakefulness, or rally to her defense—it was as if he was not there at all. There was the sound of quiet breathing on her right—nothing more; it might be Leo's or anyone else's.

She was overcome by an hysterical desire for companionship, for caresses. Why does he go on sleeping? she asked herself. Why doesn't he pay any attention to me? That lethargic breathing at her side was becoming frightening, it did not seem to be her lover's breathing, but some other man, unknown to her and positively hostile; there was in that breathing a rhythm so indifferent, a regularity so monstrously in contrast with her own anguish and her own fantasies that truly she did not know whether to be frightened or indignant. She tried to forget it, straining her ears to catch the few sounds that were audible in the flat, the slight rustling noises and creakings of furniture; she opened her eyes very wide in the darkness in search of something upon which to fix her whole attention. It was useless; the sound of that breathing, calm and almost inhuman, always reasserted itself. How lovely it would be if he were to wake up now and tell me he loves me! And she pictured to herself how this would happen—how he would draw her to his side, and with his cheek against hers murmur the sweet words in her ear, she was already feeling moved and comforted at the thought of it, when suddenly she was frozen by a horrible fear.

It seemed to her that the bathroom door was slowly opening. Either because the panes of glass in the door gave forth a faint luminosity or because the shutters at the bathroom window were open and a little light came in from the courtyard, the blackness was certainly less thick than in the rest of the room . . . and yes, there was no doubt, the door was opening very gently, was moving, as if someone were cautiously pushing it from the other side.

She caught her breath in terror and her heart beat wildly; she lay motionless, rigid, flat on her back with her eyes fixed in that direction; and the crazy thought—which she rejected immediately—flashed through her mind: It's Mother, and she's come to catch me in the act. Then the door gave a faint tinkling sound and this was too much for Carla. With eyes tight shut, with all the force she could summon, with a feeling of tearing and rending, she gave a long and mournful cry.

The light went on, the quiet room reappeared, Leo, half-asleep, sat up in the bed. "Why . . . what's happened?"

"The door," stammered Carla, white-faced and panting, "the bathroom door."

Without a word he leaped out of bed, opened the door, disappeared into the bathroom, and reappeared.

"I can't see anything," he declared; "it must have been the wind. I had left the bathroom window open." He came back to the bed, lifted the bedclothes and lay down again. "Don't think about it any more, but go to sleep," he said. "Sleep well." And he turned out the light.

His actions were so rapid, the interval of light so brief, that she did not have time to speak or even to express by an embrace or a look the extreme longing to be caressed and comforted which oppressed her spirit; and when darkness again enveloped her, she began, after a moment's uncertainty, to weep.

The tears flowed swiftly down her cheeks, and all the bitterness that she had accumulated during that night now came flooding forth from the whole of her heart. If he loved me, she kept saying to herself, he would have comforted me. But there was nothing, nothing. He switched off the light and turned away from me! The loneliness which previously she had dimly apprehended now seemed to her inevitable, she covered her eyes with her bare arm, and could feel the bitter grief upon her face. He doesn't love me . . . no one loves me. She pulled at her hair with her fingers, and her cheeks were streaked with tears, but at length the weariness that lurked within her gained the upper hand, and weeping she fell asleep.

When she woke it seemed to be day, or so she guessed from the small amount of light that the slats of the shutters allowed to trickle through into the dissolving darkness inside the room. She woke easily, at once recognized the place where she was, and was not astonished either at finding herself wearing the broad-striped pyjamas which she had refused to put on the evening before (though she did not remember at what precise moment of the night she had donned them), or, once she had got out of bed and was leaning against the wall and her sleepy eyes had grown accustomed to the dusty gloom of the room, at seeing on the pillow the dark, ruffled patch which was Leo's head. Sleep had dissipated all the fears and astonishments of the night, and it was as if she had been accustomed for years to wake up in this manner, in her lover's bed. Finished were the torment, the wonder, the impatience; finished was the melancholy, adventurous sense of unreality; with her back against the wall, her eyes wide open in the stifling darkness, Carla divined, from the unusual feeling of satiety, the calmness, the thoughtful patience that possessed her, that she had indeed entered into a new life. It's strange, she thought—whether with fear or annoyance, she did not know—it's as though I had all at once grown much older than I was before. She stood still for a moment, vaguely preoccupied, then she stooped down and shook the man by the shoulder.

[182]

"Leo," she called, in an odd, subdued voice.

Leo had pulled the sheets right up to his ears, and appeared to be plunged in a deep sleep. At first he either did not hear or pretended not to. Again Carla stooped and shook him; and then, from the dark shadow on the pillow, came a sleepy voice.

"What have you waked me up for?"

"It's late," she said, still with that new intonation, low and intimate, "it must be time for me to go home."

Without moving the rest of his body, Leo put out his arm and switched on the lamp. The quiet light of the previous evening came back again, and Carla easily recalled the furniture, the two doors, the little armchair on which lay the white heap of her most intimate garments, herself sitting on the bed, the clock under the lamp on the bedside table, pointed to half past five.

"It's half past five," announced Leo with plaintive irritation, without turning round; "may I ask why you woke me up?"

"It's late," she repeated. She hesitated, then very cautiously climbed over the body of her lover and sat down on the edge of the bed.

He did not seem to notice this, nor did he answer her; evidently he had shut his eyes and gone to sleep again. Without turning around or paying any attention to him, Carla started dressing.

But she had barely taken off that repugnant broad-striped uniform and was standing up naked, preparing to put on her slip, when she felt herself seized from behind by an arm round her waist. Startled, she dropped the garment she was holding and turned her head sharply, against her hip was the head of her lover, with ruffled hair and a sleepy, red face.

"Carla," he murmured, leaning out from the bed, raising a pair of excited eyes towards the girl and pretending to speak with an effort because of a great drowsiness he did not really feel. "Why d'you want to go away so soon? Come here . . . come back here beside your Leo."

She looked down at the face of her tempter, lit by the warm lamplight below, and her breast heaved with an inexplicable distress. "Leave me alone," she said stubbornly, striving to detach the five fingers that grasped her side. "It's late. It's time I went away."

She saw him half-close his small, excited eyes and laugh. "For some things it's never too late," he said, and Carla, without reason—for in her heart she was quite ready to admit the naturalness of such desires in her lover—exploded in anger. "Leave me alone, I tell you!" she repeated in a hard voice. Leo's only reply was to clumsily stretch out his other arm and try to pull her down beside him. With a violent jerk she freed herself, went to the armchair at the foot of the bed, and without taking any further notice of him or saying a word, proceeded to pull on her stockings.

After the stockings, the garters, and she did not raise her anxious eyes for some moments. Then she looked with a hard expression towards the bed; but Leo had turned away to the wall and appeared to be asleep. Sleep soundly, she said to herself. A moment passed, and then, as if her brief thought had in some way contrived to provoke him, a feeling of fear and uncertainty made her heart sink. After all those hours of complete forgetfulness, the old words started echoing in her head again: "The new life." She stooped and picked up her slip. Is it really possible, she thought, crushing the little garment nervously in her hand and staring straight in front of her, that *this* can be the new life?

Turning this idea over and over in the heaviness of her heart, she finished dressing and rose to her feet.

"Get up!" she cried to the sleeping man, bending and touching him on the shoulder. "Hurry up! It's time to go. . . ."

"All right," was the reply. Sure of finding him dressed when she returned, Carla went into the bathroom.

She tidied her hair with Leo's brush and comb, washed her hands, closely examined her pale face in the mirror. When I get home, she thought, I shall have a proper wash. I shall have a bath. And then . . . and then I shall have to go almost at once to that tennis engagement. But, in spite of these calm, practical reflections, the question never ceased echoing sadly through the lower planes of her consciousness: "Is it really possible that this can be the new life?"

In the bedroom a surprise awaited her. Leo had not dressed, he had not even started to get up. He was lying in exactly the same position as before, and seemed to be still asleep.

She went over to him and shook him. "Leo . . . it's late. We must go. Get up!"

He turned his head, lifted a sleepy face a few inches from the pillow and looked at her. "Eh? Are you dressed already?"

"It's late."

"It's late?" repeated Leo, as if he had not understood. "Well?"

"What d'you mean—well? You've got to take me home."

He yawned and tugged at his hair. "If you knew how sleepy I am," he began. "All night long you never left me in peace for one single moment. You kept on calling me . . . and talking to me . . . and kicking me . . . and I don't know what. I'm dying with sleepiness." He spoke slowly, drawling his words, and avoided looking at the girl. Carla on the other hand was observing him closely. It's quite obvious, she thought, calmly and without anger, that the reason why he's pretending to be sleepy now is not just because he hasn't slept but, far more, because I didn't give in to him just now.

She straightened up. "If you want to sleep, Leo," she said, almost gently, "don't bother about me. I can go by myself."

"Don't be silly." He stretched himself, lengthily. "Now you've waked me up I'll take you home."

I must show him that he's making a mistake, she thought as she looked at him, that . . . that I'm not like *him*. "No, no," she said mildly, "no . . . I don't want to disturb you. You're sleepy, it's quite right. I prefer to go by myself."

Somewhat disconcerted, Leo looked at her. "No, indeed you shan't," he said at last, with unconvincing energy. "That's what you say now, but you'd never stop finding fault with me for it afterwards. I know what you are. No, I've decided. I'm going with you." He paused, shook his head vigorously, but did not move. They looked at each other.

"And supposing I command you?" asked the girl brusquely.

"Command me what?"

[185]

"Not to come with me."

Leo opened his eyes wide in astonishment. "In that case," he replied diffidently, "it becomes a different question."

"Well," said Carla, quietly rearranging the belt of her dress, "I command you."

There was a moment's silence. "First you wanted to be taken home," said the man at last, "now you don't. You're being very capricious."

Ah! So *I'm* being capricious, am I? she thought, clenching her teeth. She sat down on the edge of the bed, close to her lover. "It's not a question of caprice," she answered, "but I've been thinking that your taking me home might possibly be compromising. If anyone saw us together. . . . Besides, Michele might be up already. So, d'you see?—it's better for me to go alone. I know the way, I shall be home in ten minutes. And you . . . you can go to sleep."

They were both silent, looking at one another. Leo, after that momentary flare-up of desire, was now in truth extremely sleepy, and nothing could have been more repugnant to him than the idea of getting up and going out into the street with Carla, perhaps in the rain; besides, it would mean getting the car out. He smiled at her, put out his hand and stroked her cheek. "Well, well," he said, "in spite of all your whims you're really a splendid little girl. Seriously, then, I can allow you to go by yourself?"

"Of course," she said, rising to her feet. Leo's tone irritated her. "Of course you needn't come. In fact, I beg you not to."

"Anyhow," Leo went on, as though talking to himself, "as you see, I tried to insist up to the last moment. If I don't go with you it's not because I want to sleep, but because, as you pointed out, it might be compromising. So don't come to me later on and say . . ." But he broke off; Carla was no longer in the room; she had gone out to fetch her hat. It's all to the good, thought Leo. It pleases me and it pleases her. So we're both content.

After a moment she came back. She had on her hat and her raincoat, and was carrying her umbrella, she drew on one glove with a preoccupied expression, and hunted in vain through all her pockets for the other. "Never mind," she said at last, "I must have lost it. . . . By the way," she added without any embarrassment, going across to him, "can you give me some money for a taxi? I haven't got any."

Leo's jacket was hanging over a chair not far from the bed. He reached out and took a handful of silver from the pocket. "Here you are," he said, holding it out to her.

I'm beginning to earn my living, Carla could not help thinking. She went over to the bed and stooped down. "See you later, my dear," she said to Leo almost affectionately, as if to make up for that unkind thought of hers, and they kissed. "Mind you shut the door properly," Leo called to her. He watched her cautiously leave the room, and waited for a moment to hear the outside door bang; but not a sound reached his ears. Then he put out the light, turned towards the wall and went to sleep again.

11

LEO'S SLEEP WAS haunted by the dismal presences of dawn, those presences that hover around people who sleep in the morning, when the sun is shining and light filters into the untidy room from every side, like water into a leaky ship. The presences came and went—Carla, her mother, Michele, with gestures complaisant and obscene; but their figures were pale, as though the light outside had discolored them. Even as he slept, Leo made every effort to detain them. "I must not wake up," he repeated half-consciously, "I must not wake up"; but a poetic, distant voice, full of feeble reproach, kept calling to him from some remote place: "Leo, Leo, wake up, it's me." Still half-consciously, he deluded himself that it was only a dream, and, with eyes obstinately closed, wrapping himself as well as he could in the blankets, he hoped, once that momentary confusion had dispersed, to enter all over again into the close, delicious tangle of sleep. But the calls were repeated, clearer and clearer, and finally a hand shook him by the shoulder. He opened his eyes and saw Mariagrazia.

At first he thought he had made some mistake, then he looked again and—yes, indeed, there could be no doubt—it was his mistress, dressed in gray, with a hat on her head and a fur around her neck, standing beside the bed. The shades of night had fled from the room and it was evidently a fine day, for cheerful splashes of sunshine lay here and there upon the dim and dusty furniture.

"You—here?" he said at last. "And how did you get in?"

"I came to leave you a note," answered Mariagrazia, "but I found the door open and so I came in."

Leo looked at her in astonishment. The door open? he thought. Ah, of course . . . that must have been Carla. He yawned and stretched, quite at his ease. "And what have you come to say to me?" he asked.

She sat down on the bed, in the half-darkness that was streaked with threads of light creeping between the slats of the shutters.

"I wanted to telephone you," she began, "but as we haven't paid the account for two months they've cut us off. Last night you promised that we should meet tomorrow. But then I thought it over——wouldn't you be free this afternoon?"

Leo clasped his arms round his knees. "This afternoon?" he repeated. This suggestion did not displease him, for he calculated that if he could rid himself that same day of the embarrassment of the mother, he would have all the rest of the week free for the daughter, but to be safe from possible surprises, he was unwilling to make any promises.

"Listen," he said. "I'll come around and see you after lunch. I'll be able to tell you by that time. Is that all right?"

"Yes, that's all right."

A long silence ensued. Mariagrazia, full of mistrust and discontent, looked around the room, examining carefully the pieces of furniture she knew so well, and then turned to her lover. His face seemed pale and rather troubled; this, and the fact of having found him still fast asleep, were quite enough to confirm her jealous suspicions. He's spent the night with Lisa, she figured. There's no doubt about it. I daresay Lisa was here a short time ago. A feeling of harsh spitefulness assailed her, and she threw a poisonous, reproachful glance at her lover.

"Personally," she said in a bitter-sweet tone of voice, "if I were in your place, I shouldn't behave as if I were twenty."

"What d'you mean?" asked Leo, dumbfounded.

"What I mean," replied Mariagrazia, "is that you're getting old and you don't realize it. You don't even realize that you can't any longer afford to commit follies like those you probably committed last night. Look at yourself in the glass," she added, raising her voice, "do please look at your eyes, and what a dreadful color you are, and how ghastly you look. Do please take a good look at yourself."

"I—getting old? And what follies?" repeated Leo, irritated above all by this direct allusion to his approaching middle age. "What follies are you talking about?"

"I know quite well what I'm talking about," she answered, with a wave of the hand, "and you know what I'm telling you—that in a year or two, at most, they'll be taking you about in a bath-chair. You certainly won't be able to walk."

Leo shrugged his shoulders angrily. "If you've come to talk this sort of nonsense to me, you'd better go away." He looked at the clock on the bedside table. "Twelve o'clock! And here I am, listening to you, when I have an appointment at half past. Go away, go away at once." He jumped out of bed, thrust his feet into his slippers, went over to the window and pulled back the shutter; the room was flooded with light.

"And my dressing-gown—don't you wear it?" demanded the Signora, without moving from the bed. "Or perhaps you've already given it away, to one of your casual lady friends?"

Leo made no reply, but went into the bathroom. Mariagrazia rose, and out of curiosity and because she had nothing to do, started wandering around the room. "And that other present of mine, that magnificent Murano vase—it seems to have disappeared. Have you given that away too?" she called out. Again there was no reply. From the bathroom came the sound of running water; Leo was taking a shower.

Discouraged but not defeated, Mariagrazia continued her inspection. Each object in that room brought back pleasant memories to her, and she sighed as she contrasted her present misery with those happy times now departed. The sight of her own photograph on top of the chest-of-drawers restored her confidence slightly. Really and truly it's only me that he

[190]

loves, she thought. When he's unwell or has some trouble, it's always to me that he turns. This is only a momentary coldness. He'll come back. She had pinned to her breast a bunch of violets that she had bought on the way over, and now, out of gratitude and with the idea of performing a kind action, she arranged the flowers in a little vase beside the photograph. Then she went into the bathroom.

Leo, in a dressing-gown, was shaving. "I'll leave you now," she said to him. "And . . . by the way . . . when you come this afternoon, pretend you haven't seen me—just as if I had really sent you a note. . . . Agreed?"

"Yes, yes, all right," he said, without turning round.

Satisfied, Mariagrazia left him. She went hastily down the stairs and out of the building; at the corner of the street she took a streetcar that was going towards the center of the city. Lisa must have been waiting for her for twenty minutes already, at the hat shop where they had arranged to meet to examine the new Paris models. . . . She sat in a corner by the window, turning her back as much as she could on the common people in the tram and looking out into the street. The pavements were crowded with a lively throng of workers going back to their homes, the cold February sunshine lit up their faces, reddened by the icy wind, beneath the worn brims of discolored, shapeless hats, and their figures in overcoats that had turned greenish from long use. It was a white and hazy sunshine, and it spread itself generously over all these rags as though it wished to give them its blessing. One after another the bright shops filed past, with their lettering in red, white or blue paint on the windows; electric signs hanging from the cornices, gray and dead, looked like ashen spectres; while the streetcar, many-colored, crowded, vulgar as a merry-go-round, advanced slowly, shaking and clanking. From time to time, under the eyes of the Signora, the shining, oblong hood of a car would come alongside with a swift movement, stop as if it were searching for a way through, with its big headlamps for eyes, then bound forward. She would see, behind a sheet of glass, a leather-clad chauffeur sitting in his place, his gloved hands on the wheel, and then, lolling on the leather cushions with a look of extreme satisfaction and a half-open eye lowered towards the crowd, some paunchy personage, or some delicate-faced, painted lady wrapped in voluminous furs. Unconsciously Mariagrazia would sigh, for she herself would never be able to drive through the ill-dressed crowd in a powerful, impressive car; her best years had vanished, her youth had fled in the shining car of her dreams. Then gradually these people that she envied, these ephemeral figures passing swift as arrows in their humming chariots, withdrew, also, from her fantasies and hopes, and, resigned, she continued on her way, with a kind of disgusted dignity, in the great painted wagon of iron and glass.

She found Lisa sitting in the back room of the shop, which was full of mirrors and new hats. In front of a pier-glass a young lady was conceitedly admiring herself, walking up and down and adopting haughty, affected attitudes; there was a sound of voices from the other room, and of glass doors shutting; the floor smelt of wax; the room was gray. In one corner was a pyramid of white cardboard boxes, large and small, some closed, others open; and in the opposite corner there had sprouted a thick vegetation of new hats, fresh, sober and delicate in color, each one perched on its separate wooden support.

As soon as she saw her, Lisa rose to her feet. "I'm so sorry," she said, "I'm really dreadfully sorry, but I can't stay with you. It's late, and I must get home."

The Signora looked at her suspiciously. "How selfish she is," she thought, "she's made her own choice and now she wants to hinder mine." "Well, I shall stay," she said aloud, with an undecided expression.

"Just as you like." And already Lisa was holding out her hand, when the other woman changed her mind.

"No, I shall come with you. The hats can wait for another day."

They went out together into the crowded street. "I'll go with you," said the Signora, "as far as the gardens, so we shall have time for a talk." Lisa did not answer. They walked on together, stopping frequently in front of shop windows, examining the goods in them, comparing prices. The jewellers' shops made the Signora feel melancholy. "I had a neck-lace like that one," she said, pointing with a sigh to a collar of pearls in their own case, "but it's gone now." Lisa looked but said nothing; her own jewels, too, had departed to remote destinations. But mine, she thought, were taken by my husband. At least I didn't sell them merely in order to live in some sort of comfort. And so they slowly came to the end of the street.

The Signora had accompanied her friend in order to be able to give vent to her suspicions about Leo; and then the crowd, the shops, the sunny morning had somewhat mitigated her spite. But when they came to the square, she saw Leo himself standing on the pavement in company with a gentleman dressed in black, and when he greeted her without looking at her and without interrupting his conversation, merely raising his hat very slightly—then her previous thoughts rushed back into her mind more tormentingly than ever.

She glanced at Lisa. No longer ago than last night, she thought, she was with him. This conclusion seemed to her irrefutable, she founded it upon the fact that, even to eyes more dispassionate than her own, it must be perfectly clear that "there was something" between those two. She looked at Lisa, examined her, and discovered that there was indeed a certain new kind of seductiveness about her, a look of physical zest that was undeniable though hard to define. This change was an indication—the Signora divined it with a morbid disgust—a sure indication of a love affair: there could be no doubt of it, it was visible in her face with the plump but delicate features that can often be seen in fair women; Lisa loved and was loved. By whom? *By Leo*, said the Signora to herself, and her jealousy, pursuing the fantasies of an indecent imagination, increased. No longer ago than last night, she thought. She found, in Lisa's moist eyes, in the sensitiveness of her nostrils, confirmation for her disgust. How could anyone love such a woman? she wondered, with genuine, if hysterical, horror. I couldn't even touch her, all full of heat, full of sex, as she is; she's not a woman, she's an animal. And her fingers curled with repugnance at the thought that Leo might have stroked and felt that body, that head, all that warm, palpitating mass.

A long, wide, straight, tree-lined avenue stretched before their eyes into the gray distance, between two rows of villas half-hidden in gardens; the trees—enormous planes—were bare, the air cold and still. There were few people walking along this deserted promenade; but large cars such as the Signora dreamed of kept passing with a sound like the rustling of silk, with a faint humming, over the smooth asphalt.

She was describing her preparations for the ball that was to take place that evening. "My Spanish costume suits my complexion marvellously well," she was saying. "I shall have a big comb—you know, one of those Andalusian combs. We've been invited to the Berardis' table. And how about you . . . will you be there?"

"Me?" said Lisa, looking down, "*Me* at the ball? I've no one to go with." She paused, anxiously awaiting her friend's reply. She thought the Signora ought to invite her to this ball; she knew the Berardis. She would dress up somehow or other, and she would drink and enjoy herself. Then, at the end, she would ask the Signora to leave Michele with her (she liked to treat him as a boy), she would get him to take her home, very late at night, and they would have jokes together, and she would spur him on and excite him; they would go home in a closed car with no lights inside. . . . It was a long drive, through dark streets; they would have time both to talk and to be silent, in fact to come to an understanding; and at the door she would invite him to come up and have a little glass of liqueur or a cup of tea before he started out again on such a cold night.

This program pleased her because of the inevitability of the things that would have to happen: it would be impossible for Michele to refuse to come up to her flat, quite impossible.

But now the Signora was speaking. She had thought over her reply, and, like all those who imagine themselves to be in possession of dangerous reserves of craftiness, she put so little of it into her words that it went unobserved. "You've plenty of friends," she said, with intention. "Get one of them to take you."

"You are my only friend," answered Lisa, who wanted at all costs to be invited. "I've nobody but you."

"Thank you—very kind of you to say so."

"By whom were you invited? By the Berardis? But I know them too," Lisa continued, "of course I know them. We went on our summer holiday together."

"Oh! Really?"

"And who is going with you two?" Lisa asked ingenuously.

"Le-o," replied the Signora, pronouncing each syllable separately, "will be at another table. The Berardis are taking us."

What does Leo matter to me? thought Lisa. "And will it be a brilliant affair?" she inquired.

"Very brilliant indeed."

They were silent for a moment. "I should like to go . . ." Lisa began again, in an off-hand manner, looking straight in front of her, "and to see the Berardis, too. It's such a long time since we've met. Over two years, I daresay."

"Ah! It's really the Berardis you want to see?" The Signora became nervous and started tapping the pavement with the tip of her umbrella. "Really *them?*"

"Yes," said Lisa, without looking at her, speaking as though she were searching her memory. "Pippo, Mary, Fanny . . . are they all well?"

"Yes, perfectly well. You needn't be afraid, their health is in no danger."

There was silence again. What is it? thought Lisa, looking at her friend's slightly flushed face, what's the matter with her now? She had at last noticed the Signora's nervousness, and attributed to it a meaning unfavorable to her own wishes. How selfish she is! she thought bitterly. She understood from the very first word that I should like to go, and, simply in order to be nasty to me, she won't invite me. She felt rather discouraged, but made a final effort.

"I must confess to you, Mariagrazia," she murmured in a cajoling sort of voice, "that I should very much like to go to this ball. I don't want to bother you—but could you possibly take me with you to the Berardis' table?" She paused, and saw the other woman laugh.

"Ha! That's a fine idea," said the Signora, between gasps of bitter laughter. "Is that what I ought to do? Thank you so much, my dear, for your delicate thought, thank you really and truly, but I can't undertake services of that kind."

"What services?" began Lisa, irritated, at last understanding the point of all these ironical remarks. But the other woman interrupted her.

"Well, d'you really want me to tell you?" she asked. "I understand the whole thing: it's not for me or for the Berardis that you want to come to the dance, but for somebody else, somebody else that interests you."

"How can that matter to you?"

"Exactly," said the Signora, shaking her head bitterly, "exactly. How indeed should all this matter to me? It matters nothing, nothing, absolutely nothing. Fundamentally you're quite right. How should it matter to me that people rob me and kill me? Nothing, nothing, and still nothing." She paused for a moment, enjoying the poisonous taste of her thoughts, then went on again. "And all this happens because I'm kind-hearted, far too kind-hearted. . . . If I'd stamped on you properly, the first time"—and she made a gesture of crushing something—"this wouldn't happen now."

"*Stamped* on me? On *me?* Are you crazy, Mariagrazia? Are you crazy?"

Quarrelling, the two women walked along the empty pavement. The Signora was wearing a gray dress, Lisa a brown; they both had fox furs round their necks, Lisa's a tawny one, the Signora's silver. They walked as they quarrelled; and the shining cars drove by, and a few couples passed them, young, elegant. Gray and gold: gray were the figures of the passers-by, whether near or far, gray the long gardens behind the railings, the deserted avenue, the plane-trees; golden the new, cold sun, still numbed by the winter frost, dripping light and water from its melting icicles, laughing and frigid like a convalescent, wrapped in cotton-wool, this golden sun, in the blue cotton-wool of the February sky.

The Signora continued her monologue.

"Too kind-hearted!" said Lisa, with a high, contemptuous laugh, "too kind-hearted—you!"

A moment's silence. "And yet," said the Signora, leaving her friend's side and looking straight ahead as if she wished to speak to a third person, "I really can't understand how men manage to make love to *some* women. That's what I can't understand."

"That's exactly what I say, too." Lisa turned pale, and her lips trembled. Why should her friend feel she must be so hard and pitiless? She had not done her any harm. And it was deplorable that a mother should take notice of her own son merely in order to injure a former rival; why in the world should it matter to Mariagrazia that she should go to a dance in order to meet Michele? And since it was perhaps the first time in her life that Lisa found herself being wrongly accused, her resentment was immense and inexhaustible. By contrast with such monstrous injustice, she felt she had gone back to the time of her innocence, that she had the soul of an angel and a pair of wings, as well as a martyr's halo. She loved Michele, Michele loved her, and how could anyone possibly find material for reprobation and scandal in a story so wholly pure?

"And yesterday evening," went on the Signora, "how did things go yesterday evening? Well—eh? He wouldn't stay with *us*, he was sleepy, he ran away. Naturally; *you* were expecting him." She paused a moment. "You know what I say?" she burst out, turning back towards Lisa, "that you ought to be ashamed of yourself!" She twisted her painted lips in disgust, looking haughtily at her friend. "You're no longer so very young."

"We're almost exactly the same age. You're slightly older than I am," replied Lisa gently, without raising her head.

"No indeed, Madam!" restorted the Signora with authority. "It's quite a different thing. I am a widow. You, on the other hand, are still a married woman. Your husband is still alive. Ashamed of yourself—that's what you ought to be!"

They were passing close to a villa with shuttered windows. Behind the house, which was surrounded by big, bare trees, a game of badminton was evidently in progress; the sharp sound of the players' strokes could be heard echoing loudly in the silence of the noonday sky, as though, with each stroke, something had burst up there behind the blueness. And when the wind scattering the white smoke from the roof-tops blew in the direction of the street the players' loud, cheerful voices sounded.

Lisa stopped for a moment to listen thoughtfully to this echo. Then she looked at Mariagrazia, and wondered at her. Was it really possible that that enraged, jealous face was a re-flection of . . . maternal love? And what kind of maternal love was it that drove to this point of fury a woman who had never shown herself excessively tender towards her children? Was it not rather a form of carnal jealousy, the jealousy of a mistress? Suddenly she understood. Her first feeling was one of relief, then she looked at the Signora and her doubts re-turned.

"Mariagrazia," she said; "tell me, you're speaking of . . . of Leo, aren't you?" She saw her friend nod her head with an embarrassed and pained expression that seemed to say: Why ask me? You know quite well. . . . I've no one but him. They looked at each other, and there was a great relief, a kind of triumphant pity in Lisa's eyes. "My poor Mariagrazia," she said; and she could have explained, exculpated herself, smooth away the furrow of suspicion from her friend's face. "My poor Mariagrazia," she repeated. Memories now came back to her, and she saw again the scene of the previous day, with the candle, and Leo and Carla embracing. She felt a certain compassion for her misguided friend, but at the same time so great a joy and contentment at not being guilty of the thing she was accused of that she did not know how to speak to her, whether with contempt or pity.

"You can be quite sure," she said at last, "you can be quite sure. I didn't have a meeting with Leo either yesterday or . . . or ever; that I can swear to you, on all that I hold most sacred."

Without speaking, the Signora went on scrutinizing her with inquisitive, suspicious eyes.

"Believe me," added Lisa, ill at ease under the other woman's stare, "it's been a misunderstanding."

The Signora bent her head. "We'd better leave each other now," she said, with a studied attempt to appear cool, controlled and very dignified. "It's late." The sharp sounds of the badminton game and the players' voices came to them. The Signora took a few steps forward.

"Believe me," repeated Lisa hesitatingly, "a misunderstanding." She looked around, as though searching some support for her arguments. The avenue was deserted, and the sunshine emphasized the solitude, lighting up the empty pavement until it was lost to view. Lisa looked round and stood still; but Mariagrazia went slowly away, step by step, looking down on the ground, with a thoughtful, absent-minded air. Believe me, Lisa would have liked to call after her, it's with Carla that Leo is deceiving you, with your own daughter, my poor Mariagrazia, not with me. But the Signora's slightly bent back showed her stubborn determination not to turn towards the truth. Lisa watched her grow smaller and smaller, lose color as she passed through the flood of bright sunshine, become fused with the receding shadows of the high garden railings; finally she was nothing more than a black speck, at the far end of the avenue.

12

WHY HAD LISA at first almost admitted that she was guilty
and then protested her innocence? Anyone else would have
been perplexed when confronted with this question—but not
the Signora: for her, all was clear as crystal, quite easily explained, for she had a profound conviction that Lisa was a
hypocrite and a liar. She did not know why—it was her face,
her words, her demeanor. It was an ancient conviction that
must have had its origin in some forgotten incident, but it
was so integral a part of the Signora's moral picture of Lisa
that to abolish it would have been tantamount to obliterating
her friend's figure from her mind.

Lisa, then, was a liar and a hypocrite, and so all was clear.
Why had she said to her, almost with compassion, "My poor
Mariagrazia?" Obviously in order to mock her and make fun
of her, or, at most, to commiserate with her on her blindness,
her ingenuousness, the monstrous faithlessness of her lover.
Why had she shown such a desire to go to the dance with
her and the Berardis? It was transparent: a Machiavellian
attempt to deceive her and make her believe that she was not
expecting Leo that evening. Lisa, in fact, with her habitual
falsity, had thought up a thousand stratagems in order to
confuse her; and had she succeeded? Oh no, it could not be

said that she had; far more than that was needed to deceive her, Mariagrazia, far more indeed. "Disillusion yourself, darling, I may be a fool . . . but not to that extent. The time is past when I believe everybody to be good and sweet and affectionate and kind. Now I keep my eyes well open, and no longer allow myself to be caught out. Ah no! my dear. . . . Once is enough. So disillusion yourself, my pet, I've seen through the whole thing. You're not taking me in; I'm too clever, I'm far too clever for that." As she talked thus to herself, she shook her head with great self-satisfaction and smiled, putting on an expression of bitter, mocking superiority. What most irritated her was the idea that her friend might believe her to be infected with simplicity and naïveté, and as she walked she screwed up her eyes and ground her teeth with rage. She had never felt so ruthless. If Lisa had been dying of thirst she would have refused her a last glass of water, if of hunger, a last mouthful of food, if her friend had been reduced to sudden poverty, she might have gone down on her knees and kissed her hand, but she would not have given her one single penny; nothing. And if she had been on the point of death and had summoned her to her bedside, she would certainly have left her to die all alone like a dog, yes, to perish alone in her filthy bed, with her face turned to the wall, in her empty room. Besides all this, the Signora felt capable of sticking pins into her, of torturing her, of dragging her along by the hair and stamping with the heels of her shoes on her belly, her breast, her face. She would have been capable of anything; never in her life had she felt so utterly, so voluptuously spiteful.

But . . . but was not forgiveness the finest vengeance? Yes, but what kind of forgiveness? The affectionate, loving, joyful kind? Or the other—cold and contemptuous, thrown in the face like a penny to a beggar?

The second, of course. Lisa ruining herself, running up debts, growing poor, becoming ragged and destitute and being deserted by everybody; or perhaps, after a serious illness, being left thin and ugly and gray-haired, and possibly—for such things do happen—feeble-minded, half-witted, perhaps even blind. A fleshless face, with blank, staring eyes and a bewildered forehead, knocking into the furniture, into other people. The finger of God, the punishment of Heaven—such things do happen. And then she would forgive her. But slowly, wait a moment; she would forgive her—yes; but only *half*—with contempt, coldness, forgetting nothing, humiliating her and not allowing her to come too near, as if to make her see that she was no longer worthy even of her hatred. And how would this act of forgiveness come about? Let us see . . . yes. . . . An evening when she was giving a party . . . a noisy band playing dance music . . . dancing couples passing and repassing in front of the gilded doors of her drawing-rooms. Under blazing chandeliers, in front of the buffet, in intimate corners, in the great halls, on the terraces where people could lean on marble balustrades and watch the moon rising behind the black points of the pine-trees—here all the best society would be gathered together. It was the culminating moment, when conversation and music are fused together into a single uproar, when passions take fire, when flowers fade, when gallant declarations are murmured into ladies' ears. Then a maid would come and whisper to her: "The Signora Lisa is here." She would rise at once. . . . No, she would keep her waiting a bit, and would then make an excuse and go out. She would go into the vestibule, full of hats and coats piled one on top of the other; not a chair free; and in the midst of all these rich garments she would find Lisa standing, poorly dressed, looking older by at least ten years, and Lisa, as soon as she saw her, would come to meet her with arms outstretched. Gently, gently now, my dear. . . . And, distances having been re-established, she would listen magnanimously to her confused excuses, her protests of friendship. Then, in a very chilly, superior manner, she would reply: "Yes, I forgive you, it's all right. But you'll have to be patient, you'll have to wait here or upstairs in the anteroom. You see, I'm entertaining a large number of people to whom I can't introduce you. Society people, you understand? aristocrats . . . people who don't care to meet just anybody, people who belong to a very select circle. Well then, that's understood, you'll go upstairs and wait for me." And she would leave her to wait the whole of that long evening. . . . At last, very late that night, she would appear before the unfortunate creature as she cowered in the dark and in her own wretchedness, she herself wearing her most brilliant smile and her most sumptuous dress. "So sorry, Lisa," she would say, "but this evening I simply can't stay with you. Come back tomorrow. Perhaps tomorrow. . . ." And with a burst of laughter she would go out. And who would be waiting for her at the door, beside a colossal car, with eight cylinders, a nickel-plated hood, and two chauffeurs, and all lined with satin?—Leo. And the two of them, diverted by this reappearance on the part of Lisa, would go off into the night.

These cinema pictures galloping ceaselessly across the screen of her mind comforted the Signora, but at intervals when she raised her eyes the landscape and the sunshine broke into her thoughts. Then she realized that she was the usual Mariagrazia and that she was as remote from these dreams as from the Indies, and that she was walking all alone through empty suburban streets. At last she found herself in front of the villa; she pushed open the half-closed iron gate and went in.

She crossed the drive hurriedly. She felt tired, but did not know whether this was the result of her quarrel with Lisa or from the sense of emptiness that always stayed with her when she abandoned herself to her fantasies. In the ante-room she found Michele sitting smoking in an armchair.

"I'm dead tired," she said, feebly pulling off her hat. "Where's Carla?"

"She's out," answered Michele. Mariagrazia left the room.

Michele was in a bad humor. The happenings of the previous evening had left him in a state of discontent and morbid depression. He realized that the time would come when he must overcome his indifference and take action; and yet there was no doubt whatever that such action was suggested to him by a logic which had nothing to do with real feeling. Filial love, hatred for his mother's lover, family affection—all these were feelings that he did not know. Yet what did that matter? When one isn't sincere one must pretend, and

[203]

if one pretends long enough one ends by believing; that is the principle upon which all faith is founded.

In short, was not some artificial device, some stratagem, required?

Yes indeed, a stratagem, that was it. Now take Lisa, for example, Michele thought. I don't love her. I don't even desire her. However, last night I kissed her hand, today I'm going to her flat. At first I shall be as cold as ice, then I shall get excited, I shall deceive myself. It's ridiculous—but I believe that by that method I may become her lover.

For him, faith, sincerity, a sense of the tragic, no longer existed; everything, seen through the veil of his boredom, appeared pitiful, ridiculous, artificial. But he understood the difficulties and dangers of his situation, and that he must needs be deeply affected by something or other, must take action and suffer, must conquer his feebleness, his softness, his falseness, his sense of the absurd, that he must develop a serious view of life and be sincere in his feelings.

What a beautiful world it must have been, he thought with ironical regret, when a wronged husband could cry to his faithless wife: "Wicked woman! With your life you shall pay the penalty of your gilt!"—and, even better, not merely think such a thing but then hurl himself into action and kill them all—wife and lover and relations and the whole pack of them, and suffer neither punishment nor remorse; when thought was followed by action. "I hate you!"—and pht! a stab with a dagger, and there was your enemy or your friend lying on the floor in a pool of blood—when people didn't think so much, and the first impulse was always a good one; when life was not ridiculous, as it is now, but tragic, and death was death indeed, and people killed and hated and loved seriously, and shed real tears for real woes, and all men were made of real flesh and blood and rooted in reality as trees are in the earth. Gradually his irony vanished and his regret remained; he wished he could have lived in that tragic, honest age, have felt those vast, overwhelming hatreds, risen to those unlimited heights of feeling. But here he was on the earth, in his own time and his own life.

He meditated and smoked. There was only one cigarette

left in the package on the table; he had been sitting for almost two hours in the anteroom. He had got up late and dressed himself with minute care: ties, suits, shirts—how many cares they represented, how many intentions to comfort himself in his miseries by raising himself to the glossy aesthetic standards of the English fashion-plate! He liked the gentlemen standing beside their sport cars, their loose-fitting overcoats, their smooth faces muffled in warm woolen scarves, their commonplace but elegant settings, with a cottage buried beneath the foliage of trees as round and rolling and soft as clouds; he was charmed by their gestures, the way their ties were tied, the hang of their clothes, the tweeds they wore.

He was sitting in his armchair in a noble, elegant attitude. His legs were crossed, his trousers pulled up to exactly the right height over his woolen socks, and his carefully brushed, glossy head bent slightly to one side towards the cigarette he held languidly between two fingers. On his soft, clean-shaven, oval face gleams of irony alternated with sudden over-cloudings, like light and shade on the face of a statue. He smoked and meditated.

Carla came in from her tennis, walking slowly up the stairs. She was wearing a many-colored sweater above her white pleated skirt, and she carried a coat, a racquet and a net full of tennis balls over her arm. She smiled. "Where is Mom?" she cried.

She stopped in front of Michele. "I met Pippo Berardi," she said. "We're both invited to dinner, Mom and I. Then they'll take us on to the dance. If you want to, you can join us there." She paused; Michele smoked and said not a word.

"What's the matter with you?" she asked, feeling herself stared at; "why d'you look at me like that?" Her voice sounded nervous, in the empty anteroom, as if it were delivering some strange kind of challenge, full of melancholy and hope; her new life was beginning, and everyone must know it; but her momentary energy was shot through with a feeling of discomfort that weakened her and made her long to close her eyes, fold her arms on her breast and plunge into the blackness of a deep and vacant sleep.

Her mother came into the room. "Oh, Mom," said Carla

[205]

dreamily, in a less cheerful tone than before, "the Berardis have asked us to dinner . . . and . . . and then they'll take us on to the dance."

"Very well," replied her mother, without enthusiasm; her nose was red and frozen-looking, the skin of her face shiny and powderless, and an icy glance shone from between her eyelids. "In that case," she added, "we shall have to get dressed early."

She sat down. "And you, Michele," she said, looking at him, "I want to talk to you."

Carla went out. "To *me?*" repeated Michele, pretending to be immensely surprised; "to me? What about?"

His mother shook her head. "You know better than I do. . . . Last night you threw an ash-tray at Leo. It so happened that it hit me; I've still got the mark of it." She raised her hand as if she were about to bare her shoulder; but her son stopped her.

"No," he said with disgust, "no thank you. Don't let's have any pointless exhibitionism. I'm not Leo." There was silence. His mother pursed her lips and her eyes darkened; she remained with her hand to her breast, in an attitude full of dignity, like a Madonna pointing to her own pierced heart, and her gesture, which had started by being ridiculous, almost acquired profound significance. It was as though she wished to display some other wound besides the one produced by the ash-tray—what could it be? Michele could not have told; and now her attitude became disarranged and she began to speak.

"I want to try and be kind to you," she said in a changed voice. "What's the matter with you, Michele, what's the matter?"

"Nothing's the matter." The boy's discomfort was increasing. She ought to know what's the matter, he thought, disturbed and exasperated. His mother's tearful voice made him shudder. If she goes on like this, she'll become ridiculous and pathetic, pathetic and ridiculous. She must be stopped, at all costs, from giving vent to her romantic nonsense. I don't want to see her weeping, or screaming, or supplicating. At any cost.

"Michele," she went on, "do your mother a favor."

"A thousand, if you like," he replied, with an amiable expression.

"Well then," she said, deceived by his irony and calming down a little, "give me proof of it. For instance, be a little more friendly towards Leo—or at least pretend to be. That's all I ask."

They were silent for a moment, looking at each other. "And what about him?" asked Michele, with a face that had suddenly gone hard. "Is he friendly towards me?"

"*He?*" she burst out, with a positively youthful smile that was touching in its ingenuousness and self-deception, "he loves you like a father."

"Well—really!" exclaimed the boy in astonishment. Such trustfulness, such lack of understanding were discouraging. There's nothing to be done, he thought, as long as we stay like this, my life doesn't belong to me, but to her. And to his mother belonged, also, that distorted world, so false, so bitterly grotesque, that world in which for him, and for his clear-sightedness, there was no place.

"*He!*" she cried again, with her clear, triumphant laugh. "He's the kindest-hearted man on earth!" Ah, well, all right, there was nothing more to be said; the earth itself, outraged, ceased to rotate, and Michele, resigned, was silent.

"Often," his mother went on, "he talks to me about you, about his worries, his hopes."

"Very kind of him," broke in the boy.

"Don't you believe it?" asked his mother. "Look. No longer ago than the day before yesterday he was telling me about his plans for you two, you and Carla. You ought to have heard him, and you would have realized then how far that man's kind-heartedness goes. 'I know quite well,' he said to me,"—and here her face took on a sorrowful expression, as if she were going to recite a prayer—"'that Michele doesn't love me very much, but it doesn't matter. I like him all the same. In a short time, as soon as Carla's married, he'll have to start working too. And then'—listen—'then there'll be no lack of recommendations and help and encouragement on my side.'"

"Did he say that?" asked Michele, interested. His mistrust

gave way before such seductions, as a woman of easy virtue
gives way, with a smile of complaisance, when she feels her
bosom and hips being pinched. Supposing it were true, he
thought, supposing Leo really wanted to help me to achieve
something, to become . . . rich? This hope brought with it,
flashing across his heated imagination, a picture of all the
things he most desired and envied—expensive women with
costly smiles, travelling, staying in hotels, an intense life
divided between business and hectic amusements; it was like a
film, with a procession of lofty cities and all their wealth,
of distant landscapes, of adventures, of the most beautiful
women and the most fortunate men, all passing across the
screen, to the accompaniment of triumphal, nostalgic music
from the orchestra, in front of the staring eyes of the multitude. The film of his ambitions moved faster and faster to
the quickened rhythm of his deluded heart. On the screen
of his imagination the images followed each other, joined
and mingled and passed each other. It was the wild race of
his hopes, taking the breath away, making the heart tremble,
deluding, and then finally melting away, leaving nothing but
the mediocre reality—exactly as in the theatre, when the lights
go on and the spectators look at one another with bleak, disenchanted faces.

Supposing it were true, he repeated to himself, *supposing
it were true!*

"That's what he said," continued his mother, "and lots of
other things too."

She was silent for a moment. "He's good-hearted," she said
again, gazing straight in front of her as though she could
see Leo and his goodness standing there side by side in the
middle of the room. "He's truly good. Of course, even *he*
has his failings, but let him who hasn't cast the first stone.
One mustn't judge from appearances. He's a man of few
words, he's brusque, he doesn't say all he thinks, he hides
his own feelings—one has to know him in an intimate sort
of way. . . ."

As you do, thought Michele, amused and irritated.

". . . to understand how expansive, how gay, how affectionate he can be. I still remember," she added, with a smile

[208]

of tenderness, "how he used to take you on his knee, you and Carla, when you were little, and fill your mouths and hands with chocolates. Or sometimes I used to come upon him by surprise, playing with you both, Michele, playing with you as if he had been a child himself."

The boy smiled with pity for her. "Tell me," he asked, in order to escape the full flood of these touching and familiar reminiscences. "Did he really say he would help me?"

"Of course," answered his mother uncertainly, "of course he'll help you. As soon as you've taken your degree. . . . He has so many acquaintances, so many friends in high positions." And she raised her hand as though to indicate the pinnacles upon which these acquaintances of her lover's sat, very upright and haughty. "Of course he'll help you."

"Ah! he really will help me?" A smile of satisfaction hovered about his lips. That good, excellent Leo! His mother was right. He was, in truth, a practical man, brusque if you like, but with a heart of gold. One fine day he would go and say to him, "Listen, Leo. Give me a note to so-and-so—you know, that important person." Or, "Please, Leo, could you possibly lend me a hundred thousand lire?" And Leo would say: "Certainly, at once, Michele. Sit down. Here's the note. . . . Here's the money. . . . D'you want it in cash or by check? And, whenever you need anything," he would add affectionately, going with him to the door and patting him encouragingly on the shoulder, "just come to me. You know I promised your mother to help you on in life . . . always and wherever you may be." Ah, Leo, Leo! Strong, reliable, good-hearted man! His heart was swelling, now, with feelings of friendship and affection. A thousand memories came back to him, a thousand incidents in which Leo figured as modest, practical, reliable and generous, all bedewed with good humor, good sense and kindness, a figure now serious, now gay, but never ridiculous; a figure sometimes mischievous, sometimes cross, but fatherly, exemplary.

"Yes," went on his mother, growing more and more triumphant, "yes, he'll help you, but only on condition that you're nicer to him. Otherwise he may end by taking offense. Look at Carla, for instance; never a word too much, or a gesture out of place. And he . . . he's taken a great affection to her."

"Ah, he's taken an affection to her?" put in Michele, with a nervous smile.

"Certainly, he's taken such an affection to her that he always thinks of her as a daughter. For instance, he realizes that we must get her married—now or never—and he's taking the matter up. If you only knew how much he thinks about it! Why, just yesterday, when we were dancing, he spoke to me about it. He was saying that Pippo Berardi would be a good match."

"He's so ugly!" Michele exclaimed.

"Ugly but very nice. As you see," his mother concluded, "we must stick tight to our Leo."

Our Leo! repeated the boy to himself, with a shiver of pleasure.

"And we mustn't drive him away by rude behavior, or worse, by throwing ash-trays at him." Completely reassured, she took Michele's hand. "Then you promise me," she said, "you promise me you'll be nicer to Leo?" Her voice trembled with sudden, sincere emotion, her heart opened like a box filled with love which she longed to pour out, under the stress of her tenderness, over everybody—Leo, Carla, Michele, Pippo Berardi. . . . "You promise me, Michelino?" she repeated. For her, this diminutive represented childhood, the little bright-eyed boy, the years long past, her own youth. It was Michelino, not Michele, who was her son.

"Yes, of course," answered the boy, writhing with discomfort under those eyes shining with emotion, "yes, I promise." He understood now, too late, that, in spite of all his clearsightedness, he had lost himself in the tangle of his mother's passions, as in a sunless forest.

Carla came in. "What are you doing?" she asked. "I thought you were at lunch."

"Not at all," said Michele, who had already repented of his promise. "We were talking. . . ."

"Yes," his mother explained loquaciously, "I was saying to him that he ought to be nicer to Leo. Don't you think I'm right, Carla? He's so good to us, in various ways, he's an old family friend, one might almost say he's watched you grow up. He oughtn't to be treated just like anyone else."

Standing erect and motionless in the middle of the room, Carla looked at her mother; and then, for the first time, seeing her so blind and so inoffensive, she realized that she had betrayed her. What would you say, she thought, if you knew the truth?

"*I* think," she answered finally, in a deep voice, half-closing her eyes, "I think one ought to be nice to everybody."

"There you are!" exclaimed her mother joyfully; "Carla agrees with me. Come over here, Carla," she added with sudden tenderness, "come here and let me look at you." She took her by the arm, made her sit on the arm of her chair, passed her hand over her cheeks. "My dear daughter," she said, "you look a little pale. Did you sleep well?"

"Very well indeed."

"*I* didn't," said her mother. "I had a terrible dream. There seemed to be a very fat gentleman sitting in a corner. I walked up and down, thinking of various things, and finally I went up to him and asked him what time it was. He didn't answer. I thought he must be deaf, and I was just going away again, when I saw that his eyes were buried so deep in flesh that he could scarcely see. His eyelids were swollen, his forehead and his cheekbones almost met, and you could only just see something bright peeping out and moving between two folds of fat . . . really horrible. Feeling sorry for him, I asked him what was wrong and he answered that he was getting fatter and fatter and would end by not being able to see at all. 'You ought to eat less,' I said to him—or something like that— but he didn't answer. Then I thought that I ought to try to open his eyes for him, and I was already putting out my hand to pull apart that mass of fat that was obstructing his vision, when it began to snow. The snow fell so thickly and so violently that in a short time I couldn't see anything; my eyes and ears and hair were full of it; all I could do was stumble about and fall down and get up again, and I was so cold that my teeth were chattering. Then finally I woke up and found that the window had been blown wide open. . . . Wasn't it curious? They say that dreams can be explained.

[211]

I should very much like to know what was the meaning of this one."

"A winter dream," observed Michele. "Well, how about having lunch?"

They got up. "Really, Carla," her mother insisted, "you *are* very pale. Perhaps you overtired yourself at tennis?"

"No, no, Mom."

They went downstairs in silence.

They sat, the three of them in the cold dining-room, around the table which was too big for them; they ate without looking at one another, with the cool, deferential movements of priests celebrating a rite; they did not speak. The silence was scarcely broken by the faint tapping of spoons on soup-plates, which recalled the chilling sound of surgical instruments put into a bowl during an operation. The coldness, the lack of intimacy that this silence held, became irksome to the sociable, talkative Signora.

"What a silence!" she exclaimed at last, with a smile. "There must have been an angel passing through the room. Now tell me honestly, isn't it true that one misses Leo?"

"Of course," muttered Michele, deep in thought, "one misses Leo."

Carla lifted her head. You miss him now, she wanted to say, but how about the future? What will you do then, when you don't see him any more? She felt unsettled and disturbed, like someone who is on the point of departure and sits down at the family table for the last time, eating hastily and thinking of the coming journey. Her mother, on the other hand, looked as though she were settled in her own place forever, petrified in her present attitude and in the regretful words she had spoken. "One misses Leo," she would be saying the same thing in ten, twenty years' time, and every day she would be sitting there at the head of the table, grieving over her lost lover.

"It's an undeniable fact," she said now, as though someone had doubted her words, "that when Leo comes we seem to be much gayer. Yesterday, for example. What *didn't* he say? What *didn't* he do? He was inexhaustible!"

"If you really miss him so much," said Michele, with a

[212]

sarcastic smile, "if you really can't get on without him, why don't you invite him to come every day? In fact you might take him in as a boarder."

"What nonsense!" replied his mother, irritated, and discerning the irony in his remark. "I didn't mean to say that I couldn't live without him, certainly not. . . ." But it's the truth, Michele would have liked to put in.

". . . But merely that I like his company, because he's gay and charming and amusing . . . that's all I mean." She paused, and went on eating. "Let's talk about something else," she said at last. "Carla, who was it who gave you the invitation—Pippo or the others?"

"Pippo."

"Ah! he was at the tennis. And did he stay long with you?"

"Half an hour."

"Only half an hour?" repeated her mother, disappointed. "And . . . what did you talk about?"

"Nothing special," replied Carla, putting down her fork. "We were watching the game."

There was silence. The maid removed the plates and brought in others.

"And . . . what do you think of him?" her mother persisted.

"Hum . . . so-so," replied Carla vaguely.

"And you, Michele—how does he strike you?" she inquired.

"Ugly but very nice," was the answer, in the same words she had used a few minutes earlier. She looked round, dissatisfied, as though she wanted to hear someone else's opinion as well.

"He's an intelligent, cultivated young man, he's travelled a great deal, and he knows a great many people. I believe," she added, with heavy craftiness, "that he has a weakness for you, Carla."

"Oh! Really?"

"They must be rich," she went on, following the logic of her own ideas, "very rich."

And therefore, Michele felt like concluding, it would be

[213]

a good match. But he kept silent, observing all these errors calmly and curiously, as though they did not concern him and he were merely a remote, disinterested spectator.

"They have five cars," went on the Signora, obviously exaggerating.

"Ten," remarked Michele quietly, without looking up, "ten cars."

"No," Carla objected calmly, "they have three—Pippo one, the father one, and a little one for the girls."

The maid came in with a second dish, which was just in time to save the Signora's already jeopardized situation.

"Signora Berardi told me," she continued as she helped herself, "that she spends eighty thousand lire a year simply on clothes for Mary and Fanny."

There was obviously a slight exaggeration here too, but Michele did not draw attention to it—what could be the use of it, anyhow? There are some things that are beyond remedy.

"They have lovely clothes," admitted Carla without envy, but as if at the back of her mind she were coming to a melancholy conclusion about the poverty of her own wardrobe. Suddenly she was overcome by a feeling of pallid faintness: was it mist, was it the muslin curtains? The white, spectral languor flowing into the room from the veiled windows seemed to be crushing her trembling heart in an enormous, swollen hand made of cotton wool; at each squeeze the yielding cotton creaked; her eyes filled with mist, and everything around her went white, with a thick, flashing whiteness in which the solitary voices of her mother and Michele, stretched out in long-drawn vowels like a phonograph record running down, gradually disintegrating. Certain gestures from the past night were reconstructed in her mind. From the mist that quickly swallowed up his face and body, Leo's hand came forth and stroked her big, sensitive breasts, her narrow belly, and in spite of her utter immobility, she seemed to shudder. Finally the mist thinned away, and in a reality that was harder and more solid after these moments of surrender, her mother reappeared to her, and Michele, and the maid who was handing her the dish.

She refused it with a feeble gesture.

"How is it you're not eating, Carla?" asked her mother.

"I don't know." She was not hungry, among all the hungry things in her life. This room, in which she ought to have been feeding herself, had been feeding upon her; all the inanimate objects around her had, day by day, been sucking out her vitality with a tenacity far stronger than her own vain attempts to break away. The best of her blood was flowing now through the dark wood of the corpulent sideboards; the milk of her flesh had melted into the eternal whiteness of the air, and in the old mirror that hung opposite her place the image of her youth had been caught and imprisoned.

"Why, that's no explanation," objected her mother. She herself was eating with avidity, looking at each mouthful before she put it in her mouth. "The father," she went on, continuing her biography, "makes a lot of money."

"In industry," announced Michele, pouring himself some wine. "Raw and worked cottons and printed cottons."

"Ah yes! In industry! An intelligent, energetic man, who rose from nothing—a self-made man." She drank, wiped her lips, and finally gazed at Michele with a curious, blank expression of satisfaction. "He's a Commendatore," she said.

"Oh! Is he really?" said Michele, astonished. "Berardi a Commendatore? And why?"

"How should I know?" replied his mother, who had missed the point. "Perhaps he rendered some service to the State."

"But how? When? Where?" insisted Michele, with the greatest seriousness.

"Ah! I don't know," said his mother, bending her head. She went on eating, then raised her uncomprehending eyes.

"Yes," she repeated, with distant, dreamy haughtiness, "a Commendatore. Carla," she added brusquely, "I was watching you the other day while you were dancing with Pippo. I though you seemed cold, stiff. You were dancing like an automaton. And, in fact, he didn't ask you again."

"It wasn't I that was cold," replied Carla with spirit, "it was he that was too hot. He was making indecent remarks to me. And so I told him to shut up and we danced in silence."

Her mother shook her head incredulously. "Get on with you!" she said with a penetrating smile. "Whatever d'you mean, he said indecent things to you? It was just the usual nonsense that young men talk to girls. No, Carla," she added, "I believe you've taken a prejudice against him."

The maid came in with the fruit. Carla waited until she had gone out again, then took an apple and examined it.

"First of all," she said in a level voice, without raising her head, "he complimented me on your beauty."

"On *my* beauty!" exclaimed her mother, flattered.

"Yes. Then he asked if I would go to his studio. I asked him what he was studying, and he told me that he devoted himself particularly to the female nude."

"Well, what harm is there in that?" put in her mother, "considering that he's a painter."

"Wait a moment. Then I innocently asked him whether he went in for painting or drawing. He laughed, and said to me in that voice of his—you know, that affected voice— 'Signorina, I don't even know how to hold a pencil!' 'Oh! what do you do, then?' I asked him; and he laughed again. 'Come,' he said, 'come just the same. As for your nude, you can be sure that something will be done about it.' And at the same time he gave me—what do you call it?—the glad eye—" Here Carla interrupted her tale, stared with comic gravity at her astonished mother, and suddenly gave her a ridiculous kind of wink. "—Like that . . . And then he asked me if I would go. I gave him a sharp 'No.' And he . . . and he exclaimed, as if he was quite astounded, 'You don't mean to tell me it would be the first time?' You see? He thought I was quite used to . . . to going to studios; of course I didn't answer him, and that was the end."

A solemn silence ensued. The Signora, very haughty and slightly ridiculous, as though Pippo in person had just been lacking in respect to her and had insulted her, or—even worse —had knocked into her in such a way as to spoil one of her famous dignified attitudes—the Signora was the incarnation of surprise and indignation. Michele looked dreamily at Carla; this tale had caught him in a mood of indifference. He wanted to convince himself of Pippo's baseness and of

[216]

the offense he had given to his sister, but he could not manage to do so; all this eluded his examination, it remained foreign, remote from his sphere of vision. . . . It was as though he had tried to wax indignant over the fate of Lucretia, the young and beautiful and good—but such a long time ago—violated by the dissolute Tarquin. *Monstrous!* he said to himself; but at the same time he realized that he did not know precisely in what this monstrosity consisted.

At last his mother appeared to find the use of her tongue again. She twisted her lips in disgust and let fall the vehement word of abuse: "Scoundrel!"

"The fact of the matter is, Mom," Carla went on, without raising her head, "many people *do* say nasty things about me."

She was completely calm. Soon, she thought, the evil tongues would triumph; she would run off with Leo, or anyhow the affair would be discovered beyond remedy; that was what always happened. And so, with thoughts of resignation on the one hand and of scandal on the other, all faith in a new life appeared to be extinguished.

"Otherwise, Mom," she added sadly, "why should Pippo have spoken like that?"

Michele never took his eyes off his sister; she looked sad and inoffensive to him, but beyond this touching discovery he could not go. Now, let's see, he thought, realizing meanwhile the whole absurdity of the question, let's see, oughtn't I to get indignant? He felt cold, speculative; he examined Carla, and she seemed to him seductive, and he thought he understood Pippo's desire better than the girl's annoyance. She's a pretty girl, he thought, with a certain superficial vulgarity; Pippo hasn't at all bad taste . . . he's evidently taken a good look at her. Besides—who knows?—possibly it wouldn't have been the first time, possibly Pippo was right. Perfectly coolly, with the imagination of a dilettante, he pictured his sister in someone's arms, with clothes and hair disarranged, legs crossed, snuggling against his chest, half-naked; or sitting at ease on his knee. Quite possible. . . . She was a woman, after all, and she too must have her desires, her likings. She was extremely well-developed physically, why not

[217]

temperamentally as well? He remembered having once seen her as she was getting out of the bath. He had retained an impression of a long, white, curving back beneath the big, lolling, wet head, and of something like a heavy, pale acorn, one of her breasts, which her stooping attitude caused to hang forward, below her brown armpit. "Susanna at the bath," he had thought, as he discreetly retired. And now Pippo . . . Well, well, that fellow Pippo . . . he hadn't at all such bad taste after all.

With these ironical thoughts running through his head, he was silent. Then he perceived that he ought to say something; he realized that the present deplorable circumstances made an imperative demand upon him to express an adequate and genuine indignation. Otherwise he would fall back, as usual, into the deadly indifference that prevented him from acting and living like other men. He had dallied long enough with his fantastic imaginings, now he must try once and for all to be serious, sincere. Now or never.

He looked at his mother. "Scoundrel indeed," he repeated, and felt himself frozen by his own voice, as cold and ordinary as if he had said "good morning" or "what time is it?" He banged his fist on the table and cried out with shrill, superficial vehemence, "I am quite capable of going to his house and slapping his face." He looked up and saw himself in the Venetian mirror on the opposite wall. Was that his own image, with its hypocritical eyes, looking down at him as much as to say, "No, you're *not* capable?"

His mother did not appear to have noticed this outburst of brotherly indignation. "Everyone knows what they are," she said. "*Nouveaux riches*, that's all."

But Carla had heard him, and turned to him. "Thank you very much," she said, "but I've already put him in his place. Better leave it to me."

This moderation increased Michele's need to get angry. "Leave it to you!" he exclaimed, and noticed with relief that he was already perceptibly more sincere. "Don't you think two words from *me* would do more to make him see he made a gross mistake?"

"Please," repeated Carla, observing him intently, "please

[218]

leave it to me." It was the first time she had seen Michele in the unaccustomed role of avenging brother; he was as awkward and exaggerated as a bad provincial actor. And if he knew I had given myself to Leo, she thought in alarm, what would he do? She glanced at him. Michele was silent now, his glossy, well-brushed head bent over his plate. He was silent, and he appeared to be thinking as he crumbled his bread into lumps; there was no outward sign of his violent purposes. What would he do? she repeated to herself. A subtle feeling warned her that there was something false in his attitude, in the fist on the table, in the words he had spoken—why, she did not understand. And when Michele lifted his eyes she thought she caught a glimpse in them of a sad and shameful secret. She shuddered, that pale spectre seized upon her trembling heart once more, everything went white again, and in the mist her mother was talking. . . .

Luncheon was over. "And what are you doing today, Mom?" Carla asked, lighting a cigarette. She waited for the answer with anxiety. So long as she doesn't want me to go with her, she thought. She wanted to spend the afternoon at her lover's flat—she understood now that to do this was necessary to her; habit had already taken the place of the desire for a new life, and she felt avidly and painfully impatient to go back to that room, to find herself again with that man.

"I?" replied her mother, in a detached, distant voice. "I don't know. I think I shall go and do some shopping." She paused for a moment, looking down at the lighted tip of her cigarette. "What about you?" she asked. Her middle-aged, deluded heart was beating fast. For that day was to be her own; her lover would come back to her, and to her old, safe love, as had already happened on other occasions (and this experience filled her with hope and comforted her greatly) after other ephemeral lapses.

"I?" answered Carla in the same detached tone that her mother had used, "I've been invited to tea by Claretta." Then they were silent, both of them looking down to hide the modestly triumphant, satisfied look in their eyes; a similar expression of relief and serenity spread over the two faces, the mature and the childish one. The hearts of both cherished the image of their common lover, and towards him, at that moment, the spirit of each stooped gently down as if to say to him, with restrained, complacent joy: "There! You see? The plot is hatched. . . . No one, my dear, no one will disturb us."

They rose and left the room. The Signora entered the drawing-room first, shivering and rubbing her frozen hands together. Suddenly she exclaimed, "Oh! There's Merumeci!" She went over to him and shook him by both hands. "Have you been waiting for us long?" she asked.

Then Carla came in, and she too exclaimed, in a tone and with an expression of joyful surprise: "Oh! There's Leo!" Last of all came Michele. He greeted Leo with a wave of the hand, stopped to light a cigarette, and went out again.

"Well," asked the Signora, sitting down and rubbing her hands together even more vigorously, as though to express her pleasure. "Well, and what good wind brings you here?"

"Not so much a wind as my own car," replied Leo, with an old-fashioned attempt at wit, and the two women laughed in the cordial, nervous manner characteristic of well-fed people who listened with pleasure, after lunch, in the intimacy of a comfortable but chilly drawing-room, to idiotic jokes.

"I received your business letter," he added more seriously, looking at the Signora, "and wanted to telephone you. But I knew your line was out of order. . . ."

"So you came here," the Signora concluded. Then she turned to Carla. "Carla," she said, "would you mind telling them to bring coffee for four instead of three?"

Carla got up and went out, with eyes lowered.

"And now," said the Signora with a flattering smile, assuming a more confidential attitude, "tell me . . . have you thought what answer you're going to give me?"

"Yes," replied Leo, carefully considering the lighted end of his cigar.

"What is it?" she asked, insinuating, anxious, suddenly rising to her feet, "what is it, Leo?" With a troubled, tender, excited expression on her face, like someone who wants to extract a confidence and at the same time make an intimate gesture, she came up behind him, put her arms round his neck, and bent her head down until she lightly touched her lover's cheek with her own. "What is it?" she repeated.

Bored, Leo bent his head to one side. "Nothing," he replied, still gazing at his cigar. She took one of his hands and passed it over her face, rubbing her cold nose and her soft mouth against it, like a faithful dog. "D'you love me?" she asked in a low voice, before he could finish what he was going to say; then, quickly changing her tone and becoming suddenly cool, as though she had perceived the danger of this show of feeling, she added, "I'll come today. But you must be good, you must be very good." Unconsciously she was repeating the very words she had used the first time that Leo had invited her, under some pretext or other, to his house. "Very good," she had said then, with her brilliant smile, as she entered the hall of her lover's flat; fifteen years had passed, and that "goodness" so hypocritically demanded had at last arrived; Leo, very good, was trying to free himself from her sinful embrace.

"We'll be good," she went on, carefully kissing his inert hand, "we'll be good children." Scrupulously she bit his thumb and passed her tongue over her lips. "Good children," she repeated, with a greedy voice and expression, and with a foretaste of the pleasurable rite implied by this conditional phrase—the phrase she spoke always with a shudder of joy and the gesture of a warning finger and an expression which sought to be childish, each time she laid herself down, all plump and white, on the yellow bedcover and called her lover to her side; and he would reply joyfully with the same excited, warning gesture, "We'll be good children." Then their licentious and complicated love-making would begin.

But Leo shook his head. "I must tell you, Mariagrazia," he murmured without embarrassment, "that we can't meet today. I have a business engagement, extremely urgent. Impossible for us to meet." He bent forward, looking at his cigar. A silly, pained, disappointed expression contorted the woman's face like a twisting hand; but she still kept up her attitude of tenderness.

"That means," she said hesitatingly, "that I can't come and see you today."

"It does."

She slackened her embrace, bringing her hands up to her breast and then to the level of her shoulders; her face went hard. "*I* can't come," she hissed, putting an extraordinary intensity into the subdued tone of her voice, "but shameless women like Lisa can. For them," she went on, "everything is possible . . . even the most urgent business is allowed to go hang. You even boast of it. You shiver and boil with passion. Boil away, Leo, boil away!" She came close to him and, clenching her teeth, gave his arm a sharp pinch.

Leo, angered, shrugged his shoulders and rubbed the injured place, but did not speak. He stared at the gently throbbing toe of his shoe, first with one eye and then with the other, and seemed to be much absorbed in this occupation.

"You know what *I* say," she continued, gazing at him, "that you're right . . . not once but a thousand times. It's I who am the fool, the imbecile, I who don't know how to enjoy life. But you," she added haughtily, drawing herself up to her full height, with a stiffening expression and a sweeping movement of the hand, "you just leave it to me. . . . All things come to him who waits. Tomorrow, you shall see." She stepped back a little to observe the effect of her threat; but there was none. Then Carla came in, carrying the coffee-tray.

"Michele has gone out," she said, "so Leo can have Michele's coffee." She filled the cups, handed them round, and then sat down. They drank in silence.

"Here's a piece of news that will give you pleasure," said the Signora, putting down her empty cup, "this morning I met your Lisa. . . ."

"*My* Lisa?" broke in Leo with a laugh. "Mine? And why, may I ask? And since when?"

"The more one understands, the less one says," replied the Signora, with a cunning, silly expression. "And she charged me," she added, not realizing that she was lying, "to give you her warmest, her most affectionate, her most cordial greetings."

"Thank you very much," said Leo, unsmiling, "but I don't understand, dear Signora, what all this means."

"Don't worry . . . you understand me perfectly," she replied, with a knowing look and as though excluding Carla from all understanding of the situation. "All too well, in fact. And I do beg you not to miss any of your appointments. That would really be a pity." Her voice, her lips were trembling. Leo's only answer was a shrug of the shoulders.

"What is all this about?" asked Carla, leaning stiffly forward from the waist. An unreasonable agitation quickened the beating of her heart and made her gasp for breath, and she would have liked to get up and leave these two people, leave this room, this atmosphere.

"It's about," began her mother, making an effort to appear cool and calm, and nervously playing with her necklace of artificial pearls, "it's about business. Our dear Leo," she explained, raising her voice and looking up into the air, while she fiddled ever faster with her pearls, "is a business man, extremely busy . . . a man of affairs such as you don't often come across. Everyone knows that . . . ha! ha!" Her whole body trembled as she laughed, and suddenly the necklace broke. There was a sharp tinkle on the floor as pearls dropped. Sitting stiffly, her body erect and her hands on the arms of her chair, she let the necklace fall asunder and the pearls roll down from her bosom and collect in the hollow of her lap; she was immensely dignified, theatrical and in spite of her innate absurdity, tragic. She started to weep; from her painted eyes two impure tears slid down over her thickly powdered face, leaving their damp traces, two more followed . . . and from her neck the pearls continued to fall like tears into her trembling lap. She remained rigid, with big folds of drapery, like a statue, and the things that were falling, the tears, the pearls, were mingled and confused against the rigidity of her face and body, both of them strained, trembling, woe-begone.

Hell take these neurasthenic women! Leo had thought as he watched the breaking of the necklace. He was oppressed by an odious embarrassment. Hell take these tears! he thought, and again tried to fix his attention on the throbbing toe of his shoe. Carla, in the meantime, had gotten up.

"What's the matter?" she asked, "what's happened?" Her voice was cold, and there was an expression of irritation on her face; Leo had the impression that the girl, as well as himself, was bored by these outbursts. Hell take these tears! he thought again. Meanwhile, with a wave of the hand and a shake of the head, the Signora had motioned her daughter away, as though she did not want her to spoil her rigid, theatrical attitude of grief.

At this moment Michele came into the room; he was dressed for going out, with hat and gloves and overcoat. "There's a woman wanting you," he said to his mother. "She's carrying a box; I think it may be the dressmaker." But he stopped all at once, seeing that she was weeping. "What's the matter?" he asked.

"Nothing . . . nothing," answered his mother. She rose hurriedly, letting the pearls drop to the floor, and noisily blew her nose. "I'll come at once," she added, and went out, flushed and slightly bent, as though she wanted to conceal something.

"What's happened?" Michele persisted, looking curiously at Leo. The latter shrugged his shoulders.

"Nothing," he replied. "She broke her necklace. Then she started crying."

There was silence. Carla, standing beside her mother's empty armchair, said nothing. Leo stared at the floor; Michele, motionless in the middle of the room, looked at Leo with eyes that were both irresolute and embarrassed. He felt no pity for his mother, no hatred for Leo; he saw himself as both useless and superfluous. For a moment he had a violent desire to react in some way or other, to ask questions, to argue, to protest. And then, with an acute feeling of humiliation and boredom, he reflected that, when all was said and done, this had nothing whatever to do with him.

"Do as you like," he said sharply; "I'm going out." And he went.

"Come here, Carla," commanded Leo, even before the door had closed, with an excited, clumsy attempt at self-possession, "here . . . beside me."

"Did you sleep well?" the girl asked, going over to him.

"Very well indeed."

He put out his arms, took her around the waist and drew

[224]

her to him. "You must come with me, later," he went on, in a deep voice. "You must make some excuse—a friend, a visit—and come with me." He pulled her closer, clasping his hands together low down, where the big, muscular thighs joined the round buttocks with a well-defined line that he could feel beneath the folds of her dress.

"How about this morning?" he said, just in order to say something; "did everything go all right?"

"Yes, perfectly," she answered, looking down—was it with repugnance or with fear?—at the head of the man sitting there, who spoke to her without raising his forehead, without taking his eyes from her lap, as though the conversation were going on between him and her belly and he took no interest except in that one, single, less noble part of her body. "No one noticed anything."

"It was early. . . ." he said, without changing his attitude, as though talking to himself; finally he shook himself out of his immobility, raised his eyes, and made the girl sit on his knee. "Aren't you afraid, now," he asked, looking at her with a stupid, obtuse expression, "that somebody might come in?"

Carla shrugged her shoulders. "What would it matter to me," she said, in a clear voice that showed no hesitation or fear, "now?"

"But really," insisted Leo, amused, "if now, at this moment, your mother came in . . . what would you do?"

"I should tell the whole truth."

"And then?"

"And then," she said in an uncertain voice, with the painful sensation that she was telling a lie in relation to a more profound truth, and playing, meanwhile, with his tie, "then I should go away with you. . . . I should go and live with you."

Flattered by this seriousness, whose reasons he misunderstood, Leo smiled. "You're a sweet child," he remarked, embracing her.

They kissed, then separated.

"We can be together from three till seven," he began again. But he anticipated this without enthusiasm; in spite of his excitement, he had an obscure intuition, as he clasped this big, youthful body, that his own powers would henceforth be less and less sufficient to satisfy its raging appetites. It was a disagreeable but precise feeling of incapacity, of approaching impotence; it was as though, in order to satisfy him, he had been offered barrels overflowing with wine, immense tables weighed down with all the most delicious kinds of food, and rooms crammed full of the most beautiful women in the world lying about in heaps, one on top of the other, like beasts. From three till seven, he thought ironically. How in the world shall I be able to manage it? He looked at himself in a mirror over Carla's shoulder—at his bald forehead, his heavy, red face, his cheeks that were puffy rather than plump, upon which the unshaven beard showed a kind of blue, metallic reflection: middle age, in fact. I really don't care, he concluded serenely, with a lively sense of reality. When I've had enough, I shall tell her so. As these thoughts went through his mind, he passed his hand absent-mindedly over Carla's neck. "How warm you are!" he exclaimed.

She was silent, looking closely at the red, hard face of her lover. "Why was Mom crying?" she asked finally.

"Because I told her that she couldn't come and see me today."

"Will you do the same thing to me, some day, Leo?" the girl asked softly.

"Why?" The thing that most interested and amused him, at this moment, was the contrast between the way in which Carla allowed herself to be caressed—not without pleasure, judging by the quivering of her docile limbs—and the indifference, the melancholy dignity, of her expression and her remarks. Just as if her body had nothing to do with her, he thought, diverted.

A few moments passed in silence. Leo raised his eyes to those of the girl. "What are you thinking about?" he asked.

"I'm thinking of the day," she replied, with a faint consciousness that she was not being quite honest, "when you'll tell me, too, that I can't come and see you."

"Rubbish," answered Leo, lowering his head again and recommencing his diligent caresses. "What have you and your mother got to do with each other?"

"You say that *now*," said Carla, "but later on?" She did

not know why she should be talking like this; truly it was
not so important for her to speculate on whether her lover
would desert her or not, as to be sure that her own fate would
not be like that of her mother. The real meaning of her question was, "Shall I be able to have a life different from
Mother's?"

He did not answer; he was delicately rumpling her skirt.
"What's this here?" he asked, planting the point of a finger
on her leg.

"My garter." She bent her head down until her forehead
bumped the hard forehead of her lover. "D'you love me?"
she asked. Leo looked at her in surprise. "What I mean is
this," she added hastily; "you never loved Mom, but you do
love me, don't you?"

The thought flashed across Leo's mind: She's jealous of
Mariagrazia. Now I understand. She's jealous . . . jealous of
her mother. Proud of his own perspicacity, flattered at the
existence of this rivalry, he smiled. "Don't worry . . . don't
even think about it," he said. "With your mother it's all over
—d'you see? All over."

"That's not what I mean. . . ." Carla was trying hard to
analyze her own obscure feeling, when the drawing-room
door opened. "Let me go," she murmured, freeing herself;
"here's Mom." With a single movement she drew away from
him and slipped to the floor.

Her mother came bustling in, quite calm now, carrying a
parcel. "What are you doing?" she asked.

"Picking up your pearls," replied the girl. On all fours on
the carpet, head down and hair hanging loose, she was busy
collecting the fallen pearls, while Leo, sitting motionless, contemplated with amusement the uplifted, moving, swelling
buttocks above her hollowed back and almost invisible head.

"It wasn't the dressmaker," said the Signora; "it was a lady
who sells materials and cushions. I bought one."

"One what?" inquired Carla, making a great effort to
reach a pearl that had rolled under the sofa.

"A cushion," her mother explained. "Look," she went on,
pointing, "there's one . . . there . . . in that corner." She de-

[227]

liberately ignored Leo; but she had obviously powdered her face afresh.

"Yes, I see it," said Carla. She bent and picked it up. Why did she feel this necessity to humble herself, to grovel, to hide, with her hand full of pearls and her eyes wide open, staring, sad? She did not know. Flushed in the face, she got up and poured the pearls into an ash-tray. "Let's have a look," she said.

Her mother undid the parcel and displayed her new acquisition—a square of blue silk with the usual Chinese dragon—flaming mouth and tail erect—embroidered on it in bright colors, red, green, gold.

"Beautiful," said Leo.

"What d'you think of it?" she asked her daughter, feigning to ignore her lover's remark.

"It seems to me quite useless," said Carla, rather roughly. "We've already got the house full of stuff like that. . . . I don't know where you can put it."

"In the hall," suggested her mother humbly.

"Well, anyhow," said Carla soothingly, "it's by no means ugly."

"You really think so?" said the other woman, with a feeble smile of self-satisfaction.

Carla took a few steps towards the door. "I'm going to get dressed," she said. "Leo, wait for me. We'll go together."

"It's early," cried her mother, looking at her watch and running after her.

"Never mind," replied the girl, already at the far end of the room.

"No, no," answered her mother, "no, no. . . ." And, chattering, cackling, waving their arms like two big, frightened birds, the two of them went out with a clatter of opening and shutting doors.

Leo threw away his spent cigar, stretched his arms and legs, yawned, and finally took a file from his pocket and started cleaning his nails. He was thus occupied when, ten minutes later, Carla came upon him.

"Well, Leo," she said, drawing on her gloves, "shall we go?"

[228]

"All right," answered Leo, in English. He rose and followed her out, and in the vestibule gave way to his usual extravagantly solemn buffoonery. "May I," he inquired with a bow, "have the pleasure and the honor of your company, Signorina?"

"Granted," replied Carla, blushing a little and smiling in spite of herself. They went out laughing and knocking into each other, leaping with agility and lightness down the marble steps, yellowed by the recent rain. In the middle of the drive Leo's car, low above its big wheels, lay in the sunshine.

With much laughter and joking the two of them went over to the glossy vehicle; they jumped in quickly, first Leo, then Carla, and sat side by side.

"Nothing forgotten?" Leo asked, as he carefully pressed the starter.

"Nothing," answered the girl. In the cold, clear air her woes and her fears had vanished; sitting beside Leo she took pleasure in the blue sky, in rain-washed nature, in the gleaming car.

The car started off and moved rapidly between the bare tree trunks of the avenue. The sunshine, the shadows of hanging boughs, the wind of their movement, struck variously upon their two motionless heads; but the same look of childish wonder, the same gay-colored, brilliant youthfulness lay on their faces. Independent of the movement of the vehicle, they appeared to be gazing at themselves in the glass of the windshield, where, above the confused variation of park and sky, parts of their fingers were reflected—their eyes, their mouths, Carla's childish cheeks, Leo's felt hat—detached and hanging in the void like an incomprehensible mirage.

13

MICHELE HAD GONE to see Lisa. All morning the idea of this meeting had been lurking behind his thoughts, creating the kind of discomfort that can be caused in a large company by everyone knowing a certain thing and no one daring to be the first to mention it; the whole morning the recollection of having kissed her hand the day before, in the dark, had haunted the lower planes of his consciousness, forming, temporarily, an atmosphere of discouragement around all his mental processes. He guessed by some obscure means that the essential question for him was not the devoting of himself to this or that occupation for those few hours, but the decision as to whether he should go and see Lisa again or not; that the important thing was not reading, writing, talking, living somehow or other, but the question of making love to Lisa. Finally, after lunch, with the excuse of going for a walk, he had left the house.

The real reason for his going became clear to him the moment he was out of doors and had looked up at the sky, which, of a pure blue a few minutes earlier, was now filling up with a quantity of tiny white clouds. Of course, he thought calmly, as he shut the garden gate behind him, I'm not going out for a walk or to drink coffee. . . . No. . . . I must be frank about it: I've come out in order to go and see Lisa. He felt he was acting in a very forceful fashion in thus coming face to face with his own inescapable weakness, and that, in a way, he was courageously accepting conditions that no will-power could have transformed. Quite useless had been the stubborn falseness, the childish pride which, for an instant, had caused him to believe in a renewed intrigue between Lisa and her former lover, and which had then weighed so heavily upon him and forced him to continue in a wrong direction. He saw now that the ironical bow he had made from the door to the dishevelled, breathless, Lisa had not been suggested to him by any genuine feeling: he might equally well have gone in, sat down and talked to them, or he might have accepted the situation calmly, as an accomplished fact, or again he might have carried Lisa off, tearing her from Leo's arms. Instead, with the instinct of a comedian forced to improvise his own part, he had chosen that attitude of irony as being the most suitable, or rather, the most natural and traditional in the circumstances—a few words, a bow, and exit. But in the street, he had felt no jealousy, no grief; merely an unbearable disgust at his own versatile indifference which allowed him to change his ideas and attitudes every day, as other people change their clothes.

The importance of the visit he was about to make was obvious and extreme: it was the final test of his sincerity and, if he failed, he would remain in his present, temporary state of doubt and inquiry, or take the opposite path, the path that everyone took, where actions are not supported by faith or sincerity, are all of equal value, and accumulate in splendid layers on top of the neglected spirit until they suffocate it. If, on the other hand, he succeeded in the test, everything would be changed: he would rediscover his own solid reality as an artist rediscovers his inspiration of happier times; a new life would begin for him, the true, the only possible life.

He turned into a larger street and found himself near the point where the streetcar stopped which ran to the quarter where Lisa lived. Should he wait for it or not? He looked at his watch; it was early, better to walk there. He started off again, and, as he went, he recapitulated his thoughts. There were, then, two possibilities: either he succeeded in his object of being sincere, or he adapted himself to a life like everybody else's.

The first possibility was clear; it was a question of isolating himself with a few ideas, a few genuinely felt feelings, a few genuinely loved people—if such there were—and beginning again, on these exiguous but solid foundations, to lead a life loyal to his own principles of sincerity. And here was the second. No change except in his own defeated spirit: he would botch up the situation as best he could, like an ugly, damaged house that one repairs here and there, when it is impossible, for lack of money, to build a new one; he would allow his family to go to ruin or to be kept by Leo; and he would make up his mind (although it humiliated him considerably that he should have to content himself with such a consolation) to carry on his messy little affair with Lisa. Dirty tricks, little acts of baseness, little falsities—who was there who did not collect such things in every corner of his existence, as though in the corners of some big, empty house? Farewell to a clean and honest life: he would become Lisa's lover.

And the villa? And the mortgage? On this matter he would come to an agreement with Leo. "You give me money enough for me and my family to live on, and I in return will give you. . . ." As a matter of fact, what was there now left that Leo had not taken? Let's see, wait a minute. There remained Lisa—with whom Leo had tried in vain to renew his former relations. Yes, Lisa, of course. Well then: "You give me the money, and I in return will persuade Lisa. . . ."

It seemed to him that he could see how this last affair would go.

One evening, after many hesitations, he would speak to her about it, and she would protest. "Do it for my sake," he would then implore her, "if you love me you *must* do it." In the end she would resign herself to it, perhaps, she would not be altogether displeased to go back to her old friendship. "Very well," she would reply, with a faint look of contempt, "send him in. But don't imagine that I'm doing it for your family. It's simply for you." He would embrace her and thank

[232]

her warmly, and would then go out into the hall and summon Leo. "Go on in," he would say to him, "Lisa's waiting for you." And he would take him by the hand and throw him into her arms. And where would Leo give him the money? There, in Lisa's flat, under her eyes, or somewhere else? Somewhere else. He would retire discreetly, closing the door behind him, wishing them good night. He would wait in the hall; and what a long, interminable night he would spend, sitting there, listening to the sounds in the room next door, where the other two were in bed; falling asleep, waking up again with a start and finding in front of him every time that overcoat hanging on its peg, reminding him that its owner was in the company of his mistress—what an endless night! And towards dawn Leo would go away, without thanking him, without looking him in the face, barely allowing him to help him into that same overcoat. He would have made place for him in the untidy, soiled bed, beside a half-naked Lisa lying in sleep and in darkness, exhausted by laborious pleasure, as though overwhelmed by a drunken slumber. And this would not be the first or the last time; Leo would come back often, every time he himself needed money. That too, he concluded vaguely, would be a solution. But he felt weary, as though all these fantasies were true and had actually happened. And supposing Leo would have nothing to do with Lisa, or Lisa with Leo? Then . . . then . . . Carla was the only one who could save the situation. Perfectly right. Carla, too, was a resource. Since it was necessary to live in that way, it was better to go to the bitter end. So there was Carla left. To be married off—yes, of course, to be given as a wife to Leo. It would be a business match, a money marriage, such as one sees plenty of, and they're often the most successful; love would come later. And even if it didn't come, there wouldn't be any harm done. Carla could console herself in all sorts of ways; Leo wasn't the only person in the world! A very good idea. . . . And yet . . . and yet. . . . Supposing Leo refused to give him his money except on condition of making her his mistress?

He's even capable of that, thought Michele, perfectly capable. He stopped for a moment. He felt his head going around, weariness and disgust weighed down upon him, and his heart sank. But ruthlessly he resumed his way, and his thoughts too. On we go, on we go, and he wondered vaguely at his own capacity for always discovering fresh miseries. When would he come to the end of them? One must go on to the bitter end. He smiled palely. Supposing, then, Leo did not wish to get married. This, after all, was quite probable. In that case a different kind of agreement might be made between the two contracting parties. Leo would give the money as before, but, in consideration of Carla's untouched youth and beauty, he would be asked for a sum twice or three times as much as would have sufficed for the middle-aged, corrupt Lisa. Every article has its price. And he . . . and he, in exchange, would certainly undertake—in such an atmosphere, on so slippery a slope, one can even reach *that* point—he would undertake to facilitate matters with his sister. A difficult undertaking, certainly; Carla must have principles —and it might even be that she was in love with someone else; extremely difficult. There were two possible plans of action to be considered: either to tell her the whole story, adducing various pretexts—family honor, poverty—and win the battle at one stroke by the sheer violence and suddenness of the pressure applied, or prepare the girl's mind slowly, making her understand gradually, creating a kind of obsession in her by dropping a word one day and another the next, so that she would at last guess, from repeated, persistent hints, what was wanted of her. Which would be the better of these two methods? The second, undoubtedly . . . much easier to let her realize certain things than to say them to her. And then, in an atmosphere of uneasiness, carefully prepared by means of hints, allusions, temptations, Carla, alone and weak, would end by yielding. It happens to so many girls. Why not to her?

As he walked along, step by step, looking down at the ground, he was able to foresee, with an illusory clearness, how this seduction would take place. A gray day, like today, a lifeless, mild day, without sun, without movement. Leo would come, as he had done that day, and would invite them, himself and his sister, to go for a drive in his car. No sooner suggested than accepted. And after the drive, where would they go and have tea? Why, to Leo's flat, of course, to Leo's flat, where Carla would quite willingly go, reassured by the presence of her brother. They would get out at his door and go upstairs together, slowly, the girl in front, then the two men. At the door of the flat, while Carla took off her hat in front of the mirror in the hall, the two of them would exchange a handshake as a token of understanding. And then, having looked around and admired everything, there they would be, the three of them, in the mild afternoon light, in Leo's little sitting-room, all with their own different thoughts and their motionless faces. Then Carla, standing, would pour out the tea, and from her hands the two men, sitting down, would receive the cups, the little floury biscuits, the sugar and milk; on her charming lips there would be an unsuspecting smile, in her eyes a look of clear innocence. They would sit near the window, because the sky by now would have become rather dark and gloom would have begun to invade the other end of the room; and there, all three together, they would eat and drink. And they would also talk, in the afternoon quietness of the house, the two men catching each other's eye, the girl laughing, all unknowing, making jokes in a loud voice. And after tea, in that moment of silence and dreamy satiety that follows upon any satisfied appetite, he would look at Leo, and Leo would return his look. Rapidly, Leo would glance first at Carla's docile, slightly bowed head, then at the door. He would understand, and would rise slowly. "I'm going to get some cigarettes," he would say, and would go out with an unusually firm step, holding his head high, leaving the other two, his sister and the man, two black, still figures against the gray, sky-filled expanse of the window.

He would go out into the hall and put on his overcoat; then he would go away, cautiously closing the door. The hours of that afternoon would pass, interminably, one after the other, without Carla, without Leo, without anybody, in the street, or perhaps in some little café or motion picture theatre. And in the evening he would go home, and would find Carla, and possibly Leo too, at the family table, and

[235]

would examine their two faces, without being able to discover, from any look or sign, what had happened in that
flat, between those four walls, after his departure. A flight
through the dark rooms, in an uproar of overturned chairs
and opening and shutting doors? A brief struggle in the
gloom of the little sitting-room, in front of the twilit window? Or, possibly, a deadly resignation in face of a surrender
that was inevitable, that had long been foreseen and now
finally accepted?

He would never know; in spite of that afternoon and of
all the other days upon which there would be a repetition
of this fruitful but reprehensible adventure, their life, from
force of habit and convenience, would go on as before. One
more misconception, one more falsity, and so on again. Or
perhaps, some day, these secret infamies, like worms in a
decomposing body, would reveal themselves in a general
burst of egoism, bringing on the final collapse. Then they
would all find themselves naked and face to face; and that
would be the end, the end of everything.

He felt he was suffocating. He stopped and looked into a
shop window without seeing anything. Now he had indeed
reached the extreme end of his imaginary future: nothing
more to sell, neither Carla's innocence, nor his own love for
Lisa, nor his own courage; nothing more to hand over to
Leo in exchange for money. After these fantasies—no more
headlong than the reality down which his existence was
hurtling—the sense of aridity that dried up his mouth and
cracked his very soul made him long to cry out and weep; he
felt tired and desperately uneasy, as if he had really and truly
left Carla in Leo's flat a few minutes before, and now, in
that closed room, the infamy were really being accomplished,
with the movements he had pictured to himself, the struggle,
the flight, the embrace; and with the same colors and shapes,
the outstretched arms, the bared breast, the prostrate body
beneath the dark, curved shadow of another body, the closed,
defiled eyes, that had appeared like lightning flashes in the
febrile heaven of his imagination. He had so strong a sensation of disgust and exhaustion that he felt an instinctive need
to cleanse himself—why, he could not have explained—a pain-

ful need for clear water, as though its fresh, purifying stream could flow through the windings of his soul . . . rivulets murmuring through the grass, white, living waterfalls leaping with continuous clamor from rocky heights, cold torrents foaming over their beds of gravel, even the rills that meander downward by hidden ways from snowy mountain-brows, at the moment of thaw, and unite in the valley below—all the freshest, coolest waters did not seem enough to assuage his unhappy yearnings.

He walked on again. He understood now that the phrase, "Luckily they're only ideas," would not suffice to purify him. He knew, from his troubled spirit, from the bitter taste in his mouth, that he had *lived* those fantasies; it would be impossible to see Carla again with the eyes of a brother, to forget that he had pictured her in the immodest guise usually associated with fallen women. It was too late, now, to return to quieter visions: for to think was to live.

But he had seen, he had felt what would become of him if he failed to conquer his own indifference. Without faith, without love, alone, he must, for his salvation, either live through this unbearable situation with sincerity and according to traditional standards, or he must get out of it for good. He must hate Leo, love Lisa, feel disgust and compassion for his mother, and affection for Carla—all of them sentiments of which he had no knowledge; or he must go away somewhere else and seek his own people, his own place, that paradise where everything—gestures, words, feelings—would have a direct connection with the reality in which they had originated.

Of this paradise of reality and truth he thought he had had a glimpse, two years before, in the tears of a woman of the street whom he had picked up and taken to a hotel room. Small and frivolous, she had a figure which was amusing because of a kind of naïve lack of proportion between the clumsy bulges of her breasts and buttocks and her slender, hollow back, so that, when naked, she looked as if she were walking in a bent-forward position in order to show off, conceitedly, like a peacock with its tail, these buxom rotundities. A further contrast was provided by her manner of offering these pink and profligate seductions veiled in tarnished black wrappings, which she wore slightly awry, like a carnival fancy dress—mourning rags gathered hastily together (as she had confided to him going upstairs at the hotel, without the smallest sign of sadness but with the indifferent simplicity appropriate to any phenomenon of nature) on the death of her mother, a week before. This doleful event, however, which had left her (according to her own expression) alone in the world, did not prevent her seeking, every evening, a companion to share her solitude: for one must live. In the bedroom she had made her little show of modesty, and with a kind of fresh and cheerful spontaneity. It was a small, humble room, and she had strewn over the floor her various articles of clothing, her black veils, her skirt, her slip and panties, like a fugitive shedding his armor piece by piece in order to run faster, and had finally taken refuge, clad only in her stockings, in the warmest, darkest corner, beside the stove. She had come out again after a great deal of simpering, and with clumsy movements of her breast and hips which looked as though she were performing a curtsy at each step; she had come out with a thousand protests, covering herself, wherever she could, with her hands; and cautiously had got into bed, with a mysterious but amiable smile that seemed to promise all sorts of refined delights. But then, when Michele had attempted to urge her to one or two acts of purely professional skill, she had refused, and finally, when he persisted, had burst into tears. Her weeping had not been of a dignified kind, nor painful and tragic; nor was it one of those hysterical outbursts accompanied by cries and contortions; no, it had been childish weeping, with big tears and violent sobs that had shaken her whole body, and, in particular, her two breasts, light and tender like two innocent riders forced into a continuous, laborious jolting by a difficult horse. He had looked at her in astonishment, unable to comprehend this sudden passage from joy to grief. At last, after he had questioned her several times, he thought he had understood that, at the moment when he was asking her to display her professional wisdom, her head, so close to his own and yet so remote from it, had been filled so completely and unbearably with the thought of her departed mother that she had burst into a noisy flood of tears. Having given these confused explanations in a mournful, sleepy voice, while the boy, still perplexed, stooped over her and looked at her without speaking, she had carefully blown her nose, had wiped away her tears with a corner of the sheet, and had become gay and serene again, and even enthusiastic, as though she wished to ask forgiveness for her inopportune grief. Everything had gone well, and after an hour they had parted at the door of the hotel and had never seen each other again.

That bout of weeping now recurred to his mind as an instance of deeply complicated, genuine life; those tears, shed at that moment, flowing down the painted face, projected from the secret fullness of that life like muscles which, at a slight contraction, come up suddenly under the skin. That soul was a complete one, with its vices and its virtues, and had a share of the quality that all real, solid things have, the quality of revealing, at any moment, a profound and simple truth. He himself, on the other hand, was not like that; across the flat, blank screen of his indifference sorrows and joys passed like shadows, leaving no trace, and consequently—just as though his own lack of substance were communicated to his external world as well—everything around him was without weight and without value, fleeting as a play of light and shade. From those spectres which traditionally should have constituted the members of his family—his sister, his mother, the woman he loved, Lisa—other figures detached themselves, according to circumstances and his own imagination, by a process of duplication that might continue *ad infinitum*. So that it was possible for him to see Carla as a girl of bad character, his mother as a stupid, ridiculous woman, Lisa as a shameless hussy; not to mention Leo, who changed completely from hour to hour as a result of other peoples' remarks and his own too objective impressions, with the result that if at one moment he thought he hated him, shortly afterwards he loved him tenderly.

All that was needed to arrest this mad confusion, to rearrange these values in their proper perspective, was one single sincere action, one single act of faith. Consequently the importance of this visit to Lisa appeared to him enormous. If he could manage to love her, all else would then become possible—hating Leo and all the rest of it.

He looked up, saw that he had passed the street where she lived, and turned back. He was tormented, now, by his own malign spirit. "Supposing," it asked him, "supposing you were really able to put things back in the places where they ordinarily belong, do you think it would be of any advantage to you? Do you think that to become a *real* brother, a *real* son, a *real* lover, a *real* ordinary man, selfish and logical like so many others, would be a sign of progress in relation to your present condition? Do you really think so? Are you quite sure of it?" There was no answer to any of these questions. "On the other hand, don't you think," went on the dubious voice, "that the road along which you are now travelling, full of doubts and perversities as it is, will lead you much farther? And doesn't it also seem to you that it would be an act of cowardice on your part to become just like everybody else?" Where would it lead me, he thought, half ironical, half despairing, where would the achievement of sincerity lead me? He stared straight in front of him, his eyes filling with tears, beguiled by his own reflection in a shop window; and it seemed to him that he understood where sincerity would lead him. The window belonged to a perfume shop, and placed among sparkling golden bottles of cheap *eau de Cologne* and surmounting a pile of pink and pale green pieces of soap was a dummy figure, designed to attract the attention of window-shoppers. It was cut out of cardboard and painted in bright colors, on a strictly human rather than doll-like model, its face was motionless, stupid, hilarious, its big brown eyes full of a candid, unshakable faith; it wore an elegant dressing-jacket and was evidently just out of bed, and tirelessly, without ever relaxing its fixed smile, it was passing a razor-blade backwards and forwards, as though sharpening it on a strip of leather. There could be no possible connection between the commonplace action and the expression of cheerful satisfaction on the pink face, but it was precisely in that absurdity that the whole efficacy of the advertisement lay; that altogether disproportionate happiness was not intended to point out the imbecility of the man so much as the good qualities of the razor; it was not intended to display the advantages of possessing only a modest degree of intelligence, but of shaving with a good blade. And yet on Michele, immersed in his thoughts, it had quite a different effect.

He seemed to be looking at himself and his own sincerity, to be receiving, from that smiling dummy, the reply to his question "what would be the use of having faith?" It was a disheartening reply. "The use of it," implied the dummy, "would be to have a razor-blade and a happiness like mine, like everybody else's, humble and stupid in origin but brilliant . . . and of course the essential thing is that it shaves." It was the same answer that any number of respectable people would have given him: "Do as I do, and you'll become like me," holding up their own stupid, clumsy, vulgar selves as examples, as goals to be achieved at the summit of the steep mountain of thought and sacrifice. "That's what would be the use of it," insisted his malign spirit, "to become a dummy, a stupid, pink dummy like this one here." He looked with tears in his eyes at the puppet, endlessly sharpening its blade with a continuous movement, with little mechanical jerks—one, two, three; and he longed to strike it in the face and smash its radiant smile.

"You ought to be weeping," he thought, "weeping big tears." But the dummy went on smiling and sharpening.

He tore himself away with some difficulty from this fascinating spectacle (and truly there was something crazy and hallucinatory about that continuous movement), and turned into the street where Lisa lived. Absurd phrases were dancing in his head. *Look, Lisa*, he kept on saying to himself, *Here's your poor dummy with a razor.*

14

THE DARK PASSAGE was filled with a familiar cooking smell. Lisa, who had obviously just risen from table, a cigarette between her lips and a troubled and excited look on her face—due perhaps to her having drunk a good deal of wine—came to the door. "This way . . . this way," she kept saying, without answering his words of greeting, and led the way to the boudoir, closing, as she passed them, open doors that revealed, here a stuffy-looking bedroom with an unmade bed, here a little black kitchen overflowing with pots and pans, here the already known drawing-room, dusty and dark. "We shall be better here," she remarked as she went into the boudoir. Into this room a blinding white light poured through the two lightly veiled windows; and at that moment the clouds had evidently cleared from the sky, for a reflection of dazzling light came from somewhere outside, beyond the window panes.

They sat down together on the sofa. "Well, how goes it?" asked Lisa, holding out a box of cigarettes. He took one without raising his eyes, maintaining his preoccupied expression. Better begin at once, he thought, looking at Lisa out of the corner of his eye. Heavily powdered, she was wearing a white blouse, yellow with age, and a gray skirt of some yielding material that had lost its shape and gone baggy with much wearing; a bright-colored tie, badly tied and not very fresh, hung at her neck, and enamelled links with heads of dogs on them adorned her cuffs. . . . But, in contrast to this rather masculine get-up, her buxom bosom swelled out her shirt in a purely feminine manner, and the blonde, pink flesh of her shoulders seemed to be bursting through the transparency of the material between the two white, common-looking shoulder-straps of her undergarment.

"Badly," he replied at last.

"Badly?" A feeling of excitement due either to the wine she had drunk or to other causes quickened Lisa's heartbeats, made her catch her breath, and at intervals suffused her solemn, troubled face wtih a deep flush. "But why?" She looked at Michele and hoped he would remember that he had kissed her hand the day before, in the darkness of the drawing-room.

"I don't know." He put down his cigarette and gazed for a moment at Lisa. "I've been thinking about various things. Shall I tell you?" He saw her make a lively gesture of assent: —"Yes, do!"—and then assumed the expression and attitude of one who intends to listen with interest and with love. God knows what she thinks I'm going to say to her, he thought ironically. Perhaps that I love her. . . . Well, well, that's what she's waiting for. He took up his cigarette again.

"I must tell you," he began, "that I find myself in a curious position with regard to you all."

"Who is 'you all'?"

"The family circle. You yourself, Leo, my mother, my sister."

She examined him with a penetrating eye. "With me, too?" she asked, taking his hand as if by chance, with perfect naturalness. They looked at each other.

"Yes, you too," he answered, mechanically pressing her fingers. "For each of you," he went on, encouraged, "I ought to have a certain feeling. I say *ought* because I realize, every time, that circumstances demand it. . . . It's like going to a funeral or a wedding: in each case a certain attitude of mind is expected, either of joy or grief, like the appropriate formal dress. You can't laugh if you're following a hearse, or weep at the moment when the bride and bridegroom are exchanging rings—it would be scandalous, or worse, inhuman. Anyone who, from indifference, feels nothing, has to pretend. And that's what I do with you all. I pretend to hate Leo, to love my mother."

"And . . . and then?" asked Lisa, seeing him hesitate and pause.

"That's all," he replied. He felt irritated and sad. I know you're just waiting for me to say something about you, he thought, looking at Lisa's face. "Only," he went on—and his voice shook as if he were on the point of raising a mournful protest, "I don't know how to pretend . . . and so, you see, what with false feelings and false gestures and words and thoughts, my life is becoming like an unsuccessful play. I *can't* pretend, d'you understand?" He was silent for a moment; Lisa sat gazing at him, and appeared disappointed. "In any case," he concluded in a confused, discouraged manner, suddenly hearing his own voice echoing, unlistened-to, in the silence of the boudoir, "none of this interests you and you can't understand it. I might talk to you for a whole day and still you wouldn't understand." He bent his head and heard the woman's voice speaking against his forehead, a voice falsely inspired, confidential.

"I *would* understand, my poor Michele. I'm sure I would understand." He seemed to be hearing the identical voice that he himself would have used if he had wanted to declare his love to Lisa. Well, well, he thought, with bitter irony, we're both in the same state. He felt a hand on his hair, and a feeling of disgusted pity, both for himself and for her, came over him. Oh, you poor woman! he thought, d'you really want to teach *me* how to play-act? But, raising his eyes, he encountered a glance and an expression so imperiously full of feeling that he was frightened. Has the moment come already, then? he thought confusedly, like a sick man who has expected long preparations and then sees the surgeon's instrument flashing in the air as soon as he has been placed on the operating table. He looked at her face, at the half-opened, imploring lips, the troubled eyes, the flushed cheeks, and saw

[244]

that if he yielded little by little to her supplications, life would once again be imposing a false attitude on his indifference. Then he felt Lisa's fingers pressing his own lightly, as though inviting him to make up his mind; and he stooped down and kissed her on the mouth.

It was a long embrace; passing clouds obscured the white radiance that had filled the boudoir, the walls quickly lost their color and became cold. And on the divan between the two windows the two figures sat still and rigid, side by side, their mouths joined, the upper parts of their bodies turned only just enough to make the kiss possible. Had it not been for the eager confusion of their lips, the correctness of their attitudes would have suggested a conversation rather than an embrace. Michele held his arms to his sides, his eyes were wide open, and his glance wandered idly over the wall opposite; Lisa, her hands in those of the boy, moved her head like one who is drinking and stops for a moment, and then begins again with renewed avidity. Finally they separated and sat looking at one another.

And now, thought Michele, gazing dreamily at the confused, excited, solemn face beside him, what now? He saw Lisa's already flushed cheeks redden with gratitude, her moist lips half-close in wonder and supplication, her eyes fill with an almost religious adoration—which only needed, to complete it, hands held up with palms open in sign of pity. Then she put out her hand and passed it through his hair, murmuring a "my dear" in a tremendous, artificial voice.

He lowered his eyes again. Lisa was sitting in an awkward position, supported by her own legs, and while stroking his head she was painfully working her way along the edge of the divan towards him, trying not to let her action be noticed. The movement, pulling at her skirt, gradually revealed a fat thigh in a slack, rolled-down stocking. A sense of uneasiness, of violent irritation, came over him, possibly from disdain at having allowed himself to be drawn into an embrace, possibly from the hypocritical contrast between her caresses and words of affection and the impure nudity which was slowly being revealed by her crafty progress towards him. What does she take me for? he wondered in disgust.

[245]

The small degree of desire that the embrace had aroused in him vanished; he retreated backwards, and then, looking fixedly at Lisa, rose with a clumsy motion to his feet.

"No," he said, shaking his head; "no, it's no good. . . ."

Lisa stared at him astonished, almost shocked, without covering up her naked leg and without losing her look of excitement.

"What's no good?" she demanded. This coldness on Michele's part was an insult to her flushed face and her abandoned behavior. Stupid boy, she thought, irritated, we'd started so well. And now, look . . . he's gone and got up. He shook his head again, repeating, "It's no good." Then she reached forward and fumbled for his hand.

"Come," she said, trying to pull him down beside her. "Come here. Sit down here. Tell me what's no good."

He hesitated, then sat down. "I've already told you what's no good," he explained in a bored voice, gazing intently at something behind Lisa's head and pretending not to notice the nervous caress of her hands and the burning look in her eyes. "I've already told you that I'm in just the same position with regard to you as I am with the others."

"And what does that mean, exactly?"

"It means . . . just as I can't hate Leo. . . ."

"Even now, after what I told you?"

Michele looked at her. "I must tell you," he began, "that, although I pretended not to know what you told me about Mother, I did really know it, all the time."

"You knew it all the time?"

"I've known it for at least ten years." He stooped down and picked up a paper-knife that had fallen from the little table; and then, as he replaced it, there came over him a hysterical urge to tell the truth. "And so, just as I can't hate Leo—and I could tell you the whole story of his relations with Mother, in every detail—in the same way I can't love you. It's always the same reason—indifference; it's always indifference. And so," he concluded irritably, "rather than pretend to fall into your arms, to be dying of passion for you, rather than make declarations of love to you—seeing that I can't do it successfully—I prefer not to do it at all."

[246]

He broke off and looked at Lisa, and saw such a perplexed and annoyed look on her face that he felt a kind of disdainful pity for her. "Try and understand me," he added gloomily. "How can I do something that I don't feel?"

"Try."

He shook his head. "No, it's no good. It would be just as if I went to Leo and said: 'Listen, my dear fellow, I don't hate you, in fact I like you very much, I have the most friendly feelings towards you, but I'm terribly sorry, I just can't help it, I must give you a slap in the face'—and the fat would be in the fire."

"But love always comes afterwards," she murmured determinedly, with a lack of modesty which seemed incredible to Michele, "when people get to know one another better."

"We know each other all too well, already."

Lisa turned pale; no one had ever repulsed her with such harshness. She was afraid that her "dear boy" was going to elude her for good, and for a moment the mad idea came into her head to throw herself at his feet, to supplicate him as a divinity. But, instead, she went on protesting. "You're not talking seriously."

"I couldn't be more serious."

She came close to him and took his hand; her heart was beating fast, her cheeks were flushed with an irrational anxiety. "Don't be unkind," she insisted, in a hesitating voice, stroking his hand; "tell me, don't you feel anything . . . anything at all, for your poor little Lisa? Tell me, won't you really give me that pleasure?" she went on, putting her arm around the boy's neck. "Michele, don't you really have a little love for me?" The composure of her expression had vanished in a harsh redness, a burning excitement, her voice was insinuating, full of feeling. As she bent towards Michele, she touched his leg with her knee; but he shook his head.

"Do please understand me," he repeated; and a violent irritation swept over him, at this pertinacious lasciviousness. "What would become of this love of yours, if I, without bothering about my real feelings any more than I would with a prostitute, if I . . . if I took you now . . . if I threw you down, without more ado, on the divan? Do understand me."

"But we haven't reached the point yet of your . . . throwing me down on the divan," she said, with a stupid, flattered laugh. She hesitated a moment, then, with a soft but irresistible gesture, flung her arms round his neck, letting herself at the same time fall back on the divan. In this first movement she was successful. Michele, taken by surprise, fell forward without resisting; but the sight of Lisa's red, excited face, of her eyebrows arched in sign of command above her burning eyes, of her throat thrust towards him, the whole weight of her body on the back of his neck, filled him with anger and disgust. He threw back his head, put the palm of his hand on that imperious, suppliant face, and freeing himself with one push from her embrace, jumped to his feet.

"If you really want it so much," he raged, mechanically rearranging his tie, "well, go back . . . go back to Leo!"

Lying back on the divan, her face in her hands, her bosom in a tumult, Lisa was making a show of grief and shamed humiliation, neither of which was real, but at the mention of her former lover, Michele saw her rise up with a wild look in her eyes and an accusing hand pointed at him.

"Leo . . . you said Leo? . . . that I ought to go back to Leo?" she cried, disregarding her untidy hair and her disordered clothes. "And, if I'm not mistaken, you also said that you can't manage to hate Leo, didn't you—even knowing what you do know?"

"Yes," he stammered, disturbed by this sudden fury, staring at her. "Yes . . . but what's the connection?"

"*I* know what it is," she said, with a brief, nervous laugh. "*I* know." She paused for a moment, swallowing the saliva in her mouth—swallowing her own impatience, too. "You know what I say?" she burst out again, reaching forward and fixing these wild eyes upon him, "that there's just one reason, and a very good one, why you *can* hate Leo and why *I* can't go back to him."

"My mother?" hazarded Michele, disturbed by that accusing hand. But Lisa burst into contemptuous laughter.

"Your mother . . . your mother indeed!" she kept saying, between peals of bitter merriment. "Why, my poor Michele, your mother has been entirely out of the picture for some time . . . for quite a long time now."

He looked at her, and it seemed to him then that he looked down upon her vindictive figure from far above, with a feeling of superiority that came to him more from the disgusted pity he felt for her than from his own greater purity, and because she was plunged in a more degraded, more hopeless misery even than his own. He felt like stooping down, smoothing back the disordered hair, soothing away the gesture of accusation; but he had no time.

"No," she continued, still staring at him with eyes that seemed to look far beyond the boudoir, beyond the house, at figures in her memory. "No, my dear boy. Someone other than your mother. Guess . . . guess!" She gave a little nervous laugh, tidied her hair and her clothes, and sat down more comfortably.

"You?" he suggested.

"Me?"

She made a gesture as if she were falling from the clouds. "Me?" But, my poor Michele, I've already told you there's a good reason why I don't go back to Leo. And you know *who* that reason is? You know who it is?" A name was hovering on her lips and she was on the point of uttering it, but restrained herself. "No," she added, shaking her head; "no . . . it's better for me not to say anything." The first moment of genuine excitement was over and Lisa was returning to her usual artificiality, in which—as though it were some subtle, absorbing game—she found the greatest available consolation in her troubles. "I don't want anything serious to happen through any fault of mine." She lit a cigarette, and looked fixedly down at the carpet as though she had made up her mind not to speak.

"Now listen, Lisa," said Michele at last; "say what you want to say—clearly you can't do more than that—and make an end of it."

He went up to her, put his hand on her hair and pushed her head back. Looking into her eyes, he seemed to detect a hardened, incurable obliquity of judgment in the fixed look of ruthlessness and stupidity with which she met his gaze, and the same feeling of disgusted pity as before came over him. If I loved her, he thought, putting her head away from him again, she wouldn't be like that. He sat down again. "What a way to behave!" said Lisa, disturbed, in a slow, stubborn voice, pushing back her disordered hair, "what a way to behave!" Michele was looking at her. The fault isn't theirs, he was thinking, it's mine. They *need* my feelings—and I haven't any.

"Then you really want to know everything?" she inquired.

"Yes. And hurry up."

There was a moment's silence. "You said," began Lisa, rather hesitatingly, "that you wanted to hate Leo and couldn't?"

"Yes," he answered, "and I also said," he added, embarrassed, "that I wanted to love you and couldn't."

She moved her hand sharply. "Don't worry about me," she said coldly; then remained deep in thought for a moment as though collecting her own impressions before beginning her tale. "There's not much of a story," she said at last, looking down at her hands. "Yesterday . . . you remember?—when Leo and your mother and sister came back from the dance, the electricity had failed and candles had to be found. Then your mother dragged me off into her room to show me that new frock that she'd ordered from Paris . . . it's a lovely frock, but there's something wrong with the belt. After a while, I decided to go. I opened the door, took a step forward . . . and guess who I saw in the ante-room?"

Michele looked at her. The whole story had been told in a cold, grudging voice, and she had never ceased staring at her hands; and he had listened absent-mindedly, without interest, as though to any ordinary, commonplace tale. But now, suddenly, he recollected that the whole preamble of the story had been concerned with Leo: it was around *his* name that all the concentric circles were drawn; and he was oppressed by a vague, threatening anxiety, so sharp that he caught his breath.

"Leo!" he said instantly.

"Yes, Leo," echoed Lisa, quietly but ostentatiously shaking the ash from her cigarette. "Leo and Carla, embracing."

Their eyes met. Michele sat quite still, and looked at her without astonishment, but with that trance-like fixity which makes a person see double or treble, as though through a defective piece of glass. Lisa's eyes held an expression of curiosity, fright, and a sort of absurd haughtiness, like one who knows he has struck a shrewd blow, or made an important pronouncement.

"How d'you mean—embracing?" he demanded at last.

"Embracing," she repeated cruelly, irritated by his lack of comprehension as though by the writhings of a wounded animal that refuses to die. "Embracing—why, just like anyone else. She on his knee, their mouths joined together. In fact—embracing."

There was silence. Motionless, Michele sat looking at the carpet, pink, like the rest of the boudoir, and threadbare at the edges. On the carpet, side by side, were Lisa's two feet, beyond them, the divan. "Embracing," he kept on saying to himself all the time, "embracing . . . that's extraordinary." He wanted to shout out: "That's fantastic!"—both amusement and curiosity being aroused by so unexpected a happening. Of indignation, of disgust he felt none: if anything, he felt a lively interest, a desire to hear further explanations, to know more about it.

This state of mind lasted only a few seconds. Then, as he was preparing to ask questions, he realized, almost with terror, that once again he was entirely devoid of the feelings that such a deplorable matter should have aroused in him. Leo and Carla embracing suggested to him merely, so to speak, a social curiosity; this new disaster failed to move him, this supreme and unforeseen trial of his sincerity missed fire; those two embracing figures appeared to him like any number of other couples, known and unknown, instead of each of them having a personality that closely concerned him. But really, he thought, this has to do with Carla, with my own sister. Lisa has seen her in the embrace of that man, who is my mother's lover. Isn't it horrible? Isn't it revolting? Surely . . . isn't it practically incest? But the embracing, incestuous Carla and Leo remained remote from his movements of consternation and disgust; he could not touch them.

[251]

He glanced at Lisa and saw from her eyes, from her whole attitude, that she was expecting, with delight and curiosity, a fine scene of virtuous, hackneyed indignation. Anger . . . rage . . . hatred, he thought feverishly. I would give anything in the world for a little sincere hatred. But his spirit remained inert, leaden; there was no inkling of anger, or rage, or hatred. Carla in tears, naked, ruined, Leo with his ferocious appetites, the shame, the misery of it—nothing had the power to shake him.

And then a desperate idea came to him. Since the final test had failed, since no other, more violent stimulant had succeeded in galvanizing his dead spirit into life, would it not be better for him to make up his mind, once and for all, to make a pretence of *everything*—of love, of hatred, of indignation—a pretence with no meanness about it, a pretence on a big scale, in the grand manner, in fact, like a man who has enough and to spare? A crazy idea. It's the end, he thought, and he felt he was really renouncing, forever, the unattainable solace of the clear, natural, ever-flowing springs of life, the end. But something is bound to happen. Something *will* happen.

He rose to his feet. "No," he said, starting to walk up and down the room, in a way suitable when a man is both indignant and preoccupied, "this is too much. No, it's impossible to go on like this. This is the limit!" He felt cool, ironical; it seemed to him that his tone of voice was not determined enough, and decided to alter it. There was a brief silence.

"Leo thinks he can do anything he likes," he went on, while Lisa, bent forward and motionless, stared at him without saying anything, "but he's wrong. No, that's too weak, he said to himself, still walking up and down, I must say something stronger than that. I am a brother whose sister's honor has been insulted by his mother's lover (all these virtuous, hackneyed words had a ridiculous, pseudo-archaic effect in his eyes); I must find something harsher. After all, why not exaggerate if necessary? But these ironical falsities merely increased his gloom and weariness; he longed to stop his play-acting, to kneel down in front of Lisa, as in front of the women one loves, and to speak the whole truth: Lisa,

I'm not being sincere. My sister doesn't matter to me in the least, nobody matters to me. Lisa, what must I do? But Lisa was not the woman he loved, nor would she understand him; she, like everyone else, demanded of him the requisite, natural attitude.

"What are you going to do?" she asked.

He stopped and stared at her, trying hard to put a look of wildness into his calm eyes. "What am I going to do? What am I going to do? What am I going to do?" he kept on saying rapidly. "It's quite clear what I ought to do—go to that scoundrel and take him by the throat." It seemed to him that Lisa was astonished by this violence on his part.

"When?" she asked, glancing sharply at him through the smoke of the cigarette that hung from her lips.

"When? Tomorrow . . . today . . . now, at once." He took a cigarette from the table and lit it, and saw Lisa throw him a quick, perplexed, scrutinizing glance.

"And what will you say to him?" she inquired.

"Oh! I shall speak very, very coldly to him," he answered, waving his hand. He was looking straight in front of him, frowning as if he could see his own destiny ahead, and now he was becoming gradually more successful at acting his part. "Only a few words . . . but he'll see that it's no joking matter." Lisa threw him another glance. What a silly fool I'm being! he thought.

"But what I find most revolting," he went on, wishing urgently that he could get warmed up and convince both himself and her, "is Leo's hypocrisy, the low way he's behaved. Quite a different thing if he was really in love with my sister. It wouldn't excuse him, but it would partly explain matters. But of course he isn't. I'm sure he doesn't love her; but he's like that, he finds her pretty and attractive and so he wants to amuse himself with her, that's all. Apart from the fact that it's always a dirty trick to take advantage of a girl's inexperience, it's doubly so when a man does it in a cold, deliberate way and in the situation in which Leo is in relation to Carla and all of us. Nobody could be more . . ."
—he searched for the most expressive word to describe Leo's conduct—"more of a swine. And as I've already said—quite

[253]

a different thing if he'd done it from real passion . . . carried away by his own feeling. But there's no question of love in this case, no passion, no affection; nothing but lust and the most odious, the most revolting hypocrisy, the hypocrisy that simulates pure, ideal feelings. It's a thing one can neither excuse nor understand, only condemn." At first Michele had been lacking in assurance, then had gradually gained it; and he brought out the last words with a strange, profound force that was surprising even to himself. "As for Carla," he concluded after a moment, "it's not *her* fault. She allowed herself to be dazzled by that man."

There was silence. Lisa, sitting motionless on the divan, her head between her hands, watched the boy. "There's no doubt," she said at last, in a tone of vague approval, "that hypocrisy is a most dreadful thing."

"Most dreadful indeed." He moved and went across to the window; the sun had now disappeared, and a low, thick curtain of gray cloud hung over the city. Lisa lived on the first floor, but the house stood on a hill, and on that side a wide panorama of roofs was visible from the window. Gables, tiles, flat roofs, sky-lights, balconies—the whole view, beneath the gray sky, was of a damp, gloomy, brownish-yellow color, and appeared, owing to the imperfect glass of the window panes, blurred and distorted like a piece of discolored, ill-painted stage scenery. In the distance, the smoke rising from each house seemed to mingle with the clouds, forming a kind of mist in which the irregular outlines of the roofs and the forest of chimneys lost all perspective, becoming jumbled and confused.

Below the window the tiles were reddish and tufts of grass grew on them. Michele stood contemplating this landscape. It was the first time he had noticed it and he could not tear himself away from it. All those roofs made a deep impression upon him. If only one could take them off, he thought, and see what's going on inside the houses. A black cat passed quickly from one sky-light to another; he followed it with his eyes for a moment. It's going to rain, he thought, looking at the gray sky and the damp, distant spaces, and he shivered. Then he turned around, and there was the faded boudoir again, and Lisa on the shabby divan, deep in thought, motionless. He went over to her. I must pretend, he said to himself, clutching again, with an effort, at his own false reality. I should like . . . I should like to go to sleep . . . but I've got to go on pretending. There was no connection between "pretending" and "sleep," but this latter word came to him spontaneously as an expression of the deadly weariness that oppressed him.

"What time is it?" he asked sharply. "Isn't it time I went to see Leo?"

Slowly, lazily Lisa shook herself out of her inertia and looked at the watch on her wrist. "Four o'clock," she said, looking closely at the boy. There was silence; then she went on, "But perhaps it would be better if you telephoned first to find out if he's at home." She rose and moved towards the door.

In the passage the blackness was complete. Lisa turned the switch and a yellowish light, like a night-light, flowed down from the low ceiling over the dark walls. The telephone was fixed to the wall, breast-high, beside the drawing-room door, and below it was the directory; Lisa turned its pages rapidly, then twisted the handle of the telephone several times.

"But you *will* go?" she asked doubtfully, turning towards Michele.

"Do you still doubt it?" he replied energetically, but he saw a look of doubt, a knowing, perverse look in her eyes.

"No, far from it," she said, then began turning the handle again.

The telephone bell rang. Raising herself on tiptoe, Lisa cried, in a throaty voice: "Hullooo . . . hullooo . . .," waited a moment, silent and tense, then began again. Michele, meanwhile, gazed idly at the passage, at its two cupboards, its nondescript, empty shelves, its chairs. Lisa was standing with her back to him, and her blouse, shot through with yellowish light, gave even more generous glimpses than previously, in the boudoir, of the pink and blonde expanse of her back between the two dingy shoulder-straps of her negligée; her hips, half-wrapped in shadow, looked less broad, her legs less crooked. All this Michele dreamily observed. Here I am in Lisa's flat . . . in

the passage, he kept saying to himself. I must pretend . . .
not a moment's respite . . . go on pretending. Hardly knowing what he was doing, he stepped to her side and took her
by the waist. "Well," he asked, in a false, insinuating voice,
just touching the back of her neck with his lips, "well, are
you still angry with me?" Then someone spoke on the telephone; Lisa gave the number, and turned towards him.

"Don't think about *me*," she said, with the same probing
glance as before. "Better think of your sister, of Leo."

"I've already thought about that," he answered, disconcerted, but he let go of her and leaned against the wall. Pretend, he thought, disillusioned, but for how long? That second glance was enough; obviously Lisa doubted the sincerity
of his indignation. What could he do to convince her?

She was speaking now. "Who is that?" she repeated, "who
is that? Am I speaking to Signor . . . to Signor Merumeci?
Ah! I'm sorry . . . wrong number." She replaced the receiver
and turned to him.

"He's at home," she said drily. "Probably, if you go now,
you'll find him." Their eyes met. She doesn't believe me,
thought Michele, examining her with suspicion.

"Well, go then," she added, at last. The boy waved his
hand with a childish, cautious gesture, as much as to say,
"Gently, gently . . . no hurry." Then he moved away. "I'm
going. Yes, I'm going," he said.

"You needn't go if you don't want to," said Lisa in a hard
voice. "You can pretend you don't know anything about it.
It's all the same to me whether you go or not."

In the hall she helped him on with his overcoat and
handed him his hat.

"Well then," he said, "I'll come back tomorrow and make
my report."

"All right. See you tomorrow."

But Michele went unwillingly. He felt that Lisa had not
believed one single word of what he had said, and he wanted
to swear big oaths, with big gestures and profound utter-
ances—in fact, to convince her. He hesitated. "I'm sure," he
said at last, taking the hand that Lisa held out to him, "that
you don't believe in my hatred for Leo, in my disgust."

There was silence. "No, really I don't," she answered simply.

"Why?"

"I just don't—that's all."

Silence again. "And supposing," said Michele, "supposing I give you proof of it—by action."

"What sort of action?"

He hesitated again; Lisa's eyes showed a mixture of uncertainty and authoritativeness. What sort of action indeed? he repeated to himself. A faint fear came over him at not being able to name the action that would have the power to convince her of his sincerity. Then, shifting his attention from Lisa to his enemy, he discovered it spontaneously, just as one finds something one has long and unconsciously sought. To kill Leo. The idea pleased him, not inasmuch as he expected to realize it, but because of its supposed efficacy upon the feminine mind.

"For instance," he remarked quietly, "would you believe it if I killed Leo?"

"If you killed him?" Lisa's first reaction was one of fright; and Michele smiled, satisfied at the impression his words had made.

"Yes. If I killed him."

But Lisa was calming down again, having observed his calm face, his eyes with no anger in them. "Oh, in that case, yes." She smiled ironically. "But the way you say it is enough to convince one that you won't do it."

He said nothing. The way I said it, he thought, annoyed at having so completely spoiled his effect. What way? Is there actually a proper way for saying one wants to kill somebody? The curtain was falling, the play had failed; the only thing left was to go away.

"So you don't think me capable of killing Leo?" he insisted, and at once saw her burst out laughing—without much confidence, but certainly not in fear.

"No, no, my poor Michele," she replied finally, her cheerfulness and sympathy restored. "There are things one says. But between the saying and the doing of them . . . Besides, I've already told you, one has only to look at your face to know that you have no intention of doing it. In any case," she added, as though to stifle, in herself, the last possible doubt, "if you had said it seriously, I shouldn't be letting you leave my house like this. . . ." She opened the door and held out her hand to him. "Hurry up," she said, "otherwise you won't even manage to see him."

"And what if I kill him?" he said again, as though it were a refrain. He was outside on the landing now.

"Ah well, *then* . . . then I should believe it," she answered, with an incredulous smile. The door closed.

15

White light poured down on to the staircase from the glass roof above it; and now the door was shut, and there was silence. Nobody believes me, he thought as he went away, nobody ever will believe me. He descended the few stairs slowly, a slight but distressing feeling of uneasiness oppressed him, and notwithstanding all his efforts he could not shake off the unhappy confusion that pervaded his mind.

All the various figures and ingredients of his misery—the seduction of Carla, Lisa's incredulity, his mother, Leo—came before his eyes with startling clearness, one after the other, like pieces torn from a single landscape by lightning flashes in a storm at night. With humiliation, he saw again the ironical face of Lisa in the crack of the door, or, more gloomily, imagined Carla dishevelled and half-naked in her lover's arms. But, if he attempted to bring together these fancies, to relate the various facts to each other, to take control of them like a puppet-showman who is able to hold the strings of all his marionettes together in his fist, if he made an effort to consider, coldly and dispassionately, the whole of the tangle in which he was involved, then he became bewildered and stifled, his feeble thoughts did not have the power to grasp the whole thorny reality, nor his eyes to em-

[259]

brace his own particular view of life fully and from every point.

He tried to reason, to contrive systems. Now, he thought, let's see. The question has two aspects, one internal, one external. The internal one consists of my own indifference, my lack of faith and sincerity; the external, of all the happenings to which I can't get any reaction. And both aspects are equally intolerable. He looked up as if he hoped to see them, these two aspects of his problem. No, he thought again, unhappily, the fault is mine; I don't know how to get passionately involved in life. He went on downstairs. But the fault was Carla's as well. Carla, he wanted to ask her, why have you done this? And his mother's too. The fault was everyone's; impossible to discover the source, the original cause of it; everyone was to blame. He seemed to see them, the whole lot of them, there on the landing, leaning against the wall. You're a lot of unfortunates, he thought, you fill me with pity, all of you. Yes, you too, Mother, with your ridiculous jealousies, and you too, Leo, with your triumphant airs. He seemed to see Leo, to take his hand. I feel compassion for you, more than anything; yes, for you. You think you're the stronger. Ah! my poor Leo! He wanted to say just those words to him, to his enemy, quietly, like that. He was possessed by a kind of intoxication; he threw back his head. You poor people, you're just a lot of unfortunates. You poor people, you're in a fix, now. You'll see what will happen to you. But when he reached the door he noticed that he was still holding his hat in his hand; and his ineptitude and absentmindedness brought him down with a bump from his attitude of superiority. An unspeakable rage and distress swept over him. It's I—there's no doubt about it—it's I who am the unfortunate one, he thought. He was smack down to earth again, and he crammed his hat on his head and went out.

The houses seemed dead, the plane-trees were mute on that still afternoon; a sky of stone weighed heavy on the crouching roofs; and for the full length of the street there was neither light nor shadow, only an arid sense of waiting hungrily for a storm. Now let's go to Leo's, he said to himself; and at this idea a sense of uncontrollable exaltation seized

[260]

him. Ah! and you think I can't kill Leo, he kept saying rapidly to himself, you think I can't. But suppose I do? He hurried along, putting great energy into his strides, giving his whole person an air of decision and assurance, absurd phrases danced in his empty head in time to his marching steps. Come along, Lisa, let's go and kill Leo. And then we'll cook him, we'll cook him over a slow fire. O Leo, O dear little Leo, you're going to die like a dog. He looked in front of him and smiled a cold, desperate smile. It's all over for you now, Leo, your fine career, your radiant future, all finished. What a pity! I myself am the first to lament it. But what can you do? It's all over for you. He felt like singing: *It's over, it's over, your beautiful life is over*—to the tune of some famous, melancholy song. He hurried along, walking with the stiff, straight steps of a soldier going into battle.

It was a humble, inferior street with small shops with poor-looking windows. He noticed a flower-shop showing funeral wreaths, a printer's establishment with specimens of visiting cards covering the walls, a carpenter's shop and a barber's. There you are, Leo, he thought, there's everything we need. First I'll buy that splendid coffin for you, then order you a fine wreath and pin my visiting-card to it. And the barber . . . the barber will give you a beautiful shave. Beyond the carpenter's there was a severe-looking house with a great, deep-set door like a convent; as he walked past it he cast a glance into the empty archway and had a glimpse of another little shop. The window was on the near side, the door beyond. At first he did not see what kind of a store it was; the shine on the glass, seen sideways, made it difficult to distinguish the objects behind it. He moved on a step, and then saw the word "gunsmith" in white letters, and, against a brown background, a rack full of sporting guns. And this is where I buy a revolver, he said to himself. He hesitated in front of the door. Then he turned on his heel and went in.

"I want a revolver," he said at once, loudly, leaning against the counter. The plunge was taken; and now a great fear came over him that the shopkeeper would see through his intentions. He assumed a cold, patient air, keeping his eyes lowered and his hands still. All he could see of the shopkeeper was the upper part of his body, clothed in black, moving slowly between the counter and the shelves behind. Under the glass of the counter he could see a quantity of bright knives arranged on a reddish background, some of them plain, others complicated, with any number of blades, some open like fans, others closed and compact. Then he looked up. The walls of the small, dark shop were hidden by glazed shelves; some of them contained racks of rifles, a few of them dog-collars. Further along the counter he noticed a block of wood in which little beads of lead were stuck according to size, looking like the sun and all the planets. And now the shopkeeper, a tired, thin, pock-marked, slow-moving man with inexpressive eyes, was placing different kinds of pistols, one by one, on the glass counter and announcing the price of each, in an even voice, as he put them down—one hundred, seventy, two hundred and fifty, ninety-five; some were flat and black, others plump and shining—the former automatics, the latter revolvers. "That's the one for Leo," he thought ironically, as he looked at an enormous pistol with a detachable butt, a sort of machine-gun, hanging on the wall. He felt calm in mind and natural in his movements; looking down again, he chose, without hesitating, the cheapest. "This one," he said in a clear voice, "and some ammunition." His pocket-book was in his hand. I've only just enough money, he thought, as he put the cash on the counter. There was a metallic sound. He picked up his parcel, put it in his pocket and went out.

Now let's go to Leo's, he decided again. The gray, still space of the street in front of him now seemed to be distorted by unsteady tears. At the corner there was a kind of workshop where they repaired machines, and in the doorway a man in dirty overalls was dismantling a bicycle wheel. It was hot. Not a sound of a human voice was to be heard. Tears from heaven, as they dropped, distorted the six-floor houses—there, he could see them, with all their windows, twisting and bending and swaying; yet those tears left no trace on the paving-stones. Yellowish spittle, but no tears. Was it a hallucination?

He turned and came out into a more important street. He

would have to walk to the far end, then cross the square, and then he would be in Leo's street. There was no hurry; he walked slowly, like any idler, looking at the people, at the cinema posters, at the shop windows, the revolver weighing down in his pocket. He stopped in front of a shop, and very gradually undid the paper covering with his fingers, and grasped the butt of the weapon. It was a strange, cold contact. That was the trigger, a slight pressure and all would be over—for Leo, one shot, two, three shots. And there, that was the barrel, and he could feel the grooves. He clenched his teeth, grasped the butt of the revolver again. There . . . there. . . . He seemed to see just how the whole thing would come about. He would go up the stairs, into the sitting-room; there would be a pause, and he would be holding the weapon in his hand. Then Leo would ask, "What is it, Michele?"—and he would answer: "*This* is what it is," and would immediately shoot. As for the first shot, all that mattered was to plug it into any part of his body—and he offered a big target—then Leo would fall to the floor and he would be able to aim at his head. He would stoop down; there would be Leo, lying on the floor, his hands, paralyzed, on the carpet, his head thrown back, a rattling noise in his throat. He would rest the barrel of the revolver exactly in the middle of his brow, and then—curious sensation—the head would move, the agonized eyes would look at him, and he would shoot again. Noise . . . smoke. . . . Quickly he would leave the room without looking back, leave that little room in which, beneath the white stare of the windows, the dead man, faultlessly dressed, would be lying on the floor with arms flung wide; he would run downstairs before some other tenant appeared, emerge into the road. The crowd . . . the traffic. . . . And upstairs, between the four walls of that little room, the dead man. . . . Then he would look for a policeman (where *are* those police stations to be found, where one can give oneself up?), a traffic policeman, perhaps, he would touch the policeman lightly on the shoulder; the officer would turn round, expecting some passer-by wanting information. "Please," he would say quietly, "please arrest me. I have killed a man." The policeman would look at him without understanding. "I have killed a man," he would repeat. "Arrest me." While he was saying this, the crowd would be moving around him in all directions, the traffic would be going past. At last the man would go with him, incredulous, uncomprehending. He would go with him, without taking hold of him by the scruff of the neck or putting handcuffs on him, to the nearest police station. A dusty room, a police register, police officers, a stale, chilly smell of cigar-smoke, a desk, a police inspector—pock-marked, coarse, vulgar—an interrogation. He had been once to report a theft; that's how it would be.

He left the shop window and walked on. After that, they would bring him to trial; all the newspapers would be talking about his crime, with huge headlines and long reports; there would be photographs of him, of the dead man, of the "diligent" police officer who had arrested him, of the room where the deed had been done, with a little cross to mark the spot where the body had been found. There would be a morbid interest in the crime, on the day of the trial the court would be thronged with the public, smart ladies in the front row, social figures; just like at the theatre. Then a pause, and the judge would enter. He could see him, a calm, rather vague old man who would talk to him from the summit of his dusty throne as a schoolmaster talks to his pupil, inclining his head towards him and gazing at him without the slightest severity from under arched, white eyebrows. He could hear him, too.

"Accused, what have you to say?"

At this invitation he would rise to his feet, and all eyes would be fixed upon him. He would tell the story of his crime, and the ladies, comfortably seated, would follow every phrase with the utmost attention—apart from an occasional frivolous movement such as the adjusting of a rebellious hat, or the crossing of a pair of tired legs. The silence would be such that you could hear a pin drop, and in that silence he would speak with absolute sincerity; each one of his words, loaded with its own sad truth, would envelop him gradually in a special atmosphere of his own, like the cuttlefish that wraps itself in the murk of its own ink. Little by little, as he confessed his want of sincerity, of faith, his dilettante attitude, he would feel that the old judge had somehow come nearer to him, had come down to his level; the gray hall would noiselessly empty; there would be no one left but the two of them, the judge and himself on the dusty platform facing the dismal sight of bare walls and empty seats; and he would go on speaking. "And so," he would finally conclude, "I killed Leo without hatred, in cold blood. There was no sincerity in the act. I might have said to him with equal indifference: 'I congratulate you, my sister's a good-looking girl. . . .' That is my real crime, the sin of indifference." Silence, and the judge would look at him curiously, as one looks at a deformed being. Finally there would be the noise of chairs being moved—an echoing noise, like the repercussions of sound in the nave of a church. The judge would leave his throne and would come over unassumingly to where he stood on the dusty platform, he would be small and slight, with big feet, and his black gown would come clear down to his heels as if to conceal some monstrous deformity—perhaps, through sitting so long on his throne, meting out justice, his legs had shrivelled—small and slight, with a large, benevolent head.

"O Judge . . . Judge. . . ."; he would throw himself at the old man's feet.

"You are absolved of your crime," he would hear him say, after a moment's silence, "but you are condemned for your want of sincerity and faith . . . condemned to life imprisonment." An inexorable verdict, and when he lifted his head again, he would realize that he was still standing before the bar, in front of the absent-minded judge, between two armed policemen . . . a dream within a dream . . . spectres.

The reality would go differently. They would give him a celebrated lawyer to defend him, they would exalt him in his quality of brother and son, at first suffering and humiliated, then, at last, the avenger. During the trial they would applaud him, there would be a string of witnesses, Lisa would come, shabby and unkempt, and would describe in that false voice of hers how she had discovered the intrigue between Leo and Carla, making a profound impression; and she would tell how he had explained to her his intention of killing Leo, and she had not believed him.

And why hadn't she believed him? Because of the tone of voice in which he had said it.

And how had he said it? Calmly, almost jokingly.

Did Michele know about his mother? Yes, he knew.

How did the deceased behave in his mistress's house? As though he were the master of it.

How long had his relationship with the mother been going on? For fifteen years.

And with the daughter? As far as she knew, only a few days.

Did the daughter know of her mother's *liaison?* Yes, she knew.

What were the relations between the prisoner and the deceased? Friendly.

Business relations also? Yes.

What sort of business? She did not exactly remember, but thought it was to do with a mortgage on the villa.

Is it true that the accused had found fault with the deceased on the grounds that he was reducing them to ruin? It was true.

What reasons had urged her to reveal his sister's intrigue to Michele? Reasons of affection for the boy and of friendship for the family.

What, until recently, had been the demeanor of the deceased towards Carla? That of a father; he had known her ever since she had been a child with hair down her back, and bare legs.

Had Carla the reputation of being an honest, serious girl, or not? No . . . she had been, in general, severely criticized.

Did witness believe there was any passion on the man's side? No.

And on Carla's side? No.

Did she believe that the deceased had any intention of marrying Carla? No, not as far as she knew.

Was it true that the deceased did not hide from the children his relationship with the mother? Yes, it was true.

And that quarrels between the lovers were frequent? Yes. Why? The mother was jealous.

Of whom? Of everyone.

Had the mother suspicions about her daughter? No, in fact she had often confided to her that her lover cherished feelings for the girl that were purely paternal.

One last question: would she ever have believed that the boy was capable of such a crime? No.

Why? Because he is too weak.

Then his mother would be brought in, dressed in mourning, much made-up, extremely dignified, but lacking assurance. She would walk past the witness box and go right up to the judge, as if she knew him personally. When questioned, she would tell a long story, going right back to the remotest origins of the matter. She would speak in a pathetic voice, with dramatic gestures, and all her black veils would be in a state of continual agitation—those black veils that looked like a fancy dress. When questioned artfully by the lawyers for the defense, who would throw themselves upon their prey like sharp-toothed sharks upon a tender whale, she would acknowledge her attachment to the deceased; and, to the question whether it was true that he had defrauded her of her inheritance, she would answer no.

And what did she know about Carla's seduction? That it was an act of madness; but whosoever does not commit such acts, let him cast the first stone.

"Let us call it an act of madness, then," Michele's counsel would stress ironically. A squabble between the two sides; an energetic call to order from the President of the Court.

And did she believe that Leo would try to make up for this act of madness by marrying Carla? Uncertainty. . . . No. . . . She was not sure.

Sensation in court. And would she have adapted herself to such a situation, with a man coming to the house who was the lover both of herself and of her daughter? Embarrassment. . . . No, but Leo had already thought about it and had already decided to find a husband for Carla.

Laughter . . . Sarcastic remarks.

Was it true that the deceased would have given the girl some sort of dowry? Yes, that was true.

"And in exchange," the counsel for the defense would observe, "he had reserved for himself, in advance, the *jus primae noctis*." Fresh squabble, whistles from the crowd, the public would now take *his* side; a threat from the President that he would clear the court. That's what always happens. . . .

Was it true that there had recently been violent altercations between the deceased and Michele? Yes, it was true.

And that Michele, one evening, had thrown an ash-tray at Leo? Yes, but it had struck *her*, on the shoulder.

And the reason? Michele had wrongly thought that the deceased wished to take advantage of the mortgage in order to defraud her.

And how had the deceased behaved on that occasion? In a paternal manner, magnanimously.

Was it true that there were frequent outbursts of dissension between herself and the deceased? No, they were united in the most perfect harmony.

But the witness Lisa had given quite a different impression? Yes, of course, she had good reasons for blackening the memory of the departed.

What reasons? Oh, only one, but quite sufficient, she had been his mistress.

Sensation. "It seems to me," Michele's counsel would remark, "that no woman was safe from him!"

When was that? Before her.

In her previous examination she had accused Lisa of instigating the crime, and now? Now she repeated the accusation.

What were Lisa's reasons? Jealousy and envy.

And she accused her also of wishing to corrupt Michele? Certainly, she was a shameless woman, without modesty or decency.

Sensation. A call to order from the President, for more moderate language; defiance on the part of the witness.

Yes, she *was* a shameless woman, she would cry, a low, shameless woman and a murderess.

[268]

A further call to order.

And was it true that, in order to account for her lover's coldness, she had suspected Lisa instead of her daughter? Yes, because she had noticed for some time that Lisa had been making up to him.

To sum the matter up, then, Lisa, according to her, was mainly responsible? Certainly, it was she who had instigated the crime, who had worked on Michele's feelings, it was she who had done everything.

And, according to her, the deceased had also done rightly in seducing her daughter? No, but—after all, human weaknesses. Besides, the fault could not have been entirely on his side.

And Michele? Michele was a poor, irresponsible boy, the tool of Lisa; he was too weak to have acted of his own accord.

Then, last of the three women in his life, Carla would appear—thinner than before, pale, a grown woman. Amid the frenzied curiosity of the public she would walk forward, without either timidity or boldness; she would be wearing a light-colored dress (it was morning), light-colored stockings, a small light-colored hat, and a fur around her shoulders; she would be made-up, perhaps, and certainly smart. The old judge would look at her without severity, as he had looked at him. She would go and lean on the bar of the witness-box, and would speak slowly. Curiosity on the part of the crowd, eager expectation of scabrous details, intense excitement. But, after a brief consultation, the President would order the court to be cleared and the proceedings to be continued behind closed doors. Disappointment of the crowd, murmurings, whistling, the hall would gradually empty, and there would be Carla, alone, a small patch of color among the gray and black trappings of justice. Then the questioning would continue.

Was it true that an intimate relationship had been recently formed between her and the deceased? Yes, it was true.

Did she know about her mother? Yes, she had known since childhood.

Since childhood? Yes, as a child she had seen them one day kissing in front of a mirror.

Did she know that the deceased could not, or would not, marry her? Yes, she knew.

Did she know that the deceased had laid hands on their inheritance? Yes, she knew that too.

And in spite of her knowledge of all these things she had given herself to him? Yes.

Why? No particular reason.

How had the deceased behaved towards her, with real passion, or like a libertine? Like a libertine.

He did not love her, then? No, he did not love her.

In what way had he first made his feeling clear to her? One day when she was alone in the house, bored, reading a book, he came and talked to her, and gradually they had reached a sort of excited intimacy; then he had kissed her and invited her to go to his flat.

She had gone there? Yes, the following day.

What had happened at that meeting? Everything.

And she had gone back again? Yes, every day.

Was it true that Lisa had come upon her in the anteroom, the evening of a dance, sitting on her lover's knee and embracing him? Yes, it was possible.

Wasn't she afraid, at that moment, that she might be discovered by her mother? No.

Didn't she think she would be ruined if she took up with this man? No.

Why? She didn't know.

Did her mother hide her relationship with the deceased from her? No, in fact she confided in her.

Had the deceased ever spoken to her of her mother? Yes.

In what way? Unkindly.

What did he say about her? That she was old and stupid and that he didn't love her any more.

According to her mother, the deceased, in spite of his relations with her, proposed to give her, Carla, a dowry and get her married: was that true? No, it was not true.

How did she know? Because the deceased had suggested

that she should leave her family and go and live in a small flat where he could visit her when he wanted to.

Would she have accepted? Possibly.

Did not the deceased think that Michele would oppose this plan? No.

Why? Because he said that if he were given a little money Michele would keep quiet.

And her mother? Her mother would have made a great fuss but she too would have calmed down in the end.

Did she know of any previous quarrels between the deceased and Michele? Yes, one evening the deceased had threatened to box Michele's ears.

And Michele? Michele had thrown an ash-tray at his head, but it had hit his mother instead.

Had her brother ever revealed to her his purpose of killing Leo? Never.

What was Michele like in family business matters? Indifferent and feeble.

Then Carla would go away too. But first she would come over and greet him. He seemed to see her—embarrassed, serious, with an imploring, troubled look in her eyes; she would ask him how he was, and they would shake hands; and then she would go away, walking in that frivolous-looking way with her high heels, in her close-fitting dress. And, from the cautious, ill-assured modesty of her gait, from the soft movement of her hips, from the details of her whole figure, he would picture the new life of which he had had a glimpse in his mother's tattered, undignified mourning .

The three women would disappear out of his life, his sister, his mother, his mistress, each going her own road; but the trial would go on; and a few days later the Public Prosecutor would speak. It would be a powerful speech; after exerting himself to depict in dark colors the corrupt and corrupting environment in which the crime had taken place, he would fully uphold the theory of its being a premeditated crime, though conceding that there were extenuating circumstances.

"Yes, gentlemen of the jury," he would exclaim at this point, banging his fist on the table, "it is a case of premeditated crime. Michele has the news of his sister's seduction from Lisa and goes off, hinting, in a joking manner—according to the witness's deposition—that he may possibly kill the seducer. Everything, therefore, was already decided, and Leo was already condemned. Michele does not go to see Leo with the object of demanding explanations, but in order to murder him, whether Lisa was speaking the truth or not. About two hours pass between Lisa's revelation and the committing of the crime—what was Michele doing during that time? No sooner had he left her house than he rushes like a madman into a gunsmith's shop in the same street in which she lives, and buys a revolver for seventy lire; after which he wanders aimlessly about the town, at the mercy of his own thoughts and his own bloody purposes of vengeance, like a ship at the mercy of a storm; you can see him, with the revolver in his pocket, stopping in front of shops, looking into the windows, walking on again, going several times up and down the street in which Leo lives, you can see him, at last, in front of the door, hesitating, then going in, mounting the stairs. There he is in his enemy's sitting-room; the latter comes forward towards him, gay, affectionate, friendly, smiling at him. That smile, gentlemen of the jury—the smile of a man who, all unknowing, is advancing to his death: holding out his hand. Then Michele shoots; the man falls; Michele stoops down, and coldly, pitilessly, finishes him off with a shot in the temple; then, with the coolness of an inveterate criminal, shuts the door behind him and goes off and gives himself up. . . ." The orator would make a careful analysis of the obstinate, implacable determination of Michele to kill Leo, in spite of his knowing that "Carla, as the evidence had made clear, was not the pure, untouched, virginal girl one might have thought —quite otherwise, in fact—and that consequently there had been no seduction in the true sense of the word." Sensation in court. . . .

"Carla," he would observe, "is one of those girls who have never been innocent: one man today, another tomorrow . . . one of the unfortunate figures of our corrupt period." He would insist on the fact that, in all probability, it had not been Leo who courted the girl, but *vice versa*; the reason being a kind of insane and morbid rivalry between mother and daughter. "Gentlemen of the jury," he would finally conclude, "no one has the right to take human, and even less divine justice into his hands. This is what Michele dared to do. Michele condemned his enemy and then carried out the sentence. This cruel, cold determination to kill is his real crime: no sudden outburst of passion, gentlemen of the jury, no explosion of virtuous indignation, but the preparation and execution of a long-meditated, bloodthirsty purpose. Remember that, remember that, for Michele, Leo was dead while he was still living, when his place among men was not yet marked by a tomb. And you, Michele," he would exclaim, turning towards the prisoner, "accept your sentence as an expiation, as a purification, after which you will be able to return again to your family and to mankind."

Michele shook his head. You're wrong, Public Prosecutor, he thought ironically, you're wrong. Neither purification, nor expiation, nor family either. Indifference, indifference—nothing but indifference. He smiled vaguely. And who would speak after the Public Prosecutor? His own counsel; that luminary, that new Demosthenes would rise to his feet. He would describe, one by one, the dingy figures of the trial, he too would paint a dark picture of the environment and the members of the family—the mother a loose and shameless woman, Leo a swindler and incestuous, Lisa a gossip, a wanton, and he and Carla, both of them victims, children of a drunkard (the father is always a drunkard, he thought), who had grown up without the love of parents, without religion, without moral standards.

"The lover, first of Lisa, then of the mother," the speaker would cry, "Leo becomes the lover, also, of the daughter—of the daughter, gentlemen of the jury," he would repeat, in a pathetic, pained voice—"whom he had known as an innocent child with her hair down her back, and bare legs, whom he had held on his knee, whom he had, one may say, brought up for his own benefit and his own filthy purposes—this house was his *harem*—and not content with this, he lays his greedy hands upon the family inheritance. . . ." And, after piling up Leo's wicked deeds like the stones of some scandalous edifice, the orator would burst generously forth in

[273]

high praise of the justice of the crime. Michele seemed already to see him, his own Cicero, with face flushed purple, hair flying, fists beating the table, seemed to hear him too. "Can they condemn you, Michele, for vindicating the outraged, the trampled honor of your own family?" When, looking up, he realized that he was in the street in which Leo lived.

A cold, deadly anxiety froze his blood. Well, here we are, he thought. Here was the street he was seeking, with its new, white houses and empty gardens, a few buildings laden with scaffolding, and some unpaved footpaths; the country could not be far off. Few people passed, no one turned to look at him, no one was watching him. And yet I'm on my way to kill a man, he said to himself. It seemed an improbable remark, and he put his hand into his pocket to touch the revolver. Killing Leo meant really and truly killing him, removing him from the number of the living, making his blood flow. I've got to kill him—like that—without too much noise—like that. Yes—aim at his chest. He'll fall . . . on the floor. I stoop down, without any noise, slowly, I finish him off. The scene which would be over in a flash seemed to him immensely long, disconnected in its movements, silent. A sickness overwhelmed him. If only I could kill him without knowing it, then—yes—then everything would be all right.

The sky was gray; few people passing; a car; villas; gardens; the revolver in his pocket; the trigger; the butt. He stopped briefly to look at the number on the door, and at that moment his own quietness alarmed him. If I go on feeling calm like this, he thought in terror, nothing will get done. I've got to be indignant, furious. . . . He walked on; Number 83 was farther down the street. I've got to get worked up, he thought feverishly. Now let's see . . . let's see what all the reasons are that I have for hating Leo. My mother . . . my sister. She was chaste only a few days ago, now she's in that same bed, naked . . . lost. Leo has had her . . . possessed her . . . my sister . . . possessed . . . my sister . . . possessed . . . my sister . . . my sister . . . treated like a whore . . . lying in that foul bed . . . horrible, horrible . . . naked in his arms . . . my soul shudders at the very thought of it

[274]

. . . submitting to that man's lust . . . my sister . . . horrible. He rubbed his hand across his neck, his throat felt dry. To hell with my sister, he thought despairingly, finding himself in the same calm state of mind as before; for all these efforts of the imagination had quite failed to move him. He looked up at a doorway; Number 65 already; and a cruel fear came over him that he would not be able to act. He put his hand in his pocket, nervously grasping the revolver. To hell with everyone . . . what do reasons matter? I've decided to kill him and kill him I shall. He quickened his pace, and the houses seemed to rush past him, one after the other, quicker and quicker. . . . It was necessary to kill him and he would kill him—that was all. Number 75, 76, a street, then 77, 78; suddenly he started running, the revolver banging against his thigh. He noticed a little girl of about ten on the pavement in front of him, holding the hand of a boy smaller than herself and coming towards him; he expected to meet and pass them; but he reached Leo's door before they did, and went in, regretting that he had just missed them. And now, he thought, as he climbed the stairs, what a joke it would be if I didn't find him at home! He ran up two flights of stairs, and on the second landing, to the right, saw his enemy's door. A brass plate bore the name *Cavaliere Leo Merumeci*.

He did not ring the bell. He wanted to be breathing quietly as he went in, and so he waited, standing erect and motionless in front of the closed door, until his panting and the beating of his heart should calm down. But they did not calm down; his heart throbbed and leaped wildly within his breast, his lungs heaved painfully, and he could not control them. O my heart! O my breath! he thought, with unhappy, nervous scorn, are you siding against me too? He pressed his hand against his ribs, trying to gain control of himself; how long would it take for his body to be as well prepared as his mind already was? He counted up to sixty, ridiculously, standing motionless against the silent door; then started again. Finally, wearying of it, he broke off and rang the bell.

He heard the sound of the bell echoing in the empty flat. Silence; stillness. He's not at home, he thought, with profound joy and relief. I'll ring once more, just to make sure, and then I'll go away. And already, as he was preparing to press the button again, already he was picturing himself going down into the street again, walking off into the town, free once more, to enjoy himself; already he was forgetting his plans of vengeance, when there was the sound of heavy footsteps on the other side of the door. Then the door opened and Leo appeared.

He was wearing a dressing-gown, his hair was ruffled and his chest bare; and he stared ungraciously at the boy.

"*You* here!" he exclaimed with sleepy voice and sleepy face, without asking him to come in. "What d'you want?"

Their eyes met. What do I want? Michele wanted to shout at him. You know quite well what I want, you beast! But he restrained himself. "Nothing," he gasped, for he was breathless again now. "Just to talk to you."

Leo looked up, and an impudent, silly expression crossed his face. "Oh, my goodness, you want to talk? To me? At this hour?" he said with exaggerated surprise. He was still standing in the middle of the doorway. "And what d'you want to say to me? I say, my dear boy," he went on, starting to close the door, "wouldn't it be better another day? I was asleep, and my head isn't clear enough. How about tomorrow?"

The door was closing. It's not true that you were asleep, thought Michele; and all of a sudden the idea flashed through his mind: Carla's in there . . . in his bedroom, and he seemed to see her sitting naked on the edge of the bed, listening anxiously to this dialogue between her lover and the unknown visitor. He gave the door a push and went in.

"No," he said, in a firm but troubled voice, "no, I've got to talk to you today . . . now."

Leo hesitated. "Oh well, all right," he muttered, impatiently. Michele went into the flat. Carla is in there, he thought, and an extraordinary agitation took possession of him.

"Now, tell the truth," he said at last with an effort, putting a hand on Leo's shoulder as he was shutting the door. "Tell the truth, I've interrupted a tender scene, haven't I?

There's someone in there, isn't there? Hee, hee! . . . some pretty girl or other. . . ." He saw Leo turn to protest, a hateful smile of ill-concealed vanity on his lips. "Absolutely no one. I was sleeping." Michele knew he had hit the mark.

He put his hand in his pocket and grasped the revolver. "Yes, I was fast asleep," Leo repeated as he preceded him into the hall. "I was fast asleep and having the most lovely dreams."

"Really?"

"Yes. And then you came and woke me up."

I can shoot him in the back, thought Michele. He drew the revolver from his pocket, and keeping his hand against his side, aimed it in Leo's direction. As soon as he turned around, he would shoot.

Leo led the way into the sitting-room, went to the table and lit a cigarette. Wrapped in his dressing-gown, like a wrestler, his legs wide apart, his head, rumpled and square, bent over the invisible match, he gave the impression of a man sure of himself and of his own life. Then he turned; and Michele, not without real hatred in his heart, raised his hand and fired.

There was neither smoke nor noise. Leo, terrified at the sight of the revolver, threw himself with a kind of roar behind a chair. And then came the sharp click of the trigger. It's misfired, thought the boy. "You're mad!" yelled Leo, raising the chair in the air and exposing the whole of his body. Michele leaned forward and fired again; again the sharp click of the trigger. It's not loaded, he realized at last, in terror, I've still got the ammunition in my pocket. He leapt sideways to avoid the chair Leo was wielding, and rushed to the opposite corner of the room, his head was going around, his throat was dry, his heart pounding. One cartridge, he thought desperately, just one single cartridge! He fumbled and snatched a handful of them with feverish fingers, looked up again as he stooped and struggled crazily to open the barrel and push in the charge, but Leo saw what he was doing, and gave Michele a slanting blow with the chair across his hands and his knees, knocking the revolver to the floor. The pain caused him to close his eyes, and then

an indescribable rage swept through him; he hurled himself
upon Leo and tried to seize him by the neck, but he himself
was grasped and thrown one way and then the other, and
finally pushed away with such violence that, after blindly
knocking against and overturning a chair, he fell on to the
divan. The other man was on top of him at once, holding
him by the wrists.

There was silence as they stared at each other. Red in the
face, out of breath, forced into a painful position against the
divan, Michele made an effort to free himself. Leo replied
by twisting his wrists. Michele made a second effort and
again his wrists were twisted. Pain and rage at last vanquished
the boy. It seemed to him, in an obscure way, that life had
never been so cruel as at that moment, and the brutal op-
pression he was suffering brought back a mournful yearning
for far-distant maternal caresses. Tears came into his eyes,
he relaxed his aching muscles and let himself go. For a moment the man looked at him; his dressing-gown was wide
open, his bare, hairy chest heaved with his labored breathing, which he expelled, every now and then, through palpitating nostrils, in a kind of savage, animal blast; he stared and
stared at him, and his whole being was expressive of a menacing fury restrained with difficulty.

"You're mad!" he ejaculated, shaking his head violently,
and let him go.

Michele rose to his feet, rubbing his sore wrists. There was
Leo, standing motionless in the middle of the room, there
was the overturned chair, and there, in the corner, a black
thing lying—the revolver. Truly all was over now . . . all
was accomplished. But he couldn't quite understand. He
didn't know whether he should show indignation or fear.
He looked at Leo and mechanically went on rubbing his
wrists.

"And now," Leo said at last, turning towards the door,
"will you be so extremely kind as to get out?" He would
have very much liked to show some sort of violence, but
restrained himself. "As for this crazy behavior of yours," he
added, "I shall speak to your mother about it."

But Michele did not move. He doesn't lecture me or swear

[278]

at me, he said to himself, he's in a hurry for me to go, because he's afraid I shall discover Carla. Carla's in there . . . in the next room. He looked at the farther door and was almost surprised to see that it was so ordinary and so like other doors, and that his sister's presence did not reveal itself in some way—for instance, by part of a garment caught in the door when it was hastily shut.

"Where is Carla?" he asked finally, in a clear voice. A very slight look of astonishment crossed the man's impudent face; but it was gone in an instant.

"Carla?" he echoed, with the greatest naturalness. "How should *I* know? At home, I suppose, or out somewhere." He went up to him and took him by the arm. "Now are you going or not?"

"Let me alone," said the boy, turning pale and looking at him, but making no attempt to free himself. "Don't imagine you're frightening me. I shall go when I want to."

"Are you going or not?" repeated Leo more loudly. He started trying to pull Michele towards the door, but the latter resisted.

"I'm certain," he cried hurriedly, digging his heels into the carpet, "I'm certain Carla's actually here in your bedroom." A violent pull from Leo. "And you, you let me alone," he ordered him, struggling to escape, but Leo did not obey.

"You *shall* go," he repeated, almost joyfully; "in my own house I do what I think and what I like. You'll go whether you want to or not." Pushed, now, from behind, Michele was unable to turn around.

"You brute!" he shouted, feeling himself forced to give way, "you brute!"

"Brute as much as you like," repeated Leo as he pushed him towards the door, "but you're going."

It was at this moment that the door opened and Carla came in.

She was coatless, and was wearing a close-fitting skirt and a brown woolen jumper; and she had evidently just dressed in a great hurry, for her hair was untidy, and she was pale, with that particular look of bareness and weariness that women have when they have been either unable or unwilling

[279]

to make a complete *toilette*. She closed the door behind her, and advanced, very erect and with a fixed look in her eyes, into the middle of the room.

"I heard a noise," she said, "so I came in."

"What are you doing here?" After an instant's surprise, Leo had let go of Michele and rushed over to her, and now was shaking her by the arm. "What are you doing here? I told you to stay in there! And yet you come in. What d'you mean by it? What d'you take me for? . . . You're all mad, the whole lot of you." He could hardly speak from rage; but managed to get control of himself. "Well, since you insisted on coming in," he went on, "here is your brother Michele, who's taken to shooting at people. You talk to him, do what you like about him. I wash my hands of the whole thing." He let her go and as though dismissing the subject, went and sat down near the window.

Michele looked at Carla. What had become of the virtuous indignation he was going to feel at such a moment? It had vanished; indeed, the idea of a seduction would not have entered his head if Leo had not seized the girl by the arm in that brutal way, and if that look of negligence had not revealed that she had dressed hurriedly. God knows what state she was in when I arrived, he thought, and he searched and searched, with painful eagerness, for the traces of her guilt. In her pallid face, the dark-circled eyes that had lost their innocent look, the lips whose color was worn away with use, the expression of confusion, of satiety—all these confirmed his suspicion, but her body, that body which had been possessed, burned with passion, twisted by lust in endless ways—her body revealed nothing; it was the same as any other day. Only the place where her breast began gave him the strange feeling that it was no longer the innocent thing he had been used to consider as something detached and separate from her other, concealed limbs; now it seemed an impure part from which her whole naked body could be imagined.

"My congratulations," he said at last, with an effort, "but you really needn't have bothered to dress. You might just as well have come in like Leo, in a dressing-gown." He pointed to the man; and Leo, with a gesture of irritation, covered his chest.

There was silence. "Michele, don't talk like that," she said in an imploring, anxious voice. "Let me explain. . . ."

"There's nothing to explain." Michele went over to the table and leaned on it. "I don't know if you love him," he went on, just as if the other man had not been present, "but you've certainly done yourself enormous harm. You knew quite well what he represents in Mother's life and what sort of a man he is, and in spite of that you've let him take what he wanted. And anyhow I'm certain you don't love him."

"No, I don't love him," she admitted, without raising her eyes. "But there's another reason."

Ah! So there was another reason! thought Leo. He looked at the two of them, the brother and sister, with a sort of amused contempt; his anger had evaporated now and there was nothing to do but await events. *I* could tell you the reason, he thought, and recalled the lascivious attitude in which he had seen Carla not more than ten minutes before; it was your desire for it, my dear, the need you had for it.

"You don't know yourself why you did it," pursued Michele, warming to his task. He felt he could see into his sister's guilt like reading in an open book. "You yourself wouldn't know how to explain it."

"Yes, I do know," she protested, looking up at him.

"Tell me then."

Troubled, Carla looked from Michele to Leo. So as to have a new life, she wanted to answer, but she didn't have the courage. That remote reason of hers, now that she saw nothing was changed except her surrendered body, appeared to her ridiculous and unworthy, and a kind of shyness, a fear of not being believed or of being laughed at, prevented her from revealing it. She hung her head and was silent.

"*I'll* tell you why it was," went on Michele, triumphant, and yet secretly, terribly irritated at the part he had to play (What am I? he thought, a paterfamilias?). "You had a moment of weakness, of boredom, you couldn't bother to look any further than Leo, and so you accepted him at once, as you would have accepted any other man if he had come

[281]

forward. You gave in to him without knowing why, perhaps just for something to do."

"Yes . . . for something to do," she repeated.

She calls it "something to do," thought Leo ironically. He felt no pity for these two. Above all, it seemed to him absurd and ridiculous that Michele, the silly boy who had tried to shoot him but had forgotten to load the revolver, and that little slut Carla, whom, he had been holding naked in his arms a few moments before, and to whom he had done everything he wanted, that these two should now be elevating themselves to the position of judges, should be assuming the wings of angels and the aureoles of saints, should be acting the role of the pure and innocent, leaving him down below in the mud. For God's sake, he wanted to shout at them, leave off those penitent faces, stop that solemn speech-making! Call a spade a spade! Be what you are and nothing more! But he refrained, curious to see how this fraternal scene would end.

"And then you realized that you hadn't accomplished anything," went on Michele, "that you'd got out of one impossible situation into another no less deporable and tedious. That's how it happened." He paused for a moment, looking at Carla standing in front of him, mute and stubborn, not like a guilty person but like one who listens respectfully and submissively, but with indifference, to an ordinary sort of scolding. And he felt himself to be so very far from the truth and so deeply involved in the lies into which he was forced by the inertia of his own spirit that he was overwhelmed by black distress, by humiliation and misery. Darkness, only darkness, nothing but darkness. He lowered his eyes. "Now everything has to start fresh . . ." he went on, in a deep but uncertain voice. "Our mistakes have been the result of boredom and of impatience for life. You don't love this man, I don't hate him, and yet we've made him the center of opposite actions." His heart was trembling, and he felt ready to cry out with the misery and helplessness that crushed him. "Everything has got to be done over again," he repeated bitterly, "it will be a new life."

"A new life?" Disheartened, Carla crossed over to the

[282]

window. The first drops of rain were streaking the dusty panes, and she looked at them for a moment, dreamily. A new life? So nothing was really changed? This dirty adventure of hers remained just a dirty adventure and nothing more? She felt stifled.

"No," she said in a clear voice, without turning. "I don't believe a new life is possible."

"I went with him"—and she pointed with a clumsy gesture to her lover, sitting motionless near her—"I did this—d'you understand?—in order to find this new life. Now I realize that nothing is changed. It's better, then, not to make any more attempts, better just to stay as we are."

"No, no," began Michele, with indifference. Compelled now to come down from his own excited state of feeling to the special case of his sister, he realized with fear that even the small amount of faith that he had was leaving him. "No, no. The reason why nothing is changed is because you don't love Leo. It's been a useless mistake. In order to live and to change, one has to act sincerely." Suddenly it seemed to him an extraordinary and a silly thing that all other cases should tend to meet in his own; it was like those invalids who imagine that everyone suffers from their own disease, and he was afraid of being selfish, of seeing only himself, of not understanding Carla. "At least, I think that's how it is," he added, discouraged, "I think you ought to leave this man you don't love. We'll sell the villa and pay him what we owe him, and if there's anything left over, so much the better. We'll give up all these parties, these people, this circle we move in, all these things that have become such a bore to us . . . and we'll go and live in a few rooms. It'll be a new life." But he was aware that he lacked what was needful—the warmth, the loud voice, the hand on the shoulder, the assured, hearty tone; he felt indifferent and tired.

Carla turned her eyes away from his—his eyes that were without faith and without illusions, and gazed towards the window. "It's impossible," she said at last, as though speaking to herself.

There was silence. The boy's remarks had frozen Leo in the very midst of his harsh, warm irony. Sell the villa, that's crazy, he thought. And indeed, if they sold the villa his own little affair would be brought to nothing; if they sold it, a valuation would be made, and then its real worth would come out, the real value of a large dwelling situated in the middle of the best quarter of the city and surrounded by extensive grounds, an area which might with great profit be sold off in lots for building sites. His whole affair would be brought to nothing. He looked at Carla, at Michele. It would be sheer ruin, he thought. A new life, indeed! Then suddenly an idea came to him, and, like a desperate remedy given by a doctor without previous discussion, he decided to apply it immediately.

"Wait a minute!" he cried; "wait a minute. . . . I'm in this too." He rose, waved Michele aside, took the girl by the arm and made her sit down. "You sit there." She obeyed with a docility that seemed horrible to Michele: *She*'ll never do anything, he thought despairingly. Leo himself sat down facing Carla.

"It's quite true," he began, with the resolution and precision that he brought into all his business dealings, "it's quite true that we've done wrong . . . that we've made mistakes. I've been thinking about it while you two were talking, I've been thinking about it, Carla. Now, what would you say if I suggested something that would make up for it, if I suggested that we should get married?" A half-triumphant, half-persuasive smile adorned his fleshy lips; he was certain he could convince her. "What would you say, eh?" he repeated, taking her hand as it rested on the table.

Carla's hand sought to disengage itself, but without success. "Get married?" she repeated, with a disappointed smile, "we two get married?"

"Yes," Leo insisted, "we two get married. What would be so strange about that?"

The girl shook her head. The idea of such a marriage was repellent to her, with her mother in the house, her husband's jealous former mistress, and besides, it was too late—she did not know why—too late for them to get married, they knew each other too well to become husband and wife. Better for her to go away . . . for them to part . . . or perhaps—why

[284]

not?—to stay as they were, as lovers. In the first rush of disgust, the first instinctive movement to defend the pure, remote idea of matrimony, it seemed to her that any situation, even one that was more degraded and painful, would be preferable to marriage. Her mind was busy but she was unable to speak, fascinated by the smile and the gaze of her lover; then she felt two hands—Michele's hands—on her shoulders. "No," he murmured to her, "say no." But his voice was not so low that Leo did not hear.

The latter dropped Carla's hand and jumped to his feet. "Will you be so kind as to leave your sister alone, once and for all?" he cried. "It's she who's going to get married, not you. Let her think. Let her answer according to what's best for her. In fact, it would be almost better if you went into the other room for a moment and left us alone, Carla and myself. We'll call you back when we're finished."

"Keep calm, I'm staying here," replied Michele in a challenging tone. The other man made an impatient movement but did not answer.

"Well, then," he said, sitting down again, "think about it." He clasped Carla's hand again. "Think it over. I'm not such a bad match. I've got capital, a good position, I'm well known and well thought of. Think it over." He paused for a moment. "Besides," he added, "how would you ever find a husband, in *your* situation?"

"What d'you mean—in *my* situation?" she repeated, looking at him.

"Well . . ." Leo twisted his mouth. "You haven't a penny, and—is it necessary to tell you?—your name is . . . somewhat discredited."

"What d'you mean—discredited?" she broke in again, in a thin voice.

"Discredited," repeated Leo. "None of these friends of yours look upon you quite as a virtuous girl. Let me explain. They would take advantage of you but they wouldn't marry you. As long as it's just a question of amusement they're all nice to you."

There was silence; their eyes met. It's your fault, yours

[285]

and Mother's, that I'm what I am, she wanted to cry, but she restrained herself and hung her head.

"I, on the other hand," went on Leo, "would regularize the whole situation, not only yours but your family's as well. We'd give your mother a home. Michele would get a job. Yes indeed, I'd make him do something, I'd find him a place." At each new promise he gazed intently at Carla, like a wood-cutter who, after each blow of the axe, examines the notched tree-trunk to see whether it is going to fall; but Carla was staring at the window, down which the silent rain was now violently streaming, and she did not answer.

A damp, cave-like gloom had now invaded the sitting-room, and, in this gloom, Michele was walking up and down. "Find a job . . . work," he kept saying to himself, agitatedly. There was no doubt that Leo was speaking seriously . . . what he said, he would do . . . he would help him to earn his living. Where he himself was vaguely well-meaning, Leo gave solid promises. How was he to choose? The temptation was strong. Money, acquaintances, women, perhaps travel-ling, perhaps wealth, in any case a life which was secure, straightforward, clearly defined, full of satisfactions of all kinds, of work, and parties, and friendly words. All these Carla's marriage would give him. He would not be selling his sister, for he did not believe in these grand and terrible words, he did not believe in honor and duty. He felt indiffer-ent, as usual, speculative and indifferent. I shan't say any-thing to her, he said to himself finally, almost without intend-ing to. I shall leave her to decide. If she accepts, well and good; if she refuses, well and good also. But a certain feeling of uneasiness warned him that these were ignoble thoughts. He looked up, over towards the window; in that uncertain light, the two heads were clearly outlined, black against the gray window-panes; he noticed it was raining; and then he started walking up and down again, stopping every now and then, and looking: where was it he had seen those two figures before, against a window like that? Each time he gazed at them a feeling of nervous unhappiness swept over him.

Here am I, he thought, here am I, walking up and down

in the dark. They're sitting over there by the window. I'm walking. They are talking. We're separate . . . distant . . . why are we like that? It's just as if we were alone, as if we couldn't see each other." His eyes filled with tears: where had he seen them before?

Leo was speaking. "If you're hesitating on account of your mother, you can set your mind at rest. I assure you that it's all been over between her and me for a long time."

There was silence. Carla shook her head. "No, it's not because of my mother," she replied, "it's not because of that."

"Is it because of Lisa, perhaps?" Leo suggested.

"Oh, no."

"Well then," he exclaimed, "why should you refuse? I can't see why you should refuse. It certainly can't be," he added, with a smile and a squeeze of her hand, "for sentimental reasons."

She looked at him, and her first impulse to refuse was followed by unhappy clear-sightedness. Really and truly, why should I refuse him my hand when I've given him everything else? There was a new hardness in her heart. Leo's promises did not convince her—we don't love each other and it would be an unhappy marriage. But Michele's promises seemed to her nothing less than childish. Life doesn't change, and it never will change. Leo is right, it's best to get married. She was on the point of yielding, of giving her consent, with a half-humiliated, half-bashful smile—she was already imagining how her future husband would take her around the waist and kiss her on the brow and was picturing a fine emotional scene, when from the far end of the room came Michele's voice: "For God's sake, Carla, for God's sake say no."

They both turned around. Michele, standing in the middle of the room, looked almost ashamed of his passionate appeal. Leo leapt to his feet and beat his fist on the table.

"Will you stop it?" he shouted. "Will you, once and for all, stop interfering in matters that don't concern you?"

Michele took a step forward. "She's my sister," he said.

"She's your sister," repeated Leo, "so what? Can't she be free to choose the husband she wants?" He sat down again.

"You pay attention to me, Carla," he insisted, "and don't listen to your brother's advice. He doesn't know what he's talking about."

But the girl made a sign to him to be silent. "Why," she asked, turning towards the boy, "why should I say no?"

She saw that he hesitated. "You don't love him . . ." he began.

"That's not enough. One can get along without love."

"There's Mother. . . ."

"Oh! She," Carla shrugged her shoulders, "she doesn't trouble me."

"Carla," persisted Michele, after a brief silence, "you must refuse him because I ask you to. If you married Leo—well, it would be absolute ruin." His voice was trembling. Certainly, she thought, as she looked closely at the boy, it would *not* be a very fine thing to do. But, after her intoxication with the idea of a new life, she was possessed with a sad, paltry need for reality.

"And in exchange," she asked in a harsh voice, "what should I have?"

"What would you have?" He looked at her. Carla's eyes were calm and vacant, her cheeks shadowy, her face surrounded with an untidy mass of shaggy hair. "What would you have? You would be free . . . free to make yourself a new life." He paused. "Don't imagine that what I say is false," he added, struck by the emptiness of his own words, "in some ways I'm in the same position as you are. . . . I know there are many difficulties ahead, but in the end we shall get there. We shall achieve our own life." He saw Carla shake her head, without taking her eyes off the window. Have faith! he longed to cry to her.

Leo, sure of himself, was smiling. "Words!" he said. "Life is neither new nor old, it's simply what it is."

Finally Carla shook herself and turned towards her lover. "And so, Leo," she asked, with forced casualness, "you want us to get married?"

"Certainly I do," he replied emphatically.

"And you're not afraid of its being a failure?" she insisted.

"Personally, she went on calmly, "I'm convinced that you'd deceive me."

It's you who would deceive *me*, my little slut, thought Leo, gazing at that youthful head in the half-light. He would have liked to give her a slap right on her big breasts, a gay, teasing, joking slap, for he visualized her as she had been a few minutes earlier, naked and white and with the clumsy, animal-like movements that come from inexperience. I'm marrying a slut, he said to himself, then put out his hand to her.

"I swear to you," he said solemnly, "that I'll always be faithful to you."

"Carla," insisted Michele, "say no." He went up to her and put his hand on her shoulder. "Say no. There *is* a reason. I'll tell you afterwards."

Carla stared at the window and said nothing. Her big, round head looked out of proportion on her thin shoulders. It was quite dark now; the little light that remained—a kind of vague phosphorescence—was receding from the wet window panes; it was still raining. They were swallowed up in the darkness of the house; there was nothing to be seen of them but hollow, half-obliterated faces and hands lying on the table.

"It's time to go," she said at last, and rose to her feet.

"And the answer?" asked Leo. He too, rose, and felt his way to the wall and turned on the light; and for a moment they looked at each other, in that brightness, with dazzled eyes, as though astonished to see each other—Carla and Michele side by side near the window, Leo beside the door. It was then, for the first time, that Leo observed a certain resemblance between brother and sister: there was the same undecided expression, the same timid movement of the arms; but Carla's face looked merely tired—and now she drew her hand across those no longer innocent eyes—whereas upon Michele's face was a nervous, fanciful sadness. They stood close together in the bay of the window and seemed frightened of him.

"The answer?" echoed the girl, after a moment. "Tomorrow, Leo, tomorrow. I've got to speak to Mom." She turned towards her brother and placed her hand on his chest. "Michele, wait for me here," she added, looking at him closely, "I'll go and put my hat on and come back." She slipped between Michele and the table with a kind of easy, frivolous agility, passed in front of her lover and opened the door on the right; she did not shut it behind her. Then that room was lit up, and Michele saw a wardrobe with a mirror, a carpet, a chair upon which a man's shirt had been thrown, with one sleeve dangling. Carla walked back and forth in front of the mirror with the manner of one in familiar surroundings. She turned on the lamp near the wardrobe and carefully combed her hair, then she went away and returned with her jacket and hat, put them on and disappeared again, came back with her bag, powdered her face. During these preparations the two men did not move or speak. Leo stood near the door in his short, full, belted dressing-gown, his legs apart, his chest bare, his head and eyes lowered as though he were absorbed in thought; the fine, ruffled hair on his bald brow looked like a little dark cloud. His hands were clasped behind his back, without lifting his head he would raise himself on tiptoe and fall heavily back on his heels. Michele did not move from the window, whence he watched, with dreamy eyes, his sister's familiar, frivolous movements in front of the looking-glass. It seemed to him that a heavy, corrupt atmosphere filled that adjoining room; he knew there must be a sort of indecent disorder in there, with trailing sheets, garments thrown over chairs, pillows on the floor, perfumes and the smell of tobacco and sleep. In that atmosphere, in the midst of that disorder, Carla was moving freely about, almost cheerfully, on those agile legs of hers. She looked dissolute, tired, pale. And now here she was, ready to go out, with her hat pulled well down over her eyes, her face powdered, fresh, rosy, her lips reddened, two pointed curls on her cheeks, here she was coming towards him, leaving behind her the tarnished mirror, the stuffy air, the wall, the chair.

"Let's go," she said quietly. She held out her hand to Leo. "Good-bye, Leo."

"Then it's *yes*, isn't it?" he murmured as he kissed the tips

of her fingers; he felt contented and secure. Carla looked at
him but did not reply. They went into the hall, first the girl,
then the two men, and Leo, well satisfied, almost excited,
hovered about her. "We'll get married . . . we'll get married,"
he whispered to her while Michele, in the opposite corner,
was putting on his overcoat; he wanted to see her smile, or
at least concede him a glance or a sign that would reveal
her possible consent, but Carla was inflexible, absent-minded,
as though she had neither heard nor seen him. "Good-bye,
Leo," she repeated as she went out. He watched the two of
them through the crack of the half-closed door as they went
silently downstairs without turning back, followed, on the
wall, by two slanting shadows; then he shut the door and
went back into the sitting-room. He caught sight of Michele's
revolver on the floor, picked it up, looked vaguely into the
air as he weighed it in his hand, and remembered that he had
an invitation to a dance at the Grand Hotel. The Signora
had decided to go, too. It will be a good opportunity to encourage Carla in this idea of marriage, he said to himself.
Completely satisfied, he walked in front of the looking-glass
in his bedroom and gazed at himself. "Nothing much wrong
with *you*," he said aloud, and felt like giving himself a slap
on the stomach. "Even when you're married, you'll still be
the same old Leo." He went into the bathroom and started
to wash.

16

WHEN THEY reached the threshold of the outer door they found that it was pouring rain, not violently but with a careless abundance. A great rustling sound like a torrent filled the darkness, a leaden sheet of water boiled on the paving-stones in the street, the heavy rain was venting, in every direction, in cascades and trickles and rivulets, the dirty flood that had fermented so long in the bosom of the clouds. Houses stood straight and black beneath the downpour, the lamp-posts seemed drowning, the flooded pavements took on the amphibious air of half-submerged quays in a harbor.

Bent under the rain they walked hurriedly close against the walls, striving for shelter beneath a single umbrella. At a corner, the straight beam of a taxi's headlights caught them. It was free; they jumped in and were off.

Sitting side by side in the darkness they looked straight ahead and said nothing; the jolting of the vehicle made them jump up and down and knock against each other like two lifeless puppets with wooden limbs and staring, ecstatic eyes. Michele lay back in his seat and appeared to be meditating; Carla sat stooping slightly forward, trying to see where they were going—in which she was unsuccessful, for the glass of the windows was wet and dimmed over by a cold mist, and it was impossible to see anything. She felt she was shut away, out of the world, alone with her brother in that black box, and that she was being carried at a great speed towards some unknown place—where? So the day was finishing and, with it, her old life—finishing with a question to which there was no answer. Where is one going, by day or by night, in darkness and rain or in full daylight? No one knows. She was afraid; she wanted to restrict her aims, make her world smaller, see her whole existence as a narrow room. I shall marry Leo, she thought. She fixed her tired eyes upon the glass in front of her, and seemed to see little shining figures appearing and forming upon that dark, luminous surface. Ah! the windows of houses, on rainy nights; train windows, talkative, monotonous, with mysterious showers of sparks; windows open upon the dark country of dreams! There . . . there, now she saw, coming to the surface from the shadows beyond, the sun-warmed steps of a church, and herself all white in her long bridal veils, her eyes cast down (it must be a bright, sunny day) as she clung to her companion's arm; and behind them the figures of the wedding procession emerging, one by one from the shadow, casting off the darkness like a garment. Her mother, far, far off (she would certainly be weeping, but one couldn't see), holding a round, glistening bunch of flowers; Michele with his head down, as if he were looking where to place his feet; Lisa in an extraordinary, spring-like costume; and many other guests whose faces could not be distinguished, the women dressed in white, the men in black, crowding confusedly behind them, some still half in shadow, others in the full sunlight, all of them very elegant (one could see the impeccable creases in the men's trousers, and each of them was holding a glossy top-hat that reflected like a mirror; and one could distinguish, flower by flower, the women's brightly-colored, round bouquets). They all came out from the invisible porch of the church and walked down the steps behind the bride and bridegroom; and the steps were full of sunshine. Then there was a sudden burst of slow, religious music, that seemed to follow the bridal procession step by step—an organ? She seemed to hear these triumphal sounds that accompanied her; they were solemn sounds, but overflowing with a sadness both bitter and exultant, as though she, dressed as she was and clinging to her husband's arm, were going not towards joy and happiness, but towards a harsh renunciation, towards a life filled with troubles and difficulties insuperable.

She shook herself as Michele's hand grasped her own. The shadow of the glass flowed rapidly over the little bright figures of the wedding procession, as when a photographic plate is exposed to the sun. The car had slowed down and stopped, waiting to cross a crowded street. Rain, noise, bicycle bells and horns, voices, lights, faces, and at last, with a jolt, the taxi moved on again.

"Well," she asked, turning to him, "what is it?"

Her brother made an awkward, convulsive movement with his hand. "If I'm not mistaken," he said with an effort, "if I'm not mistaken, I never told you the reason why you must refuse Leo."

She glanced at him. "No."

"Well, here it is." The boy leaned forward and began hurriedly and without any transition to tell his tale. "Here's the reason. Today, before I went to see Lisa . . . By the way, it was she who told me the whole story about you and Leo."

"Ah! It was Lisa, was it?"

"Yes, it appears she came upon you yesterday, together, in the anteroom. But let me go on. . . . Yesterday, before I went to see Lisa, I started thinking about our affairs and the state we're in, both of which are really very bad. Gradually I became so deeply involved in my arguments that I lost—how can I express it?—I lost all restraint, and caught myself thinking more or less like this. 'Here we are, ruined. There's no remedy. In a year's time, if things go on like this, we shall be in complete poverty. In order to avoid this disaster, would it not be advisable to make some sacrifice or, at any rate, come to some compromise?' The only person upon whom one could count for an arrangement of this kind was Leo. And so I went on to think that, considering the man's character (he being so mad about women), he would give all he's got for a woman he really likes; wouldn't it be a good plan to give him to understand that I, in exchange for money, would undertake —d'you see?—to bring my sister Carla to him—you, in fact— to bring her to him in his own home?"

"You thought that?" she asked, turning sharply and looking at him. At that moment the light from a lamp-post lit up Michele's face for a second or two, and she saw his staring, dilated eyes and a look of repugnant, awkward humility on his white face as he nodded. She turned away her head, and a sudden sadness and distress clutched at her trembling heart. The cab was moving swiftly now, and Michele began speaking again.

"Yes, I thought that . . . and, you know, I could see it, too." He made a gesture as if he wanted to seize hold of something. "I could see how we would go, all three of us, you and I and Leo, to his flat. When I'm troubled I seem to see the things that I think. How we would have tea in Leo's sitting-room, and then finally how I would go away, discreetly, according to our pre-arranged plan, leaving you alone with Leo. . . ."

"It's horrible," she murmured, frightened; but Michele did not hear.

"And so when I saw you just now, sitting facing each other in front of the sitting-room window, and heard Leo asking you to marry him, I seemed actually to see the scene I had imagined. It's a thing that happens to everyone: you go along a street, you think you're going to find certain people in certain attitudes, and you *do* find them. But in my case there was that piece of calculation as well, the calculation with regard to Leo's money. Now, I said to myself, everything's turned out as I thought, as I ought *not* to have thought; it's just as if I had really said to Leo, 'Look, Leo, here's Carla, my sister; she's a beautiful, blooming girl.' Don't be offended. . . . That's how I imagined myself speaking to him. . . ."

"No, I'm not offended," she murmured without turning. "Go on."

" 'A beautiful blooming girl,' " Michele repeated. " 'You give me some money, plenty of it, you undertake the support of my family, and I, in return . . . in return I'll leave you a free hand with Carla . . . do just as you like with her.' "

"But what did you think?" she burst out, feeling both sad and irritated. "What did you think I was?—an inanimate object? An animal?"

"No, but I knew," replied Michele, with a faint, victorious smile, "I knew that you were bored—how shall I express it?— that you were in a suitable state, that you would yield easily."

"You knew that?" she murmured.

"The fact that I hadn't taken any action," continued Michele, without answering her, "was no longer of any importance. I should have just the same feeling of remorse. Seeing you there, married, living, myself, on that money, I should always suffer, just as if I had really been guilty. D'you understand? . . . D'you understand?" he repeated, seized with sudden exasperation, taking hold of her by the arm, "d'you understand? One thinks of some ugly, evil action, but doesn't perform it. Then everything comes to pass just as one had thought, but not completely, only up to a certain point, in such a way that one can still prevent its happening. What ought one to do then? One will try to stop it, to prevent that horrible thing taking place. If one doesn't do that, it's just as though one had been implicated in it from beginning to end, it's as though I had really handed you over to Leo for money, had really taken you to his flat. . . . D'you understand now? If you marry him, for me it's just as though I had really aided and abetted you in your union, in your guilt, as though I had, on the one hand, thrust you into Leo's arms and, on the other, taken the money. D'you understand? D'you understand now?" A jolt of the taxi threw them, all unwillingly, against each other; there was silence until they had gone some distance.

"Forgive me," the boy said at last, in a voice full of feeling and humility, bending forward beside his sister, "do you forgive me, Carla?"

She sat silent, looking straight in front of her, then she gave a dry, forced laugh.

"There's nothing to forgive," she answered; "you haven't done anything to me . . . you haven't done me any harm.

What should I have to forgive you?" There was silence. "I haven't anything to forgive anybody," she went on in exasperation, in a tearful voice, never taking her eyes from the window of the car, "not anybody at all. All I want is to be left in peace." Her eyes filled with tears. Everyone was to blame and no one was to blame, but she was tired of examining herself and examining others, she did not want to forgive and she did not want to condemn, life was what it was and it was better to accept it than to judge it, let them only leave her in peace.

Michele seemed to see, in these words, his own complete and final condemnation. I've done nothing, he kept on telling himself with astonishment, for it appeared to him that he had grown older, that he had lived through much in that one single day. It's true. . . . I've done nothing, nothing except think. A shudder of fear shook him. I haven't made love to Lisa, I haven't killed Leo. All I've done is to think. That's the mistake I've made. He bent down and took the girl's hand.

"But you *will* refuse him, won't you?" he inquired anxiously. "Tell me you'll refuse him."

There was silence. "I shall marry him," she said at last; and again there was silence. "What would happen to me if I didn't marry him?" she said, in a hard, sad voice. "What would become of me? Just think a moment . . . in our present situation." And she made a gesture as if to show herself as she really was—naked, lost, poor. "It would be madness to refuse him; the only thing left to me is to marry him." She broke off, again staring straight in front of her.

The inflexibility of her tone convinced Michele more than any reason. It's all over now, he said to himself, looking at Carla's childish cheeks, lit up by the headlamp of a car. She's a woman. He felt himself vanquished. "And so, Carla," he asked again, like a child that refuses to be convinced, "you'll marry him?"

"Yes, I'll marry him," she repeated, without turning her head.

They had nearly reached their destination. The streets were wider and there were few people in them; and they were lined now, not with rows of houses, but with bright villas and dark, rain-dripping gardens; there were few street-lamps and the pavements were broad and deserted. Carla followed their route attentively, and thoughts were whirling in her tired, excited mind with an equal speed. The taxi was her life, launched blindly into the darkness. She would marry Leo. A life in common with him, sleeping together, eating together, going out together, travelling, sufferings, joys. They would have a lovely home, a fine apartment in a smart quarter of the town. Someone comes into the drawing-room —a room furnished with luxury and good taste—a married lady, a friend of hers, and she goes forward to receive her. They have tea together, then they go out; her car is waiting at the door; they get in and drive off. She would be called 'Signora'—Signora Merumeci—how strange, Signora Merumeci. She seemed to see herself, a little taller, larger, her legs bigger, her hips wider—for marriage makes people fatter —with jewels at her neck and on her fingers and wrists; harder, colder, splendid but cold, as though behind her un-moving eyes she held a secret, and, in order to keep it hidden, had killed all feeling in her heart. With this demeanor, in her smart clothes, she enters a crowded room at a hotel; her husband follows her: Leo, slightly balder, slightly fatter, but not much changed; they sit down, they have tea, they dance, many people look at them and think, "She's beautiful, a beautiful but an evil woman . . . she never smiles . . . her eyes are hard . . . she looks like a statue . . . goodness knows what she's thinking about." Other people, standing over by the pillars, murmur to each other: "She married her mother's lover . . . a man much older than herself. She doesn't love him and of course she ought to have a lover herself." They all whisper to each other, and think things, and look at her; and she sits there beside her husband, her legs crossed, smok-ing; her legs, indeed, are much in evidence, and her dress is close-fitting, with a deep *décolletage*. All the men watch her desirously as if they wanted to bite her; and she answers them with glances of utter indifference. And now a bed-room: here is the Signora Merumeci, late because of some visit she has had to pay, running to meet her lover; in his

[298]

arms she loses all her statue-like hardness (these stiff-looking women are always the most ardent), and becomes like a child again, weeping, laughing, stammering; she is like a prisoner released who sees, at long last, the light. Her joy is innocent, the whole room is white, she is without stain in her lover's arms. Purity is found again. Then, when the time comes, she returns, tired but happy, to her conjugal abode and her face reassumes its habitual expression of coldness. And so her life continues, for years. Many envy her: she is rich, she has many amusements, she travels, she has a lover—what more can one want? All that a woman can have, she has.

The car stopped and they got out. It was no longer raining; the air was cold and misty, and a moist wind moved ceaselessly in the dark foliage of the gardens. Carla jumped nimbly over the wide puddle between the pavement and the street, and, standing under a lamp-post, waited while her brother paid the fare. Then she noticed a long, black shape lying high and dry at the edge of the road, like a whale deposited by a flood—a large car with a glistening head, and the driver slumped in his seat with his cap over his eyes. The Berardis' car, she thought wonderingly, and then remembered the invitation to the fancy dress ball.

"Michele," she said to her brother as he stepped cautiously towards her over the puddles, "the Berardis' car."

"So it is," he said, with a quick glance at it. "They must have come to fetch us."

They went in at the gate and crossed, in silence, the space in front of the house, looking carefully where to place their feet. There was a sound of crunching gravel; a feeling of dampness; dark, fantastic, shadowy shapes against the misty sky; a vast, ocean-like rustling in the great trees; and a sense of respite, for it was no longer raining.

In the warm, brightly lit vestibule Michele took off his coat and hat. "Carla," he said at last to his sister who was waiting for him in the doorway, "when are you going to speak to Mother about this marriage?"

She looked at him. "Tomorrow," she replied quietly.

They went through into the corridor, and a sound of voices and laughter came to them from the drawing-room.

The girl went over to the curtains that concealed the door, parted them cautiously, and peeped in for a moment. "They're all there," she said, turning round; "all three of them, Pippo, Mary and Fanny."

They went upstairs, and as they came into the anteroom their mother and Lisa came to meet them. The Signora was already dressed in her Spanish costume. Her soft, pathetic-looking face was plastered with luxuriant make-up, her cheeks flaming and dotted with beauty-spots, her lips scarlet, her eyes swimming in a languid blackness; the Spanish costume, long and entirely black, billowed about her, with its soft, full folds, at each swaying movement of her hips; a sumptuous lace-embroidered veil flowed down from a broad tortoise-shell comb over her fleshy shoulders, over her wide, flabby, bare arms; and in her hands she held an ostrich-feather fan. Smiling in a silly way, and as though afraid of upsetting the balance of her head-dress by a careless movement, she walked with her head erect and rigid; and at her side, like day at the side of night, was Lisa, fair and of a floury whiteness and all dressed in pale colors.

As soon as she saw Carla and Michele, their mother went towards them. "It's late," she cried, even before they had reached the top of the stairs. "The Berardis have been waiting a quarter of an hour already."

She was satisfied, well pleased; for Lisa had passed the whole afternoon with her, and consequently Leo had told her the truth and had not been deceiving her. Her joy had made her behave in an extremely affable manner towards her friend, to whom she had told all sorts of secrets, and for a moment she had almost thought of inviting her to the dance that evening; but she had given up the idea, partly from mean selfishness, partly because the Berardis knew Lisa only very slightly and might have been offended at her taking such a liberty. "Hurry up . . . hurry up," she kept saying to Carla who stood there quite still, staring at her; "quickly, go and dress up."

"Have I got to dress up?" asked the girl, in a deep, hesitating voice, looking down at the floor.

Her mother laughed. "Wake up, Carla," she said fluttering her long Spanish veil; "what are you thinking about? You surely don't want to go to the dance *without* dressing up?" She took her daughter by the arm. "Come along," she added, "come along, or we'll be late."

Automatically Carla took off her hat and, shaking her big, lazy, untidy head, followed her mother, whose Spanish veil undulated elegantly from the two swaddled protuberances of her buttocks. Carla looked at her and it seemed then, as she saw her so like herself, so unchangeable, that nothing during that afternoon, had really happened at all. And yet, she knew I shall have to tell her about this marriage. And so, one dragging the other, they left the room.

Lisa and Michele were left alone. The former, from the first moment, had been watching from her corner with eager, troubled curiosity, as the pair of them, brother and sister, came in together; and now, after waiting in vain for the boy to speak first, she went up to him.

"Well?" she inquired, not attempting to conceal her indiscreet interest, "tell me . . . how did it go?"

He turned and looked at her. "How did it go?" he repeated slowly, "how did it go? Badly, it went. . . . I took a shot at him."

"Good gracious!" exclaimed Lisa, with exaggerated terror, throwing a lively glance at him, "and did you hurt him?"

"I didn't even touch him."

"Come over here." Excited, she drew him to the divan and sat down beside him. "Sit down here. Tell me. . . ."

But Michele moved his hand in a weary, impatient way. "Not now, later." He observed her rosy, fair skin, her buxom bosom, and an insatiable longing came over him to forget, just for one single moment, his wretchedness. "Are you going to the dance?" he asked at last, when he had ceased examining her.

"No."

"Well, then—" he hesitated—"well, then, as I'm not going either, I'll come and have dinner with you. And then . . . I'll tell you everything."

He watched her enthusiastic assent. "All right, that's splendid, we'll have dinner together." And he smiled bitterly.

[301]

"This time," he thought, irritated yet pleased, "don't worry, don't be afraid, I won't rebuff you."

He was oppressed by a feeling of dull disgust. His thoughts were arid, his mind a desert; there was no faith, no hope there, that he might rest and refresh himself in their shade. He saw, always, in others, the same falseness, the same shabbiness that filled his own spirit, and it was impossible to rid his eyes of the film of discouragement and impurity that interposed itself between him and life. A little sincerity, he kept saying to himself, clutching again at his old fixed idea, a little faith, and I should have killed Leo. And now I should be clear as a drop of water.

He felt himself suffocating. He looked at Lisa, who appeared content. *How do you live?* he wanted to shout at her. *Sincerely? With faith? Tell me how you manage to live.* His thoughts were confused, contradictory. And yet, he thought, with a sudden, despairing return to reality, perhaps this is all simply the result of my own shaken nerves, perhaps it's only a question of money or of time or of circumstances. But the harder he tried to reduce, to simplify his problem, the more difficult and frightening it appeared to him. It's impossible to go on like this. He felt like bursting into tears; the forest of life, tangled and impenetrable, surrounded him on every side; no light shone in the distance. Impossible.

Carla and his mother came back. Carla now dressed up as a Pierrot, her face half hidden by a black satin mask, an enormous, swaying ruff round her neck, and a loose jacket and trousers and white silk slippers with big black pompons on them. She walked on tiptoe, her three-cornered hat on one side, and smiled mysteriously.

"What d'you think of us?" demanded the Signora.

"Splendid . . . splendid," said Lisa. "Have a good time."

"That's what we intend to do," said Carla with a burst of laughter. She was a different person in her fancy dress—gayer, lighter. She went over to her brother and tapped him on the shoulder with her fan. "You and I will have a talk to-morrow," she said in a low voice. The confession in the taxi had left a painful impression on her, she felt that Michele was ruining his own life. And yet it's all so simple, she thought, as she'd slipped into her Pierrot trousers in front of the mirror, and the proof is, that in spite of what has happened, I'm dressing up and going to the dance. She wanted to cry out to Michele, *It's all so simple,* and she was already thinking that she would make Leo find him some work, a job, an occupation of some kind, as soon as they were married. But her mother was dragging her away.

"Come along," she kept saying; "come along. The Berardis are waiting."

They went downstairs, side by side, the white Pierrot and the black Spanish lady. On the landing the mother stopped her daughter. "Remember," she whispered into her ear, "remember to be . . . what shall I say? . . . to be nice to Pippo. I've been thinking it over. Perhaps he loves you . . . And he's a good match."

"Don't worry," answered Carla seriously.

They went on down the second flight of stairs. Carla's mother was smiling with satisfaction. She was thinking that *her* lover, too, would be at the ball, and she looked forward to a pleasant evening.